MOSAICS OF A LIFE

MOSAICS OF A LIFE

TIBOR GERSTL

Pittsburgh, PA

ISBN 1-56315-108-1

Trade Paperback

First Printing—1999
Library of Congress #98-85309

Request for information should be addressed to:

SterlingHouse Publisher, Inc.
The Sterling Building
440 Friday Road
Department T-101
Pittsburgh, PA 15209

Cover design & typesetting: Drawing Board Studios

Printed in Canada

I dedicate this book to the memory of my parents, who died at Auschwitz, two among the six million victims of human bestiality, and to my comrades in the labor camps, with whom I served in the Headquarters of XI KMSZ. Its final roster I reproduce on the following page. Most of them died in Csajta (Shattendorf), just inside the Austrian border. Others perished on the road in a forced march. Those stalwart few who survived the journey did not survive their destination: the scorching confines of Mauthausen concentration camp.

Humanity should not forget.

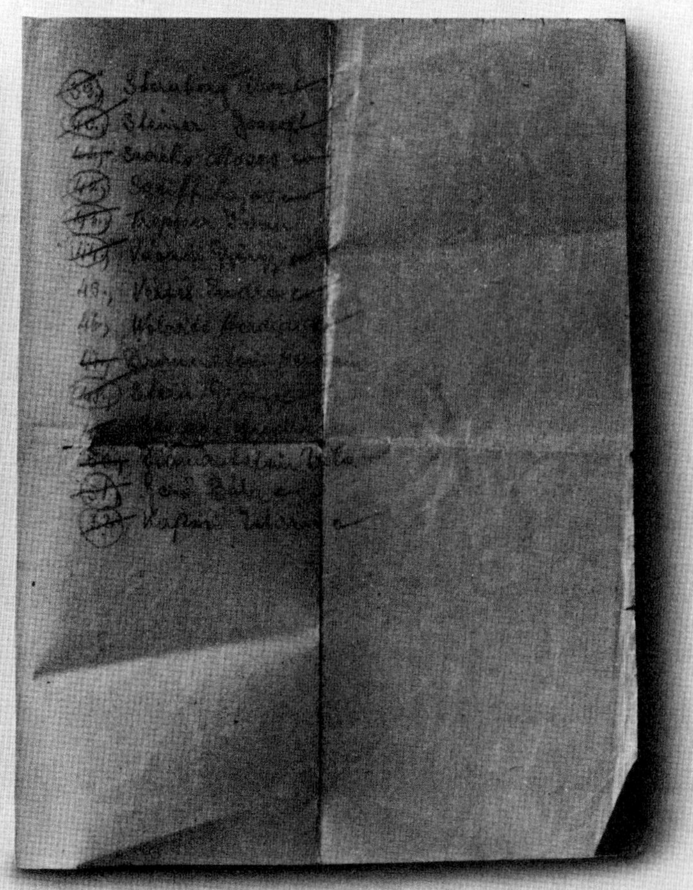

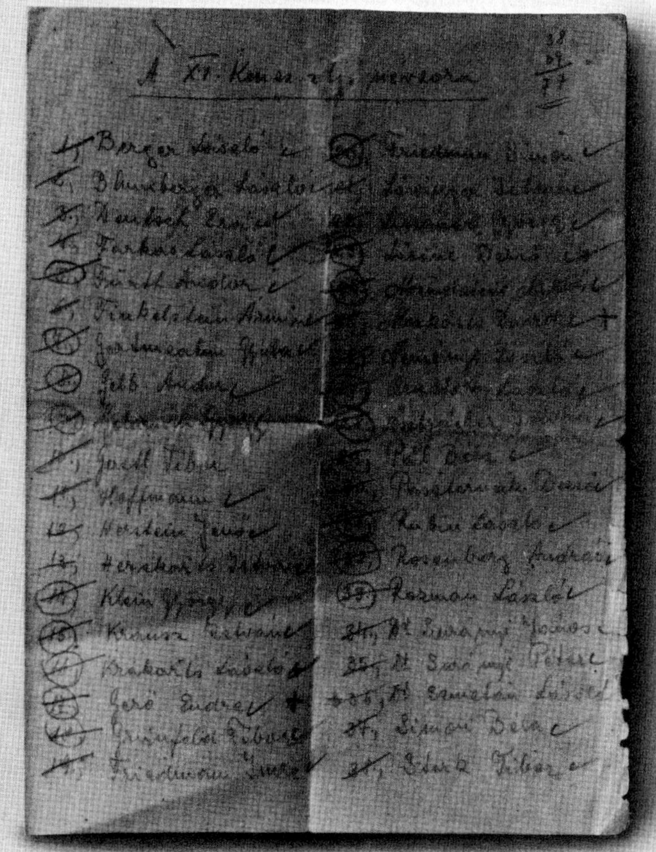

ACKNOWLEDGEMENT

My mother tongue is Hungarian, my life companion is Belgian and we speak French at home. We have lived in the United States for forty years and speak English outside the house. Unfortunately, by now I don't speak any of these three languages perfectly.

I could not have accomplished this book without the invaluable help of Barbara Baumann and Mario Mattich, who corrected and edited this book. I am also indebted to Ruth Sultan, who struggled to enter my poor longhand into the word processor. I am grateful to my friends, mostly Eddy and Beverly Picker and my lifelong companion Ida, who encouraged me from the beginning to write my story, which I would never have done without their prompting.

FOREWORD

I am not a writer. I am an artist. A graphic artist by profession, a tinkerer with fine art painting. I am not a historian. I can't write the history of World War II. War experiences are as many and varied as the individuals who live them. Consequently, hundreds, if not thousands of books relate their experiences. So why add another one?

In my case, I have no children to tell my story to, so I commit these pieces of paper in testimony to my existence. But I also add my voice in witness to horrible and harrowing events which the world is in a hurry to forget.

References to historical, political, military and social events are strictly to situate my own experiences. These references are fairly accurate and were precious morsels of news, hungrily devoured to nourish the spirit of those of us who struggled to survive the forced labor camps.

All events in this book are based on actual happenings, although dates and places may have been mixed in my memory from a distance of more than 50 years. Some names are real, others are purposely changed. Most of the people I write of have died. A few still live, but I have not seen them since our liberation. My story, I believe, if not unique, is greatly different from other stories I have heard about the war and the Holocaust.

Despite the strong anti-Semitism prevailing in Hungary at the time and, most likely, to this day, I was extremely lucky to be in a place and under the authority of an exceptional human being. He and a few like him, spared me from the worst atrocities. As a consequence, I am able to write this survivor's remembrance.

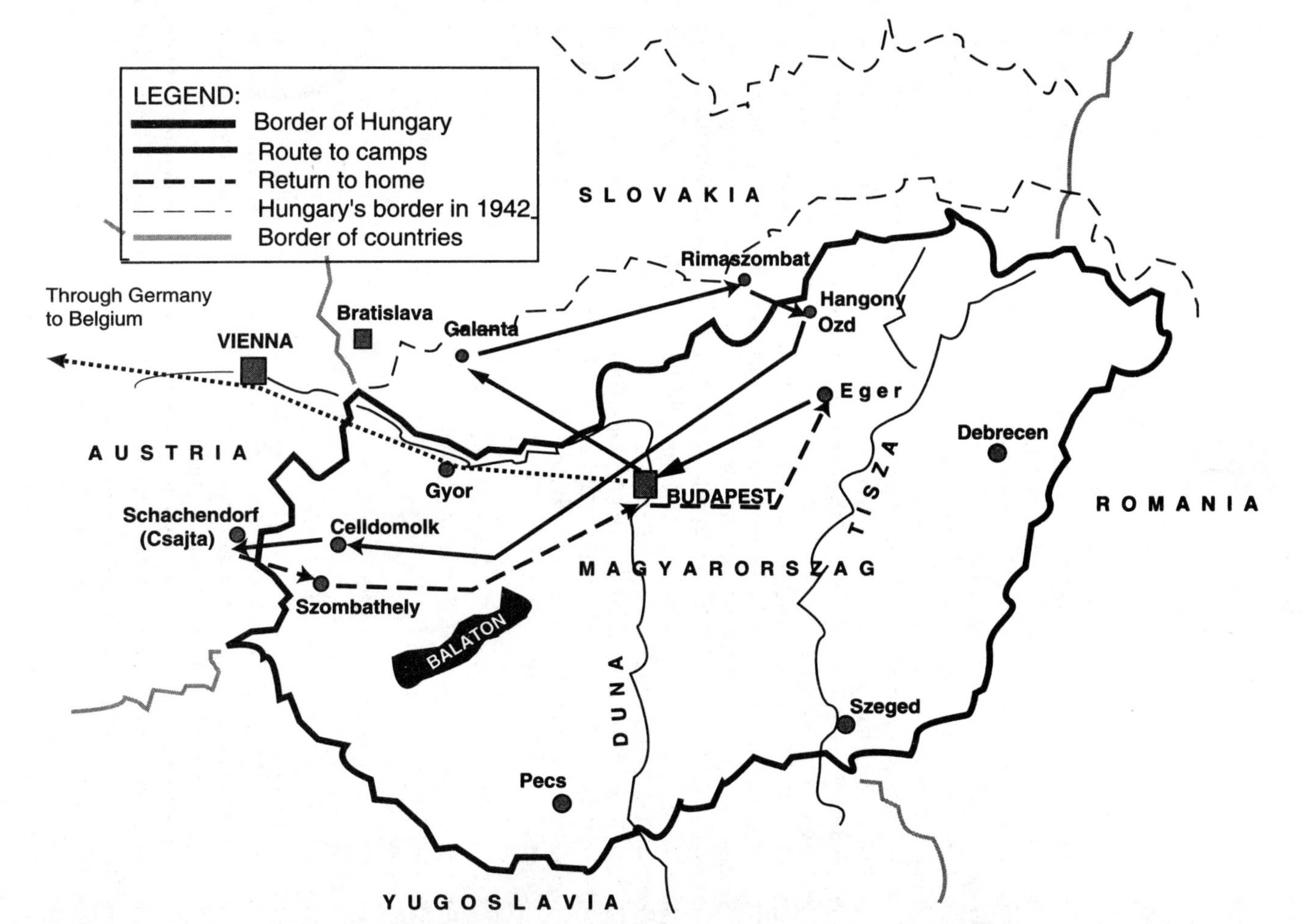
LEGEND:
Border of Hungary
Route to camps
Return to home
Hungary's border in 1942
Border of countries
SLOVAKIA
ROMANIA
AUSTRIA
YUGOSLAVIA
MAGYARORSZAG
Through Germany
to Belgium
VIENNA
Bratislava
Galanta
Rimaszombat
Hangony
Ozd
Eger
Debrecen
Gyor
BUDAPEST
Schachendorf
(Csajta)
Celldomolk
Szombathely
BALATON
TISZA
DUNA
Szeged
Pecs

THE EDGE OF WAR

I touch the swimming pool's end, finishing, I believe, eighteen hundred meters of my two thousand meter daily backstroke routine. I wouldn't know for sure, if not for Mr. Frederik, who gestures desperately to make me go faster for the last two hundred meters. It's easy for him, walking on the edge of the pool, his big belly well filled. He surely had a good lunch at noon, and he continues to nibble, even now finding food in his seemingly bottomless pocket.

Mr. Frederik will be disappointed again today, as he often has been lately. I feel too tired to accelerate. I make a great effort, but my arms and legs feel too heavy, as if each limb weighed ten kilos. Of course, if, like Mr. Frederik, I could eat a good dinner, all this would probably go better.

He's a good buddy, Mr. Frederik. I like him a great deal. He has been my protecting angel since my recent arrival in Budapest from my home town of Eger. He has done everything he could to fulfill his promise to find a job for me if I would join the team of his water polo club, known as III KER TVE. (Literally translated as Gymnastic and Fencing Club of the Third Borough.) I joined, but it's not his fault that he can keep neither his word nor his promise.

"Move, old buddy, move." Coach Frederic prompts me with enthusiasm. "Just twenty-five meters more! Accelerate a little more! Push! Last ten! Push! Last five!"

"This is very good," says Mr. Frederik, looking at his chronometer and affectionately patting my head. "This is excellent. Your best time this year! Now, out of the water, rest. In a half hour, we start the water polo. After we're finished, we can talk about your problems."

I can't believe my ears. Best time yet? Is he joking or teasing? It must be true, since friends are gathering around with amiable pats on my back. It seems incredible. Where does the energy come from, the strength to do better, to go faster? I feel more tired and less well-disposed than on previous days.

Maybe I have drawn from some mysterious source of energy the vigor which permits an athlete to jump higher, run faster, or throw farther in conditions of adversity, competition and tension; the power of the mind which causes an average person to become a hero in time of natural disaster, or in time of war. In any case, I am content. I put on my warm-up robe, to relax at the edge of this magnificent pool on the island of St. Margarite which divides the Danube as it flows majestically through Budapest. I sit satisfied, but ever so lonely, looking at the daredevil divers, champion swimmers and frolicking girls.

Fred, Gabor, Bushy and the others who join me are new friends. My teammates are more or less my age, with the exception of Bushy, who is about ten years older, and a veteran at the age of thirty-two. He is the team's father figure, a colossus weighing over two hundred pounds and an incredible swimmer. It is impossible to sink him in water polo. He seems a force of nature with the heart of a baby. He takes me under his protection and shelters me from the vicissitudes of the big city and also, a little, from my new friends.

They are relaxed, uninvolved, and not troubled at all, my friends. They do not yet feel the economic pressures, the new Hitlerian laws. They are the elite of the Hungarian bourgeoisie, the Lipot Varos, the Park Avenue of Budapest. They believe they are rich enough to overcome the country's, even the world's temporary difficulties.

My non-Jewish friends are innocent bystanders to the events which are affecting all European Jews. With varying degrees of anti-Semitism planted in their hearts since childhood, they do not mean to do harm to anyone. In any case, they consider me an exception to the propaganda that dictates how a Jew is supposed to look, feel, or behave. To them, I've been part of a privileged group of sportsmen for whom the fighting, competition, and fair play are natural. They hate only other, unseen Jews.

It seems to me that all Christians have at least one good Jewish friend whom they consider an exception to the stereotype. There are only five Jews to each hundred Christians in Hungary, but this simple arithmetic does not deter them from hating "Jews" of their imagination.

The generally jovial Coach Frederik is serious and concerned as he approaches me. "Come with me Tibor, sit down. As you know, I've tried everything to keep my promise and hire you in our firm as a textile designer. Being the director of the company, I didn't expect to have any problem with this, even just a few months ago, but the anti-Jewish laws hit me just as bad and, as things are going now, quite soon I may have to look for a job myself. Nevertheless, I promise you again that I will continue to search. I hope, with my connections and your design talent, we will find something. In the meantime, take this little bit of money and eat a good dinner somewhere. I will arrange something for you so that you are able to eat at least one good meal each day."

I listen with bowed head, my eyes furtively staring at the floor in embarrassment. To be so poor and unable to find a solution to my problem!

"Thank you, Mr. Frederik."

* * * * *

Those last few months had brought about major changes in the established order which were much more important than my difficulty in finding a job. The seeds of fascism that Hitler started to sow in Europe only a few years earlier had taken easy root in the fertile soil of Hungarian anti-Semitism. The Fascists started to reap the first fruits of their sinister harvest in the form of legislation in the Hungarian Parliament.

The first laws against Jews appeared in the summer of 1938, just one month before I successfully completed my baccalaureate in June at the Dobo Istvan Real School in Eger. My Jewish friends and I resigned ourselves to not being able to pursue our studies at the university. The Numerus Clausus, permitting only six percent of university students to be Jewish, in existence since the 1920's, now became Numerus Nullus. No Jews could attend any university at all. In consequence, in order to earn a livelihood I had to find a manual job, a trade where the proportion of Jews relative to gentiles was less than six percent.

Every day the poison of Nazism seemed to creep more and more into our daily life. Aside from the difficulty of finding even a menial job, there was the hurt of insults we did not dare answer. Even good friends distanced themselves, either by their own conviction, or because of peer pressure or the general atmosphere created by the fascist press which held Jews responsible for all the ills of the country.

The first anti-Jewish laws in May 1938 were primarily directed against the press, industry and the professions. The second, in May 1939, affected all Jews, who by April 1944 were ordered to wear their yellow star of David.

The victorious Western Powers buried their heads in the sand of false stability and security established by the Versailles Peace Treaty after the First World War. Parcelling up Germany, Austria and Hungary, disregarding demographic, language and cultural considerations, they sowed the seeds of future troubles.

Hitler ably exploited the desire of minorities in the "victorious" nations of World War I to reunite with their original countries. German and Hungarian nationals detached from their mother countries by the 1920 Versailles Treaty considered their situation temporary. The mother countries stood ready to welcome and reclaim them. It was not surprising then, that when Hitler offered to help Hungary liberate her occupied territories, the country, having suffered a nationalistic fever for twenty-five years, was ready to march with the Germans.

The Anschluss in Austria, already a fait accompli, made the Germans next-door neighbors of Hungary. In September 1938, the well-intentioned but disastrous Munich agreement was signed by Britain's Chamberlain and France's Daladier. It sanctioned the dismemberment of Czechoslovakia, with the occupation of the Sudetenland followed by Hungary's advance on the Sub-Carpathian Ruthenia in March 1939. At the same time, Germany renewed its demands for Poland to cede Danzig.

The war did not affect us directly in the city. Active recruitement of young people was already at a maximum. We were only spectators of the hostilities through newspapers and from the radio which broadcast the latest developments minute by minute. By such means, Hungarians savored the heroic exploits of their soldiers, who advanced practically without resistance to a new border more or less determined by Hitler in advance.

Along with war news, the country enjoyed reports about the enthusiastic welcome expressed by Hungarians living in Czechoslovakia who were being "liberated from oppression" by the military campaign. These hearty endorsements were genuine, in spite of the fact that Czechoslovakia was one of the most democratic countries in central Europe, and the economic situation also was better than in Hungary. The newly-annexed Hungarian population had always felt Hungarian. They shared our history, culture, language and personal outlook. As a result, these people rejoined the motherland with enthusiasm.

Hungarian language and culture had retained their vitality in Czechoslovakia, in Yugoslavia, and even more so in Rumania. Ironically, this cultural integrity was preserved by indigenous local Hungarian publications, which were run, in very large measure, by journalists, financiers and literary personages who were Jewish.

* * * * *

I went home without spending the money Mr. Frederik gave me for my dinner, hoping someone from my family, or a friend, would invite me to dine. The funds could then be put aside to pay for a possible date next Sunday.

I rented my furnished flat from a Jewish bourgeois family. Mr Braun, my impoverished landlord, tried desperately to maintain the appearance of better days. He rented two of his four rooms to supplement his income. The pain of injured pride was written on his face as he watched boarders pass through his dining salon on the way to their rooms.

Nobody invited me to dinner, but when I passed through the living room, Mr. Braun's beautiful daughter, Agnes, invited me for tea, which was served with a few cookies. As dinner, it was a meager consolation for my stomach. Still, Agnes' beautiful red hair, her round firm breasts, and the "accidental" touch of her delicate skin under the table, at least rekindled my vanishing morale.

The following day, I spent my time unsuccessfully looking for a job. I went to evening swimming training tired, but comforted, as if I were going home. The pool was the only place I found myself surrounded by friends. I also continued to nurture the hope that "grandaddy" Frederik might have found me an occupation.

Mr. Frederik greeted me with a big smile at the entrance to the swimming pool. Surely he had found a job for me. Noticing my eager expectation, the smile suddenly froze on his face. Poor man. All he could announce was that he had found a very beautiful restaurant owned by an ex-sportsman and that arrangements had been made for me to be fed there every day.

Within seconds, vivid images flashed in my mind. I saw myself humiliated, begging for soup or a meager dinner in a chic restaurant. My mother prepared food packages at our home in Eger with great love, and sent me these from time to time especially to avoid such humiliation. Images flashed back of the traumatic experiences I had when the director of the Dobo School, following a practice accepted as normal, ordered me to stand up with three or four other students. In front of the class, he announced to us that if our fathers would not or could not pay the tuition for the semester, we would be sent home. Would I ever be able to protect myself from such humiliation and embarrassment?

But I also saw myself going home tomorrow with an empty stomach.

"Do you hear me?" Frederik yelled as he grabbed my shoulders. "I found a place where you can eat a dinner every night. Don't you understand?" Mr. Frederik noticed my hesitation and embarrassment. "Listen, young man," he said, "I will give you a bit of advice which, maybe, will serve as a lesson for the rest of your life. You must survive first, and improve your existence after, as you can. You cannot reverse this order."

When the words were first out of his mouth, I did not realize the importance of this simple truth. I think it was my instinct to survive which responded.

"Can I go tonight?

* * * * *

Mr. Alexander, the restaurant owner, was impeccable in his tuxedo. He radiated self-confidence and, although retired from swimming for a few years, was still well-built. After observing him through the chic Restaurant Victoria's enormous window, having passed the door numerous times with hesitation, my chest pounding, I entered and headed toward him.

"I am Tibor ..."

"I know who you are. You played an excellent match last Sunday. Mr. Frederik talked to me about you. Relax and follow me."

We walked between the tightly packed tables set for dinner, past the beautiful people dressed in the latest fashion, flashing gold and diamonds as they reached for crystal glasses filled with champagne.

Off the main dining area there opened a narrow, short corridor with one row of tables on each side. A chess set sat on each table. Some of the habitues were deeply involved in their games, while at other tables lone players awaited a partner. The opponent could be anyone willing to play. At the end of the row near the kitchen entrance, a few tables were set for dinner. The waiters ate dinner there during their breaks.

"Here we are! Please sit down. You will be served shortly. You are welcome every night," the owner said.

My face burning and my body shaking with emotion, I managed to squeeze out my thanks.

The empty stomach has its own logic, embarrassment and bruised ego notwithstanding. With a full stomach you can concentrate more sharply on your own problems, as well as on the world's.

* * * * *

The news from Germany and Austria was getting worse and worse. Germany was pressing its demands against Poland. England and France guaranteed Poland's territorial integrity at the end of March, 1939. However, the Western Powers' diplomatic maneuvering, including Roosevelt's demand that Hitler and Mussolini guarantee they would not attack twenty-nine countries, accomplished nothing. In May, England and France literally begged the Russians to sign an alliance with Poland; but Litvinov, more pro-western in outlook, was replaced by Molotov, who sought accommodation with the Germans. In August, they signed a non-aggression pact. Germany offered half of Poland to the USSR. Jews fleeing from Poland found temporary rest in Hungary. The possibility of an extended war became more and more a reality.

Yet for me and my friends, these developments were only newspaper articles or radio news from far-away places; the war was not yet in our streets. I was filled with fast-growing concern over world events, but more immediately, I was worried about not having a job.

After dining at the Victoria restaurant, when my belly had declared a truce with my mind, these thoughts fought for my attention as I strolled on Avenue Rakoczy near Budapest's Eastern Railroad Station. As I walked, lonely and silent in the crowd, amidst the noise of tramways, cars and people, a sudden voice broke into my consciousness.

"Hi, Tibor, how are you? What are you doing in Budapest? You don't remember me, of course. You were too young. How are the folks at home in Eger?"

"I'm sorry, but ..."

"I'm Zoltan Reich," he said.

"I'm afraid I don't recognize you, but it's nice to meet someone from Eger."

"That's alright," he said. "Are you on vacation?"

"No, I'm not. I'm looking for a job," I said.

"A friend in Eger told me you were one of the best designers in High School," Zoltan said.

"Maybe so, but what's the difference? In the present situation, I can't go for any kind of higher education, and I can't find a job."

"Do you like to design?" he asked.

"I think so."

"Do you want to help me out? I have a graphic art studio and I could use a pair of hands."

"I don't think I'm good enough. What can you do with an amateur?"

"Don't worry. Come to my studio, have a drink, and let's talk."

I felt my heart in my throat. Hope, anxiety, opportunity and self-doubt assailed me at once.

Zoltan was at least fifteen years my senior, stocky, strong as a bull, and already bald. He wore a constant grin on his face. I followed him, talking about our home town, the folks in Eger and the great opportunities in the big city. By the Eastern Railroad Station we turned into a side street—a modest lower-middle-class neighborhood. He turned the key in his apartment door and we entered.

I was shocked not by the unbelievable disorder, but rather because he emphasized that this was his apartment, not just his studio. The mess, paint in bins, pots and ash trays on the floor, and the scribbling on the wall would satisfy a layman's notion of how artists are supposed to live and work. Besides the tools of his trade, there was a three-legged semi-high stool at his work table. The opposite corner had a beautiful sofa, in marked contrast with the general mess.

"Make yourself comfortable. Sit down," he said, pointing toward the sofa. Feeling tired, I let myself drop into what I thought was its cushiony embrace. My bottom hit the unyielding surface so hard that my tailbone still ached two days later. Zoltan exploded with a tremendous belly laugh. He flipped over the beautiful velvety cover, which revealed a shabby wood-frame construction filled with three straw bags. I laughed, too. It was a small price to pay for his offer.

"You can start working with me tomorrow or right now. In exchange, you can live here with me and I'll give you some pocket money ."

Hurray! I had a job!

"Incidentally, where can I sleep?"

"We can buy a folding bed if you're fussy; if not, the bathtub next door, with some cushions, will do fine." I opted for the folding bed. "One more condition. When my mistress comes, you hit the movies, but I pay."

"It's a deal," I said.

A few months of apprenticeship sharpened my technique and my taste in graphic art. We did catalogs, advertising, window displays; anything that came our way. To save money, we mixed our own colors—pigment plus dextrin plus water made "gouache".

We liked to have catalog work, not because of its artistic value, but because we kept most of the samples sent to us to be illustrated. The chocolate and canned food contributed to our sustenance, the clothing to our appearance, and the sofa's cover to our "interior decoration."

I met Lola, Zoltan's girlfriend, the second day. She was a lovely, attractive woman, slightly less bohemian than he, and pregnant.

"Hi! Nice to meet you," she said. "Zoltan told me about you, how talented you are, and how hungry you are. So here's some food. Let's eat. Zoltan! Set the table!"

"Yes, love." Zoltan responded.

He proceeded to push aside the jars and cans full of colors, knocking over one or two in the process. Lola unpacked her basket and served us good, warm food. She did that very often, since we had no kitchen. Other days, we ate in cheap restaurants or had cold cuts with wine. We also shared the food packages my mother sent; they were always the highlight of our culinary adventures.

The telephone rang. Zoltan answered it. An important customer, a liquor distributor, wanted him to come over immediately. He changed in a hurry, and was in the doorway when Lola noticed a big hole in his socks.

"Zoltan, change your socks."

"There's no time now." He grabbed a brush, matched the color of his socks and painted it on his skin. "Okay? Goodbye!"

* * * * *

It was almost a year since I left the safety, love and warmth of my home in Eger and began the struggle to survive in Budapest. Zoltan was an excellent artist, but certainly not a businessman, and neither was I. Lola stayed more and more often at the studio, and I had to go more and more often to the movies. After his baby boy, Jancsi, was born, it was obvious that the time was near for me to move on.

* * * * *

While I was innocently struggling to make a living, long-established Jewish businesses, brilliant careers, and fortunes were crumbling under the pressure of increasingly vicious anti-Jewish laws. The choices were few for those who wanted to live and eat tomorrow. There were those who preferred not to struggle, and committed suicide. But I remembered Mr. Frederik, "First survive, then we'll see."

Our last hope for peace vanished fast, that September. Hitler claimed that Polish troops attacked German soldiers, but everybody knew the attack was made by S.S. troops disguised as Poles. Germany made no reply to the mediation efforts of Belgium's Leopold III—in the name of six small European countries—nor of Roosevelt, nor of Pope Pius XII, nor even of Mussolini.

On September 3, 1939, within a few hours of each other, Great Britain and France declared war on Germany. On September 5th, to the consternation of the European governments and their people, the United States declared itself neutral.

These events encouraged the Hungarian Nyilas Party to commit greater atrocities. The Hungarian Nyilas (Arrow Cross) Party had been created in 1937 with a platform calling for the creation of a Hungarian Empire and the expulsion of all minorities. By 1939, it already had considerable power. With the advent of the war, its leaders flagrant abuses against the Jews, even though it was not until 1944 that, with the help of Hitler, it became the ruling party under Imre Szallasi.

Under their auspices, to hold any job, or just to exist, a Jew needed more and more "proof" as to the degree of Hungarian he was. For a short while, different categories were created: Jews in mixed marriages; Jews who converted to Christianity; Jews who arrived recently from the Polish and Czechoslovakian persecutions, or those absorbed by Hungary's expansion of the border to the Sub-Carpathian territories; Jews who lived, but were not born in Hungary; and the most desirable, those who were born and had lived for generations in Hungary.

Proudly, I belonged to this last group. It did not matter for very long. Still, the scramble was on for all papers, legitimate or false, to prove one's deep Hungarian roots.

* * * * *

My refuge and salvation continued to be the National Swimming Pool. There I continued to live one of my childhood dreams; to be a champion. I seldom missed training, nor did I miss the free dinner at the Restaurant Victoria that followed.

One day I arrived a little late. My teammates were already in the water warming up. Mr. Frederik was yelling at them, as coaches do, urging the swimmers to try harder. To me, he shouted, "Get going! Ten extra laps for being late! Move!" I jumped in.

Years ago in Eger, I realized that I would never be a world-class swimmer. I was a backstroker. Backstroking often tempts you to watch the sky, the passing clouds, and swim "junk laps" instead of concentrating. But I did become a world-class water polo goalie. I loved being a goalie. While doing my laps, I imagined myself already in the goal thinking about the weekend championship games, hearing the enthusiastic crowd when I stopped a murderous shot.

We finished the warm-up. "Five minutes rest," Mr. Frederik called.

Bushy, Fred and all my other teammates were unusually polite and solicitous toward me lately. I was the only Jew on the team, besides Mr. Frederik.

Such politness contrasted sharply with the general boisterous and madcap atmosphere of this rough sport. My teammates were embarrassed about what was happening around us. Fred slapped my head gently.

"Hi, Tibor. How are things with you? I hope you've had no serious problems with the Nyilas thugs."

"Ya," joined Gabor, "you know, our constant arguments about anti-Semitism don't mean we agree with what's going on, especially with the treatment of real Hungarians from the country, like you."

"Cut it out," Bushy interjected. He was always the pacifier, either by verbal persuasion or by virtue of the muscles of his two-hundred-pound body.

"Five minutes are up. Tibor in the goal! The rest, line up!"

What's so great about being a goalie? Certainly not the finger bones broken against the goal post, or the ball shot in your face from two meters away, which occasionally knocks you out. It's the feeling of being the last hope of your teammates. It's facing the attacking line that outplayed your defense with calm concentration, muscles ready to spring; seeing suspense in the eyes of your teammates and hearing the tense silence of supporters, the relief and the roar of the fans at a successful stop, all in a fraction of a second. It's concentrated delirium.

Defeat also has its own emotional impact and is not completely negative. Terrible as defeat may seem, solace does come if your peers recognize that you have done your best. I learned early, through those games, that there is no excuse for error; a goal is a goal and there is no way to undo it. But it was only a game. Outside the pool, an error, good or bad judgement, could mean life or death.

Coming home from the pool, I often stopped at Csaky Street, where Cica, my childhood girlfriend, lived with her mother. Ours had been a semi-innocent courtship with romantic interludes on St. Margarite Island. Her mother, Aranka, had great ambitions for her.

I was accepted as a friend from Eger, but certainly not as a contender for her daughter, who was destined for a rich professional, preferably an American.

In the meantime, while her mother would entertain a friend in one room, we had our freedom in another. Our freedom at that time was limited to "everything but." If that was not enough to satisfy, there was the additional reward of dinner.

One of my best friends, Zoli, had been a schoolmate since kindergarten. He and Klari, his girlfriend, provided the so-badly needed real friendship in my otherwise harsh life. Klari was the daughter of a well-to-do chemical engineer with his own independent petro-chemical laboratory, who was not yet unduly affected by the anti-Jewish laws. He was part of the comfortable Jewish intellectual bourgeoisie in Lipot Varos, living in a plush turn-of-the-century environment. Such people had the most to lose, but were also least likely to believe they could lose everything. Weren't they true Hungarians, after all? But for the moment, theirs was a quiet, well balanced family, with everything I didn't have. For a long time, the only place, other than at the pool, where I felt at home since I had left Eger, was in their professional upper-middle class atmosphere, listening to classical records in warm comfort, with elegant and sophisticated girlfriends. I never had money to invite them to the movies or for coffee, but it didn't matter. We walked endlessly on the streets and in the parks, eating frankfurters at Uncle Sarvari's terrace, which was a two-foot extension of his pushcart on Kiraly Street. We cuddled, kissed and philosophized... about religion, politics, and art with the fervor and conviction of our eighteen or twenty years of life experience. Could we ever have realized at that time that those early convictions would stay with us all our lives?

I also had friends among my swimming pals. One of them, Fred, was a knowledgeable guide to Budapest's bordellos. After one disappointing training session, as we walked home over the St. Margarite Bridge, he suggested that we forget polo. "Let's go to see the girls of O Street."

"How much does it cost?"

"Two pengo."

I started to count my money, reaching deep in my pocket. I didn't have much, but I rationalized the expense as food for the soul. "So let's go."

This was the first time I had gone to a bordello and I was rather nervous. It turned out to be a fairly nice cafe where girls in low-cut, semi-transparent evening gowns lounged at little round tables, sipping coffee or drinks, waiting to be asked to dance. This romantic prelude was a kind of testing, and gave the customer a better feel of the merchandise.

Broad-minded as I was, I still felt somewhat disgusted by the whole affair. But as the mind has needs, so does the flesh. After a few minutes, either one changed partners or went upstairs to the rooms. I chose. We danced. Then it was time to climb the steps. We passed a cashier at a turnstile and I paid two pengo.

Upstairs in the room, my "beautiful conquest" immediately started to undress. I was shy and embarrassed by her nonchalance. When she was half undressed, with her large breasts hanging out, she asked for her fee. "I trust you, young man, but the rule is to pay in advance!"

"I'm sorry ... I just did at the turnstile ..."

"That's for the room, little idiot. How about me?"

"I'm sorry, madame, I thought ... I have no more money ..."

"You bastard! Do you take me for a fool? You want to fuck free? Don't waste any more of my time! Get out of here before I call my pimp!"

For a moment I was petrified, then I grabbed my things and scrambled out in record time, my face burning with embarrassment. Fred came down later and laughed at my story. "That's okay. You can always go back to the pool and have a cold shower."

"Thanks!"

That was the first and last bordello experience of my life.

* * * * *

On our way home, Fred and I stopped at a terrace cafe at the Place Berlin, the social, intellectual and commercial center of Budapest. It was the preferred meeting place for lovers, artists and businessmen alike. In the center of the Place was a large newstand on the "Banana Island", a popular rendezvous for lovers. It was also one of the few places in Hungary where you could buy bananas and pick up some sad or angry girl whose lover had stood her up.

Many people at the cafe tables around us, as well as the passers-by, reflected the city's nervous anxiety. Bent over their newspapers, they spoke in hushed tones, pointing at the disquieting headlines. On the street, greenshirted "Nyilasok", alone and in groups, paraded confidently. They wore their version of the swastika on armbands, a flashing crossed arrow. Yet others in the cafes, including well-to-do Jewish women, continued to savor their coffee and chocolate in ignorant beatitude. They showed little concern for the symbols of hatred surrounding them.

The daily papers featured large headlines above stories detailing the German army's glorious victories in Poland. The Poles resisted heroically, especially around Warsaw. The city was devastated by heavy bombing and held out until the 27th of August, when it was finally overwhelmed and overrun. By September 17th, the Russians occupied Eastern Poland. They met the Germans at Brest-Litovsk, and that was the end of Poland. We learned only after the war about the secret clause of the German/Soviet Non-aggression Pact dividing Poland between the two countries.

* * * * *

"What do you think, Fred? What will all this lead to?"

"You Jews are not the only ones to worry. I can be drafted anytime.
So can the others on the team. Everything may fall apart, but I hope now that England and France have entered the war, they will take care of Hitler pretty fast. They should move faster, damn it, before I'm drafted."

But they didn't.

"You know what, Fred? I'm almost more concerned about the local fascists like those you see here than about the war. They get more and more vicious and bloodthirsty; they intimidate the more moderate Gentiles. Very few are like you."

* * * * *

I was proud of my progress in the graphic arts and I wrote about it to my parents. Their feelings were very different. My parents' letters arrived more and more often. They expressed great concern about my well-being, my health, and the course I was taking with my life. They looked upon my flirting with the arts as suspicious, worried that it wouldn't lead to anything. If, because of the anti-Jewish laws, I could not become a doctor or an engineer, as a Jewish boy is supposed to, at least I should learn a decent trade. But the options were very few. The only choices available were manual labor in typical Jewish trades like those of a tailor, furrier or leather worker, or self-employment as a small businessman.

In my letters, I tried to mention only the good things. "Everything is fine," even though I might be starving or had seen some new brutality. I was too proud to acknowledge that I might not succeed, and I knew they couldn't afford to help me. But a mother always knows, and the food packages kept coming. Concerned about the increasingly frequent atrocities in Budapest, they pressed me to come home, at least for a visit.

* * * * *

So I took the train for a short visit with my family. Since the railroad station in Eger was far from my home, I took a carriage. The old horse trotted slowly through the streets past old friends' houses. The monotonous clopping of horseshoes on the cobblestones filled me with the comfort of my home town's familiar sounds. I drifted into a dreamlike recollection of my childhood and school years. They were so recent, only one and a half years ago, yet they seemed so far away. I pulled the coarse horse blanket around me against the chill.

I was looking forward to seeing my family after eighteen months, especially my mother. She was always loving, light-hearted, understanding, tolerant of our childhood weaknesses and cautiously optimistic about everything. She was one of seven children: on her side I had six uncles. My grandparents lived two houses further down the street, as had their own grandparents for many generations.

My father was always concerned about our future, since his past had been so unfortunate. After having owned a fairly successful haberdashery store, he lost everything in the great depression, and struggled desperately to provide for the family and for his children's education. A bad mark in school or a bad remark from a neighbor would upset him. For him, hope for the future, as in most Jewish families, was in learning, reading and understanding.

Everything that distracted from this meant jeopardizing the future. He loved us desperately and wanted us to succeed. Of course, when he forbade me occasionally to attend swim training, I didn't look at it in that light. Characteristically, my mother would sneak my trunks out to me.

I loved my mother for her lightheartedness. I loved my father for his concern and his heroic effort to provide. I loved my brother, who struggled with many childhood sicknesses and who had to be protected. I saw myself as the strong guy who could take reprimands or slaps, both for myself and as my brother's surrogate, if I did not keep him out of trouble. In fact, I preferred a spanking to the lengthy admonitions and reprimands of my overly-concerned father.

The carriage approached our neighborhood. The silhouette of the ancient fortress erected in 1241 stood proudly against the cloudy sky, always reminding us of the heroic people of Eger who had defended the city. In the foreground on the Market Square was the statue of Istvan Dobo, defender of Eger against the Turks in 1552, with a woman figure at his side. It symbolized their contribution to the defense of the city, pouring boiling oil on the assaulting Turks climbing the fortress wall on their ladders.

My father was waiting in the middle of Servita Street, along the base of the fortress, with both joy and fear written on his face. What had become of his son? I jumped from the carriage and set down my cardboard valise. We shook hands and hugged, but just for a second or two. Showing more emotion would not have been manly. We passed through the arched door which opened onto a long, narrow interior court, full of flowers that pressed against the massive, forbidding walls of the fortress. My mother, in the kitchen doorway, stretched out her arms with a big smile, awaiting my embrace.

"You look terrific. A little skinny, but a real man. Come in." We kissed. My brother looked at me with awe, searching for the telltale signs of big city experience.

Within five minutes, a welcoming party had started that included all the neighbors. I looked around. Nothing ever changed. Amid the centuries old houses were people young and old: Catholics, Protestants and Jews, soldiers, teachers, the lesser nobility, rich merchants, peasants in their semi-feudal society, and gypsies at the edge of the city. All fitted properly together like a jigsaw puzzle, each piece tucked safely into its niche.

Coming back from the big city, I found all this so boring, yet so blissfully secure, familiar, and so much my home. But the foundation was shaking. Almost imperceptibly, Gentiles began more and more to avoid Jews. Fear created by propaganda and a few local fascists permeated the air, even this far into the country. People whose families had lived in town for many generations were forced to begin a humiliating search for birth certificates. For the elderly, it was a particular hardship. There had been no records kept, aside from the religious registers. These the fascists tried to destroy. But such assaults on human dignity were benign compared with the brutal persecution recounted by the Polish refugees who had managed to escape the repressive regime of Hans Frank, new Governor of Poland. Their stories filled us with anxiety for the future, although we resisted acknowledging that the handwriting on the wall would apply to us.

* * * * *

"Mom, I'm running over to see Grandpa and Grandma and I'm going to drop in at the pool, okay?"

"You've hardly arrived, but go ahead. Just don't be late."

I kissed her and ran.

My grandparents lived on the road to the pool, and Grandma was also a grandma to all my friends. They always stopped at her house to be fortified by her delicious chocolate cookies or strudels.

My Grandfather, except for his religion, could have been the symbol of Hungary. He was like those marvelous works of art which have come to represent a people or nation. Close to six feet tall and wiry, he had a big handlebar moustache and was strong as a bull. At the age of seventy-one he did not need eyeglasses, had all his teeth, braved sub-zero temperatures without a coat or a hat, and turned to admire every pretty girl who passed. He enjoyed life. His father, a horse trader, had bought stolen horses from the gypsies and sold them to the hussars and the clergy. It was, arguably, a reputable occupation: He even gave Eger's archbishop a horse as a gift. This event, duly recorded, was my grandfather's "proof" that he was Hungarian.

Yet time had begun to take its toll while I was away. Grandfather was losing the fiery spark in his eyes.

"What's the matter Grandpa?"

"It's hard to say, son. The world seems to be going crazy. They tell me I'm not Hungarian, nor your father, although we were decorated heroes in the First World War and the war before it. See that airplane flying there near the church tower? It's menacing. I don't like these new things. Does Hitler have many of those? It spells bad news for us and for the world."

He died a year later of natural causes, the only one in my family to have a grave in Eger.

* * * * *

At the swimming pool, which was my playground from age six, nothing had changed. Young people did their laps, the polo players passed the balls in circles or drove them toward the goal. The coaches still barked and tore their hair out in desperation over poor performances. It was a timeless scene I knew well.

Walking to the far side of the fifty-meter Olympic pool, I hailed old friends and revelled in my good reputation as a goalie in Budapest. I headed toward the locker rooms. There was one for each of the city's two swim clubs, the ETE, all Jews, and MESE, all Gentiles. This segregation had nothing to do with the recent rise in fascism. It had always been like this; one club supported by well-to-do Jewish merchants and professionals, the other by the city and clergy. Relations were normal and sportsmanlike between the two teams. The clergy even helped us out in the winter with a carriage-load of firewood to heat our lockers.

We swam outdoors all winter since the entire city enjoyed natural warm artesian springs, bubbling out of the ground at a comfortable 33 degrees celsius. Even drinking water had to be cooled in caves. Swimming was the principal sport in Eger, and the city was home to many Hungarian champions.

Everything seemed the same. Or was it? Some familiar faces were not around. Dispersed or drafted, some of us had already been wounded in Hungary's march on Czechoslovakia and Rumania.

A few players gathered around. “Hi, Tibor. Feel like jumping in the goal for just a few minutes?”

“Okay.”

We started talking about the coming Olympics in Tokyo. Would I make it? My old friend Sandor pressed. “I may, I’m in a good position to make the team, at least as a substitute. But with all the things going on now, who knows?” It did not take long to find out.

With the expanding of the war to so many fronts, the 1940 Olympic games, which were supposed to be held in Tokyo, were cancelled. On the way home, my nostalgic mood mixed with anxiety about the future. I took the main street and came across many friends and acquaintances. Some were already in uniform, proud as peacocks, and they talked with amiable condescension to me, a Jew, but still a “friend”. Suddenly, turning into a side street near the post office, I found myself face to face with an old schoolmate, Varga.

* * * * *

I had meant to say “szervus”, a friendly salutation, but the words died on my lips as a flash of memory reminded me of the first anti-semitic incident in our class. Varga was the second son of a hardworking but poor blue-collar family. His father was a blacksmith and his mother cleaned houses occasionally for well-to-do merchants who sometimes were Jews. Now they saw their salvation, as so many others in a similar situation, in the promise of the Arrow Cross party. His older brother, a low-level city clerk, was already openly active in the party and obviously had to demonstrate his militancy to his brother and the party.

Out of twenty-four students in the class, ten were Jews and eleven were Catholic, which was very unusual. The average was three or four out of twenty-five. So we had strength, especially when, occasionally, the three Protestants joined with us. We were well matched. We had our muscle man, so did they; we had our sharpshooter at paramilitary exercises, and so did they. Whether in chess championships or in studies, it was all very even. Too bad that we could not take each other’s measure in a sportsmanlike, friendly competition. Instead, little by little we drifted apart, and our old classmate friends became the “master race,” our masters.

Varga and I looked in each others eyes without saying a word; I with contempt, he with the proud superiority of his race. Neither of us blinked. We passed without looking back. The drama of our generation was played out in three or four seconds. No doubts. We were enemies.

Just a few months before our baccalaureate in 1938, the class had returned from a ten-minute recess after the religion period, which was held one hour each week by the respective clergymen in separate rooms for each of the three religions. Steiner, a classmate, pointed to his seat. “Tibor, look at this, and that, and Miska’s and the seats of all the other Jews!”

Swastikas had been drawn with crayon on all our seats. Steiner proceeded to wipe his seat off. “Stop!” I yelled. “Don’t touch it! Let the one who did this step forward and wipe it off.” Nobody budged. After insults had been exchanged, and just as a scuffle was about to break out, the math professor entered the class.

“Sit down,” he said routinely. I did not.

“Why are you standing?” I explained what we found on our chairs.

“Who did it?” No answer.

“Cowards,” I said, and sat down.

We learned later that Varga was the instigator, but he had not executed his crime alone.

* * * * *

The Dobo Istvan Real School placed an emphasis on living languages. French and German were obligatory, English and Italian optional. We also studied mathematics and design. The school director, Dr. Fejer, was a former Catholic priest who read and understood Hebrew. He often visited our religion class, which was taught by a Reform rabbi. When Dr. Fejer was in the class we were taught religion. When he was not, which was most of the time, we were taught Zionism and Hebrew to rebuild Israel.

Rabbi Roth also headed the Jewish Youth Club called Ohel Sem. Although seemingly it was mostly fun and games, it was actually almost a paramilitary organization whose purpose was to prepare us for life in Israel. Opinion in the Jewish community was split on the issue. Most of us, even in 1938, felt that we were Hungarian first, of the Jewish faith second, and what happened in Germany would not happen to us here, in spite of the anti-Jewish laws.

How wrong we were.

* * * * *

I spent many of the daytime hours of my few vacation days with my old buddies. We swam laps or played polo in the swimming pool reserved for competition only. Sometimes I went to the solarium, a larger co-ed pool that was also a social hub. There, I met with friends, including the Jewish girls from the Catholic girl's gymnasium. Since there was no co-ed schooling at that time, the Catholic nuns accepted Jewish girls and were quite open-minded about socializing with boys. Evenings, I stayed at home with my parents and my brother, mostly talking and worrying about our future.

My parents felt strongly that art, commercial or fine, was a bohemian "gypsy" occupation, not a serious way to live. Since there was no way to go to the University, I had to learn a trade, like my brother, who was apprenticed to a tailor. But my parents suggested that I learn something which would allow me to use my talents for design. A few years later, this advice would get me in and out of a lot of trouble.

The end of my vacation came all too quickly. On the eve of my departure to Budapest, we gathered for our last meal together, grandparents, granduncles, aunts and cousins, chatting and eating. Anxiety and concern about each other was heavy on our minds, but unspoken. Only my mother, grandfather and brother tried heroicallly to lift our spirits. Night descended. The many church bells which toll for joyous as well as for tragic occasions, or just to give the time, seemed to harmonize with their message: It was time to retire.

We said our good-byes and dispersed with hidden or not-so-hidden tears in our eyes. I climbed into my cozy bed in my little room, and pulled the feather filled comforter over my head. The fresh air and the scent of flowers poured in through the open windows, along with the bugle call of "Takarodo," the taps the soldiers played each night atop the fortress. I remembered the games we played, running on the top of the crested walls of the old fortress, beating the Turks, and the sound of the flutes, when young soldiers played beautifully sad or wild Hungarian folk songs. Finally, I fell a sleep.

* * * * *

The distance from Eger to Budapest is only a hundred and five kilometers but, in the minds of country people, it was like traveling to the moon. When I arrived back in Budapest, I dropped my luggage off in my flat and headed for the swimming pool. The training was in full swing. We were preparing for the Hungarian championship which, at that time, was almost equivalent to the World Championship, so strong was the Hungarian team.

After workout, I stopped Mr. Frederik. "I would like to talk to you about some serious matters concerning my future."

He answered, "None of us knows now what the future will be. We all act like automatons and try to ignore the reality. Like in an earthquake, everything shakes from its foundation, objects fly around us, there is nowhere to run, and we hope that nothing collapses and crushes us."

"It's true, but we still have to go on living," I said.

"What's new at home? How are things in the countryside?" he asked.

"Not great, everything is tense. My parents would like me to learn a trade. I must find a job, Mr. Frederik, and I need your help to do it. You remember I told you about my second cousin, a printer. He mentioned that steel engraving needs a lot of artistic skill."

"What the heck is that?" he said, "I never heard of it."

"It's a kind of sculpting. A bas relief in reverse, engraved in steel; sports medals, coins and the like. They also make steel and rubber stamps, all in reverse negatives for reproduction," I said.

He smiled and nodded, "Since everything else is in reverse, it seems to fit our times. I'll look into it and let you know."

It took months before he could find me a job. Meanwhile, I landed a few free-lance accounts, mostly catalogs and window displays.

I spent a lot of time in the pool. I also met a few nice girls, especially Agi, the sensitive, intelligent daughter of a rich Jewish family from Lipot Varos. She was warm and affectionate, just the opposite of the many snobs from that part of the city. Through rose-colored glasses of love she saw my everyday struggles as those of a country-boy hero. She was the antidote to my troubles and my cheerleader at the polo games. When she entered my dreary flat at Csaky Street, she transformed it into a palace. We tried to talk about the future, but we knew it was unlikely that we would be together. Some days we weren't sure there would be a future at all.

Every day the papers and radio reported events galloping at incredible speed. Having been successful in Czechoslovakia and Poland, Hitler decided to attack the West. That was confirmed by the Mechelen incident, in which two officers carrying documents to German army commandants were captured in Mechelen, Belgium.

On May 9th, 1939, the Germans invaded the West through Holland and Belgium. Goose-stepping around the Maginot line, they mounted an assault through the Ardennes, a feat which had been described by the French a few months before as impossible.

Just about the time we were fearing the fall of France, Mr. Frederik, after much diligent effort, found employment for me at the Bojti Engraving Company. The firm was located in the basement of a relatively modern building. Mr. Bojti explained that, thanks to my baccalaureate, I was to be an apprentice for only one year. Otherwise, it would take three years—at minimum salary. I would have to attend a trade school two half-days per week. At the end of the year, I would be required to take an examination by completing an assigned engraving. This system, while it had its negative aspects, produced excellent craftsmen who were appreciated all over Europe.

I also had to attend the "Levente" once a week. This was the paramilitary organization of Hungary, like Germany's Hitler Jugend, but minus its blatant anti-Semitism ... at least in the beginning.

"So there it is," concluded Mr. Bojti. "Let me now introduce you to my crew of three. You won't have it easy. Don't show off your better education or your design capabilities. Just be an apprentice under their orders, and nothing else."

"I will," I said.

We entered the workshop from his office. "This is Janos, senior master engraver; Geza, junior master engraver; and Peter, stamp specialist. And this is Tibor, our new apprentice."

First, a long silence, and then a murmured "Hi!" from Geza and Peter. No sound from Janos. "This is your work table," continued Mr. Bojti, pointing to one niche of the three which were cut out in a semi-circle at a large work bench. "Janos will assign your work to you." Mr. Bojti left.

My co-workers did not receive me well. I tried to reintroduce myself with a handshake, which Peter and Geza accepted grudgingly, but which Janos refused. Spreading his feet apart, with hands on his hips, he declared from the full height of his five-foot frame, "I don't shake hands with Jews. I'm a member of the Nyilas Party."

I froze. His words brought back the memory, with all its accompanying emotion, of the incident of the swastikas in the school classroom. The hostility of my co-workers was not due to religion alone but, in part, to their resentment toward a system which permitted someone with a high school education to accomplish in one year what it had taken them three years to achieve. That this person was a Jew flew in the face of all the propaganda defining Jews, like gypsies, as an inferior race. The gypsies, however, unlike Jews, were seen as embodying a part of the mythic Hungarian soul—the romantic dream of freedom and vagabondage hidden just beneath the surface of a rigid, semi-feudal society, and celebrated in countless poems, tales and music.

Of my three colleagues, only one seemed capable of separating me as an individual from the stereotype of the group to which I belonged. Geza, the younger of the master workers, was clearly torn between his instinctive decency, and his need to conform to his colleagues' attitudes. Later, I learned that I was not the first Jew to belie his expectations. Mrs. Bojti, the boss's wife, was Jewish, and Geza, who had a "subversive" tendency to think for himself, had already observed the disparity between the sinister figure of propaganda and the rather ordinary woman married to his boss.

"Maybe there are exceptions," Geza suggested.

This was always a dangerous proposition. Those whom they didn't know and had never met were supposed to be villains.

Peter was, in the most basic sense, a man of letters: a typesetter and specialist in the making of rubber stamps. Although he was a rather grey figure, he had a special status because of the sensitive nature of many stamps he created for the government, foreign embassies and private organizations. His trustworthiness had to be beyond reproach, for it was not too difficult to make a copy once a mold was created. It was the rule that special molds be destroyed in the presence of the boss. Peter was always non-commital. Either he didn't know, or had no opinion on anything. Yet you could detect, if you observed him carefully under his visor, his approving or disapproving expression on the comments of others, accompanied by some murmur under his moustache.

Eventually, I searched for words of reply to Janos. "Not to shake hands, or to dislike me, is your prerogative. But Mr. Bojti won't take it kindly if he loses his right to have an apprentice." (According to law, if the firm's apprentice did not qualify for junior master in three consecutive cases, the firm would lose the right to have the cheap labor of an apprentice.)

"You see," he said, turning to Geza, "we have a clever Jew here; he hardly walked in and already tells me what I can do. We'll see!"

We sat down at the bench and I was watching without anything to do. They all ignored me. I became more and more tense and disturbed. I could not beg, however unbearable the situation became. After a good thirty minutes, I summomed my courage and asked, "Can I help anybody with anything?"

"Sure," said Janos, grinning maliciously. "Grab the broom and sweep the floor." I did. Peter asked me to sort a bunch a mixed lead letters according to typeface. Geza asked me to hold a piece of steel while he prepared it for engraving, sawing and polishing.

This type of routine had been going on for days when my opportunity came. Janos was a real master of his craft. He created beautiful medals and ornate baroque designs for silverware, stamped from steel molds, but the company bought the basic design from an outside freelance artist.

The artist had just delivered one of these designs for the personal seal of an old nobleman. Bojti and Janos did not like it.

I took a deep breath and interjected with fear and anxiety, "I can do it better." A great insolence on the part of an apprentice. The unspoken words were written on their faces. Bojti: "That's right, he's an artist." Geza: "Really?" Peter: "Hmm, hmm." Janos: "The bastards! They always know better."

Bojti agreed to let me try it, but insisted that it be done quickly. From that time on I became the official design specialist. Months passed and the tension eased. Our familiarity was like that of victim and kidnappers: the longer they kept their victim, the less likely they would kill him. Between my supervisor and myself, silence dissolved into conversation, argument, and even confrontation. This was a dangerous risk, since Janos could have reported me to his party, creating untold trouble for me. But he didn't. Instead, he endlessly recited fascist propaganda concerning horrors the Jews committed against the world; capitalist bloodsuckers in one argument, communist mad dogs in another. He produced his contradictory statements without blinking an eye. Jews were the cause of all evil and misfortune in the world, in the nation and in his family. He quoted from Mein Kampf as if it were the Bible, which may have been the only book he had read during the last ten years. Now he was a proud member of the master race, with a growing fellowship of brazen instigators to give him direction and courage.

Naively, I tried to challenge his firm convictions with rational arguments. Statistics, analysis, logic, history, examples of proof to the contrary; it was of no avail. Reason against faith? What a laugh. No chance.

Nevertheless, little by little he assigned me real jobs and accepted my help with drawings and their transfer to the polished steel. Within about eight months, I had become a very good engraver and produced on a par with my colleagues. Peter also welcomed my help with typesetting, mixing the mold medium for rubber stamps, and heat-curing the rubber. Conscientious by nature and education, I learned my trade well. My time was now spent at work by day and at the pool in the evenings. Usually, I would eat at the Cafe Victoria or at my current girlfriend's house, since an apprentice's salary was almost zero. Some pocket money, that's all. I would dream, "In a few months I will become a master engraver. Then it will be easier if ... if the firm where I have to take my test is not fascist, if I do a good job, if the war does not sweep us all away."

* * * * *

The water polo championship matches began, and after the first rounds we were in fourth position. Not too bad. We won our last game against one of the toughest clubs and we were jubilant. I was heading home with friends and we stopped in at a patisserie for coffee and cake. Fred pointed to a newspaper headline: DRAFTING THE CLASS OF 1920. My heart sank. My thoughts raced. I imagined the terror in my mother's eyes, the crumbling of my father's dreams; and all my efforts so far, for nothing.

"Tibor," Fred exclaimed, "how can we finish the championship without you?"

"I have another year to go. I'm Class of '21. But you'd better call Mr. Frederik."

"I'll speak to Mr. Frederik tomorrow. Let's go."

* * * * *

From 1940 on, The Hungarian forced labor camps (KMSZ) were established gradually. First, the Jewish soldiers' weapons were taken away and replaced with picks and shovels. Later, their uniforms were taken away, and they had to wear their own clothes with a yellow armband (white for the converted Jews). But aside from the humiliation, it did not seem different from the army, at least in the beginning.

We were walking down the Grand Boulevard past Kiraly Street when a nervous young man furtively pressed a leaflet into our hands. It said that horrible death camps had been established in February in Auschwitz, Poland. Thousands of Jews, gypsies and others were being tortured and killed in gas chambers. It urged one to join the Communist Party and fight the greatest crime the human race had ever seen.

"Look, Tibor, this is typical communist propaganda. Who can believe this?" Fred exclaimed.

"You're right. I'm aware of the atrocities in Germany, Poland and Czechoslovakia, and that people certainly are killed, but this is not possible, let alone believable."

* * * * *

As we avidly scrutinized the news, from the propaganda of the fascist papers and radio to the objectivity of the BBC, we tried to convince ourselves that the Allies could and would stop the Germans. But we heard only the BBC's confirmation of German successes.

The Germans advanced at lightning speed. Belgium and Holland collapsed. Churchill flew to Paris for consultation. French and British troops were ordered to retreat and the world feared the fall of Paris. A brave counter-attack by de Gaulle's mobile armored division slowed the German attack for a few days only, but earned de Gaulle the rank of general. France was considered lost and, at Dunkirk, the largest sea rescue in history was under way to save the British and French forces. Churchill told the House of Commons, "I have nothing to offer but blood, toil, tears and sweat."

We were amazed at and fearful of the German successes. At the same time, we were comforted that the front lines were moving further away and not toward us. Our suffering was mostly mental and moral.

We had experienced no physical harm, except for isolated incidents with the Nyilas during their increasingly frequent rampages, when they would break the windows of Jewish merchants, or gang up on a victim, a dozen of them beating up a lone Jew. Their numbers were growing, as was their acceptance by the population. All we could do was try to live with it.

* * * * *

I became proficient in engraving. Janos showed me every trick of the trade. He was impressed by my national status as a water polo player, which kept my name in the newspapers. "You're a nice guy, Tibor," he kept saying. "It's too bad you're a Jew." At the time of major German victories, he proudly pushed the Nyilas newspaper's headlines under my nose, as if they described his own accomplishments. It was always a good starter for comments and debates about fascism, communism, capitalism and socialism. He never failed to underscore that he was basically a socialist, just a national socialist. I could not make him see the distinction, or explain what that simple adjective "national" meant for me or what I feared it meant for the country. While these confrontations were risky, I found them irresistible. I also sensed that he categorized me as the exceptional "good Jew" and would not denounce me.

Geza returned to high-school evening courses and appreciated my help in solving trigonometry and other mathematical problems. He bought a chess set and we played at lunchtime; Janos, Geza, the boss and I. One lunchtime, I played Janos. While I beat him easily most of the time, this game was tight. I was down a pawn at the end game; the queen and rook each had been captured. He was sure to win, but I overcame his advantage with good king moves and a few small errors on his part.

Chess is a most cruel, vicious game. Neither football, boxing nor rugby can equal its mental torture. Tricks and chance play no part. Everything is in the open and, little by little, the loser must acknowledge his adversary's superiority. It was too much to accept for Mister Master Race. His voice trembled and he broke into an avalanche of abuse: "Why is it that Jews are the best chess players, merchants, bankers, and best in all the other bloodsucking, unproductive activities?"

"Not all of them are, Mr. Janos," I answered. "Some are. If you would just understand that, I would feel better about our future. You and the likes of you have always excluded us from so many activities; we can't own land, can't go to the university, can't gain rank in the military, and on and on. So here I am, hopefully, getting better at engraving. Is that unproductive too?"

"Okay, guys, philosophy is over. Back to work!" directed Mr. Bojti. Perfect timing, since these arguments never solved anything.

* * * * *

My romance with Cica continued, but it was more friendship than love. And despite some very beautiful and passionate adventures, I felt lonely, or maybe a loner. I realized early in my life that I liked the conquest, the challenge, but did not want to be attached. I set high—maybe too idealistic—standards for myself, as well as for a potential mate.

After swimming, I roamed the streets looking through the windows of rich apartments in Lipot Varos, catching here and there a glimpse of what I thought was happiness. On a nice summer night, when most windows in Budapest were open, curtains hardly drawn, a family dinner, kisses and embraces, sexual play. The more I saw, the more alone I felt. From day to day, from hour to hour, I vividly imagined being a water polo hero, a great artist, a scientist or philosopher answering life's great questions.

I had avidly read Kant, Spinoza and Aristotle since early youth when the great questions of human existence tease inquiring minds the most. It helped me form a view of the world and has continued to confirm my belifs throughout life. These early convictions were reinforced by later events; random happenings, erratic and unpredictable human behavior. Wildly alternating fear and anxiety were my constant companions.

We are certainly not born with such a burden, but I watched my family struggle to make ends meet, saw their inability to pay school tuition. The uncertainty of one's career in the pre-war years, expecially for a Jew, clashed with my strong personality. I desparately wanted to control my destiny. I needed to dominate any kind of situation and do the impossible, to make the best of a bad situation. I could not tolerate excuses for myself. No predestination, no help from heaven; a situation is given and action or reaction is to be chosen. There is no excape from making a decision, be it right or wrong. It seems to be quite a pessimistic view of our existence but it has great rewards too. It made me feel strong and determined, or at least it gave me that illusion.

Such was the Aristotelian notion that there is no possible proof for the primacy of the spiritual or the material universe. Both can describe eternity, and the acceptance of either one could explain everything that follows. So, it is just a matter of faith. I had chosen a materialistic course. It was a harsh, merciless philosophy, harder to live with than with a spiritual view because it did not give any excuse for failures or allow a belief in miracles. I was depressed by lonliness, yet in a strange way it comforted me.

But those were the nights. The days always brought me back to reality. My feet stood solidly on the ground even if my head was in the clouds. The trouble was that the ground was shaking. The news that Paris, the city of my romantic dreams, center of art and culture and liberal thought, had fallen, hit me like a sledgehammer. For my generation and cultural milieu, Paris was the center of our spiritual universe. While Hungary had strong political and commerical ties with Austria and Germany, the cultural influence of France on the upper middle-class was profound. In school, French and German were required for eight years. The free French spirit became my ideal in those very early years, and made me a lifelong francophile. Thanks to Mr. Fejer, our severe and doctrinaire professor, I knew French history, literature and especially art. One year, we had a young professor who had lived in France, whose class consisted of describing the magnificence of Paris, Montmartre, the cafes and his romantic adventures in France. We never learned so much.

* * * * *

Hungary was quickly drawn into the war as an ally of Hitler, who easily exploited the irredentism drilled into the mind and heart of every Hungarian since the end of World War

I. Hitler promised to correct the injustices of the Versailles Treaty by which Hungary lost two-thirds of its territory; it was a perfect argument to induce Hungarians to cooperate and be used for his own political purpose in reaching the Mediterranean through the Balkans.

In November, led by Prime Minister Count Teleki, Hungary, together with Rumania and Czechoslovakia, joined the Tripartite Pact of Germany, Italy and Japan. By December I saw, for the first time, German troops moving through Hungary on the way to Rumania.

TA... TA ... TA ... Taam, TA ... TA.. TA.... Taaam. These soothing bars of Beethoven's Fifth, a rallying call for the evening news, came through on the BBC like a glimmer of hope to dispel the depths of despair. We surrounded Klari's radio, listening to the forbidden BBC broadcast with tense expectation of better news, but fear of worse. Often in complete silence we listened to the bad news month after month. Occasional deep sighs gave away our anxiety over tremendous losses of commercial vessels and battleships to German submarines, and our sympathy for the victims of London's bombardments. Only the British victories over the Italians at Tobruk provided welcome relief.

What saddened me most was to learn about France's anti-semitic Vichy government. I countered the cynical remarks of my friends about my pro French attitude by championing de Gaulle, the Free French Army and the Maquis. I argued (with not too much conviction) to save face. Yet, I also placed my faith and hopes in symbolic acts, like de Gaulle's departure to London and whatever the Maquis could accomplish.

In January 1941, Roosevelt decided to bring all American warships to full readiness, and in March the U.S Senate passed the Lend-Lease Bill, with Britain and Greece as the first beneficiaries. One day our hopes were raised by relatively good news, to be dashed the next by some new event. When the Germans attacked Yugoslavia and Greece in the same month with the help of three Hungarian divisions, Miklos Horthy, Governor of Hungary, decided to collaborate with Hitler in the invasion of Yugoslavia, even though just a month before, his Prime Minister, Count Pal Teleki, gave assurances to Yugoslavia that Hungary would not attack. Teleki felt dishonored and committed suicide. He was succeeded by the fascist Laszlo Bardosy, who became Foreign Minister as well. This was very bad news for all of us of draft age. The war was inching closer and closer.

Thus, Hungary was drawn deeper into the war and Horthy became a puppet, dancing at the end of strings manipulated by Hitler. Constitutionally, Hungary, after the breaking up of the Austro-Hungarian monarchy in 1848, remained a kingdom, but without a king, whose place was "temporarily" occupied by the Governor.

As war raged around us and Jews were persecuted in other places, we could not believe that pogroms like those in Russia and Poland could happen in Hungary. Ignoring the obvious, I buried myself in the daily routine of survival. I continued my profession as an engraver and became really proficient. Escutcheons, heralds, griffins, eagles, bears, medieval symbols constituting the stamp of foreign embassies, portraits of historical, political, art or sports celebrities: watching them emerge from a slab of steel gave me great pleasure. I enjoyed creating these negative molds, these matrixes from which a new and unique positive came into being.

The act of struggling with the material, the craft, the metier which permits you to bring forth your vision from its resistance, separates the artist from the dreamer. Of course, the dreamer may have imagination and deep feelings, but to quote Oscar Wilde, "All bad art springs from genuine feelings." Without this struggle, at the point of a pencil or brush touching paper or canvas, or at the finger tip on the keyboard, the dream, the vision disappears leaving only blank paper or canvas or a false note. No art is born. Similarly for the scientist; the logic, the power of new associations of words, ideas, concepts, spark of the "aha!" of discovery, but those concepts must be learned and stored in the recesses of the brain. Nothing is created from nothing, except in metaphysics, if you can believe in it. I have never been sure whether I should be an artist or a scientist. I feel an intimate connection to both fields. I dreamt of being a Churchill who paints, an Einstein who plays music, a Leonardo who does it all. But just then there was no choice. My test for certification as a master engraver approached.

When I was in the mood for art, I visited Zoltan. He always argued that I had been crazy to leave the graphic arts. One day when I visited he was in a very bad mood. He hardly said hello, and just stared out the window with glassy eyes. His girlfriend sat almost motionless. Only the baby made an occasional noise.

"I'm going back to Eger for a visit," I said. "Any message to your family?"

"Yes, there is. I'm drafted by decree." A powerful silence. Finally I interrupted, "Labor camp?"

"Yes."

The half-finished liquor and Belgian chocolate advertisements stared at me daring me to complete them. A large window display, a mural hailing the common Polish-Hungarian border, the result of Hungarian occupation of the old Sub-Carpathian territory, sent chills up my spine.

"Anything else I can do?"

"No, thanks," said Zoltan.

"I'll see you before I leave."

I left Budapest for a second visit with my family in Eger. My visit home wasn't joyous, unlike those in the past when my mother and my brother, optimists by nature, lightened my mood, or old buddies at the pool made me feel at home. Gloom was everywhere. The economic situation of my parents had worsened. My father was struggling as a shoe salesman. My mother, bending over an old Singer sewing machine, worked for starvation wages producing beautiful crushed velvet three-quarter length coats with lots of elaborate trim. It was a local folk costume for rich peasants. My brother was apprenticed to a tailor for almost no pay.

Most of my buddies had already been dispersed from Eger. Now I walked the main street, our traditional promenade, with Cele and Fules, younger swimmers who beat me regularly in back stroke. They were good friends, Christians who assured me of their disapproval of the fascists, and demonstrated their resolve by promenading with me. A classmate in officer's uniform saluted me smartly. We exchanged a few polite words and passed.

I also visited Zoli's parents but spent my few days mostly in the pool. Although I loved my parents and grandmother, I was not unhappy to leave the gloom washing through my home town.

* * * * *

On June 22nd, Hitler launched "Operation Barbarossa," breaking through on all fronts and surprising the Russians. Within weeks, the Germans were menacing Leningrad and Moscow, hoping to occupy both before winter. Hungary now declared war on Russia, as did Finland and Rumania.

As German troops advanced on Russia in the occupied territories, the Germans mandated that Jews in all territories under their control should wear a yellow Star of David. In Poland, during October, they decreed the death penalty for all Jews leaving the ghetto. At about this time, Hitler assigned to Himmler the study of "the final solution to the Jewish problem." But I did not know about that, nor did my friends, Jew or Gentile. We viewed the plight of Polish, Hungarian and Russian Jews as representing isolated local atrocities, like the pogroms which flared up at different places periodically throughout history.

We assured ourselves that we were Hungarians. I continued my daily routine: work, swimming, girls, work, swimming, girls, hoping that the storm would pass, that somehow the Germans would be stopped. We hoped that their victories were exaggerated, that tonight the BBC would offer only good news. But it didn't. During all of 1941, with a few exceptions, the Nazis were advancing victoriously, and the end of the year brought them to the doors of Moscow. The BBC confirmed German reports that Leningrad was surrounded, but that its heroic people resisted despite facing starvation; that Moscow was in imminent danger of falling to the Germans only forty miles from Red Square. But with December came the Russian winter, which had defeated many invaders throughout history. The Russians mounted tremendous counter-attacks and turned back the Nazis . Was it the beginning of the end? There were other events in faraway places: naval battles in the Pacific, Atlantic and Mediterranean, and the terrific beatings taken by the American Navy at Pearl Harbor, Malaya and the Philippines.

Serves them right, we muttered. Maybe they will wake up finally and respond with money and supplies, send some troops too. Maybe they will begin to understand what is at stake. Finally, on December 10th, the U.S. declared war officially on Japan and the Axis powers. On January 1, 1942, the Atlantic Charter was established, forming a real alliance that was to outlive the war from which it had been created

* * * * *

In spite of the war, in Budapest the swimming and water polo competitions started a new season. More and more familiar faces were missing. My class of 1920 had been drafted: the Gentiles served in the Army, the Jews in labor camps. I played water polo with special permission because my team had no other goalie. Coach Frederik still was able to use his influence to delay my draft, but I had to "Hungarianize" my name so as not to draw too much attention from the fascist public. When my parents learned that I changed my name to Garami, they were not happy. It was not easy to give up my identity for the sake of water polo. But I was in great form. I had just passed my master engraver's test and began to draw a full salary. This permitted me to eat better, if still not well, which surely helped my game.

The company to whom the trade association assigned me for testing was of German origin, but had been established in Hungary for a few generations. The owner's political alliance with the fascists was obvious, but he was also recognized as the best in the business. Even in normal times, passing the test at this firm was a real achievement and a strong endorsement of an apprentice's ability.

I reported to his shop exactly at 8:30 A.M., as ordered by the trade association.

"Good morning, Mr. Schafner. I'm reporting for my test. Here are my papers and my trade school attendance record."

"Morning. Come with me to the shop." A dozen workers were already sitting at their workbenches, arranged in neat rows of three.

"Mr. Gerstl," thundered Schafner. "You have a German name ..."

"Yes, but I'm Hungarian." (I used Garami only in sports).

"No, Mr. Gerstl, you're a Jew."

"Yes, I'm of Jewish religion. Mr. Schafner, are you German?"

"No, I'm Hungarian," he declared proudly, but still in a German accented Hungarian typical of the Schwab minority in western Hungary.

"Mr. Gerstl, I don't care what you are for the purpose of this test. You will be assigned a job. It should be completed by 5:00 P.M. and be of high quality. You know my company's standard."

"Yes, I know, and I'm proud that the association assigned me to your company for my test."

We stared intensely into each other's eyes. Finally, he said, "Fine." I sensed a switch toward me in his attitude. He blinked, and I began to feel he would be fair.

After he left, the foreman gave me a photo of a "turul", an eagle, the emblem of numerous Hungarian ministries. I was to make a reduced-size engraving, about one and one-half inches, in reverse bas-relief in copper, to be used for blind-embossed stationery. I was very tense and nervous. Workers stood up occasionally to look over my shoulder. Some nodded approvingly. Many others sneered or made offensive remarks like, "Now that they can't be bankers or lawyers, they invade our trade."

It was not my job to react. The foreman came over at noon to notify me of the half-hour lunch break. He took a piece of plastiline and pressed it into my engraving to check the progress.

"Not too bad," he murmured.

I sighed, and ate the lunch I brought with me at my bench. I resumed working quickly out of fear that I would not be able to complete the job in time. Exactly at five o'clock, my head was still buried in my work when Mr. Schafner cast his shadow across my bench.

"It's 5:00 P.M. Let's see what we got." He took the piece of metal, not larger than two by three inches, with my craft and career in it. While he examined it with the help of his foreman, probing it with plastiline, peering at it through a magnifying glass, comparing it with the original photo, my initial anxiety gave way to wandering thougths. Vicious wars were raging around us. Hitler, on the occasion of his ninth anniversary in power just a few days before, announced that Roosevelt was a mad fool and that the Jews of Europe would be destroyed. Cardinal Himsley's broadcast from London announced that 700,000 Jews were murdered in Poland alone. And I could be drafted at any moment. And Mr. Schafner was probing my "turul" on a two by three inch piece of metal. How important; how unimportant!

"Mr. Gerstl, Mr. Gerstl ..."

"Yes, sir?"

"It's a fine job. Too bad you're a Jew but it's a fine job. I will recommend that the association endorse you as a master engraver. Come into the office and I'll give you your workbook."

Love for the trade and a job well done appeared to be stronger than his hatred of the Jew.

"Thank you."

* * * * *

The 1942 championship games drew to a close. My team, the III KER TVE, finished in fourth place. I felt in great form despite the depressing news from around the world and from home. With success in my job, my sport, and my bittersweet love affairs, I felt indestructible.

Our semi-final game against FTC started at four in the afternoon, following the Hungarian championship swimming preliminaries. The Margit Sziget (Isle of St. Margarite) swimming stadium was full. We tried to relax at the edge of the pool before the start. First, the goal line ropes were drawn at thirty meters in the fifty meter pool, then the goals were placed, and finally the referee's three sharp whistles called us into the pool.

After a few minutes' warm-up, we lined up. Another whistle, and the game was on. All fought well and as clean and sportsmanlike as water polo players ever will be. It's a tough sport. But the public was tougher. I heard more and more obscene anti-semitic yelling: "Shoot out the bastard Jew! We know who you are!"

At halftime, FTC was leading two to one. I was swimming to the side of the pool for the halftime rest when a fascist, who had been yelling throughout the game, threw garbage at me. I jumped out of the pool heading toward him, but three teammates grabbed me, pushing me back and yelling at me to relax. "You have to rest. We'll take care of him. You concentrate and play ball." A short melee ensued in the stands, then a strange silence.

We evened the score in the second half. With about one minute to go, one of our defense men, in desperation, drew a four-meter penalty against James Nemeth, FTC's center forward and Olympic champion. We did not protest. The call was right. A four-meter penalty cannot be stopped unless it is shot badly. James, with the ball on his extended hand, readied himself. I attempted to edge myself forward from the goal line to try to cut the angle, but the referee impatiently backed me to the regulation distance. It's incredible the volume of thought that can be squeezed into a few seconds. I was the last chance for my team. My teammates were literally frozen in place. The crowd was silent. I had only the faintest chance to stop the shot of this polo superstar. Glory. Who knew? It could be my last chance, my last game.

The referee slowly put the whistle to his mouth, holding out the baton with black and white flags. Decide, I ordered myself. I moved an inch to the left to make him attempt a shot to my right. Sharp whistle. In that fraction of a second, I jumped to the right upper corner, and I felt the sweet pain of his murderous shot in my face. Unbelievable! It's still two to two. The rest almost did not matter to me. We lost anyway on overall goal averages.

We had a small party after the game at a Budapest restaurant. Players, swimmers, fans, wives, girlfriends, and the primarily Jewish industrialist backers of our team, gathered in both celebration and sadness. We congratulated each other and analyzed what we could have done better. We discussed organizational and funding problems. Then, Mr. Frederik tapped his glass and lifted it for a toast.

"My friends, we have proved ourselves. In spite of political pressures, economic difficulties, hardships for individuals and the team, a divisive climate which sets Jew against Gentile, husband against wife, parents against children; despite insults from the steps of the stadium, persons lost to the draft and death on the Russian front, we finished honorably. But times are becoming even harder for us all. The war and political climate will not permit us to continue as usual. Take a few weeks of rest, then pursue your training individually, as best you can. As long as I am able, I will be at poolside waiting for you and, despite the turmoil, I want to set a date for restarting routine training. Thank you, friends." In a hardly audible voice, he added, "Let's hope we will have still another season."

We never did, and everyone knew we wouldn't. In deadly silence, with wet eyes, we stood up, shook hands, hugged one another, and dispersed into the night.

Just a few months later, I found myself with Brody and Sarkany, two Jewish world and Olympic champions of the Hungarian national team, in a labor camp. Kabos, the Olympic champion of fencing in the category of saber, was there too. The entire class of '21 and most of the class of '20 were in the army and labor camps.

* * * * *

News of the tremendous battles in Russia was reported by the papers and confirmed by the BBC. Atrocities against Jews, civilians and POW's were confirmed by unfortunate eyewitnesses who had lost a leg, an arm or, even worse, had returned home.

The Russians had some initial success containing the Germans during the winter and spring of 1942 to 1943, but the Germans mounted renewed concentrated attacks on most fronts. A murderous attack at the end of June brought them to Sebastopol and, in July, the German Sixth Army and Fourth Armored Army advanced as far as Stalingrad, while the German Army Group A attacked in the direction of Rostov.

On July 12, the Russians established the Stalingrad Front under the command of Marshal Timochenko. It was the first major battle we heard of in which the Hungarian army was heavily involved, and their heroic advances were hailed by the Germans. But eyewitnesses, one of whom was a Gentile schoolmate, Virag, who came home without an arm, told us some horrible stories. At the bend of the Don, where the Hungarian army was engaged, the Russian resistance was ferocious. Germans pushed the Hungarians ahead as cannon fodder, and the Hungarians pushed their Jewish labor-camp prisoners ahead of themselves to dig anti-tank trenches and fill sandbags in a constant hail of fire from the Russians. Jews who tried to protect themselves by ducking drew fire from the Hungarians. By Virag's firsthand account, there were perhaps three survivors from a brigade of one thousand Jews.

A July decree announced over the radio and in the newspapers demanded the remaining

Jewish members from the Class of '20 to report to labor camps. I called a few friends and relatives in Budapest and we exchanged encouraging words. "Maybe this won't last much longer. Maybe the Russians will stop them. Maybe the U.S. will become more involved." Maybe ... Maybe....

I met Cica and her mother, who was now sorry to have been an obstacle to her daughter's marriage.

"What's next, Tibor?"

"I'm going home to Eger to see my parents and my brother, who's three years younger. Not that it will matter too much for long. He'll also be drafted shortly. I'm prepared to go."

"Write if you can."

"I will."

"Will I see you again?"

"Who knows?"

"When do you leave for Eger?"

"Tomorrow at two o'clock."

"I'll be there."

"I'd like that." We kissed warmly, and I kissed her mother too.

"You know," she said, "you're the toughest young man I ever met. It's one of the things I didn't like about you, or rather didn't want for my daughter, but I tell you, if anybody can survive, you'll be the one to make it."

I forced a grin. "Very few resist bullets or bombs ... "Bonne chance" and bye ...bye."

Cica was at the station and, to my surprise, Mr. Frederik, Bushy, our team captain and muscle man with his tiny Jewish wife, as well as Mr. Bojti and his wife, all came to see me off. The few minutes we spent at the station were heartwarming and heartbreaking. At the time, I had wished to slip out of Budapest without fuss, but years later their images on the platform became moral support in my miseries.

I stayed in Eger only two days, and saw my parents, grandparents, brother and a few other relatives. My mother tried to swallow her tears. My father remained silent most of the time, sitting in his usual chair at the end of the table, with infinite love and concern in his eyes. He tried to give me advice based on his First World War experience, when he served Hungary as a corporal and was twice decorated for maintaining telephone communications behind enemy lines. But we knew that the labor camp was not a regular army; at best, it was slave labor.

I loved my brother very much. He loved me even more, or expressed his emotion more openly. Everybody loved "Ocsi"—little brother.

My grandparents still held on, though my grandfather was in declining health. Nevertheless, he went every day to the shoe shop, sitting on the three-legged cow stool hammering wooden pegs into the custom-made shoes with precision. He was my number one fan at swimming competition and in everything else.

The call-up decree requested that all Jews report to camp with a good pair of shoes, their own clothes, two sets of underwear and socks or leggings, one blanket, jute bags to be filled with straw, a razor and other personal items. My mother assembled all of them and much, much more, neatly packed in a rucksack. It looked almost like what she would pack when, as a teenager, I went on a hike or an excursion.

On the afternoon of the second day, accompanied by my family, I said good-bye to the small railroad station, to the fortress, the Turkish minaret, the cathedral and synagogue and, of course, to the pool and solarium—the brightest spots of my youth. The carriage stopped at the station. The old horse knew the road, knew where to stop without command. Just a few minutes more. We kissed, we hugged, we cried. The conductor's sharp whistle cut through our emotions. This was no longer a referee's signal, but the clarion call of a new battle—this time to survive.

THE DANCES OF GALANTA BUT NOT BY KODALY

I had to report the next day to the Eleventh KMSZ (Kisegito Munka Szolgalat), literally Auxiliary Labor Service, commonly known as labor camp. The camp was at Galanta in northwestern Hungary. To reach it, you first had to return to Budapest. To travel to Budapest from Eger required changing trains at Fuzesabony, a small village about twenty kilometers from Eger. It became a major railroad distribution point in the '20s because Eger's archbishop wanted to keep the clergy's domain isolated and undisturbed by progress. The clergy and a few noblemen owned just about all the land in our county, as the nobility and the clergy have always owned most of the land in Hungary. And they used all their influence to protect the magnificent orchards and fields from the railroad, principally the famous vineyards of deep red wines called "Bikaver", Bull's Blood of Eger.

It was late when I arrived in Budapest. I headed directly to my Csaky Street flat for a night's sleep. The next day, my landlady broke out in laughter on seeing me in heavy boots, compliments of my grandfather, toting a rucksack and with my blanket wrapped around me, reminiscent of soldiers in World War One. Since I had only a furnished room, I had few belongings. I brought some letters and photos to my aunt in Budapest for safekeeping, but I added a little box to the already heavy weight of my rucksack. It contained items of importance to me which I would not entrust to anyone: my swimming medals, photos of my mother, father and brother, some engraving tools and a small sketchbook.

In the early afternoon, I continued my journey from the eastern railroad station. The old steam engine made a valiant effort to pull the squeaking wagons from the station. It gradually gained its cruising speed of about thirty kilometers per hour, only to stop and start its labors again at almost every little village, town and city. It proceeded, picking up well-dressed ladies and gentlemen, military officers in the first class coaches, and workers and peasants with large food baskets and even live chickens in third class. There were also beautiful young peasant girls tightly bound at the waist, with their wide multi-layered short skirts and red boots; a feast for the eyes.

Through the window I watched the passing landscape of small mountains, red-tiled roofs alternating with thatch-roofed farm houses, peasants laboring in the fields, drawing water for their horses or cows from ancient forklike wells, guards in civilian garb with uniform caps, pompously signaling for the passing train at crossings. I fell into a light sleep. The clicketing rhythm of the steel wheels faded into the beautiful folk melodies of Kodaly's "Dances of Galanta." How fantastically vivid is the feeling this music conveys the smells of the passing landscape, the colors of the embroidery adorning the blouses of the peasant girls, the rhapsodic dances, from the slow and sad to the exploding turbulence of the Csardas; the soul of a nation in a few bars of music.

Filled with warm feelings, I was drawn closer to Galanta. The sun was well past its zenith; the shadows of the forked wells became quite long. A few more kilometers and the train would start to slow down. Suddenly, my throat got dry and my heart raced a little faster. Calm ... calm down, I said to myself. What could be so bad about the dream of Kodaly? I was concerned, but unafraid.

The long train with its heavy load rolled into the station and came to a slow stop. The steam engine sounded as if it were expiring with its last breath. There were no dancing girls or beautiful colors, and no music at all. The station was the same as many stations in small villages, a small whitewashed old building succumbing to the passage of time, with wooden letters on its facade: "Galanta." I let the few local people off ahead of me. A bunch of soldiers were hanging around. I could not tell whether they were on duty. Then I saw a dozen other recruits jumping off from different coaches. Some had rucksacks like myself; others carried elegant valises as if they were going on vacation to a nice resort. There were those who looked like they were going on a safari, and one with a cardboard valise, blanket across his chest, and a pair of shoes which certainly had seen better times. Instinctively but hesitantly, we drew together.

"Hi, you too?"

"Ya, hello, hello."

"Any idea which way?" another asked.

"Looks like there's only one road."

As we started to walk, two soldiers detached themselves from their group and approached us. "Recruits to the camp?" they asked. Nothing could have been more obvious.

"Yes."

"Follow us." The camp was about a half-kilometer from the station on the dusty macadam road. Even after just a few hundred meters, some of the men were in pain from the heavy weight of their fancy valises, and were being prompted forward more and more impatiently by the rearguard soldier. The soldier leading us made cynical and sarcastic remarks about them.

"They must be lawyers or rich merchants from Lipot Varos or someplace, but they're certainly dumb, aren't they?" Nobody answered. Then he turned to me because I kept pace with him and I was closest, "I'm talking to you!" he yelled. "Are they?"

"Yes, they are."

As the sun went down this late September afternoon, it became chilly. Clouds started to gather, and as we arrived at the gate of the barracks it started to rain. The main receiving buildings were large and made of brick. All others were typical army barracks. We entered and passed a number of long tables.

"Your conscription papers, I.D., name, address. Any weapons? Go wait in the right corner."

The last two of the group, with heavy valises, reached the tables. One of the sergeants roared at them, "You idiots! You know you're only allowed two changes of clothing. Open them!" Vicious laugh. "All right, take out half of it and we'll take it in custody."

"I'm sorry, but ..."

"Move!" Finally, we mustered together in the corner. Our soldier rejoined us.

"Follow me!"

We crossed one of the large drill fields surrounded by barracks. It was heavy with mud from previous rains. We did not see a soul, just a few soldiers passing between the barracks, bayonets fixed, and a few frightened faces in windows and doorways. The silence was chilling. No movement. Automatically, we lowered our voices and looked around cautiously as if this were a dark alley, wary of a bad surprise and the trouble it might bring. Robi, the recruit with the bad shoes, made worse by the mud, whispered in my ear. "What the heck is going on here? It doesn't look good."

"No, it doesn't."

We entered one of the smallest barracks. Along the narrow, long corridor every door was closed except one on the immediate left. It opened into a room that measured about twenty by twenty meters, in which a few recruits were huddled against the walls, holding onto their belongings. They had arrived just a few hours before.

"Get in, put down your belongings, and follow me, all of you!" We were led behind the barracks. "Grab from the shed one jute bag each, and fill it with straw from that pile," the soldier commanded us, pointing to the farthest one. "Fill it good; that's your bed. You have ten minutes." We started frantically to press the wet straw into the bags while the rain continued its slow drizzle. I could not help but laughingly remember Zoltan's fake living room sofa stuffed with straw.

"Ten minutes are up! Close it, line up and follow me." We returned to our barracks, number nineteen, room thirty-five. "Put your things in order; settle down. Nobody may leave the room except to go to the latrines. Somebody will take charge of you. Not a nice guy like me, either!" He left and banged the door shut behind him.

We could barely squeeze our belongings and straw-filled bedding into the room. After some mild pushing and shoving, we settled somewhat. We left hardly a footwide channel between mattresses as a corridor to reach the door. By now it was 6:30 P.M., dark and raining, and nothing was happening. A half-hour later, we heard the bugle call for supper; an unusually late supper, given our knowledge of the military. Within minutes, hundreds, if not thousands of people were pushing out of the barracks yelling, bumping and being struck by the "smassers" (the pejorative term we later learned referred to the guard soldiers).

We looked out the window to see men trying as quickly as they could to form their brigades of about fifty, by rows of three behind each of the big cauldrons. The slightest misalignment, unnecessary movement, or talk was instantly punished. Some unfortunates were randomly pulled out and ordered to run around the drill field; some were ordered to do push-ups. Each unit was led by a Jewish "octato" (literally teacher), or drill leader, and supervised by a "smasser." Through the window which opened on the drill field, I saw the octato of the closest brigade report to the commanding officer of the day, who stood between the cauldron and the cook. Saluting smartly, he moved with the angular steps and turns typical of parading military, which I recognized from the paramilitary training in school and the Levente, the paramilitary youth organization. "Octato Goldberg of Brigade Twenty-four reports fifty men, three in sickbay, forty-seven present. Request permission to proceed!"

The officer saluted. "Proceed."

The replacement for our corporal never came for us. Half the men had already disappeared from the drill field. They returned to the barracks, their aluminum canteens filled with pretty good food, as far as we could see and smell from that distance. A few were around each cauldron awaiting seconds.

We started to become restless, and pretty hungry too. Should we go out in spite of the order, to draw somebody's attention to the possibility that we were forgotten? Who should go? Maybe as the latest conscripts, we would be called when all the others were finished ... but nobody came. For many of the well-fed men, to miss a meal was a major tragedy, while for others like myself and Robi, who were accustomed to skipping meals, it was a minor annoyance, as much because of the principle as from real hunger.

By now it was pitch dark and all hope for dinner had surely disappeared. The guessing started. Are they testing our discipline? Were we really forgotten? What do we do if tomorrow morning it continues? At the same time, clusters of three, four and five men formed within our group. They created exclusive circles, drawn to each other by sympathy, by a sixth sense, or because they were family or friends from home. With exploratory small talk we tried feel each other out.

* * * * *

I had placed my sleeping bag right under the window. I like fresh air, and I just might need a fast exit. I didn't care who was next to me. It happened to be Robi, with the bad shoes, followed toward the left corner by the twins, Joska and Mihaly, and their close friend Bela. They were all lawyers from Budapest. Toward the right were Janos and Otto, with their expensive valises, followed by both blue and white collar workers, from Csepel and Ujpest near Budapest. Some engineers came from the same area. Two men wore yarmulkas; one of them had a big beard and looked like a rabbi. It seemed an almost unbelievable mix for such a small group.

We all settled down except for one man who stood innocently in the middle of the room. He looked around with a frightened face, unable to decide what to do.

"Set your ass down. Robi yelled at him.

"What's your name?"

"Moric."

"Sit down, damn it!"

"May I sit there?" pointing to the one empty space.

"You have my permission," said Robi who burst out laughing. Moricka (we all referred to Moric by this affectionate diminuitive) seemed a bit slow-witted. He appeared uncoordinated and had a funny smile. Maybe he was too frightened.

It seemed obvious that we had been forgotten. Valises and rucksacks were opened and the smell of good Hungarian salami, roasted chicken, smoked kielbasi and ham filled the crowded room. The food came with the good-byes of thoughtful wives, mothers and lovers, and brought tears to more than one eye. Everyone was carefully measuring the slices, hoping to have enough left over for another day. We all ate, but not with equal relish. I ate very little.

Finally, we all lay down, tired from the travel, the uncertainty and the anxiety. The room had quieted down. Some were already asleep when, for the first time since we entered Room Thirty-five, the door opened and a uniformed guard looked inside. "Takarado," taps. He closed the door immediately, not providing any chance to ask a question. The familiar sound of the bugle playing "Takarado" brought back childhood memories of the fortress at Eger and, while others were tossing and turning, I fell sound asleep.

"Tam . .. Tratam Tatatratam! Tam Tratam Taratratam!" A bugle again, but this time the clarion for alarm. Were we being attacked? There was an enormous sound of a crash in the corridor, accompanied by yelling and swearing. I looked out the window. It was pitch dark. "What time is it?"

"Midnight," a voice called from one corner.

"Look out!" Joska yelled half hysterically. People poured from the barracks, wearing only their trousers, carrying shoes in their hands, trying to step into them on the run. They were chased by smassers with fixed bayonets, who were swearing madly and foaming at the mouth like wild animals. They hit or kicked everybody within reach and barked orders. "Form your brigades! Line up! Report for roll call."

Since nobody had opened our room yet, the uncertainty about what to do, the absence of action, froze us in panic. Mihaly and Joska, the twin brothers, held onto each other petrified with fear. Two orthodox Jews and some others started to pray, rocking back and forth and sideways, as their forefathers had done throughout the centuries. They moved faster and faster calling with urgency for God to intervene. Janos suggested going out. "It's better to be with the others than caught here trying to escape the storm, and punished more."

Others disagreed. Disagreement suddenly escalated into a cacophony of arguments, then slight pushing and shoving. Robi was swearing with all his might at the madmen around us.

"Attention!" I shouted as loud as I could, "Everyone to his bed!" A moment of hesitation. "Now, listen!" I yelled. "We stay put until somebody fetches us. If they come, we get out with as much order as possible. As soon as we're outside, we assemble at the nearest tree in formation. You hear? In order! Whatever happens! I take responsibility and you can blame me. I'll claim that I'm a temporary 'octato,' if it's all right with you."

"It's all right. Okay," murmured the group. Robi hit me in the back, and I wasn't sure whether it was affection or disapproval. It was the former.

Minutes passed like hours, when suddenly our door burst open. Four or five guards poured in; two more were swinging their gun butts through the open window. "Kurva, bastard Jews! Are you hiding here, you motherfucking assholes? Get out! Move with the rest! Move, damn it! On the double!" A few near the door started to run out, collecting hits on the way. I walked to the door and saluted smartly to the corporal.

"Corporal, sir, we're not hiding; we've just arrived." He hit my side with the gun butt, but he did not have a good swing because it was too crowded.

"We have no guard. We don't know what to do."

"I'll tell you what to do. Shut-up! Exit on the double, or I'll chop off your head!"

I ran out with the rest to the nearest tree and commanded, "Formation! Line up!" When the five guards caught up with us after emptying our room, the corporal took command.

From other brigades we heard the question barked: "Why are you being punished?" A chorus answered: "We hit a Hungarian soldier!"

"Down! Up! Down! Up! On your stomach flat! Up!" The guards were running between the rows, kicking one, hitting another, running over backs.

"Up! Down!"

Now it was our turn.

"Why are you being punished?" There was some hesitation because we really did not know, but we guessed by now, mostly through latrine contacts; I gathered my courage and in a moderately strong voice I said, "We don't know!"

"You Kurva Jews, you don't! Down! Up! Jump! Why are you being punished?" This time in a chorus we answered "We don't know!"

"You, Octato!" pointing at me. "When did you arrive? Late yesterday afternoon? Where have you been hiding?"

"We were not hiding, sir!"

"Shut up!"

"We were brought to Room Thirty-five!"

"One of your bastard Jews hit a Hungarian soldier yesterday afternoon and he will pay for it, and you, damn it, will have an early lesson of one-for-all and all-for-one. Bend your knees! Up! Down! Up! Down! Jump! Up. . . . "

* * * * *

It was around 1:30 A.M. when, exhausted, we staggered back to our barracks, covered with mud from head to toe. We tried to clean ourselves as best we could, and slowely settled down. There was almost no conversation or comment; Robi was swearing in a low voice, almost non-stop. Moricka was crying. The lawyers were thinking, I suppose, they stared straight ahead. The orthodox did not pray. I was thinking too, about the morning to come.

I never dwell too much on what has passed, but I often try to anticipate the future, or at least prepare for the next possible steps. How should I behave? What could we do? How would we get our breakfast if we still did not have a guard? Would the smassers come back for a second round? I wanted to talk but I was hesitant. Finally, since nobody spoke, I could not hold back.

"Is anybody injured?"

"No, not seriously," they answered.

"What should we do in the morning?"

After a long silence, Joska stood up. "I suggest that Tibor lead us to one of the kettles in the same orderly manner as the other brigades we saw at last night's supper. It looks like Tibor has the military manner they like."

Szabo, as spokesman of a suddenly loud group, disagreed. "We should stay, unless a guard comes to fetch us officially."

"That's what we'll do," said the orthodox.

"Screw you!" shouted Robi. "Everybody else is coming. You can stay if you want to."

"Okay, with your authorization I'll take temporary command, and then we'll see. Now I suggest we try to sleep."

At the first sound of reveille, we rose and followed the people from the other rooms to a long shed next to the straw piles. The shed contained long pipes with holes, serving as faucets or shower heads. While awaiting our turn to shave and wash, we learned more about the incident for which we had been punished. Peter, an octato of another brigade, explained that the days were filled with constant drills, cleaning inside and outside the barracks, and disciplinary punishments because there was really nothing to do, or to learn. The poor guy who was probably being tortured at the guardhouse had been slapped in the face by a sergeant, whom he hit back. Our little night outing was the price for this. It was well worth it.

"He became a hero, but who knows at what cost? Now you'd better hurry. You have only forty-five minutes to prepare yourself and the rooms and line up for breakfast with your men. Who's your smasser?"

"We don't have one."

"Hmm?"

"Hey, you guys," I called, "I was just told by an octato that we'd better clean everything spic and span. Line up the beds. Put the blankets at the head ready for inspection so we don't have to run around the field or do push-ups to warm up for breakfast. We have only fifteen minutes. Please move, everybody." I noticed that Szabo and his little group were deliberately moving slowly. "Could you move faster? We'll get into trouble."

"Who the heck do you think you are, the camp commandant?"

"I'm nobody, but you chose me to be the temporary octato."

"Look, Szabo," Joska interrupted, "if you don't want to cooperate with the majority and we get into hot water, we'll point you out as a troublemaker." Good to have a lawyer around, I thought.

With his customary delicacy, Robi chimed in, "If I have to do one push-up because of you, you'd better ready your ass!"

"Okay, you guys, five minutes. We'll run to the tree and line up in threes according to height. Put Moricka in the middle to hide his two left feet."

We moved out quickly. We heard loudly barked commands. "Brigade fifteen, fall in! Brigade twenty-five, fall in!"

We were not a brigade, so I yelled, "Room Thirty-five, fall in!" The other brigades marched up smartly to their assigned kettles, but I did not know which one our group should go to. Joska suggested that we wait a little and then go to the shortest line.

Pali, the tallest in our group, prompted me to go. "Room Thirty-five, attention! March! One, two, one, two, left, right, left. Room, stop!" We stomped on the ground as hard as we could, since most of us had learned to march at the Levente. "Halt!" I raised my hand to my cap in salute. "Tibor Gerstl, temporary octato of Room Thirty-five. Present, thirty-six men; none in sickbay. I ask permission to proceed."

The commanding officer of the day was astounded. "What the hell are you talking about? What is this? Are you crazy?" I explained our situation. He consulted the cook and surprisingly said, "Proceed." Then he added, "Line up your group at 8:30 A.M. sharp by the tree you stood near before and be ready for drill practice."

"Yes, sir."

We dispersed to eat our breakfast of porridge. Some sat under the awning of the barracks, some, like myself, in the room at the foot of our beds. Joska, Mihaly, Robi and Bela sat nearby. Others were eating while standing around us. We tried to assess what was happening. A majority wished that someone in authority would take charge of us for better or worse, but at least would relieve us of the burden of uncertainty.

"I think this will be resolved in a few minutes," Szabo interjected, "and so much the better."

"Why are you in such a hurry to submit us to our executioner rather than keeping us relatively free as long as possible?" Mihaly argued.

It was a good point. I worried about the situation I had allowed myself to be sucked into. I had to act on behalf of my group and assume responsibility for them by virtue of their trust in me, and now also by order of the commanding officer. My thoughts had to be oriented to the immediate situation and the steps to follow to avoid reprisal.

"Okay, guys, fifteen minutes to finish breakfast, then let's wash the utensils and line up at the tree. May I have your attention? How many of you have been in the Levente?" About three-quarters of my troop raised their hands. "Let's try to maintain the best military discipline we can, even without having trained together. Let's try to refute their prejudice that all Jews are soft bookworms or fat, cigar-smoking capitalists. I think it will help us. Does everybody agree?" Nods and murmurs of agreement. "Okay, let's do it. Szabo, how about you?" He looked at his friends.

Robi yelled, "He agrees or ..."

"Shut up!" Szabo shouted at Robi. "I can speak for myself. I agree." Joska, Mihaly and I looked at one another with relief.

We lined up five minutes ahead of time. This gave us a chance to organize, fall in properly in straight lines, three deep, and leave an equal arm's length from each other. The least athletic, or those who had no Levente training, were hidden in the middle. As the officer approached from the right, I barked commands. "Attention! Salute! Heads right!" He stopped and faced me. "Tibor Gerstl, temporary octato, Room Thirty-five, reports thirty-six men, no one sick, at your command."

He was impressed. "Your unit is being formed. There's no assigned guard yet. From now on, Tibor Gerstl is the octato and will report directly to me. I have no time to fuss around and try to make men out of Jews, but since you are reporting to me, I want this unit to be the best. If you embarrass me you will regret it. Octato!"

"Yes, sir!"

"Practice marching drills, stops, turns, proper attention, at ease, dismissal, falling in and a proper salute! Got it?"

"Yes, sir." And so our routine was established, with some variation, or so I thought.

* * * * *

The morning passed relatively quickly. Around the kettles, we became known as a special brigade with no smasser, attaching to us a certain mystique. After supper, we had a little free time. We used it to get better acquainted within our group and with the other brigades. Our spies tried to learn about the camp, its routines, and who was who. I welcomed the evening, to collect myself and reflect on what had happened to me. What had I gotten myself into? ... and rest, I needed rest. Action is a terrific substitute, an antidote for thinking. But you can sustain it just so long. Physical pain is tiring, but what really exhausted me was being alert all the time, anticipating possible troubles, avoiding incidents; using the right words and intonation towards my peers as well as superiors; being firm, yet not offending anybody; showing courage when I was afraid; smiling when I wanted to cry.

The bugle sounded to retire. We settled down slowly on our straw-bag beds which, even after only one night, were considerably thinner than the night before. We were just a little more comfortably spaced than sardines in a can. With a deep sigh, I closed my eyes and pictured my worrying father. He always tried to foresee the future, and could be calmed only by my mother, who was more optimistic. She was so proud of her healthy, strong progeny.

I dreamed of Cica and me at Isle St. Margarite, of the times we spent in her room, while her mother remained in the other. Then I was doing laps at the pool, playing polo, stopping impossible shots, accepting the admiration of my teammates.

I sat up in a daze. What am I doing here? Why can't I live my own life? What is that madman doing to us, doing to the world? I suppose we Hungarians should understand. Our country, as well as his, was chopped up by the Versailles Treaties. We were taught from kindergarten on never to forget. But what does that have to do with the Jews? What can he possibly have against Hungarian Jews? What do they all have against us? Throughout the centuries, Jews have been cast in the role of scapegoats, of outcasts who unify their enemies. By our exclusion they achieve solidarity. My Gentile friends, the schoolmates I grew up with, my teammates, my buddies from work- why don't they realize that? They do, but marching to the common drumbeat is easier.

To be different requires active conviction; it is easier to sit with a faceless crowd than to stand up alone. There is more exhilaration in "Heil Hitler" than in "Good morning, Mr. Smith." There is security in belonging ... by excluding.

"Don't worry, fellas," sighed somebody across the room. "It won't last long, and we might escape." Miki, the engineer, announced this with the assurance of one who has inside information.

"Wishful thinking," responded someone else. "The Germans are advancing everywhere."

"Not everywhere. Just read the papers about how our "heroic" Hungarian soldiers moved to defensive positions at the big bend of the Don, awaiting reinforcements. Leningrad, Moscow, Stalingrad are still standing. The German war machine is stalled. I tell you, the Russians resist, and their winter is coming."

"It's too far away for us, and the Russians move very slowly. Maybe the Germans can't occupy all of Russia, but we're stuck here."

"That would be good news," someone interjected. "Otherwise, we might find ourselves on the Russian front faster than you think. What then?"

"I'm telling you," Joska insisted, "people heard on the BBC that tremendous battles are going on in Stalingrad and the Russians are threatening to encircle the Germans. Both sides suffered enormous losses, but the Russians are holding and counter-attacking. The English are pounding the German cities, and in North Africa the Allies are advancing as well. Some French forces, after plenty of confusion, seem to be lining up with the Allies too."

"How about the Americans?"

"Ah, they're struggling with the Japs somewhere in the Pacific, like New Guinea and Guadalcanal, places I had trouble locating on the map in school."

I was listening, half asleep, thoughts flashing in my brain in confusion ... home ... girlfriend, art, polo, human bestiality ... escape. Why always the Jews? What happens tomorrow morning? Why did I have to stick out my neck so I have to worry if Szabo is late in getting up or Shmuel, the orthodox, finishes his prayers? Why?

Because I care! No. It's a lie. Because I care about myself; because I feel in better control of my own security and destiny by commanding; leading rather than following, regardless of the risks.

"Shut up everybody, damn it!" Robi yelled. "I want to sleep." He released a tremendous, two-horsepower gas explosion generated by the bean and cabbage mixture called "Szecska". Within minutes, everyone calmed down and struggled off to sleep.

The following days were relatively uneventful. The daily routine gave structure to our lives: meals at regular times, cleaning ourselves and the barracks, and the time spent mastering drill exercises outdoors, spiced with push-ups or runs for real or invented foul-ups or an incorrect reaction to command. We learned that senior recruits could be given leave to go home or permission to go to town. This was made easier by greasing the palms of officers, with the obvious result that the rich went and the poor stayed behind.

All who passed the guard were subjected to the usual military inspection for shined boots and buttons, under the threat of losing permission to leave. There was also the sex-pen inspection. This was a tube-like container filled with a fluid to protect against venereal diseases. It was assumed that one would persuade his girlfriend to inject herself with it. It had to be full leaving our living quarters, and empty when returning. If it was not, one was treated like an idiot at best or, at worst, punished for not using it. The punishment ranged from the mild inconvenience of a few push-ups to running, jumping, or climbing trees to the point of exhaustion. One could even spend overnight in the cooler, depending on the viciousness or drunkenness of the guard.

One Sunday morning, the officer who had appointed me octato called for me to see him at the guardhouse, on the double. He ordered me to line up my unit at our usual spot on the drill field. When we were arranged in formation, he approached with a determined, assured, haughty gait, followed by a soldier holding a cardboard box.

"Attention!"

"By order of the Hungarian government, all Jews in the KMSZ must wear a five-inch yellow armband and all the converted or Christians must wear a white one at all times. Any deviation from this rule will be punished mercilessly. Those tainted with Jewish blood will not bear arms. Your weapons will be pick and shovel, to help accomplish the goals of the glorious Hungarian army. "Chris-ti-ans," he yelled sarcastically, dragging out each syllable, "step forward."

Three stepped forward. The soldier opened the box. He handed out white armbands.

"Everyone else, pick up your yellow bands!" We went to the box and in a few minutes were labeled unfit, undesirable, the scum of the earth.

"Fall in!" We did, quickly. The Christians stayed put where they were, not knowing what to do.

"Fall in!" he thundered at the three. "Are you deaf? Are you disobeying?"

"Sir ... ?"

"Shut up! Down! Up! Down! Up! Let me see you run three times around the field. On the double!"

"The bastards," he said, ostensibly to himself, but actually for all to hear. "They think they can hide behind their armbands. The rest of you sit, and nobody moves."

Out of breath, they finally finished their laps and reported, half collapsed, to the officer.

"Fall in!" They reintegrated into the group. Or did they? "Fall out!" the officer yelled.

I was astonished that Joska and Mihaly, the twins, were anything but Jewish. Somewhat less surprised about Bela. During our tumultuous first days in the camp, I had established an unspoken communication with Joska, a kind of understanding about what to do and how to behave. He was about 5'8" and well-built, with gold rimmed eyeglasses. He looked a little older than the rest of us and impressed me as an intellectual. His twin brother could not have been more unlike him. Six feet tall, heavy as a bear, with thick tortoise-shell eyeglasses, clumsy and contemplative, he seemed always to be standing in his brother's shadow.

I returned to the barracks depressed. A few minutes later, Joska joined me rather hesitantly. "I saw your expression when I stepped forward," he said. "I was born Christian. I didn't convert."

"So it was your father who tried to escape from Judaism."

"There's no point in being sarcastic," he said. "Maybe my father's instinct for survival, or his love for us, was stronger than his faith."

"How about his principles?"

His face turned red. Obviously, he had been tormented by this question more than once. He lowered his eyes and slowly turned around to walk away. "I apologize," I said, but it was too late.

I laid down on my straw cot with some guilt of my own. I had just violated my own conviction not to be doctrinaire, to search for truth in diversity ... but at the cost of moral commitment? In any case, here was a perfect example of the way religion divides people and raises needless conflicts.

A yellow or white armband, red, green or multicolored flags; these powerful symbols of our insanity were used to try to make us believe that wearing this color, or being under that flag made us better. As I had argued many times with my "religious" Jewish and Gentile friends, religion was the worst of evils. It exploited people's psychological need for comfort as well as their fear of the unknown after death. It was a game of power played on all levels of society. Religions do have their redeeming values. Their moral precepts, the ten commandments or their equivalents, are clear enough and practical enough for all to understand. But if there was a need to shroud this message in mystery, punishment after death, it is understandable and acceptable as long as the diverse faiths do not create more harm than good by inciting war, or killings because of their different methods. The psychologically troubled do not mind by what method they are cured, whether Freudian, Behaviorist, witch doctor, religion or voodoo. And neither should we, as long as people don't go for each other's throats, and the psychologically sick are dying rather than being cured.

Yes, since the beginning of organic life the struggle was on for territory, for dominance. The plants for a place in the sun, pack against pack, tribe against tribe, nation against nation and beliefs against beliefs. And this last is the worst because the faithful don't know, but they do believe that they are better, superior, more valuable than the "unenlightened." If we could ever believe that although the "others" are different, they are equally beautiful and valuable, it would be a different world. But people don't, and there I lay on my cot, victim of the war between beliefs, I with my yellow armband and Joska with his white. We were both victims.

"Joska! I'm sorry. Let me explain."

"It's not necessary," he said sadly.

* * * * *

A dark, heavy sky hung over the camp and above the fields of Galanta, which extended beyond the drill field to the horizon. The snowy clouds had flattened to a uniform silvery gray, casting an eerie light on the landscape. Soon the first snowflakes of the season appeared on this late afternoon in mid-November.

The camp was like a beehive all day. Carrying strawbag bedding and personal belongings, people moved from one barracks to another, or to the newly emptied bunkhouses. We had to vacate a section of the camp and prepare it for new arrivals. These were not fresh recruits, but veterans, the class of 1919. From the time of our arrival at the camp, we had heard stories about the class of 1919. They had been sent to the Karpath mountains on the Polish-Hungarian boarder to build roads at one of the few mountain passes near Turjaremete. These men, nearly one thousand strong, were under the command of the most vicious guards and the worst commandant of the Galanta camp, nicknamed "Rumlis." In Hungarian this means something like a "busybody" or "troublemaker." Cruel and sadistic, he used any excuse to unleash his smassers on the Jews.

Rumors of their misery circulated ceaselessly, based on the stories told by the few sickly members of this class who had previously returned. Equally telling was the attitude of their smassers who were sent back to headquarters, who arbitrarily chose people in the courtyard for exhausting pushups, frog-walking, and the like. Their cruelty accompanied hateful admonitions warning of the lessons they would teach us once we came under their authority.

My group was assigned to a small barrack on a little hill. The whole camp was under orders to clean everything spic and span, inside and out. We had to landscape the ground in front of the barracks in expectation of Rumlis' inspection over the next few days, and were even promised a reward for the best barracks. We completed the moving and cleaning before dark, leaving the landscaping for next morning. After we retired for the night, I suggested that we create a big herald of Hungary in bas-relief in the earth on the side of the little hill. I volunteered to sculpt it if others would help me move the earth with shovel, pick and wheelbarrow. Most volunteered, but a few grumbled, "What's the purpose? It's ridiculous. Let's just clean up and that's all."

The next morning we started in earnest. We were finished by noon, and ours was by far the best looking barrack in the camp. By two o'oclock, the camp was ready for pre-inspection by our smasser and the day officer. They moved in and out and around the barracks, yelling and screaming, dissatisfied with everything, in spite of our best efforts. Of course, our civilian baggage, disparate clothing, and bedding could not give our bunkhouse a regimented, uniform, military appearance.

It is almost unbelievable how fast priorities or values can change. Almost imperceptibly, the military routine, the stupid drills with shovels and picks, as if those were guns or sabers, the preparation for parade marches, became goals in themselves. We wanted to do it right, to do it perfectly. Clean the barracks, shine the shoes, whatever the task, one takes pride in a job well done. In civilian life, the bosses know that employees will do twice the work, and do it better, if they appeal to their pride.

So we were somewhat offended at not being appreciated, and I said so to smasser Bako. He got furious and ordered all octatos to line up in front of the barracks. There were six of us. We did as we were told. Smasser Bako was a small five-foot-four and stocky, with a bushy, irregular black moustache. When I saw him for the first time, I almost took him for Janos, my fascist engraver colleague from Bojti, they resembled each other so. After a few minutes, he appeared with a bunch of dirty papers, cigarette butts and tin cans, which he had supposedly found in and around the barracks. He began to shout at us about how ineffective we were as supervisors, just scoundrels protecting our damn Jews. He worked himself into an extremely excited state, launching into grotesque political oratory. (I suspected that he drank more than a little.) Suddenly, he faced the first octato, nose to nose and, after a few insults, slapped his face. Then he stepped sideways to the right, clicking his heels with Prussian precision, and slapped the second, and the third octato. I was last in line. The surprise and shock of his action wore off, and I had time to think before he arrived. As he advanced, my anger and fear mounted in equal proportions.

I could not take such an insult without budging or reacting. If I hit him back they would beat me badly. Maybe they would kill me. I tried to calm myself. We never knew what ultimately happened to the recruit who hit a guard the day of our arrival. My mind was racing. "I can't take it. I won't take it. I'll never be able to face myself. Coward! Hit him back!" My heart was pounding as he approached the fourth in line. "No, don't be a fool. It's insane. Remember Mr. Frederik! Survive first! But at any price? Are all of us just cowardly Jews, as they believe?" He passed the fifth man. Again he clicked his heels, this time in front of me. I leaned forward at attention, as if ready to bolt. I looked down deep into the eyes of the little gnome. I would kill him if he hit me. I felt the blood rushing in my temples, ready to burst. I fixed his eyes; he mumbled some insanity and moved away.

"Fall out and disappear!" he yelled. A tremendous sigh escaped my chest. I was sick to my stomach, but felt enormous relief having avoided an incalculable danger. I couldn't move. Thankful as I was for my good fortune, I suspect I knew, though I will never be certain, why he did not hit me.

Many years later, when I describe this incident to friends, they often ask whether I would really have hit him back. I find this impossible to answer. In subsequent years, I have experienced a few life-threatening situations. I have discovered that there exists in the fight or flight reaction a kind of suspended animation, a freeze, just for an instant, which can make an aggressor hesitate. This can be sufficient to change the dynamics of the situation. During this moment, a facial expression, body language, an intonation of voice could make the difference. When facing Bako, and in critical moments since then, I somehow disconnected my intellect and let my animal instinct prevail. It seems to know best.

The camp was now anticipating the "homecoming" of the people from Turjaremete. And they came.

In late November, with a heavy gray sky hanging overhead, they marched in long lines from the railroad station, looking like Napoleon's army returning from Russia. Their bodies weak and filthy, dressed in rags, their shoes held together with twine, they bent under the light weight of the few belongings in their rucksacks, cardboard valises or boxes. The village dogs, who followed them on the road, were barking in concert with the guards prompting them to move. The headquarters brigades were lined up in front of the guardhouse and the smassers of Turjaremete faced them at attention, creating an honor guard for the arriving Commandant Rumlis, who passed like a conquering hero, saluting smartly.

From afar, we observed this tragi-comic posturing with concern. As he arrived at headquarters, the guards started to round up their Jews as sheep dogs round up their sheep. There was a bite here, a bark there. Suffering from fatigue and hunger, his "troops" moved slowly toward the barracks we had prepared for them.

For the next few days, they were kept isolated, so we could not communicate with them. We lingered in small groups near the single barbed wire, which was the demarcation line. Robi, Joska, Bela and I yelled questions to them in order to gather information about their experiences. We threw over food and clothing, as the guard looked the other way in exchange for a few "pengo". We found to our satisfaction that the rich guys with the fancy equipment, whom we had ridiculed when they reported to camp, now were able agents and contributors to paying off the guards.

* * * * *

We had been standing at attention for close to half an hour. The entire camp, nearly a thousand men, waited freezing on this cold Sunday afternoon in December. About three inches of snow lay on the ground. On the surrounding trees snow crystals scintillated in the pale sunlight. Three gallows, erected that morning by prisoners under the supervision of guards, loomed dramatically against the white ground and ragged sky. All Sunday leaves for the guard had been cancelled. We were lined up at elbow distance, side by side; at arm's length front to back. The guards, with bayonets on their rifles, were moving in fast steps between the rows, yelling, swearing, and punishing the slightest movement with a blow from their rifle butts or by ordering push-ups or frog jumps in the snow. Punishment was meted out even for trying to rub fingers or ears against the cold. Many poorly dressed men in a hodge-podge of civilian clothes unfit for winter suffered badly.

We were all being punished, forced to watch and "learn" from three unfortunate comrades. We didn't know who they were, what they had done, or if they would be hanged by the neck or by their hands tied behind their backs.

Finally, Rumlis appeared with his officers. He took a position on the highest point of the little hill and informed us of the reason we were assembled. "In my absence, while I was serving the glorious Hungarian army, this camp became soft, undisciplined. Revolts brewed, probably inspired by your communist cells. One of you Jew-bastards has hit a Hungarian soldier in the face. You are all responsible for this act and that of his two communist comrades who tried to excuse his offense. I want to assure that this never happens again. This demonstration will serve that notice."

"Bring them forward," he ordered. Framed by six guards three men marched underneath the scaffolds, their hands tied behind their backs. "Up with them!" he yelled. The "executioners" attached the long ropes dangling from above to their tied hands and pulled them up just one or two inches off the ground. "Next time offenders will be hung by their necks," Rumlis thundered.

A muscular, good gymnast can hold this position for four or five minutes, before pain and numbness will overwhelm him. Accelerated by the cold, the stress and twisting disjointed their tired shoulder muscles. One by one, the men broke out in sweat and passed out, only to be revived by a splash of cold water in the face to continue their suffering. One was growling, another howled, and the third was silent. Ten, fifteen, twenty minutes passed like hours as they dangled half-dead on the ropes, trying desperately to reach the ground only two inches away from their toes. Weaker men in the formation passed out simply from standing at attention in the cold. These were permitted to make one run around their line and return to their places. I believe my anger and frustration kept me warm. In a low voice, I tried to inspire Joska and the others near me to liberate the dangling men by running en masse to their scaffolds. But after being labeled crazy, and unable to gain support for my idea, I did nothing but feel terrible about my impotence.

After half an hour the men were removed to the infirmary. Dejectedly, my friends and I returned to our barracks, frozen more in soul than in body. Thousands of us had been unable to do anything against one man's whim. You don't have to be a Jew, I thought, to experience the power of an established order like the military.

Their friends kept the curious away from them when they returned to their units a week later.

* * * * *

Galanta was a recruiting and training camp. Once brigades were formed, they were sent out to military units who needed their labor for constructing roads, digging anti-tank trenches, cutting firewood in the forest and the like. It had seemed innocent enough until we heard that units of the 1919 class had been completely wiped out digging trenches between the Hungarian Second Army and the Russians at the bend of the Don.

About two weeks after the hanging incident, rumors started to circulate that we would be shipped out of Galanta, and the interminable guessing game began about where we were going. On December sixteenth it was announced that visitors would be permitted the following Sunday. We were convinced that we were destined for the Russian front.

The visitors arrived. Parents, wives, children, friends and girlfriends. Most were loaded with food and warm clothes, and we had a fast glimpse of our new friends' families. The camp was invaded for this one day with everything from high heels and mink coats to worn boots and ragged mismatched clothing, representing the full range of the society we used to live in. With them they brought fresh news of the rapidly deteriorating situation of the Jews. My father came with a sad smile and a hundred questions in his eyes. He hugged me. "Everything is alright so far, Dad," I said, trying to alleviate his fears.

"Your mom sent this. She couldn't ... she didn't want to come."

I recognized the terrific food package, prepared with so much love, and I knew the contents. We walked around the grounds, filling the few hours of visiting time mostly with small talk about my experiences. Then we settled on my barracks bed. Joska came by with his elegant wife and Robi stopped in with his girlfriend, who looked like a streetwalker. Gabi arrived with his father, mother and fiancee. I was introduced to them like some mini-hero; the self-appointed octato of our special group.

Moricka came by with his mother who, with tears in her eyes, supplicated me to take good care of her son. My father was surprised and concerned. "What can you do?" he asked.

"Nothing, Dad, but some of the weaker ones need to believe in and rely on someone. So against my will and my own concern, I'm the one."

The visiting was drawing to an end. I walked with my father across the drill field to the exit. We passed couples, little groups drawn closer to each other; we passed tears, admonishments, hugs, prayers and frozen smiles. I hugged my dad in silence.

"I pray that God helps you," he said.

"May he help you too," I responded. "We can use every bit of help, even God's."

Half an hour later the camp was empty of visitors and silent. Deadly silent.

The next day the order came to be "combat ready" because we were to be moving out of Galanta during the next few days. We ganged together in the barracks, convinced that we would be sent to Russia. Joska asked if everybody had warm clothes and shoes. Despite the provisions brought by the latest visitors, many were still unprepared. I suggested that those who had enough should share. It was not enough.

Robi, who was lying on his bed, stood up ceremoniously. “Don’t worry fellas,” he said. “Get me a pass to town tonight and you’ll have warm clothes. I need some too.”

“What do you mean?” I asked.

“I’ll explain, but only to you and Joska. Over the last few days, guys from unit fifteen have been at the railroad station loading and unloading wagons of warm underwear, shoes, gloves, everything. We’ll help ourselves.”

“You’re crazy!” Joska said.

“No, I’m not. Trust me. I’m a professional. I go alone, but you have to wait for the ‘szajre’ on this side of the fence, when I throw it over.”

“What do you mean, you’re are a professional?” Joska asked.

“I’m a professional burglar, a good one and a respected one,” he said proudly. “Only two arrests in five years, and no killing of anyone. I won’t do that. I have a strict morality.” We were shocked, not sure whether to believe him. He raised his voice. “So do you want clothes?” We looked at each other, then I said okay.

Joska called Weinberger, the money-man. “Weinberger, we need cash to buy a pass for tonight. It’s important.”

“Who’s going?”

“Robi.”

“Robi, why?”

“Don’t ask too many questions. It’s important. Spit it out or I ask Greenwood, or we’ll collect it among ourselves.”

“Okay, okay, here it is. What’s the going rate now? Three pengo? Okay.”

At 2:00 A.M., according to plan, we started to go to the latrine at ten minute intervals. Joska, Bandi and I passed at the nearest point of the designated fence to pick up the bags. At 2:15 Robi appeared with one loaded bag, and with two others a half hour later. We dragged each one into the barracks. There were very few guards and the plan worked without a hitch. Robi came through the guardhouse legally, except that he was punished with twenty-five push ups for being late, and twenty-five more because his sex-pen was still full. He returned to the barracks furious.

“Shit, the bastards! That I had a tough job was okay, but doing push-ups was not part of the bargain.” He slapped me on the back so hard that I almost fell forward while he exploded in a belly laugh.

THE MORGUE OF RIMASZOMBAT

We arrived in Galanta by passenger train and left by cattle cars. This was nothing abnormal; for military emergency transports, eight horses or forty men was the rule. We were on the road for two days traveling east, if you could call it traveling, since we spent more time waiting on side tracks than moving. Barracks number thirty-five, had become truly unified through our common experience, and in spite of the diversity of our backgrounds, we had managed to stay together. As we grew to trust one another, individual characters surfaced and expressed themselves freely: the constant complainers; the hypochondriacs; the tough ones; the engineer who always had to have a corner of the barracks for his bedding; the pious ones praising God all the time; the rich guys whose paid servants helped them with everything; the withdrawn who suffered in silence; the love-sick, tortured by a girlfriend's image; the intellectuals who thought too much, riddled with anxiety, constantly trying to figure out the next move; and the ones who cared only about the next meal. They were all now galvanized, trying to answer the crying question of Moricka, the idiot: "Where are we going?" Was it really Russia, which already had become the burying place of thousands of Jewish labor auxiliaries?

And the Germans continued to advance.

The last Sunday visit brought more than food and warm clothes. We all had fresh news from our visitors. Most of them had listened to the BBC and received illegal pamphlets distributed by socialists or communists. It was difficult to know the truth, yet we were able to piece together the general situation. It was not encouraging.

We were able to hear or gather news from letters, papers, and the soldiers who boasted about the German victories. We heard only rumors about Jews. Frightening, unverifiable and unbelievable rumors. Mass deportations were said to be taking place in Vichy, France, which the U.S. protested. We heard few details, but reports circulated in England that two million Jews, mostly Polish, were exterminated. Who could believe such a thing? It was too difficult to grasp. Miki, the engineer, was a main source of news. We might doubt him, but he always knew specifics, and his news was usually verified by other sources or by new events weeks later. He constantly drew little sketches of battle situations, earning the title of "Napoleon, our resident strategist." He too was convinced that we were going to Russia. It would take some time though, and maybe, just maybe, the Allies and especially the Russians would beat back the Germans.

* * * * *

It was late evening. Our boxcar was cold, dark and motionless. Our daily ration, either bread, kielbasi and some canned food, or a warm meal of soup made from dehydrated vegetables was long since digested, and most of us were nibbling on the contents of the previous Sunday's packages. Suddenly, we heard the car's metal "butoire" click against each other. The few lights of the darkened station started to move by very slowly.

There were only four small windows in the upper part of our car, and we assigned a "guetteur" to each side twenty-four hours a day to see where we were heading and to report on anything unusual. We were really moving this time. The rhythmical clicking of wheels on rails got faster and faster, and the cold winter night forced us to bury ourselves in our blankets, coats or whatever else we had managed to bring along. "We're definitely heading east," announced Bandi from his station at the window. There was silence. Everyone tried to steal a little sleep, but the noise of the train, the cold, and the smells of our bedding of humid straw mixed with human odors were not conducive to relaxation.

The pale winter sun had just risen behind the hills of Buda when I opened my tired eyes. We were approaching Budapest. All of us became excited. What did this mean? Were we coming back or just passing through? A few of us thought that maybe we could jump off and disappear into the crowd. "Cool it, fellas," said Bandi. "They locked the wagons from the outside an hour ago."

When our wagons rolled in on a side track, away from the main station, we were surrounded by the fascist Arrow-Cross guards, in addition to our own cadre of guards from Galanta. After a short stop of an hour, during which time we received our ration of bread and hot ersatz coffee, and attended to our natural functions, we continued our journey eastward. We pressed our eyes against any crack in the wall of the boxcar to catch a glimpse of the Budapest landscape. By early afternoon, we began to see familiar villages; that is, familiar to a few of us from the Eger area. At Fuzesabony we passed just ten miles from my home town. I noticed that I was not the only one who tried to hide his tears. What was my mother doing at this moment? Bending over her sewing machine? And was my father fitting a shoe on the foot of an anti-Semitic former friend to eke out a living? Was my brother still apprenticed to a tailor for practically no pay? And what unknown destiny was I speeding toward?

Our train slowed not far from Eger at Miskolc, a major commercial city of the region. Then it picked up speed again, still heading southeast. After half an hour we turned north and crossed the old border between Hungary and Czechoslovakia, now, thanks to Hitler, reoccupied by Hungary. We stopped on a track overgrown with crabgrass, seemingly abandoned a long time ago. We were arguing back and forth as to what this meant, when our doors opened on the Rimaszombat railroad station.

We stepped down, and spent the next few hours speculating whether this was our final destination, hoping it was not just a stop-over on the road to Russia. When the sun had slowly descended behind the small hills, we were marched through the abandoned streets on the sleeping city's periphery.

Rimaszombat, or Rimavska Sobota in Czechoslovakian, is one of the many small towns and cities which in my lifetime alone have changed nationality at least three times. Before World War I, it was Hungarian; after the Versailles Treaty in 1920, it became Czechoslovakian; in 1938, Hungarian again; and after World War II, Czechoslovakian yet again. The population was at least ninety-percent ethnic Hungarian, and had a small but prosperous Jewish community. Small industry and crafts, local commerce, the schools and military establisments provided the economic base for this rather well-to-do community.

The casern was just outside of town, a quick fifteen minute walk from the station. It had more stone buildings than Galanta, plus some shoddy barracks, well equipped offices, medical facilities and a real kitchen.

We walked around on the casern grounds to familiarize ourselves with our new home. It was a great relief that wherever we were, at least it was not on the Russian front. Consequently, everything appeared just fine, even though the uniform buildings of yellow-ochre and the eight-foot high stone wall surrounding the grounds were rather depressing and gave the feel of a prison.

"This doesn't look better than Galanta," Joska remarked. "It's less open; the buildings are crowded together and look as permanent as a long-term prison."

"But it isn't Russia," Robi answered. "Don't forget," he said philosophically, "a prison protects you from the outside as much as it closes the outside world to you. Take my word for it."

*****

Heavy fighting continued in North Africa, but the Allies were winning. Eisenhower had won the cooperation of the Free French, but the Germans took a more aggressive stand with the Vichy government and actually occupied Vichy, France.

Miki religiously kept tabs on his little maps of the war's progress, especially in Russia. The Russians had launched a great counter-offensive from Stalingrad, and Hitler ordered Von Paulus to hold out, whatever the cost. Our hopes were hinged on events in Russia. Maybe the Russians could break through and advance fast; then maybe we would be saved.

Inside our casern the atmosphere was generally relaxed. While the smassers pressed their authority, they also appreciated the fact that they were not on the Russian front. Our daily chores and disciplinary drills were done by 4:30 and we were normally permitted to go to town, although we had to be back by 10:00 P.M. Coming or going, we were stopped only occasionally by the guard or day officer because of dirty shoes or improper clothing. These obstacles were generally overcome at the price of a few push-ups or a few pengo, depending on who was the victim of the day, someone like me or one of the rich guys. The guards knew very well who the "money bags" were.

There were over five hundred young Jewish men aged twenty to twenty-eight in the camp, and some thirty to forty girls of similar age in town. We competed against one another and against the few local boys who were still home, for their favors. All of us, however, were invited in small groups of three or four by the local Jewish families. This was Jewish solidarity at its best. As always in our history, when in trouble, we banded together. I was twenty-three and, notwithstanding my few successes with women, I was basically shy, and did not make advances for fear of being rejected or creating an obviously artificial situation. I felt that love should happen in an unexpected romantic encounter, as it does in movies or dreams. So I was often lonely, maybe a loner, but not withdrawn. In company, I could be a good conversationalist, holding forth on my interests of art, sports, science and philosophy with the depth and ardor of my age. My senses were always tuned to pick up the signal of an eye, a voice, a word, a gesture of an interesting female, but I was nevertheless usually too timid to respond.

I had been invited for the fourth time to visit the Klein family, each time together with two or three other friends. Mother Klein would always invite me when we met on the street. "Why don't you come over for dinner with your friends?" she would say.

"I don't want to be ..."

"Don't worry about imposing. You're welcome anytime."

The Kleins were a well-to-do bourgeois family. Since Mr. Klein had been drafted, Mrs. Klein ran the bottling company, which was located in an attachment to their house. Her daughter Edit, whose studies were restricted by the Jewish laws, helped at home. She was an attractive blonde, slightly on the heavy side, whose piano playing impressed me, as I have no musical talent. She was bubbly and laughed easily, in contrast to my rather heavy and serious character. Nevertheless, we hit if off well, spending more and more time together. But as teasing and flirtatious as she was, she always found a way to escape closer sexual contact. We were limited to holding hands and exchanging little kisses. Frustrated, I started to avoid visiting so frequently.

Almost a week had passed without a visit from me, when Mrs. Klein stopped me in the street a block from their house. She asked what was wrong between Edit and me. Receiving no answer, she invited me to come home with her. Nobody else was home. After some small talk she sat down facing me, took my hand and, with obvious embarrassment, searching for words, started to talk. "It's difficult to tell you this, but it will be better for my daughter's sake if I do. She likes you and cries a lot because of your absence. But it's difficult for her to show affection because of something terrible that happened to her as a child. She was nine years old, playful, lively, well developed for her age, and very warmhearted and trusting.

One day, in the little office in the corner, one of our workers took advantage of her. She was raped. The man is still in prison, but the case soon will be reviewed by the fascist administration and I'm sure he'll be freed. This is a small city, Tibor, and the stigma will never be removed. The label 'the one who was raped' will stick as long as she lives here. You're the first person since that she has cared about, but she's afraid. I beg you, please understand. Be patient. You seem to be a very sensitive person. Help my daughter ..." and she broke into tears.

"I will, Mrs. Klein, I like her too." I left in confusion. I liked Edit but I was not in love. Yet now a melange of sympathy, love, challenge and curiosity brought me closer to her.

I started to visit her again, sometimes with friends, but more and more often alone. We became very good friends. She played the piano, while I'd kiss her neck, her lips, and eventually her vibrant hard nipples when she finally abandoned herself.

* * * * *

Within the labor camp, the standard routine continued: the same stupid time wasting typical of all our labor camp activities. There were the useless drills with no purpose other than to maintain discipline; the domestic chores, necessary to maintain ourselves and the casern's barracks; and the task of serving our officers and smassers who took it as natural that, as part of the master race, they be served by the Jews.

Rimaszombat, the town in which the camp was located, lay in the territory which for the past twenty years had been part of Czechoslovakia, but which was now re-occupied by Hungarians. The Czech (although not the Slovak) influence was reflected in the generally liberal and democratic attitudes held by the inhabitants, both Jewish and Gentile, who would freely exchange news and gossip when one met them in the street. People referred openly to news reports heard on the BBC, and returning veterans reported their war experiences frankly. (These veterans, it must be said, were all soldiers. No Jews came back from the labor camps to report their experiences). There were a number of Arrow Cross fascists who, when they encountered us, would do what they could to impose their authority; for example, requiring us to do push-ups in the middle of the street. But these were a minority.

Rimaszombat was also the home town of the camp's Commandant, Captain Koranyi. The town was reputed to have a fairly liberal background. Naturally, we were anxious to see whether this liberal attitude would be shared by our new Commandant. Bela asked some of the old-timers, "How are the officers here?"

"Not too bad," was the reply. "Dr. Miklos is from Eger and is pretty good. Sergeant Kovacs is just a dumb sergeant who follows orders but is basically not bad. The worst smassers are gone—they were sent to Russia via their brigades three months ago. The rest vary from neutral to vicious, when they feel they can get away with it, but Koranyi usually keeps them at bay. He's a most reasonable man, and does not appear to be anti-Semitic."

This was welcome news indeed, but nevertheless we remained skeptical. As matters turned out, not only was the characterization of our Commandant accurate, but it was the greatest understatement, as we were to discover during the next year and a half. Behind an unassuming appearance, Koranyi concealed a hidden moral strength, the equal of which I have never seen again.

* * * * *

One Sunday morning, without warning, the entire camp was ordered to line up on the drill field for review and a head count. All leaves were cancelled. Our immediate reaction was fear of going to the Russian front. The panic abated with the announcement that our comrades were returning from the Russian front and would be put in quarantine in our casern.

"They're sick and in pretty bad shape," Koranyi announced. "Many have typhoid and dysentry. You will be responsible for seeing that they receive the necessary help and care as directed by Major Doctor Miklos.

Dr. Miklos was a big man, some six feet tall and massively built. He was from Eger and, although I had never met him there, I became his favorite. He shared Koranyi's liberal attitude and his actions saved a lot of our people. "Here's the general directive," echoed his deep, strong voice between the buildings. "We'll build fences to isolate those returning, in order to stop the spread of disease. Any unauthorized contact will be severely punished, and whoever breaks this rule will automatically go behind the fence. Tonight everybody will line up here. All, including officers and sub-officers, will receive a preventive shot. No visitors will be allowed to enter the casern territory. Medical and food supply units, and clothing and bedding supply units will be formed. I need volunteers for nursing duties. Volunteers, raise hands!" Every Jew raised his hand. As I followed the eye of Dr. Miklos in the direction of our smassers, almost in disbelief I saw a raised hand there. Dr. Miklos seemed to be surprised too. "That's courageous of you, Corporal!" A few more hands went up in their ranks. They were our new guards. "Await further orders tomorrow morning! Dismissed!"

The cattle cars arrived the following morning with more than a thousand wretched, sick and dying Jews. This was the first labor camp contingent ever to come back from the Russian front. The train pulled in on an isolated track of Rimaszombat's only railroad station, in the late afternoon. Altough they had been on the road for weeks, it was not permitted to open the cars until 11:00 P.M., in order to disinfect them and avoid curious eyes. Newspaper and radio reports attempted to play down the event, but the news spread like wildfire through every Jewish community in the country. Families and friends descended on Rimaszombat, filling every hotel and all available beds in the local Jewish houses, everyone hoping his loved one was healthy and with the group. They were loaded with packages, and lined up on the front of the casern entrance to deliver them.

Jewish organizations from Budapest shipped bed sheets and hospital material. Doctors and nurses volunteered but were not accepted. It was impossible to find words adequate to describe these wretched, miserable men as they filed into their assigned quarters, the gaping holes in their shoes showing cracked and bleeding feet. One half carried or supported the other half, most of them skin and bones, looking as if they would expire at any moment. We stared at them, stunned, horrified, and filled with pity, but we could not touch or approach them. We just threw food over the quarantine fence and offered a few encouraging words. Their smassers and officers were in far better shape and yelled orders almost non-stop, but nobody seemed to pay attention. They were beyond caring. Hopelessness was written on their faces, and they reacted only with lethargy to the bread thrown over the fence.

The next morning, twenty volunteer nurses were ordered to enter the quarantined areas. Robi and Janos were among them, together with six professional guard nurses and Dr. Miklos. The officer in charge of the returnees, Lieutenant Barocy, well fed, spic and span in his smart uniform, requested permission to leave the quarantined area with the sub-officers. Dr. Miklos refused. They immediately began swearing, damning their Jews. Miklos warned Barocy and his men that if any Jew suffered injury or death because of a weakened state or mistreatment, there would be a court martial.

Joska and I stood with a small group just outside the fence, witnessing the scene. "You know, Joska, I've begun to realize how lucky we are with our new officers."

"Yes, it's slowly sinking in to me too, how exceptional our situation is."

"How many are they?"

"Nine hundred fifty-two," Joska explained. "We've started gathering their names in the office. Their officers didn't even have a list of names, just the number. This afternoon we'll post the list of names at the casern entrance so that visitors can see it. So many will be disappointed, not seeing the name they came to see. Do you have a special assignment, Tibor?"

"Yes, we're handling the personal packages from relatives and organizations. We'll distribute them with the help of the volunteers in the quarantined area." The response for help, the solidarity of the Jews in town and in the country was overwhelming. There were far more packages than people.

That night, I couldn't sleep. The vision of the suffering, misery, sickness and mistreatment of our unfortunate comrades filled me with anger. I felt guilty for being able to stay at headquarters while others were dying in Russia from mistreatment and hunger, even more than from bullets. The deep silence of the night was broken again and again with painful cries, hurled epithets or muffled moaning from behind the fences. I got up, took my sketchbook and walked out into the night. I was not alone. Joska and others were already there, staring at the fences. Slowly, the day broke with fiery red glory. My tired eyes fastened on the silhouette of two bodies on stretchers being carried by nurses to the infirmary, which Dr. Miklos had transformed into a morgue.

How do you capture so much suffering or inhumanity in a single drawing? Is it the artist's role to depict, to tell a story, or really just express his own state of mind? How do you concentrate in a single line, how do you express with color or texture all that moves you or inspires you to take up the pencil in the first place? How can you symbolize, abstract, or simplify this scene in order to transcend this one episode so that the suffering in it becomes The Suffering, and its pain The Pain; so that the work may penetrate the barrier to understanding the scene, even those responsible for it.

Although many died of typhoid, Dr. Miklos had decided to perform an autopsy on all who died, to learn how to help the living. He imposed stringent measures inside and outside this inner camp to avoid an epidemic. He also made sure that the sick received maximum care. We admired his courage and determination to save everyone he could. What a difference one man can make in spite of inhuman laws and hostile environment.

The morgue wall was the extreme perimeter of the quarantined area. Curiosity drew me to the high window and, on the tips of my toes, I was able to just peek inside. I wished I hadn't. I saw the dissmembered body of a man I never knew, with the top of his cranium next to his body, and his thorax as well as his abdomen open. Dr. Miklos was staring into a microscope. He suddenly turned, and our eyes met. He came to the door and yelled out. "Are you curious? Come in," he ordered.

"No, I'm not, Sir!" But it was too late. He motioned me inside. I tried not to look, but I could not avoid the spectacle. Here was a clump of flesh and bone such as one finds in a butcher shop, where a few hours before there had been a human being. Who knows what careers, what inventions, what works of art had been killed by Hitler and his cohorts.

"This clump of flesh, this brain tissue," Dr. Miklos said, pointing to the open cranium, "had the potential to encompass the world, to understand the stars, the universe, create revolutions or be a saint. I want to make sure what the cause of death was to save others, to make sure that it was not negligence. Do you know what Mr. Jacob, the first one, died of?"

"No, Sir!" I was struck by the reverence with which he said the name. "A piece of food, meat stuck in his throat. He was too weak to eat. Negligence!" he yelled. "We will find the guilty one! Grab that pail, take the body behind the morgue and dispose of it. Dig a hole, spread this lime in it and over the body, and cover it with earth. Then call your rabbi."

"We have no rabbis, Sir."

"You know that religious guy in your unit?"

"Shmuel?"

"Yes, whatever his name is, tell him to bury the dead as they should be buried."

My head was spinning, the stench was terrible and I could not escape the shocking sight. That was all we were. I thought I was going to pass out any second, but I didn't. I just staggered out with the pail and threw up. Yes, that was all we were. Some organic matter, some heriditary traits, and the sum of our experiences. There was no thought, no God, nothing but the perceptions of these dead brain cells when they were living.

When did a living being become conscious of itself?

Death in the Rimaszombat quarantine

If we could, most of us would like to live forever, whatever the course of our lives. Happiness, misery, suffering, are just ups and downs of life. Religion offers eternity in the beyond. But what of the non-believer and the materialist? The world, the universe exists for us as it is perceived by our consciousness, by our senses, our instruments of measurement. But our consciousness is the function of our material brain, which, when it disintegrates, means the universe doesn't exist for us. So the best we can hope for is the transformation, the degradation, the degeneration of our physical being, through its atomic and subatomic stages into free energy. A poor substitue to our present state. Yet consciousness can exist at many levels. The objective reality of a tree is very different for each of us. It may be perceived by man as organic matter, plant, wood, or as an object of aesthetic beauty; for an ant who crawls on it, it may seem the universe or, at the other extreme, some form of super-consciousness in a pre-existent energy state of which we are unaware.

The morgue of Rimaszombat had a deep influence on my entire life.

* * * * *

Four weeks of care, better food, the help of camp volunteers and the kindness of the local Jewish community, nursed the returnees back to life. The typhoid epidemic had abated and no new cases had been reported for three weeks. In small groups they received permission to exit their quarantine and the casern, and the rest of us were able to go out again. During these weeks, I had seen Edit only through a fence, but had been able to receive her letters, although we could not send mail out. Her letters were warm, loving, and full of anxiety about the war, about the future ... about our future.

Weekend visiting was again permitted, resulting in a wide range of emotions, from crying to laughing. Families and friends appreciated our efforts, as well as the wisdom of Koranyi and Dr. Miklos.

They looked on us as mini-heroes and expressed loathing for the smassers and politicians who had caused unnecessary suffering.

My father came to visit with a big package of food prepared by my mother.

"She couldn't come," he said.

"Why?" I asked.

"You know how emotional she is. She couldn't bear it. She fainted again a few times lately, and ... and ... you know."

"No money?"

He nodded, with tears in his eyes. My father did not talk too much. He never had. Only his eyes revealed his sorrow and shame that he could not help himself or his family. With his arm draped over my shoulder, he talked about his infinite love for us all.

"Grandfather is sick in bed," he said. "They don't know the reason."

Grandpa sick? He had never been sick. I could never remember him sick. I thought he must be sick in his heart. Sick from the ugliness of the world, sick of the insults to the Jews, although he was never very religious.

"There's no cure for these illnesses, son. Ocsi is such a good boy. He's drafted too, as you know. You should write more."

"How is your life now at home? What do they say about the war?" I asked.

"All of us are frightened. The fascists are more and more aggressive. Old friends distance themselves from us Jews. Many of us are trying to emigrate, but it takes money, much money to be able to do it. Still, we are Hungarians, and perhaps the storm will pass."

I did not believe it would, and I was sure that he didn't believe it either. But we needed hope, in order to keep our sanity.

* * * * *

The sights I had seen in the morgue and the words I had exchanged with Dr. Miklos continued to haunt me. The rationalization that Dr. Miklos had lost only eleven human beings out of close to a thousand could not alleviate my nightmares of torn, chopped-up flesh which had been human just minutes before. I began to sketch, not just the reality, but my hallucinations and dreams. How would this fit in the mosaic of life? The answer eluded me.

Camp life became settled again. Leaves were authorized more readily. The guards of the Russian detachment were sent back to the front, and the Jews gradually were assigned to other labor camps inside Hungary. We were back to our original number in the camp, plus the few who were retained at headquarters. I continued to go to the city more often to see Edit. I also became acquainted with more people in town. I talked with many non-Jews, including one city policeman who was obliged to wear the Arrow-Cross uniform, but who revealed himself to be no fascist at all. One Saturday afternoon, Edit invited a small group from the camp: Joska, Mihaly, Miklos, Shmuel, Tamas (who had stayed with us from the Russian group) and myself. We discussed our situation relative to current events, and our hopes of gaining time until the German collapse, which sometimes seemed so close, yet was so very far. Seeing or hearing about atrocities, we nevertheless underestimated the determination of Hitler's gang to destroy the Jews.

"It's nice to see there's still a warm Jewish home, after all the destruction I witnessed on the Russian front," Tamas said with a sigh. "Destruction of people, monuments, homes, works of art, nothing is left at the bend of the Don, except the Russians' determination to resist. Nothing is valued or worth sparing to the western barbarians."

"What is permanence or value anyway?" Mihaly asked, with his head down and defeat in his voice. He was answered with silence. All of us retreated to our thoughts.

"There are only two things a human being can do which outlast him and which ensure permanence and value," I said.

"What?" Joska asked.

"Two aspects of creativity; a baby who carries the potential of a better future, and art which bears witness and links the past and future."

"How about science?"

"Science, literature and philosophy all have their creative or artistic moments. A moment of inspiration and an elegant solution: that's art."

"But who can care about art in the midst of destruction, when we fight or fear for our survival?" Edit asked.

"The individual and his sex drive compelling him to reproduce are inseparable. The need for beauty is also innate in the individual, even though its expression may not be obvious. The desire to possess something beautiful doesn't arise after the necessities of existence, but exists from the beginning. A person will select between the objects presented for his choice, the 'plus beau' in his concept."

"To make a choice is a complicated procedure psychologically, in which all our character, education, milieu, temperment are engaged. As Camus wrote, in each moment of our lives we are "condemned" to choose. And we choose from among the objects, ideas, systems, philosophies submitted to us, which are proposed by a relatively few creative minds."

"Are they aware of their power over the noncreative masses?" Edit asked.

"Certainly not," I answered. "The artist doesn't create for any interest or any person. He expresses his ideas and sentiments in the language most comfortable for him. One of my high school professors defined art simply as the "jeux des grands enfants," games of grownup children. This is significant when others question, then forbid the artist to "play" with his ideas and express them freely. Such repression occurs not only in the political arena but is also practiced by vituperative critics and the uneducated public, who cannot understand new movements or styles like cubism, abstraction, surrealism, or atonality in music or existentialism in philosophy."

"These aren't times for artists' games," Shmuel interjected. "It's the time to pray and be humble about our capabilities."

"Not so!" I retorted. "The artist, through his sensitivity, illuminates. He's not essentially different from other people, nor more sensitive, but, as Malraux expressed it, differently sensitive. This distinction is important. The artists' sensibility is rather a great capacity for perception, observation, simplification and synthesis, conscious or otherwise, to ably express his sensibility with emotional fire."

"You're right, Tibor," Joska said. "We need artists now more than ever."

Edit's mother opened the living room door. "Having a good time, fellas?"

We looked at each other. "Yes, Mrs. Klein." For over two hours we had been in a different world. How refreshing!

"It's close to five o'clock. You're welcome to come again but you had better return to the casern."

"Thank you for your hospitality."

We said goodbye and walked back to the casern in a reflective mood. I was assailed by guilt for having relaxed and enjoyed a few hours of pleasant conversation. People were suffering all around. Men were dying by the thousands in Russia, in the Pacific, in Italy. Jews were being murdered everywhere. My family, my father and mother were struggling like beasts of burden just to survive. How could I feel good even for an hour?

We can understand intellectually, we can feel sorrow and sympathy, we can get angry and upset; but we can't feel the bullet in the other man's head, the knives ripping a friend's flesh, the agony of hunger and thirst. Ultimately, we become totally involved in our daily existence. Ours was defined by the casern's order and routine, with misery or well-being determined in that context. Perhaps this was morally outrageous, but it was probably part of survival instinct.

* * * * *

Returning one day to the barracks, I found my friends gathered around a tall, good-looking guy, in surprisingly good shape.

"New recruit?"

"No."

"Hi, I'm Tibor."

"I'm Barabas."

"From where?"

"From the Russian front," he said laughing. He had been telling of the incredible battles at the bend of the Don and the even more incredible story of his escape. Barabas and two smassers were the only survivors of an entire labor camp regiment.

The Russian counter-attack at Stalingrad had been successful, forcing the Germans and Hungarians to retreat to the Don's west bank. The labor camp recruits, who were forced to stay put to dig anti-tank trenches, were shot at by the advancing Russians; and if they tried to move back or toward the Russians to escape, they were shot at by the Hungarians.

"We were able, with a few others, to retreat, and decided to float to the other side of the ice-cold river between the hundreds of floating bodies of Russians, Germans, Hungarians and our labor camp comrades. I made it. The others didn't."

"How about the two smassers?"

"They were transferred, both slightly wounded, back to headquarters here. Out of sympathy, or maybe because they're awakening to the fact that they may be losing the war, they brought me with them, probably thinking it would be advantageous for them to have at least a few Jewish friends. So here I am."

"What do you do in civilian life?"

"I'm a mechanical and civil engineer. I build roads, bridges, sewers and the like."

"That's terrific!" Joska said enthusiastically, winking at me as if he had some idea. Barabas would integrate into our group very quickly.

Koranyi had known Barabas before he was moved out to the Russian front, and two days after his arrival he called him into his office for an eyewitness report on the events in Russia and the fate of our regiment. Then Koranyi gave him written permission to rest until he was ordered on a special assignment.

Barabas knew only about the events in which he had participated. Even so, he had little understanding of their meaning, having been so isolated, and he was eager to know how those events fitted into the larger picture. One summer Sunday afternoon, a dozen of us along with Miki, our strategist, gathered in front of the barracks and tried to piece together events of the last three to four months.

We knew that on January 7, 1943 bayonet fighting was going on in every house and block in Stalingrad. On January 8, Von Paulus had not dared to accept the Russian ultimatum for fear of Hitler, even though he knew his troops were lost. A few days later, the siege of Leningrad was broken; the Russians had opened a narrow corridor south of Lake Lagoda through which supplies could reach the city. Although Volklov secured it over the next few days, the Germans kept pounding it incessantly with artillery fire, and it became known as the "death corridor." In mid-January, the Russians broke through the Hungarian Second Army, the weakest link in the chain around the Don. Most of the Hungarians and both Jews and Gentiles were wiped out. "I'm aware of that," Barabas interjected, with sadness. The best news we heard in many months was that on January 31, 1943, the Germans surrendered Stalingrad. This would turn out to be the turning point of the war.

Following Stalingrad's collapse, the most vicious propaganda was undertaken by the Germans against the Bolsheviks and Jews, as Hitler urged his people to renew their efforts.

The next morning, the entire camp was called to assemble on the drill field. There was tension as the smassers took their head count, and it was obvious that something important was happening. That none of our spies in the offices knew anything about it was disturbing. Then Koranyi announced that the glorious Hungarian army, fighting alongside our German allies against the perils of communism, needed our casern and facilities. We would have to evacuate within a very short time. Our withdrawal date would be announced later. All leaves were cancelled. The casern could be left only with special permission.

It was a shock. We had become complacent from months of easy living. My first thought was about Edit. What would become of our romance? Then the idea of escape came to me, as it had every time we moved. Was this the time to escape and try to join some partisan group? Where in hell were they, anyway? My thoughts next went to my family, whom I had seen seldom lately. Where would the rapids of destiny put us on shore?

Koranyi granted me permission to go to town. Rimaszombat was his hometown. He knew Edit's family and he knew about our romance. "Here's your permit until 10:00 P.M." Then, looking deeply into my eyes, "Make no attempt to escape. You could jeopardize all of your people and me. Do you understand?"

"Yes, Sir."

When I met Edit and her mother, they had already heard the news. Edit didn't talk. She gave me a kiss on the cheek and held my hand. Her mother asked, "When are you leaving?"

"We don't know."

"You can stay here," she said.

"No, I can't." Silence.

She left the room. Edit and I sat down on the sofa very close.

"What will happen to us?" she asked in a low voice.

"We can't tell. I'm more concerned about you. We at least are in a military organization. For the moment, we have food and shelter and decent officers. But what's happening to civilians in eastern Europe is terrifying. In Poland, Lithuania and Ukraine the Jews are being confined in ghettos and deported from their homes and homeland. Who knows what's happening to them?"

Would we see each other again? Would we survive? We asked the question hundreds of different ways, without wanting an answer. Obviously, we could not know the future, but our odds did not appear very good. By asking questions for which we wanted no answer, we had already begun to part from one another. We had already accepted the inevitable. After a tense dinner, interrupted by Edit's sobbing, with a final kiss I returned to the casern.

* * * * *

In the last few months great changes had taken place on all fronts. Beginning with Stalingrad, we had better news to rejoice about, but our fantasy of a quick end to the war was not about to come true. In April of 1943, Leningrad saw tremendously heavy air battles. During that same time, the German radio announced the discovery of a mass grave of 4,150 Polish officers in Katyn, near Smolensk, and accused the Russians of the massacre. Russia denied it, and later broke diplomatic relations with the provisional Polish government in London on the issue. From the Pacific, we heard news of important battles and great American successes. As we learned after the war, the Americans broke the Japanese codes, the famous "Tokyo Express," and learned their every movement.

On our Russian front map we moved our flags to the Kuban region, where in great battles the Russians were pressing westward. A Churchill warning to the Germans threatened reprisals if they used poison gas against the Russian advance.

One day, Miki ran to fetch me, Barabas, Joska and the others. "I heard terrible news," he said, out of breath. "Terrible massacres are going on in the Warsaw ghetto. Over 50,000 Jews have been killed. It was some kind of uprising."

"How do you know about this?"

"From friends in town I can't reveal, but they're reliable."

"You'd better not spread rumors if you can't reveal your sources," Barabas warned him menacingly.

"So far I've seldom been wrong, have I?" he retorted.

He was right. The Jews had revolted. It was even acknowledged in the fascist press, but we knew very few details about it.

"What can we do?"

"Wait for our opportunity," Joska said, calming everybody.

"Why don't we join the partisans? They're around us," Mihaly, the most unlikely guy, suggested.

"Because we can't find them," said Barabas with regret.

"Where is all this news coming from, anyway?" Mihaly asked.

"Maybe we should establish a news bureau or, more to the point, a rumor bureau to consolidate everything we hear," I said jokingly.

"It's not such a bad idea," Joska jumped in. "Why not? These are the sources: official fascist news from papers and radio; the BBC, when we can gather it second-hand from the village; Koranyi and Dr. Miklos, who often volunteer news different from the official line to Bela, Joska and other office workers; Miki, from wherever he gets his information. Bela! You'll be the bureau chief, assigned to interpret, read between the lines and summarize the available information."

What we assembled thus far was not necessarily the most important news or the most timely, but whatever we could gather from second and third-hand sources. We knew that at the end of April and the beginning of May major battles took place in Tunisia, and that the Allies had conquered Tunis during that month.

All through May we had encouraging news. The Trident Conference between Roosevelt and Churchill decided on the invasion of Sicily. General Marshall promised air support to Chiang Kai-shek to use against Japan. The German announcement of major battles against Yugoslav partisans was especially encouraging for us: we always hoped to do something similar. And the Free French created a council of National Resistance. A surprising piece of news via Bela's wire service was that the Russians had announced the dissolution of the Comintern, obviously to please the West.

I helped Koranyi to establish the new front on his map and, based on his information, we moved the little red flags to the area of Kursk, where one of the war's greatest battles took place. From June to July, incessant attacks by the Germans, by air and on the ground, were repulsed by the Russians, who scored a major victory and established their air superiority for the first time. Zhukov and Vasilivsky became the generals most feared by the Germans. We learned with satisfaction that the Free French had become more active. On July 10, the Allies landed in Sicily and, by the end of July, Mussolini was forced to resign. We were pleased with all this good information, but what we were most interested in was how well the Russians were advancing.

As the Russians neared the Hungarian border, more and more German troops crowded on Hungary's eastern frontier, preparing major defense lines behind the Carpathian mountains, which provided a natural obstacle to the Russian advance. We let our imaginations go wild. "This may be the time," we thought, "to make real escape plans."

"They're only a few hundred miles away," said Miki, pointing to his ever-present situation map. Barabas, who always had been very action-oriented, felt that we should organize our partisan unit and find a connection to the Russians or the Czech partisans who were operating not too far from us. Partisan movements were now active all over Europe, especially in France, but also in Italy, Czechoslovakia and Greece. There were also Yugoslavian chetniks and Tito's communists. But not in Hungary. "Those other countries were occupied by Hitler. The Hungarians are Hitler's allies," pointed out Robi.

"Where the heck do you go if the population doesn't support you?"

"He's right," Joska added. "We have a rather exceptional situation with Koranyi as our camp commander. He's extremely liberal and is able to control our immediate environment and contain the anti-Semitism of his subordinates, but the population in general is hostile."

"Maybe Koranyi himself can help us," Barabas insisted laughingly.

"Anyway, we cannot undertake this kind of action unless all of us agree, and move at the same time," Joska pointed out. "Otherwise, we would make the life of the others unbearable, since it would mean the end of Koranyi's liberal policies."

"I feel guilty, damn it. I sit here doing nothing, while Jews in Poland are massacred and others flee in all directions from persecution ... but to where?"

"The irony is," Mihaly remarked, "that many people, mostly from Rumania and the sub-Carpathian area of Czechoslovakia, are crowding into Hungary. We haven't seen the worst of it yet."

"Don't worry," Barabas said angrily, "it will come; remember the Warsaw ghetto. We'd better be ready. We must organize now."

"Okay, I'm ready," Joska challenged him. "What do you want me to do? Make a grenade or a bomb and blow up the trains full of ammunitions and war machinery which pass here almost every night heading to the Russian front? So get me one. All it takes is one grenade to kill our smassers and rob the ammunition depot in the concrete blocks."

"Maybe we can buy them," Mihaly said, "or we could let Robi organize a break-in."

"I have a better idea," Miki said, "why don't we just derail the trains?" Silence.

All of us were thinking: this was a real possibility.

Barabas faced me and looked me straight in the eye: "You're the field octato; designate someone and let's move."

"Okay with me. Let's call in the other council members. Lajos, call them in."

We explained our ideas to Bela and the others. They were astonished, to say the least. Doubts were raised and objections offered. After some give and take, I asked for a show of hands. There were three dissenters who argued that we would accomplish very little and risk a lot; but they agreed not to hinder us if we went ahead. We agreed that whoever executed the plan must assume personal responsibility, as if it were their own undertaking. They must take any punishment alone.

"All right then," I said, "any volunteers?" Barabas, Joska, Robi and Miki raised their hands alongside mine. We agreed that Barabas and Robi would act for us all.

No two men could be more dissimilar in background, education or personal experience. Barabas was a cool, super-intelligent engineer from Budapest's famous Polytechnic Institute. He was from an upper-middle-class family. He had thin, pinched lips, and always walked straight, head up, self-confident, ready to confront the world. He was also the only one who had experienced the Russian front. Robi was streetwise, opportunistic, a little furtive and secretive. He had been fatherless from an early age, raised in a crime-ridden outer suburb of Budapest, Angyalfold, "Land of the Angels." He also had a criminal record.

They shook hands with sincerity, and I saw in their eyes and the strength of their handshake that they felt equal, with as many similarities as differences. Each was principled in his own way, although they obeyed different rules in normal life. They were determined that they would not back down from whatever they undertook. "Let's get together with you and Joska to discuss the details. Nobody else needs to know anything," Barabas said. "Okay?" Yes, we all agreed.

We decided that our target would be about one to one-and-a-half kilometers outside the city, in a fairly long arc of the track, before it hit the straight line leading to the station. "All we need," said Barabas, "is to loosen a few railroad spikes. We can lift the track with a strong crowbar on one side to get leverage. We can then attach a molotov cocktail with a two-wire detonator, which will close the circuit as the wheels press on it." We agreed to start to assemble the materials, mostly with help from outside the camp.

* * * * *

Although it was almost 10:00 P.M., Barabas and Robi were waiting for me at my bunk.

"While you were out with your Edit," Barabas started, "we received orders to pack everything in the casern starting tomorrow morning. Personal belongings are to be march-ready; all the offices, furniture and papers, all the ammunition in the cement bunker, will be loaded on horsedrawn wagons. It will be the perfect opportunity to steal one or two hand grenades for our mission."

"To tell the truth, I had almost given up hope of carrying out our decision. Do you think we'll be able to get away with it in the confusion?"

"You bet!" Robi said excitedly.

"We need two things from you," added Barabas, "A pass, first of all; and tomorrow you must assign Robi to the group loading ammunition."

"I'm sure it will be heavily guarded."

"That's my business," Robi snapped proudly.

We all smiled.

Koranyi would not give me another pass, especially for two people, but Bela and his team of office workers had stolen blank ones. Barabas, Robi and Joska looked at me. "We need a signature."

"Ja?" I shrugged.

"You're an artist and engraver, so what's the problem?"

"All right," I said, "but try not to use it if you can avoid it. Give me the pass and you will have it signed in half an hour. I smeared a soft lead pencil over an old signature of Koranyi's, placed a semi-transparent piece of toilet paper from the officers quarters over it, and traced the signature with a hard pencil. The lead was picked up on the other side. I rubbed it on the new pass, went over it with a fountain pen, erased the lead and there it was, a perfect signature. Or certainly good enough for casual examination.

We agreed that they would sneak out on the side of the morgue where a wire fence surrounded the camp, and would use the pass only if they were caught. "If you can get some explosives, we can get started tomorrow evening," I said.

"It's no good to keep explosives in our quarters, especially now. I'll get a crowbar from the warehouse," Barabas said. "It will be no problem to steal one with all the people coming and going."

We awakened to the bugle call the next morning. We prepared for the daily routine, lining up for breakfast and assembling for headcount as usual. The smassers were unusually impatient, barking and yelling unecessarily. After we had assembled, we noticed the day officer talking with two Arrow-Cross officers, who left after a few minutes. Then he ordered all to assemble at the drill field. "Octato Gerstl!" he yelled. "Send ten men to Officer Gerely for work in the offices, twenty men to the ammunition bunker, twenty men to the warehouse, and ten men to the kitchen. Everyone will get further orders from the officers; we will start orderly packing, loading and inventorying all material!"

"Yes, sir."

It was no problem to send Barabas to the warehouse and Robi to the ammunition bunker. After midday, as I was making my rounds to check on my different groups, Robi motioned me toward the latrine. I met him there and he pushed into my hand three objects wrapped in newspaper. "Get these into the barracks," he said, "and be careful, too!" He laughed. I went to the barracks immediately, supposedly to check whether anybody was goofing off, and placed the package in my rucksack.

That evening, we assembled around my bed. The plan seemed to have worked perfectly. We had the explosives, including a timer device, and Barabas reported that he had dropped a heavy crowbar near the morgue and hidden it in the bushes. Everything was ready. There would only be a problem if they shipped us out before we could do anything. Tonight was too late, all of us agreed. Tomorrow, as soon as it was dark, we would have to act or forget the whole thing. "Then tomorrow it will be," Barabas said quietly.

At 10:00 P.M., Bela returned from the office where they had just finished packing. "Fellas, I saw the orders. We have to move out and evacuate everything by tomorrow night."

"Shit!" was Robi's comment.

"Perfect," Barabas said. "Let's go to sleep."

The order was given in the early morning. By afternoon, everything was ready to move to the railroad station. Our people went to load and unload. The freight cars to be loaded were on an isolated track at the opposite end of the station, near the spot we had planned for our action. By 6:00 P.M. it was quite dark, and we decided that Robi and Barabas had to move. They cautiously sneaked out of the casern by way of the morgue, cut two wires near the wall, and reached the designated curve in the track in just fifteen minutes. The timing of their return was critical. They had to return through the same hole in the wire to avoid using the false pass. When the order came to line up at the drill field, they were still out. Minutes passed like hours. Orders to march to the train might be issued any minute.

Some forty minutes passed since they had left, when the day officer ordered roll call. "Szabo," Present. "Weinberg," Present." "Barabas," No answer.

After a second of hesitation, I stepped forward. "Sir, Day Officer, I sent Robi and him to make one last round in our quarters to check if anything was left behind."

"Look after them and keep them moving." The roll call continued. The minutes passed and my fear and anxiety increased. Should I speak with Koranyi? No! I could not involve him in this.

I was desperate to find some diversion to delay our departure, when I finally saw their silhouettes struggling back outside the wire. As loud as I could, I yelled, "Hey you, finish the search and get back to the line on the double! Day Officer, they're here. We're all ready." He reported this to Koranyi, who gave the order to march. The entire Jewish population had lined the street, and many walked with us up to the tracks. There we were swallowed one by one into the freight train, which departed with us to an unknown destination.

Once in the boxcar, we surrounded Barabas and Robi. "Did you do it?"

"Yes, the timer is set for between 10:00 and 10:30 P.M. Those German ammunitions won't reach the Russian front tonight."

At nine o'clock, our boxcar started to move back and forth, from one line to another, until we couldn't tell which track we were on. Around 10:15 we started slowly but surely to move westward, but we were still convinced that we were ultimately headed for the Russian front. With a humorous glint in his eye, Miki said to Robi that it looked as if he had done an excellent job of getting us blown up. By 10:20 we passed the curve where the track had been rigged, and we saw the German train heading east on the opposite track. A minute later, we heard a tremendous explosion, as the explosives hit the ammunition stores through the bottom of the boxcars. Smiles of satisfaction and an exchange of congratulations went all around. Nobody could blame us. We were underway.

THE HANGONY ELECTRIC COMPANY

We were heading south this time. After a short while, we came to a halt at a small, dusty town. The night turned to day and day to night again before our train started to move through seemingly familiar landscape back to the west. As it slowed down again, "guetteur" Toni announced that he could see tall industrial chimneys and big open flames of a steel smelting plant. We were heading toward Ozd. Perhaps they needed labor at the railroad terminal there, or for the industry. That wouldn't be so bad. At least we were still in Hungary. Of course, they could just be moving us to another side track.

As soon as the train came to a stop, we heard the military barking orders and the rough metal of the boxcar's locks being opened from the outside. Soldiers pushed the doors open with great force and began yelling, "Out! All out! At once! Move! Line up in front of your car!" Our legs numb, we jumped off, pushing each other in confusion. Joska and Bela tried to calm everyone, and I heard Joska yelling at me to take command. "It will be dangerous with these people," I said, "It won't be as easy as with our old smassers, who would accept it as normal."

"Do it! Now!" he retorted, "or we'll lose all our options! Move!" I pushed myself to the front of our two carloads, a group of ninety. "Attention!" I yelled as loud as I could. Lifting my right arm high, I ordered, "Everyone line up by threes. Move fast, damn it! After I count six, nobody moves!" At six I turned back; all were lined up. "Right turn! One, two!" I marched up to the sergeant with clicking steps.

"Sir Sergeant, Octato Tibor Gerstl reports Unit Two is ready for your orders!" He was perplexed, to say the least.

"Where is your commanding officer?" he asked in a rather normal voice. I pointed to our corporal. He called him over and, after a few minutes of talk, ordered him to the head of our group. When everybody was out of the train and in line, the sergeant thundered that we had a ten-kilometer march to our destination, the village of Hangony.

We passed through Ozd, an industrial town. Its uniformly small workers' houses were pressed against each other. These were interrupted occasionally by business sections, comprising the baker, butcher, tailor, shoemaker, almost all owned by Jews, who seemed to be going about their business undisturbed. Their wives and daughters waved to us with encouraging enthusiasm.

Leaving behind the last houses of Ozd was like stepping from mud to cleansing, crystal clear water. The vista now opened onto dormant agricultural land covered by snow. Our marching step on the frozen dirt road echoed in the silent landscape. We passed some small farmhouses, and our arrival was announced far ahead at each one by a "puli" or "vizsla," those terrific sheep and hunting dogs. Here a neat peasant girl, there an old peasant with a big bushy mustache pressed their heads against their windows with curiosity. A young boy watched us, leaning against a prairie fence.

We reached Hangony after dark. I saw the silhouette of a two-story stone building, standing out between the small farmhouse roofs of thatch or red tile. It was the casern. As we arrived, except for the moon, the only light in town consisted of a few candles or kerosene lamps twinkling in small windows. The town had no electricity. We were ordered directly into long barracks which stretched all around the main building. Food was distributed as we filed in. We settled in for the night, and were told that we would be organized the next day.

* * * * *

It was a chilly and dry morning. The sky was bright blue, and as the winter sun climbed higher it warmed our backs, and our hearts too. We cleared the quarters assigned to us and were happy we were able to keep our unit together. The camp was surrounded by a low wire fence. Beyond it, a few thousand meters away, was the village of Hangony, with its dormant vegetable gardens and open fields between the houses. We saw its inhabitants, sturdy, colorful Hungarian peasants going about their business, the men feeding their livestock in the stables and the women shaking baskets of grain, calling the chickens, or bringing buckets of feed for the pigs. It was an idyllic pastoral scene as they moved in a measured, unhurried, almost rhythmical tempo. This was the heart of Hungary, its soul. These were the stubborn, tenacious, romantic men and women who had maintained the Magyar identity. Throughout thousands of years of history, they had kept alive the unique language, folk songs, dances and traditions, while the nobles spoke Latin in the Middle Ages, or Latin and some Turkish during a hundred fifty years of Ottoman rule, or German during the Austro-Hungarian Emplre.

The camp sat squarely in the valley of a fairly steep and moderately high mountain range. As I started down on a small path between the barracks to explore the area, I was joined by Joska, Bela and Miki. We walked toward the camp's edge at the foot of the mountains, but before we reached it we were stopped by another wire fence with a small, open gate. The path continued past a half-collapsed bridge over a narrow but deep gorge to a small building about a hundred meters up the mountain side.

"It's better to stop here," Joska advised. We agreed and headed back. Beyond the casern territory, just a few hundred yards outside the fence, we noticed somebody gesticulating behind the bushes and moving toward us.

"Hey! Hey!" she yelled, approaching in her colorful dirty skirt and half-open blouse. "Hey, any left-overs? Any old boots?"

"No, love," Miki yelled back, "we have nothing, we've only just arrived!"

"Shit," she responded casually, and turned back.

"Look," Bela pointed after her. Where she had disappeared we could see tents, freely running horses and campfire smoke. "It's a small gypsy camp at the foot of the first hill."

"Happy people," sighed Joska.

"Happy or miserable, but certainly free," Miki added.

"Not freer than anybody else," I thought. They are restrained by their own clannish traditions and economic pressures. In their struggle to survive, they have to compromise too, live outside small cities and villages and suffer the abuse of townspeople and the police. They are free, nevertheless, because they have the option to pick up their camps and leave, which we haven't.

Walking back, we passed some of the military cadre, whom we saluted smartly to avoid any problems. One of them stopped us and engaged in a friendly conversation about Galanta. He said that our original cadre of guards, or most of it, would return to Galanta and his group would take over. We continued toward the main entrance, but suddenly all of us stopped, frozen, as if commanded to do so. On the opposite side of the main building and the main entrance was a smaller stone building which we thought was occupied by the guards, our future military cadre. Instead, some eight "Csendor"marched out in fancy uniforms, with their typical elongated melon hats decorated with colorful rooster-tail feathers. They paired up, and some took off on foot, some on bicycles, as they dispersed in different directions outside the fence.

If ever there was unity among Hungarians, between Jews and Gentiles, middle-class, lower-class, rich and poor, it was in a common hatred of the Csendor. They filled the role of military police, state troopers, CIA and FBI, all rolled into one. They executed every dirty job the central authority required.

"It's not very encouraging," said Bela in a low voice. We nodded in agreement.

* * * * *

There was a lot of coming and going in the main building by military personnel of all ranks, from soldier to brigadier. Only Sergeant Kovacs and a few others seemed to be veterans of field activities. The handful of Jewish laborers appeared to have very good relations with their guards.

Joska, Bela and I greeted one of them, who was pushing a wheelbarrow full of shoes and boots. We introduced ourselves and, hesitantly, he gave his name as Feri.

"Are you an old-timer here?"

"Yes."

"We don't see too many old-timers."

"No, there are only craftsmen attached to headquarters."

"How many of you are there?"

"About forty. I'm the shoemaker. There are tailors, mechanics, blacksmiths, a cleaning and maintenance unit, cooks and the like."

"The smassers seem to treat you well."

"Ah, yes, since we do all kinds of illegal, private jobs for them."

"We're fortunate. These are the better smassers. The others are on duty in Russia, somewhere around Stalingrad. They're guarding about a thousand Jewish laborers."

"Do you hear anything about them?"

"Yes, all bad; there have been many casualties, and much bad treatment. It's a disaster. I have to go now. We're sure to meet again."

In mid-afternoon, the sharp sound of the bugle called for attention. We were ordered to assemble on the drill field for review at 4:00 P.M. between the barracks. We were all ready on time, filling the small rectangular court completely. Each unit was headed by an octato and a guard, including the old-timer headquarters unit on the extreme right. A detachment of about twenty soldiers led by Sergeant Kovacs marched to the middle of the drill field, stopped, and turned with precision on the sergeant's command. They were followed by a group of high brass, who took their places on the porch steps of a facing barracks.

The sergeant addressed the entire camp, pulled his sabre from it's sheath, yelled, "Attention!", and with parade steps approached the brass. "Sir Camp Commander, Sergeant Kovacs reports seven hundred thirty-five auxiliaries (that was us) and twenty-two guards ready for your command."

Commandant Koranyi finished chatting with the other brass, stepped forward and saluted, addressing especially the old-timers and the new guards. "Welcome to the Eleventh KMSZ. Although you don't wear uniforms, you are military personnel and will be treated as such. Your contribution to the defense of the Motherland is important. Laziness or sabotage will be severely punished. After proper training, you will join the army wherever your labor is needed. Your unit's guards have been assigned and will relieve the ones from Galanta. I want to see heads held up, confident and proud. You are to maintain strict discipline and follow orders precisely. Sergeant! Take charge!" He saluted, and turned to continue his interrupted chat.

Commandant Koranyi was an unassuming figure, perhaps five-foot six and slightly hunched, with an oversized nose, suspiciously red, under which an always short cigarette butt was ready to burn out. He continued to chat as he promenaded across the field with his aides: Dr. Miklos, some lieutenants and commissioned officers, who were followed by sub-officers, many of whom we either met or had seen in the office building.

Now it was Sergeant Kovacs' turn to admonish us about discipline and work. For five long minutes, in his nasal voice caused by a harelip, which he tried unsuccessfully to cover with a bushy mustache, he droned on. He assigned a guard to each unit. They then led us to the dinner kettle, and we were dismissed for the day.

That evening, we gathered in our barracks to assess our new situation. We invited Feri and his friend Toni in order to learn about the camp and the local customs and idiosyncrasies. We were mostly concerned about the commander's reference to out-placement. Although nobody openly discussed it, the threat and how to avoid it was on all our minds. The obvious answer was to try to stay at headquarters. Naturally, the competition for the few openings for craftsmen would be fierce. Getting such a job could literally mean the difference between life and death. "I'm sure there are plenty of jobs for someone with my kind of background," Robi declared assuredly. We all laughed, and Feri was wondering what it was all about.

Feri and Toni left. A dozen of us crowded into a corner to try to figure out what we could do to influence our destiny. We learned in Galanta and Rimaszombat that units with a strong octato were better off than units with strong smassers. So we decided that starting the next morning, I should make every effort to maintain my command. We also agreed that if the opportunity arose to get to a headquarters' job, it would be acceptable to pursue it individually, even if it meant not staying with the group. An objection came from the most surprising person, Robi. "We have to try and get those jobs for the weaker guys like Moricka, if we can. Otherwise, Bela or the other rich guys will buy their own safety." A deep silence followed.

"Okay, lawyers," I prodded. "Mihaly, what do you say?"

"A life is a life, and nobody has the right to ask another to commit suicide." It was not fair, but it was a matter of survival. We all agreed.

* * * * *

Reveille awakened us to the day's reality. We anticipated the usual boring, stupid drills: march... step left ... right ... run ... stop ... push-up ... jump ... sing, spiced with arbitrary punishment, barracks cleaning and potato peeling, over and over again. But I approached this line-up with great apprehension. While we were readying ourselves, Joska, myself and our inner circle told everybody that we would try to maintain the Galanta routine, under my command.

Before we left our room, I called for attention. "Fellas, please help by being very fast and accurate with drills and work. Try not to give any reason for the smassers to intervene. If I have to 'punish' to put on a show, Joska will be first, Robi second, then I'll pick according to the circumstances. Is everybody ready? Moricka, make sure your shirt doesn't hang out. Robi, check him. Shmuel, finish with your damned prayers and get ready. Ready? Move out! On the double!"

With my stomach in my throat and my chest pounding, I led the troops. I kept telling myself, "That's it. No more hesitation! Action! Just act! Just do it the way we did it in Galanta!" Our smasser, a corporal, was waiting outside the barracks with legs spread as if anchored to the ground, and an air of superiority over a bunch of civilian Jews. My brain switched gears into automatic. Instinct took over. Before the smasser could open his mouth, I stopped abruptly, raised my hand high and called, "Unit Twenty-four! Attention! Line up! One! Two! Three!" I turned back toward them.

"Hey! You! Octato! What the hell ...?"

He tried to intervene, but I pretended I didn't hear him. "Attention!" I continued, "Salute! Right!" All heads turned right in frozen attention. With hard marching steps, I moved to face him at the regulation distance of five meters. "Sir Corporal? Octato Tibor Gerstl reporting. Forty-eight men, none in sickbay, ready for your command!"

"Not bad for civilians," he noted with sarcasm. Then he took five long steps toward me, measuring to see if I was at the proper distance.

We stood nose to nose for three or four intense seconds before he stepped back. "I am Berci Veres, your unit commander. I will teach you the work you have to perform, discipline, drill and competition. If you are good, I am good. If you are not, I will eat you alive." He leaned forward, "Is that understood? Right turn! And let me see you sprint to the drill field." He obviously expected his order to be executed immediately, but nobody moved. This was the moment of truth. The critical fraction of a second for me to play my card. As he began to recover from his surprise, I yelled, "Right turn! In a gallop! After me! One, two, one, two, one, two ..." We headed to the drill field and our smasser followed with long measured steps.

When he arrived we were again lined up.

"Octato! I will take command!"

"Yes, sir!"

"Left turn!" The unit executed the order, but not me. I lined up slightly behind him as his adjutant supervisor, and he accepted it. When he ordered us to gallop around the field, he ordered me to lead while he stayed put, observing us as a circus master watches horses run around the ring. But I dictated the tempo. Thus, our effort to make them accept me as a smasser-helper proved to be extremely useful in minimizing the unit's misery. It saved lives, but it also angered and bewildered the new recruits, to whom our motives could not be explained.

The daily routine was established, and my role as octato maintained. Still, every day we had to be alert and walk a tightrope, balancing between the smasser's need to be rough and my desire to protect my troops.

A few weeks later, the born or converted Christians, identifiable by their white armbands, were reassigned to office duties. They had daily contact with the top brass, exerting important influence on their thinking, and providing us with important inside information. For example, they were able to influence the commandants by having them explain to the smassers that it was beneath their dignity to command Jews directly, and they should do it through the octatos. Although this was not an order, most of them obliged, even though some were skeptical of the recommendation and only partially applied it.

The drill field between the barracks was small. One day we left the casern around 8:00 A.M. for the soccer field, marching smartly to the beat of Hungarian military folk songs. Each hundred men were led by an octato, and I led all of our nine hundred people. The smassers marched at the sides of the columns and kicked the behinds of a few people to make sure that nobody forgot who he was. At four in the afternoon, we marched back to the casern along the same route. For the townspeople, all this razzmatazz was a great event, a distraction from their daily routine. They liked to watch us march and drill. The main street was always lined with people, especially in the afternoon. The atmosphere was friendly in general, and the boys and girls were out in strength. There were no Jewish inhabitants in Hangony, and the only time we met Jews was when we went to Ozd to shop. If there was any anti-Semitism here, I had yet to see it.

Mariska was a beautiful peasant girl, about nineteen years old. She had a typical Hungarian face, with high cheekbones and jaw tapering to a point at her chin. Her blouse was tightly laced at the waist, and her multi-layered skirts would swing from left to right with each step, revealing a little of her legs between her skirt and her shining boots. I noticed for the second day in a row that she was marching with two giggling friends at the roadside, exactly in line with me leading my group. The only difference between the side path and the road was that the former had more footprints while the latter had more horse, cow and wheel prints in the dirt. Mariska was reserved, but it was obvious that she was flirting with me. Although I was concerned about how the smassers or the townspeople would react even to the possibility of us walking together, by the third day I could not resist and, just before we turned into the casern, I indicated with hand signals that she should meet me at five on one of the street corners.

* * * * *

In the casern, the usual routine had continued for more than a month, and our relationship with the officers was good. Joska, Mihaly and Bela reported good news about our new big brass from their offices. Of course, we loved Koranyi, who often at great risk tried to persuade his sub-officers to curb their anti-Semitic tendencies and convictions. Once an officer under him denounced this policy to the Arrow-Cross in Budapest, but Koranyi was able to clear himself of the charges.

A few very special recruits joined the camp. There was Kabos, many times an Olympic fencing champion with the sabre, and Sarkany, also an Olympic medalist as the star of the world champion Hungarian water polo team. They wore the armbands of the national colors, red, white and green, as a special privilege for their service and contribution to the prestige of Hungary.

People often received leaves to visit Budapest or their home towns. Kabos was sent home by the officers to collect some fencing equipment. Then he taught them fencing.

Miki, our engineer, wanted a leave very badly. He had a terrific idea which we filtered up to Koranyi through our office workers. He proposed that we electrify the casern, and eventually the town. He suggested connecting a series of twenty or thirty car batteries in the small, concrete, bunker-like building behind the little bridge at the base of the mountain. An automobile motor could feed the batteries. After some explanation, he got permission to leave and buy the necessary material. A week later, he was back with a small truck and began the job in earnest.

He was permitted to select four permanent helpers, and more if necessary. He chose one electrician, two strong men, and Moricka. Berci Veres, our smasser, asked why Moricka, the idiot with two left hands, was chosen.

"There's an easy, monotonous job to be done. It's just right for him." Everybody was happy to get him out of the way, and maybe he could be kept safe there in case of outplacement.

A week or so later, to great jubilation, the first twenty-five-watt light bulb illuminated Mr. Koranyi's office. Congratulations were showered on Miki and all of our unit. Some of the sub-officers bit their tongues with jealousy: "The damned Jews they're clever!"

In another two weeks, all the barracks had at least two light bulbs, as did all officers' rooms. The townspeople had permission to see the miracle the Jews had accomplished, which the government had never been able to do. Seeing the good will generated by this project, our four office workers and myself as head octato got together with Miki to discuss how we could exploit this further to our benefit.

Mihaly suggested offering it to the Csendor through Koranyi. Bela suggested bringing in some movie equipment and films to play for the officers and smassers. Joska jumped up: "How about movies for the town?"

We all loved the idea, but how should we go about it? The Csendor refused the offer, and reproached Koranyi for what had already been done in our camp. But the town's mayor welcomed our plan enthusiastically and offered his help, even money. Most important, he gave us a large barn a few doors down from the casern, which was set up with benches and podium for town festivities.

We needed somebody to go to Budapest to buy a projector, sound system and screen. Szabo, who was a reluctant teamplayer in the beginning, now cooperated, but grudgingly. He knew about film mostly as an avid movie goer, but supposedly also knew a little about equipment. We suggested that he be the one to go. He was surprised and very appreciative of the unexpected opportunity to see his family and girlfriend.

Two weeks later, the first film was projected for the officers and townspeople. No Jews saw it except Szabo, who was the expert, and his two assistants. To make sure that nothing went wrong, Miki turned off most of the lights in the barracks. It was a tremendous success, and my unit became the heroes of the town.

* * * * *

I met Mariska at 5:00 P.M. at the corner I had indicated. She was very shy, and I was afraid of harmful gossip. We introduced ourselves, and she pointed to her house in the middle of the same street. We walked up and down the main street a few times. When we again reached her street, she stopped and reached for my hand. "Why don't you come in? I'll introduce you to my family." I was surprised, and asked if I would be welcome, if my visit wouldn't create problems for her family, for her and for me. She said it would not and, as the invitation was very tempting, I accepted.

We walked to her house, on a street without a name. Spring had exploded in a riot of colors and smells; wild flowers, geraniums, and poppies carpeted the field between the houses on both sides of the street. We entered her family's house through a small door in a low, aged wooden fence. A narrow dirt road dividing a large vegetable garden led to the thatch-roofed, whitewashed house. Red peppers, onions and grapes hung under the awning; geraniums adorned the windowsills.

The inside was stark. Benches were pushed against clean, white-washed walls. A heavy wooden table with matching chairs stood in the middle. The floor was compacted earth, but it was so hard that it hardly produced any dust when swept. Shelves filled with ornate ceramic plates, ustensils and flowers ran all around the room about two-thirds of the way from floor to ceiling. In the corner opposite the door by which we entered sat a potbellied stove in brick, covered with a mud plaster mixture that had also been whitewashed.

Her father came out of an adjoining room with his big, calloused hand outstreched toward me. "I'm Temesi Geza. Welcome." He pointed toward the woman working at the stove, "That's Maria, my wife." We all shook hands.

"I have the same initials," I said jokingly, "Tibor Gerstl." We laughed. While we were chatting about the country versus the city and the present political situations of which he disapproved, Aunt Maria was busy preparing a "snack" of home baked bread, Hungarian kielbasa, ham served with paprika so hot that the fire of purgatory could not match it, and a wonderfully aromatic home-made wine.

A younger son joined us at the table. The conversation quickly turned to Jews. They didn't understand why Jews were still persecuted. "Yes, they nailed Jesus to the cross, but that was a long time ago. Schwartz the tailor and Rosenfeld the butcher in Ozd are good people."

The time passed quickly and Mariska, who did not talk too much, was as alert as I to grab the other's hand for a warm squeeze whenever the family seemed somewhat inattentive.

Not wanting to overstay my welcome on this first visit, I said good-bye. Uncle Geza and Aunt Maria insisted that I was welcome any time without invitation. "We know what life is like in the casern," they said. Mariska accompanied me to the fence, and with a quick kiss on the cheek she disappeared. I felt as if I were in heaven.

Mobilization had reached its peak in Germany, and Hitler pressed his allies for more soldiers. New Hungarian recruiting sent Christians and Jews to the front and more Jews to the labor camps. Koranyi called all uniformed guards and administrative personnel, as well as all Jewish octatos, to line up on the drill field for an announcement, the subject of which a few of us already knew. "Starting next week, probably on Thursday, thousands of new recruits will arrive at Hangony by train. As casern barracks are already cracking at the seams and cannot contain more people, all available space in the village will be requisitioned by immediate order. This will include all available empty rooms, stables, pigpens, shacks, caves, animal sheds in the field, the movie house and anything else you can find. Sergeant Kovacs, immediately after announcement, will assign a segment of the village to each of you except the administrative personnel. You are required to canvas and report the number of spaces available."

"When the recruits arrive, you will take them to the appropriate house and, whether five, ten or twenty, you will squeeze in as many as you can. For meals, you will pick them up twice a day, lead them in order and escort them back. Any incident or discourtesy toward the villagers will be most severely punished. Attention! Is everything understood? One more thing! The reassignment to Russia to help our brave army will accelerate, starting with the best trained among us. Sergeant Kovacs! Proceed!"

His last statement fell like a hammer blow. That's us. Some thousand people from Galanta. That's me and Joska and Mihaly facing real bullets at the front. Of the previous thousand sent to the Russian front, just three survived, and only one had made it back to headquarters. I hardly heard the barking of Kovacs.

We lined up awaiting his orders. He was well intentioned, but he was a poor executor. He was certainly not an organizer. After struggling five or ten minutes to divide up the village, he pointed to me. "You, octato, take this over. I have other things to attend to!" And he shoved his clipboard in my chest.

"I will need a half hour with a few octatos and guards and the plan will be ready."

From that moment, I became head of all the operations. I even gave orders, carefully, to our guards. In half an hour the simple plan was ready, and I made sure that Mariska's house was in my territory. The hectic activity started immediately, with the villagers grumbling and swearing at the war and the government; yet their underlying patriotic feelings made them responsive to the country's call for help. For the peasants of Hangony, just as for others throughout history, any government meant taxes, plus requisition of food, horses, livestock and their sons. They were ambivalent about what to do, but orders were orders.

Most people cooperated. In only a few cases did officers need to intervene. While canvassing, we had unlimited time in the village, which I used to see Mariska as soon as we dispersed to our territories. The moment I entered the house, she jumped in my arms, and without a word we kissed with wild passion. We were alone and felt free to abandon ourselves to our repressed desire. "Mariska," I said after a long, ecstatic embrace, "I have a mission to accomplish over the next few days."

"What kind of mission?" She asked me.

"Don't even worry a minute. I can organize the neighbors for you in twenty minutes. Let's take a walk in the garden." She grabbed my hand and we walked through the vegetable garden toward the collapsing, low wire fence at the back of the house. We passed through an opening where a small footpath led downhill between high grass and wild flowers to a small creek. The late spring's abundance of flowers, the aroma of jasmine, acacia and honeysuckle, the blood red poppies and the yellow and white margarites made me forget the war, the casern and my assignment. There were only the two of us rolling in the grass. Making love to her felt like making love to Mother Nature herself. Relunctantly, we walked back to the house and started to seek out the neighbors to find accommodations for the new arrivals. Within half an hour, I had commitments for more than a hundred spaces. It was late afternoon when we said good-bye.

* * * * *

We gathered in the casern guard-house. I collected the results of the first canvassing and handed them over to Sergeant Kovacs. We had more than a thousand spaces committed. "Not bad," he said.

Back in the barracks after takarodo, there was not too much talk. A sad, resigned mood had descended on our unit. It was obvious, even without the confirmation of our spies in the office, that while we were canvassing for space for new arrivals, our move to the Russian front grew near.

Three days later they arrived, and we were ready for two thousand people. Boxcar after boxcar arrived during those two days. All the Jewish youth, in fact every male up to the age of fifty arrived wearing civilian clothes of all kinds, like ouselves in Galanta. Each wore a yellow or white armband. We awaited them in Ozd and marched them to Hangony with either a smasser or octato leading each unit. Many of them were shocked upon jumping from the train, when as many octatos as smassers yelled at them, ordering them into line and making them march to the order of an octato, another Jew like themselves, who would not engage in open conversation even with recognized friends. They could not understand what was going on, what our role was.

We could not explain on the spot, certainly not in front of officers, that our yelling and aggressive posture was their safeguard against real and severe atrocities. We did, however, try covertly to explain to friends we saw in the crowds, about our real role. It was only moderately successful.

An ex-schoolmate of mine, Kardos, found himself in my group. On the road to Hangony we had a real confrontation. I called him to the front of the column. Marching next to him, I explained the situation. But he was livid. Indignantly, he raised his voice to curse us all. "You bastards, it's not enough to suffer our miseries from the fascists; we have to take this shit from Jews and friends!" I tried to explain, but he wouldn't listen. We didn't realize that the smasser had overheard his loud protest. He ordered him out of the line and put him through a severe routine of frog jumping, push-ups and running around the column on the march. Then the smasser fell behind, to await another unit.

"Do you understand now what I meant?"

"You fucking collaborators," he said in a low voice.

My heart sank. "I hope you'll understand ...." I retook my position at the head of the column. "One, two, left, right, one, two, left, right ..."

By darkness every new arrival had been placed under some kind of roof. Within two days a routine was established. Every morning and evening, three thousand people had to be lined up, counted and fed. In between, we did the usual drills in the casern or on the town's soccer field. People who were quartered in peasants' houses were permited to help them in their fields or around the house, if requested, which they did gladly for the benefit of both.

Corruption found its way to the surface quickly. Rich Jews paid the farmers in order to stay out and loaf, or to send the farmer's son to Ozd to call the recruit's family, since there was no phone in Hangony. Encounters between the sophisticated metropolitan Jews and Gentiles, whose minds were colored with legends about the Hungarian peasants' life, produced a deep culture shock when they were forced to learn the realities of their hosts' existence.

The iron smelting plant of Ozd had been built during the first industrial revolution. It was old, smelly, an unhealthy for the workers as well as for the inhabitants of this drab city. Soot seemed to cover everything and everybody. The small houses of the workers crowded each other as they climbed up the small hills around the factory.

Our brigade of fifty men left Hangony at five-thirty in the morning. We were to join the workers who were converging on the factory from all directions. Dressed in dirty gray work garb and carrying lunch boxes, they showed their misery and poverty as they lethargically passed through the iron gate. The early fog mixing with the noxious gases spewed by the open chimneys made breathing hard. We were soon coughing in concert with the local workers. The doors to the smelting furnaces opened periodically, shining a red halo around the silhouettes of tired workers.

We stopped at the gate and were directed by a foreman to the plant's railroad yard, where tracks branched, rebranched and branched again, like multiplying snakes. Slow moving freight cars of all variety, flat, semi-closed, and coal carts loaded with iron ore, coke, or coal, headed into the factory or came out either empty or loaded with waste material. The foreman led us to a large pile of earth and rocks, ordering us to load the cars on the track next to it. He explained that we had to load each one until the concave wing suspension springs were flat, and I imagined this would happen when the car was fully loaded. But I quickly understood it differently, as I bent down to pick up a football-size rock to throw it on the wagon. I could hardly lift it. Only a small pile of the iron ore in the middle of the wagon was sufficient to straighten the car's spring. It was a backbreaking job, struggling all day to fill our assigned quota, then marching the ten kilometers back to Hangony.

Nevertheless, whenever we could, we tried to go to Ozd for leave. We were always welcomed by the few Jewish families. The Friedman family was especially kind. They were moderately well-to-do by local standards, and they had two pretty teenage daughters who had the time of their lives with so many boys around, although fear of the future would poison their minds as it did every Jew.

I went less often than most of my friends, but when I went, usually I was able to borrow a bicycle, either from the casern or from the villagers, to make the ten kilometer distance more pleasant. It was far superior to walking, except for the dogs from the few farms on the road, which invariably ran after the bicycle barking ferociously and trying to bite ankles and calves. It always scared the hell out of me, especially when I was biking home at night. One Friday, I was invited to the Friedmans with two other guys for Sabbath dinner. We had just finished the excellent chicken soup that Mama Friedman served with the traditional chalah, when suddenly the shrieking voice of sirens broke loose. The iron smelting plant whistle added to the frightening cacophony. We all ran to the bomb shelter under the house, where we were joined by other neighbors. Within minutes, we heard the heavy laboring of American bombers, anti-aircraft fire and the bombs hitting nearby. It was the first time I saw what war really meant.

* * * * *

Day after day, new military recruits arrived in small groups. They were formed into a separate unit trained by Sergeant Mihaly Rabai, a vicious anti-Semite who was kept under control only by the general atmosphere created by Commandant Koranyi. But now he had a field day transmitting his poison to the future smassers.

At the same time, Sergeant Kovacs and Lieutenant Bodo were recruiting professionals in road and bridge building among the Jewish population. There were a few training manuals on the subject in the camp's library, but Barabas was the only one with this skill, so he shortly became the recruiter and organizer of training sessions. He was authorized to go to Budapest to find more training kits and manuals of bridge and road models. When he came back, he chose Pali, Janos, Miska, an artist, and myself as "professors" of the subject. "Here is what we do," he said. "When we get together in our barracks and there is nobody around, I will teach you. Koranyi wants us to have a few weeks of class. Two hours in the morning and four hours in the afternoon for the smassers and a dozen octatos."

"But we know nothing about this subject," Janos interjected nervously.

"What does it matter?" laughed Barabas. "Here's the manual. We'll get together every evening, and I'll teach you the next day's lesson. You rehearse it at night, or as needed. Miska and Tibor are artists; they will nicely reproduce illustrations on the board. It's simple." We hardly believed this could work.

"We'll start in two days; Monday, nine-thirty, after the drills. Don't worry, fellas. The level of education of most of the smassers is just above elementary school, except for a few sub-officers. Just make sure that you're experts."

We would try our best and hope. So one Monday morning, in front of some thirty smassers, I began to teach the elements of temporary bridge building, while in the other barracks Joska was teaching road building to another group of thirty-five. In the afternoon we changed groups.

By giving the class over and over, and assembling, disassembling and reassembling the scale models again and again, we became proficient and were regarded as real experts, since nobody knew better. We went so far as to field-test actual size bridges with improvised materials like chains, ropes and lumber.

While we had fun with the classes, a suffocating atmosphere surrounded all other activities. We still felt the uncertainty and the fear generated by constant rumors about being sent to the Russian front where, in spite of recent Russian successes, a seesaw battle continued.

Three thousand people moving around in a small place like Hangony created irritation among the townspeople as well as among ourselves. More and more often, smassers took groups of Jews and punished them for minor offenses or for no offense at all, sadistically, mercilessly, and when no octatos were around who could report it to higher brass. It was obvious to them by now that the top leadership, meaning Koranyi, would not stand for their methods.

Early one afternoon on a hot summer day, while most men were on the drill fields, Barabas, Joska, Mihaly, and I were in the classroom with the smassers. Robi was helping us haul bridge material outside the barracks. I saw him through the window talking to Bela, who suddenly became agitated, ran to the window and gestured to me to come out. I excused myself and ran outside. "What's happening?"

"Tibor, bad news. Bela saw orders in the office for our out-placement to the Russian front, effective immediately. He asked you to get our inside group together immediately after class. Can I come?"

"Sure."

"So, here we are, fellas. What we feared most has come," Bela said with a big sigh.

"Can we do anything?" Miki asked.

"Yes," said Robi, "wait for the train and go."

"Maybe not," I said.

"Workers like you, Miki, with the 'Hangony Electric Company,' or you people in the office probably will stay. The bridge and road building training gimmick probably will end because the smassers are going. Barabas will stay, but I'm afraid that having become in their eyes the principal octato, it's almost assured that I'll go with the first group."

"Koranyi and Dr. Miklos, like you and me, believe they want familiar Jews around them just in case the future doesn't go well for the Axis. We're the best witnesses of their good intentions."

"That's an unfair remark," I objected. "They're genuinely good."

"True, but they may still need witnesses."

"We'll see. Bela, how many people know about this?"

"Just a few, but by tomorrow, everyone will know."

"That fast?"

He nodded sadly.

The soccer field was lined with people. The entire camp, including the Jews lodged in the houses in town, converged on it at the order of the camp commandant. Koranyi and the top brass arrived. Sergeant Kovacs drew his sabre, and in a screeching voice commanded attention. Everyone was ready by now for the bad news. It was no secret; we were heading to Russia and few would return.

What would determine which of us would stay and which of us would go? Where was it written that I should stay here and survive at least for the time being, or go to the Russian front and be killed? Statistically, being killed was almost a certainty, since only a few came back out of a thousand in the 1919 class. On the other hand, I might be stronger, or have a little more will-power to survive the starvation, mistreatment or cold, if not to resist a bullet. In any case, chance was the determining factor which overrides both statistic and probability. Isn't that a contradiction? "Determinism and Chance." No. Just as in the universe, infinitely small changes can create infinitely large effects, so minute elements in one's personality, a smile or a minor service rendered at the right time or place can determine whether you live or die. While today this phenomenon of minor changes is explained by scientific discoveries on the state of chaos, old folk tales knew it a long time ago.

"For want of a nail, the shoe was lost:
For want of a shoe, the horse was lost:
For want of a horse, the rider was lost:
For want of a rider, the battle was lost:
For want of a battle the kingdom was lost."

Koranyi routinely went through an exhortation of our patriotic duties as auxiliary laborers helping the great Hungarian army. I could almost detect in his voice his malaise about the double standard of asking people whose civil rights were taken away, and who were treated as enemies of the country and the world, to serve and give their lives for the victory of their torturers.

But what was moral in the way of wars or even peace when people were willing to enslave and sacrifice others for even small personal advantages?

"The entire camp will be dispatched to Russia in groups ranging from three to five hundred men each day, starting next Monday," announced Koranyi. "About a hundred men will remain for headquarters duties." He started to read the names of the old-timers, craftsmen like Feri, the shoemaker, Toni, the tailor and some twenty others, then he seemed to stop. "That's it, we go." I said to myself.

But after a moment he continued "... and Brigade Twenty-four to take care of the Electric Center, teaching of bridge and road building, administration and other chores." We looked at each other with tremendous relief. Again, as I had so many times in the past and would in the future, I relived my entire life during the stress and suspense of a few seconds. I saw myself on the Russian front maimed or dead, and seconds later felt relief to be able to face tomorrow, the next incertitude, always tense and always ready for fight or flight, although the inability to actually fight made the tension even more unbearable.

* * * * *

As the Russian counter-attacks on the eastern front succeeded, they inspired and encouraged partisan activities, especially in Czechoslovakia, which was the most western oriented and democratic country among the central and eastern European nations. Hangony is situated only a few kilometers from the Czech border. During the day, we had begun seeing small planes flying low overhead, while at night we heard loud but dull noises of airplanes dropping heavy loads just beyond the border.

Rumors were circulating that strangers, presumably partisans, had been seen behind the casern trying to make contact or infiltrate into our camp. We were excited at the prospect of doing something to influence our destiny, altough we did not yet know what. Escape? Join them and fight the Germans as partisans? Barabas, the only one with combat experience, suggested that he and I, being least likely to be interfered with by our guards, should go in the late afternoon to "help" Miki in the Hangony Electric Company behind the casern. We could sneak outside the fence and venture a little further into the woods to try to make contact with the partisans. So we went in the biggest secrecy—only Joska and Miki knew of our intentions. At five that afternoon, we passed the little bridge and met Miki. After some encouragement, and after Miki assured us that he would not put the operation on his map yet, we dashed the fifty meters into the woods behind the building.

Suddenly, a wonderful feeling inundated my whole being. This insignificant little act generated a marvelous sense of freedom, of doing something for myself rather than just suffering at the hands of others. Looking at our camp and the neighboring gypsy camp from the small hill outside the fence, I had wild visions of combating Hitler's evils and liberating our camp.

"Tibor, catch your breath and let's move," Barabas prompted. We started slowly to move deeper in the woods, stopping every ten or twenty meters to look for signs of human presence. After an hour, we gave up and were heading back when I noticed the corner of a wooden crate hidden under some bushes. We approached it very carefully. At the same moment, we both pointed to the Cyrillic lettering. We looked around suspiciously and nodded to each other. The box was empty, but we knew that our "friends" were somewhere near.

We continued to walk back, but now made noise purposely, speaking loudly and waving our yellow armbands high above our heads. We reached the edge of the woods without seeing anybody, except Corporal Rac, one of the guards, standing half-way between the electric company and the edge of the woods. He was staring us straight in the face. Twenty yards behind him, Miki was observing the scene with concern.

"Where have you been?" Rac asked.

"We were just taking a walk, getting some fresh air."

"Looking for partisans?"

"What partisans?"

"Don't give me that shit. Did you make contact?"

"No. We just walked ..."

"Are there any in the camp?"

"We don't know."

"The next time you go outside the fence, you will be court-martialed and shot. Is that clear?"

"Yes, sir."

We were surprised Corporal Rac acted so tough. He was the nicest and the most understanding of our guards. However, we were more surprised to see him outside the wire fence.

The next few nights low flying airplaines and the landing of supplies like unexploded bombs made it obvious that serious partisan actions were taking place in the surrounding mountains. Local newspapers were talking about food and drug supplies and similar nonsense for the population of Czechoslovakia.

In the middle of the week, a detachment of a hundred-fifty regular army men and some fifty Arrow-Cross soldiers arrived at our camp with only a few hours advance notice to Koranyi. Oddly enough, Bela had heard about this possibility the day before from his office "colleague," a devoted Arrow-Cross officer. It was very disturbing that the Arrow-Cross officer knew about it before Koranyi. We reported this to Koranyi.

Two barracks had to be emptied hastily, and their occupants crowded into the remaining ones and the village quarters. The Arrow-Cross commandant wanted to take over the camp immediately. He issued orders to everyone, barking about discipline, catching anybody who passed, and ordering disciplinary runs, jumps, and sit-ups. Koranyi, who had a superior rank, made an obviously bold decision and confronted him in the middle of the drill field. "Lieutenant Gero! Attention! I am the camp commandant here, and don't forget it. You take care of your detachment, and the guards take care of the camp people. Is that understood?"

"Is that Jew a guard?" asked Gero sarcastically, pointing at Gabi.

"He's one of the octatos. They're useful auxiliaries and you will keep away from them. That's an order. Dismissed!"

The lieutenant made a sharp left turn, and walked away smiling cruelly.

The next day all hell broke loose. A dozen Arrow-Cross high brass arrived with special orders to take over the camp and organize a campaign to liquidate the partisans in the surrounding area. First, they surrounded the camp with their own men, cancelled all leaves, and took over from the Csendor, whom they assigned to duty inside the camp. The next few days we saw soldiers leaving every morning for patrol duties, mostly to the north of the camp into the surrounding mountains, and past the electric company, which continued to operate.

Two evenings after they had arrived, we were startled by the sounds of gunshots. Exploding hand grenades were followed by the firing of sub-machine guns, then we heard grenades again, landing closer and closer to the camp. This lasted at least an hour. We couldn't sleep, and around five in the morning Barabas asked me if I was willing to go with him to the latrine behind the barracks to try to see what was going on. We went and, near the small bridge, we saw two Arrow-Cross guards patrolling between two barracks. We also saw the bloodied body of a civilian.

"A partisan," Barabas sighed.

"No doubt," I murmured. "Maybe a Czech, maybe a Hungarian, maybe a Russian?"

"No, it couldn't be a Russian."

Heading back, we had almost reached our barracks when a burst of sub-machine gun fire erupted. We dashed into the barracks. Everybody was up and tensely awaiting our description of what we had seen. Out of breath, our hearts pounding from the fear and the thought that we may just have escaped the last round of fire, we told them about the death of the civilian, probably a partisan. The reaction was wild confusion. Only whispering, small groups pressed their suggestions: "Let's join the partisans now," "Let's break out now," "There's nobody to join. They're only individuals," "Are you crazy?" We did nothing, just awaited the certain reaction of the guard.

A little earlier than usual, the bugle sounded urgently, menacingly. Almost immediately, the Arrow-Cross and our guards rushed into the barracks and ordered us to line up outside with all our belongings within half an hour. Nothing was to be left behind; we were to be ready to march. We all tried to guess what this meant; whether we were going to the Russian front, or whether this was a punitive measure because of the partisans.

When assembled, barracks by barracks we marched through the corridor of Arrow-Cross soldiers, camp guards and Csendor. As we passed the camp entrance, they drew their small arms, rifles and sub-machine guns, and pointed them at us without a word, not even the usual swearing or insults. This made the atmosphere even more frightening. We were heading to the soccer field when we saw all the Jews who had been quartered in the village herded out to the street the same way.

Many townspeople were walking up and down the street pretending to be going about their business, but watching us with tense curiosity. Mariska made a small gesture to catch my eye; her frightened expression just tried to tell me, "I'm here."

Joska, who marched next to me, poked me with his elbow. "You at least have a living witness."

The entire camp was assembled on the soccer field. Armed guards surrounded us, their guns pointed toward us. The Arrow-Cross' general repeated his now familiar insulting lecture on capitalist-communist conspirators, enemies of the world, and source of all the pain of humanity. Then he ordered all of us to strip naked and place our clothes, two sets of underwear, our shoes and a blanket in front of us. Everything else, including money or jewelry of any kind, was to go behind us. "Anybody who does not comply, or who cheats, will be shot on the spot!" he thundered.

The few faces I was able to see to the left and right, or in a few rows in front and behind, reflected the emotions of the thousands. Robi was smiling derisively; he had nothing to lose. Bela and Janos and the rich merchant, who could not imagine life without the security of money or gold, were also natural risk takers. They toyed slowly with their belongings in obvious indecision and fear, looking left and right to see how the order was being enforced. Shmuel, the orthodox, had his "tefilin" in his hand, holding the leather prayer boxes tensely, his eyes riveted on the sky. Moricka, the idiot, had no problem: he did what was ordered, and cried. Joska and Mihaly folded everything neatly, even what they put behind them, but then Joska searched through the clothing behind him and put something from it in the front pile. Photos and letters, he told me later. My mind was focused on one thing, the small box which I had added to my already heavy rucksack in Budapest before departing to Galanta. Standing naked with thousands of others, I sought my swimming medals (remembering the way I earned them), the photos of my family, and the few engraving tools that held the only possibility for my livelihood. No! I would not give them up. I snatched the box from my bag and placed it in front of me under the permitted clothes. And peace descended on me.

Standing naked with guns pointed at you is a hundred times more terrifying than it is when you are clothed, as if a cotton shirt, jacket and trousers would be much of a shield. To be murdered this way seems both more likely and more indecent (as if it would make any difference which way you are murdered). Guards moved up and down the rows of naked people, randomly poking their bayonets into the mounds of clothes, yelling, barking orders, and pushing people with their gun butts. But no shot was fired.

After half an hour or so, we were ordered to dress and take up the belongings in front of us. We were lined up and led back to our quarters. As we marched away, a few grabbed anything they could reach during these last unguarded moments. Less than an hour after we returned to our barracks, we saw our stolen property brought into the camp piled high on horse drawn wagons. Then it was loaded onto trucks and disappeared, together with the special units of the Arrow-Cross and army. We did not, however, observe the Csendor or our guards taking anything; that is, we did not see them take any larger objects. As for money, jewelry and the like, we did not know. Before their departure, the Arrow-Cross brass had announced that the partisans were cleared from the area, and our belongings, which were acquired by cheating and exploiting the Hungarian people, would be given back to the people. It was obvious that the Hungarian people meant were themselves. They left, and we settled down again in our barracks, bewildered and frustrated by our inability to defend ourselves.

"It was a well-planned highway robbery," Joska said to Robi.

"I can testify to that. And with no risk!" Robi confirmed.

"It looks like it was planned just before the departure to Russia," I interjected.

"Possibly, or maybe it was just a coincidence," Joska said, incapable of imagining such callousness. As a lawyer, he should have known better.

"Did you salvage anything?" I asked Joska.

"Yes, I did," he said, without being specific.

"So did I," Miki laughed, as he showed a box. I, too, showed what I had saved. Surprisingly, more people had salvaged things which they considered valuable, materially or sentimentally, than I would have imagined.

"How did you dare take the risk?"

"How did you?"

I believe that people in situations like this don't think. They act on impulse without really considering the risk.

Shmuel moved closer and, in a low voice, with his hand shielding his mouth, he said, "I didn't take any risk, but I have my package. Come with me."

Three of us followed him outside the barracks. He led us to the latrine, pulled up his shirtsleeve and reached under the third round hole in the rough wooden plank which served as seat. He pulled out a small package which he had plastered under the seat with his own feces. Our stomachs recoiled from the stench.

"For that small package, this mess?" I asked in disbelief.

"Small, but valuable," he said, winking conspiratorially. We laughed. He opened it cautiously, revealing two gold and diamond rings.

The seizure of our property postponed the departure of the units to Russia for a few days. But soon the first group of five hundred men was ready to depart, with two officers and a dozen smassers. In a deadly silence, they lined up at the small drill field with the remains of their belongings. What words could be spoken? "I hope you make it," was the biggest encouragement one could offer.

"Attention!" the officer yelled. "Line up. Ready, march." He saluted the superior officers, and the group disappeared on the road to Ozd, where the train awaited them. Three days later, almost the entire camp had dispersed, ordered to the Russian front, and the village of Hangony regained its pastoral nature, its quiet charm, and the normal rhythm of its peasants' everyday life.

* * * * *

The quiet did not last long: new events stirred up the population. It was confirmed that the "civilian" who was killed had been a partisan. Furthermore, the last burst of sub-machine gunfire, which had sent me and Barabas scrambling into our barracks, had killed two guards. We feared additional retribution, but, since only a small group remained at this headquarters and they had already taken everything they could from them, nothing more happened.

Some hundred-fifty people remained at headquarters, including senior craftsmen, our group of fifty, the guards and the administrative officers. We tried to settle down in our new unsettled situation, not knowing what we would do here or for how long. Miki returned to his electric company the next morning, but came back almost immediately.

"Hey, Tibor, Joska, come here!" he gestured excitedly. "You won't believe this."

Just outside the fence at the little bridge, exactly at the spot where the partisan was killed, there was a beautiful bouquet of fresh red roses, and another somewhat faded bouquet, as if it was there from yesterday. "What should I do? We could get into trouble. They may think that we're doing it."

"Don't get excited," Joska said calmly. "There are surely no florists here."

"That's pretty clever, but it doesn't help me, you idiot," Miki retorted, a bit irritated. "I think it's terrific, isn't it, Barabas? It's now that we should escape. The partisans are certainly around!"

"It's too dangerous now. Let's wait a few days to see what happens."

I suggested going back with a smasser. Let one of them discover it ... and discover it they did. Within fifteen minutes, guards, sergeants and officers had examined and removed the roses. They ordered all the Jews to line up on the drill field. The day officer, Nagy, immediately accused us of conspiracy, arrested Miki as a suspect, and cancelled all leaves. From Koranyi's office, Bela reported that Koranyi was not in and had not been informed about the flowers incident. Then, with his big red nose, and his cape thrown nonchalantly over his shoulders, Koranyi appeared unexpectedly at the edge of the drill field, just as Miki was being led away handcuffed.

"What's the commotion about?" he asked the officer.

The officer approached him and explained in a low voice. Koranyi raised his hand to his forehead, saluted, and turned, still nonchalantly, but I noticed that the ever-present cigarette butt between his lips was turned upward. He was smiling! The next morning, a fresh bouquet lay at the same spot, even though Miki was in the cooler. He was released later that day.

A new daily routine was established. Most people worked either in the offices or in the shops. About thirty-five men were under my command, doing all the odd jobs in the kitchen or sweeping the grounds. Every morning and afternoon, it was drill for all.

* * * * *

My background as graphic artist was known to all, and "the artist" became my second name, which did not displease me. One day I was called on by Koranyi to design a large map of the Russian and western fronts. When it was done, the officers pinned little colored flags to it so as to follow the events, which they could not influence, just acknowledge. With the exception of Koranyi, Dr. Miklos and one smasser, they rooted for the Germans. Official news and propaganda came not only through the radio in the offices, but also from the BBC, although we never knew just who had access to the news, which was spread by rumor. So we had three different colored flags for the positions of the different armies: red for Russians, green for Germans as per the official fascist propaganda news, and blue as per the BBC news. We had no maps for other parts of the world where the war was raging just as ferociously. The Pacific or China, or even North Africa were too remote for us to follow.

I felt frustrated, helpless. "The entire world is on fire. Our friends are dying somewhere around the Don. Jews are in ghettos everywhere, and we're rotting here, cleaning the grounds and peeling potatoes for our guards. We're lucky so far, but I feel guilty to be here."

"Don't," said Joska. "You won't help anybody or anything by dying with the others." Suddenly, Mr. Frederik's advice in the swimming pool flashed through my brain. "The first thing is to survive, then we will see."

Finally, the commotion subsided and we were again permitted to go to the village. The movie projections started again. Occasionally, a smasser came back from the front bringing terrible news about death and destruction, but people spoke little about the Jews there, and we feared the reason. I saw Mariska again, more often, and one day she asked me to come to a get-together at her house.

Every week she and her friends met at somebody's house, and that week was her turn. When I entered, I thought I had walked into a dream world. A dozen girls, dressed in their beautiful Sunday attire of multi-layered skirts with long embroidered aprons and blouses, and wearing red or black boots, sat on the benches along the walls, doing needlepoint or embroidery on their future wedding garments and singing sweet or tearful folk songs. Legenyek—lads in their teens and early twenties—sat around the rough wooden table talking and drinking. Some were doing woodcarving, shaping the handles of whips that had a long leather "pattantos", or frayed tails. In their black trousers, vest and boots and white, pleated shirts with very wide sleeves, they looked like figures in a painting. Inside, but still holding the door handle, I felt like an intruder. They hardly looked up. Only Mariska motioned for me to come and sit down.

One of the boys pushed a chair under me and poured glasses of wine all around. We introduced ourselves formally, although we had met before in the streets. I was deeply touched. What should I say? How could I thank them? How could I make sure not to disrupt their routine? Soon the boys started to sing, and the girls and I joined in. From the kitchen, people brought kielbasi, salami, paprikas szalonna, warm homemade bread and a big kettle of goulash. They ate and I joined in. Was this real? Was there really a war going on out there? With Jews being killed by Gentiles, Russians by Germans, Americans by Japanese? The world was mad! Why was there not more understanding and kindness, like that which these simple people were spontaneously showing. Why couldn't people enjoy diversity, rather than insisting on boring uniformity? Why couldn't they understand that people can be different, and yet equal in virtues or shortcomings? Why not Utopia? Why must we be competitive, intolerant and defensive, when this leads to what we have? War.

* * * * *

The flag on the Csendors' building was flying at half staff. Eight of the twelve men at the station had been killed by the partisans who had supposedly been wiped out by the Arrow-Cross. Although we shed no tears for them, we worried about the consequences for us. Even the village people were concerned about the anticipated unpleasantness of search and interrogation as a new contingent of Csendors arrived and started to investigate.

Tante Rosa, a civilian employee of the gendarmerie, cleaned their offices twice a week.

Occasionally, they asked our officers to provide Jews to chop wood or paint buildings and fences. Otherwise, Jews were never permitted to go inside their premises. Joska, Barabas, Miki and I gathered in the home of Mariska's best friend, Anna, who was a neighbor of Tante Rosa, to learn what had happened. She was afraid and reluctant to talk. "I like you boys," she said, "but you'll get me into trouble."

"Don't be concerned. If anybody gets into trouble, it will be us. What happened? You were there that morning."

"A young man came to the station," she said, "a stranger. But he looked like any peasant here or in the neighboring villages."

"How did he speak? Did he have a Czech accent?" I asked.

"Not at all. He spoke perfect Hungarian like we speak here, a little Paloc, a local dialect. He reported that there are partisans in the surrounding mountains and he is one of them, but he was forced to join them. This was his first opportunity to escape and he was looking for protection."

"How do you know this, Tante Rosa?"

"I was in the office for a while, then I heard the gendarmes discussing it between themselves."

"What happened then?"

"They pushed a local map in front of him and asked him to show their location. He said he didn't know exactly, but he knew where their arms, ammunition and cash were. Then they brought him into the torture room, where he was interrogated for at least two hours."

"Did you see anything, Robi, Gabor?" I asked.

"Yes," Robi answered, "we were in the back yard cleaning their pickup trucks when, at about 2:00 P.M., eight of them under Sergeant Bodo, the head of the local unit, loaded themselves and the partisan into the pickup truck. The partisan was attached to the truck's bench. The motor had already started, when suddenly Sergeant Bodo yelled at us. 'You two Jews! Jump on the truck!'"

We looked at each other. "Shit," I said to Gabor, "I don't like this, but we have no choice."

"We were driving fifteen to twenty minutes on smaller and smaller roads until there was no road at all in the mountains. The partisan indicated the direction once in a while, and then said we had arrived. They untied him from the truck and handcuffed him to one of the gendarmes. We all got off and started to march, following the gendarmes, who were armed to the teeth."

"The partisan stopped at a small clearing in the heavily wooded area and, with a sweep of his hand, indicated a half circle in a general area where the arms were. Here and there a wooden box was visible under the bushes, indicating that maybe some mines had been laid nearby. The Sergeant ordered his men into patrol formation, one behind the other, with some twenty feet between them. He ordered the partisan and us ahead of them, just in case a mine exploded, with an admonition that at a sign of the slightest suspicious movement we would be shot. As the partisan passed me to move ahead, he whispered,' Just do as I do,' which I then told to Gabor." Robi continued:

"The entire group started to move toward the edge of the wood, but we had hardly traveled twenty yards when suddenly we heard a whistle, which I thought came from the sergeant. But at the same moment I saw the partisan hit the ground, jerking his gendarme with him, so Gabor and I did the same. Two seconds later, a salvo of submachine gunfire erupted from the woods. TRRR, TRRR ... and not more than ten seconds later, the eight gendarmes were dead or dying."

"It was terrible. Gabor picked me up. I was sick and shaking. Actually, I shit in my pants." We did not laugh.

Tante Rosa started to cry. "The poor young boys. They were nasty, but they were just doing their job."

"They did more than their jobs," Joska interjected hesitantly.

"I don't want to hear any more," Tante Rosa complained. "We'll get into trouble."

"What happened after?" I asked.

"A few minutes later, six other partisans came out of the woods. They shook hands with our partisan, patted him on the back, tossed him a submachine gun, and congratulated him for a job well done. Then they turned to us and asked what we were doing there. We explained, and begged to stay with them because nobody would believe that we were not accomplices, since there was nobody left to testify."

"Sorry, fellas," said the one who appeared to be the leader. "It's your tough luck, but you can't stay. You must go back. It may be dangerous for you, but if you stay, your entire camp will be accused of collaboration and, anyway, we need well-trained people here, not amateurs. You'd better get going. They'll surely be back shortly with the other gendarmes to pick up these guys. Don't worry, we won't be here," and he laughed. Before we left, I decided to ask them why this killing was necessary.

"You Jews are either naive or badly misinformed," he answered. "I'll tell you this much: these are the ones who called in the Arrow-Cross, who killed one of our men near your camp, and another one not far from here."

"Were these partisans all Hungarians?" I asked.

"You bet, one hundred percent."

"How did their weapons look?"

"Like short, stubby guns with a drum-like ammunition case in the middle."

"That's it," Barabas exclaimed. "The Russian Davaj Guitar."

"We made it back on foot, exhausted by the experience," continued Robi. "I've done many things in Budapest not very kosher, but for this you need a strong stomach. The gendarmes were patrolling the road, and arrested us at the edge of town. They interrogated us for hours, but aside from a few slaps in the face, we weren't harmed. But their beds, the concrete floors, were a little incomfortable, damn it. As you know, thanks to Koranyi's intervention, they let us go."

Almost routinely now, when there was a crisis, the first thing they did was to close the casern and cancel leaves. Usually, we were unhappy about being confined, but this time it felt almost like protection from the outside world. The rumor mill was going strong, and the guards and cadre had an unbelievably mild reaction. It was as if we had gained some respect in their eyes by the possibility that we might have had a hand in the partisan action. I never completely denied or discouraged this speculation, and neither did Joska or the others in our group.

Aside from this incident, very little happened around the camp. The days passed with routine chores and drills, leaving us plenty of time to ourselves, especially now that we were closed in. Hundreds of thoughts which had been crowded out of my mind, or which I had supressed in order not to deal with them, appeared as fleeting images or waking dreams. Pictures of loved ones now surfaced one after another, while I was sadly questioning our place in this mad world.

As I lay on my cot late one afternoon, the low sun's rays created ever-changing images on the opposite wall, throwing shadows of foliage, flying birds, or a passing smasser, officer, or comrade.

"My sketch book! Take the sketch book," an inner voice accused me. "You're a day dreamer, just like millions of others who don't leave traces of their imagination." I jumped up laden with guilt, frantically searching for my sketch book in the little box with the engraving tools and photos. I grabbed the book and some pencils with determination, and jerked it open to an unused page. "No, I'm not just a dreamer; I'm an artist." The pencil touched the paper " ... or am I?" The faint noise of my pencil scratching the white surface told me I was doing something.

It took a long time to consider all the episodes we had lived through. I searched my mind furiously to choose one to give solid form and permanence to. The heroic partisans? The dead gendarmes? The naked brigade, and the Arrow-Cross poking their bayonets into piles of clothing and belongings? The frightened eyes of Moricka? The barking sergeant? Our archangel, Koranyi, with his red nose and cigarette between his lips? Perhaps some pastoral image? Or a love scene with Mariska? "It doesn't matter; just sketch one."

A guilt-ridden conscience pressed me on. I filled five pages with fast sketches. At the sixth, the pencil stopped touching the surface and I started to dream again. What if one day after the war ... if it ever comes and if I make it ... what if I create a gigantic mosaic composed of thousands of little tiles, each showing one of these sketches of our experiences, the whole becoming a picture itself, creating the essence of our lives, the essensce of our actions, ideas, emotions, and dreams? "Quickly, move the pencil, sketch another ...," which I did until the bugle's raucous sound calling the line-up for supper broke my dream.

* * * * *

It was impolite to visit at the time of a family's Sunday dinner. People have just returned from church, and are settling down around the table. It's likely that at the same moment, as the church bell strikes the noon hour, the fresh home-baked bread is broken in every house.

I stared at the embroidered tablecloth that added to the Sunday tradition and festive mood.

"I'm sorry to disturb you, but I just couldn't wait to give you my news."

"Sit down and eat with us," Maria insisted. Without waiting, she fetched another plate.

The noon bells sounded. Geza Bacsi stood up and perfunctorily murmured five seconds of a prayer. "So what's happening in your palace there?"

"It's not very good," I responded. "There are rumors that we're leaving Hangony very soon."

"To go where?"

"We don't know. Maybe to the Russian front or, if we're lucky, they'll move our headquarters to another location behind the lines."

There was complete silence, interrupted only by the sounds of forks hitting plates or the slurping of soup. Finally, I spoke again. "I like Hangony ... and you people. It will be very hard to leave."

"Hmm," answered Geza Bacsi. "That's what war is all about, I guess: displacing and killing people. We got used to you people here. A lot of you helped around the farm, you were good workers too, and you learned fast. Mariska, do you have nothing to say?"

"No!" she said, as if he had offended her. "I already heard about it in church." She stood up abruptly, and left the table crying. When she returned a few minutes later, she was slightly more composed.

"Let's eat," Maria prompted again.

After dinner, Geza wiped his mustache on an embroidered napkin and cleared his throat two or three times. "You're a good boy, Tibor. I hope we see you before you leave. Don't worry. Just live day by day, like we did in World War I. And remain what you are." He thrust his heavy, rough hand forward and I shook it with humility. In that fraction of a second, our eyes met and we communicated hundreds of years of shared subjugation. They, by their feudal lords; we, because of our religion.

* * * * *

Miki, who treated the electric company like his private business and brain-child, worried about abandoning it. Bela and Peter felt they still had a good chance of staying at headquarters, no matter where the rest of us were ordered. Shmuel accepted God's will, as he always had, burying his anxiety in rigorous prayers. Still, he was concerned about maintaining his kosher diet in the future. Here, he had been able to barter or buy kosher food from Ozd, or

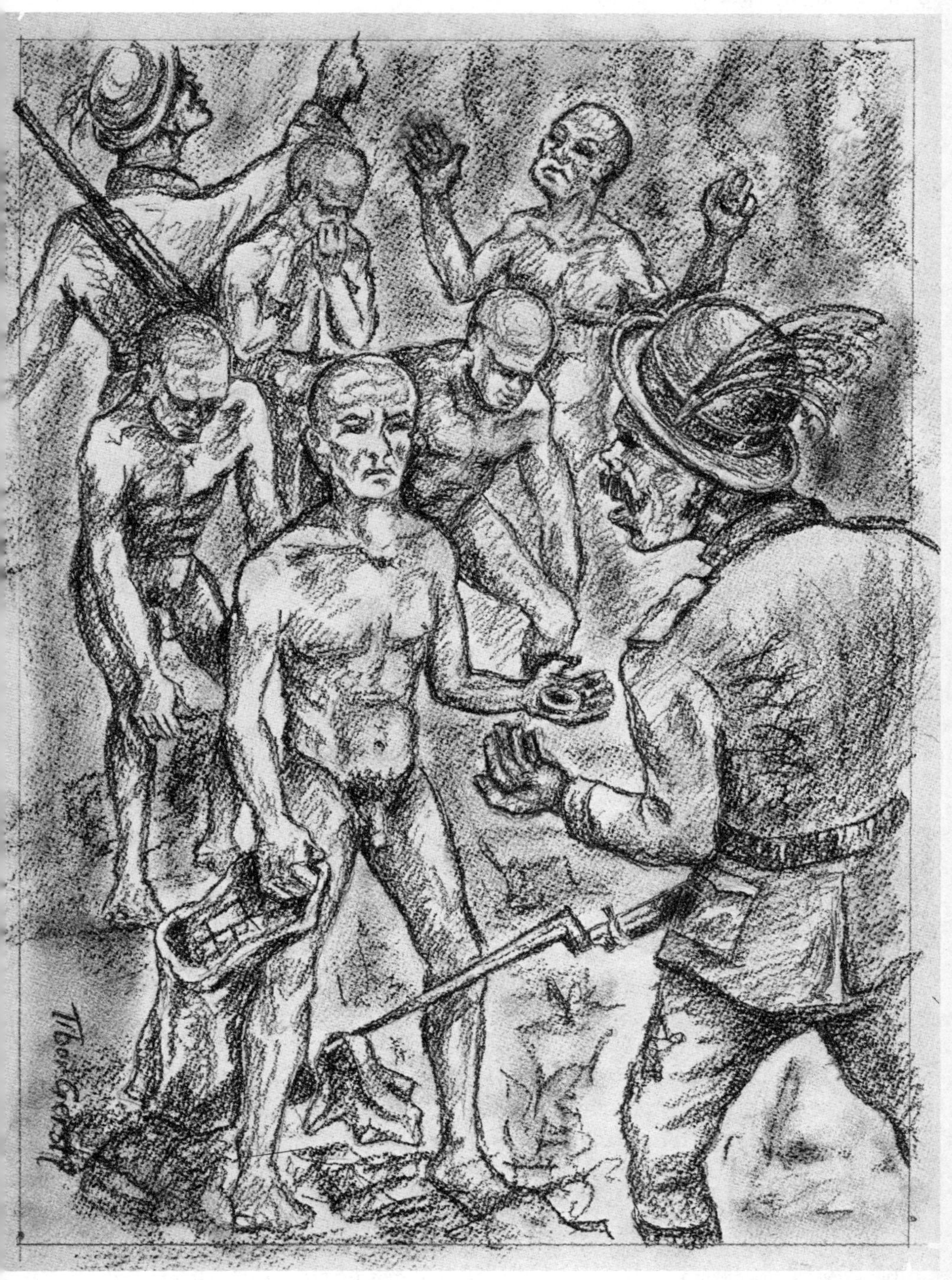

The raid of the Arrow-Cross gendarms

receive packages from home. He would do what he had to in the future to remain kosher, but he knew it would not be easy.

I said nothing. I was reflecting on the irony of my situation. Since I had left my parents' home, I had never lived so well. I didn't need to worry about where the next meal would come from, I had no rent to pay, and I had a nice girlfriend in town who provided a pleasant and romantic environment. I felt I had the most to lose, but I was ashamed to say so.

The next few days were spent packing. Packing our belongings was pretty simple by now. The Arrow-Cross raid had considerably lightened the rich guys' valises, although they had found ways to re-supply their losses.

Packing and loading the camp supplies on trucks took much longer. The trucks were to go to the Ozd railroad station in advance of us, and were filled with all sorts of things: dehydrated vegetables, beans, carrots, the dreadful "szecska" (a mixture of nobody knew what), smoked meat, potatoes, salt and, of course, paprika. They also carried jute bags for the straw beds, military uniforms for the smassers, small weapons, pistols, grenades, submachine guns, ammunition, office equipment and files. Many of the officers had furnished apartments in town, and we had to pack and load their belongings as well. With two days left before we moved, all barracks, except where we slept, were empty, clean and disinfected, and the last truck left for Ozd.

I saw Mariska every day. We often sat together in the grass near the creek at the back of her house. We watched the clouds pass, saying very little. There was nothing to say. We understood how wonderful and how terrible it was that only a few encounters in a lifetime are engraved in our minds, never to be forgotten. A sentence, a word spoken by friend or foe, an eye meeting another in approval or disapproval, a handshake which says "Welcome" or "I don't really care about you" may haunt us to the end.

On the last night, we were confined to the camp, and hung around the barracks in small groups. Some were playing cards for pebbles since money was forbidden. Others played chess sitting on makeshift benches of planks and stone. Everyone tried to divorce himself from the reality of our situation. Joska, Robi and I walked around aimlessly, inspecting the place for the last time. As we approached the far side of one barracks, Robi suddenly told us to stop. We slowly approached the open door, listening to a lone man crying out a beautiful song.

"What the heck is that song?" Robi asked quietly, so as not to interrupt. Joska clutched my arm, as the beauty enchanted him. My musical knowledge did not go too far. I had never attended a concert, an opera or even a play. My knowledge of classical music extended only to a few songs and overtures, or arias from the best known operas. This was one I recognized. We stepped inside carefully, and the words and sounds of Tosca's famous "Letter Aria" tore into my heart. Moricka, alone in the barracks, was singing with a poignancy which no tenor I have ever heard has been able to duplicate.

* * * * *

In 1943, the bombings of German and Italian cities became routine news. Other bombings attracted our attention, offering new hopes of quickly ending the war. Rumania's Polesky oil fields were forty percent destroyed, and the first American bombs hit an Austrian target near Vienna. Clearly, the war was getting closer. We also celebrated when the Flying Fortresses of the USAF flew their first mission over France. In those far away places in the Pacific, on which the BBC reported great battles, the Americans, Australians and New Zealanders were making progress. As fierce as the fighting in Italy was, so were the battles between American and Japanese troops in the Solomon Islands for the Munda airfield.

When the news was good we moved Miki's little red flags with delight, but our destiny depended on events along the Russian front, so we were just as angry with the Americans and British and French for not opening a western front as the Russians were.

In the political arena, we picked up two news reports; a bad one, that SS Officer Himmler was named Interior Minister, and a good one, that the Allies recognized de Gaulle's Committee of National Liberation as the de facto government of France. We hoped this was a prelude to open the western front.

* * * * *

The good news of military successes during the latter part of 1943 was mixed with the terrible news of German massacres, burnings and atrocities committed in the wake of their withdrawal. For us, the Russians were still far away.

The disaster which hit Hungarian Jews with full force in the middle of 1944 was made even more tragic because the Germans had clearly lost the war. It was obvious that for many of Hitler's hatchet-men like Eichmann, extermination of Jews became the most important goal of the Third Reich. With a cooperating population and a collaborating government, this task was simplified for them.

The French revolution and turmoil of 1848 had encouraged liberal trends throughout Europe. One consequence was that Hungarian Jews enjoyed almost full rights of citizenry until the 1920s. Then, Horty's counter-revolution broke the trend, and the Jews were equated with communism. Few people remember that the first communist state in the world was not Russia, but Hungary. In 1919, Bela Kun's communist government lasted about three months.

After the initial "white terror" of Horty's reign, and after the regime had settled down, Jews regained most of their civil rights. Among other sanctions, they still could not obtain high ranks in the army, and there were numerous clauses in the universities. Jews were active in politics, the press, the arts and sciences, and were generally prosperous and influential in the country's economic life.

In spite of the fact that my parents could hardly make ends meet, my childhood had been happy. Our poverty was due more to the effects of the depression than to anti-Semitism. The social climate of the Jews started to crumble in 1938, and collapsed completely with the deportations of 1944.

As early as 1935, Ferenc Szallasi had floated the concept of a "New Hungary," based on a federation of national socialist minorities in a Hungarian empire. In this, he included the Slovacs (Toth), Rutens (Karpat Russia), Transylvania (Szekely), inhabitants of the southern territories (Delvidek) and those of Burgerland (Swabok), the German minorities in the west. This last group's inclusion put him at odds with the Germans, especially after the Anschluss, when the Swabs became more and more influenced by the Germans and formed the Volksdeutche Kamaradschaft. In February 1939, the authorities dissolved Szallasi's party and jailed him. During the time he was in prison, Hubai reorganized his party under the name of "Arrow-Cross". In September 1940, Szallasi benefited from an amnesty, and pursued his idea of a Hungarian Empire with a new twist. He wanted to resettle all the minorities: the Slavs in the Volga area, the Rumanians in the Dnieper and the Berg area, and the Germans in an area designated by Hitler "Warthe Gau" (to establish a German presence and as an excuse to protect them).

As a result of three consecutive anti-Jewish laws starting in 1938, the Jews were barred from all economic, political and intellectual life. Perhaps worst of all, these acts destroyed all illusions that Jews had been accepted as Hungarians. We had never thought that what had happened to Jews in other countries would happen to us. It did. We realized that the destiny of the Jews in Rumania and Czechoslovakia would be ours too, and a feverish quest to emigrate began. But it was too late.

The western powers, especially an extraordinarily callous United States, cut their immigration quota under every imaginable pretext, just as the Germans began the implementation of their "final solution" in 1938. For the next few years, immigration policies became more and more severe. Quotas shrank, despite a meeting in Evian, France, where the Allies promised help for Jewish refugees. Whatever may be said about anti-Semitism in France, the fact remains that a large percentage of all European Jewish refugees migrated to or through France, when the U.S. and Great Britain refused to accept them. Additionally, the British, to please the Arabs, cutt off all but token Jewish immigration into Palestine.

* * * * *

Our train rolled westward at a good clip as we debated the chances for survival of the Jewish population, ourselves and our loved ones. We saw more and more German military equipment and more Wermacht and SS troops passing on the eastward tracks.

As the morning broke, we were far from the Danube, moving slowly through the rolling Badacsony hills, a land famous for its Riesling wine. Then we turned southward, inspiring new guesses as to where we were heading. It was still indirectly west, a mixed blessing, as Joska noted. We moved away from the shooting, but also further from liberation by the Russians.

The train stopped and started all day long. We stood on side tracks next to Hugarian and German army units. Arrow-Cross and SS Soldiers moved in all directions. It was chaotic on the rails, with hardly anyone paying attention to anyone else.

Our boxcar doors were opened and we were relatively free to move around, go to the toilet, or buy things at the station. When we started to move again, it was at a steady pace. Every little village we passed seemed to be full of military personnel of one sort or another. It was already dark when our train stopped for the last time at a tiny railroad station. We could hardly make out a small sign indicating that we had arrived at a place so small that nobody in our group had ever heard of it.

Our guess was that we were not far from Celldomolk, a small city of the Dunantul (literally, beyond the Danube; an area west of the Danube). Exhausted, we jumped off the train without ceremony. We unloaded our supply trucks near the tracks. Three smassers were assigned as guards overnight. While we lined up, ready to march at the command of our officer Lantos, Koranyi and Miklos appeared, accompanied by a civilian, and announced that they would meet us in the morning at our new destination. Then they disappeared by motorcycle with sidecar.

We started to march in the dark on a dirt path under the heavy winter sky. We marched for over an hour that seemed more like ten because we were so tired. Finally, the silhouette of a few farm buildings appeared; we had almost run into them.

Around one o'clock in the morning, with the help of local peasants, we were directed into pig pens, stables, granges, and hay lofts to bed down for the night. Joska, Miki, Shmuel, Bela, Robi, myself and the others were lucky to find ourselves in a stable among cows, who provided central heating, and cracks in the mud wall provided unnecessary air-conditioning. After suffering the aggressive welcome of a nearby cow's wet tongue, I rejected her with a kick and fell soundly asleep.

Smasser Berec, who had the last overnight shift, yelled at 6:30 with all his might, "Everybody up!" As we had slept in our clothes, in whatever spaces were not occupied by cows, with our rucksacks under our heads and covered with our blankets, it was not very difficult to get ready. Of course, a good warm shower would have been nice, or the chance to brush our teeth, but that would be for another day.

The morning was crisp and beautiful. Daylight slowly pushed back the stubborn darkness and revealed picture postcard scenes of the small hamlet. The main house, built during feudal times, had certainly seen better days. Small, thatch-roofed, whitewashed houses had housed the serfs then, the peasants now. Pens, stables, granges, agricultural tool shacks, all in bad repair, completed a large circle, the center of which was dominated by the symbol of the Hungarian rural landscape: the country well, and a long trough with food and water for the animals.

Morning toilette at a friendly farm

While the peasants were heading slowly and deliberately toward the stables to milk cows and feed pigs, we went to the well to wash our faces. The peasants were polite, although somewhat reserved. We said cordial good-mornings to each other, but, as we learned later, they were angry with the government and military for requisitioning their homes, horses and wagons.

We had a royal breakfast of fresh milk and homemade bread with "szalonna," thickly cut lard. Just the smell of it could satisfy a person for a day. By 7:30, we were lined up ready for orders. A long line of horse-drawn wagons filed in, each driven by a peasant; some were young teenagers, some old grandpas.

"Octato Gerstl," Officer Lantos commanded, "assign six to twelve men to each wagon. Corporal Berec will lead all of you back to the railroad station. Your men will load the wagons. Nobody is to sit on the wagons going or coming. If anything is lost you are responsible!"

"Yes, Sir!" By the time we left the hamlet, all the animals were outside around the well. A big bull was mounting a young cow, who casually walked away after the successful act, dripping with semen. "What a lucky bull," Robi remarked. We all sighed with envy.

Most of the day was taken up unloading, loading and bringing the supplies back to the hamlet. We were ordered not to unload upon our return, which indicated that we would move again soon. The "cocher" unbridled the horses and led them to the stables for the night.

We finished our chores by early evening and I had the opportunity to rest and think. What is our new condition? Why are we here, surrounded by fascist military and Arrow-Cross, rather than on the Russian front? What's going on at all the fronts? Unable to answer such questions, I took up my sketch book and, from the corner of the pigpen, I started to sketch another piece of the mosaic of our existence.

It was announced at the evening roll call that the following morning we would march to Celldomolk, some forty kilometers away. So we would share another night with the animals, although this time we were a little better organized. We laid a good layer of straw on the floor, and settled down for the night. Conversation continued in the dark in low voices. Our press corps, that is, Miki and Bela, had mostly good news to report from all fronts; but about the Jews, the civilians and our peers in other labor camps, there was only the most meager information.

"The military situation can be pieced together," Miki reported, "from the Hungarian and German press and BBC reports, but who makes announcements about the Jews? Nothing gets mentioned but exceptionally brutal killings. Never do the announcers give an overall view. At least we could not gather any."

Slowly the voices died down, and absolute silence and darkness surrounded my stirred up emotions. My highly tensed senses reacted to the slightest rustle of the straw as if it was the mysterious noise of an entire forest. The tranquil ruminations of a cow sounded like an earthquake. Moricka's quiet sobbing mixed with the cows' peaceful urinating made me feel as if the tears of all the Jews were inundating me. Exhausted, I fell asleep as if falling into a bottomless pit.

Morning came too early. In spite of the smassers yelling and general commotion, Joska had to shake me to consciousness. "Get up, damn it! You have to line up our troops." I jumped up and rushed to catch up with the morning activities.

We had another good breakfast. The peasants brought out the horses and bridled them, and we waved goodbye to the children and women. I felt sad to leave this peaceful place with its lucky bull, dirty pigs, and chickens that were scattering in all directions ahead of the horses. We were on our way again.

The narrow country roads were filled with moving military units, green-shirted Arrow-Cross units and civilians with Arrow-Cross armbands. Our group and the local civilian population hated all these strangers in their midst. Sergeant Boros led our convoy. Ten steps behind him walked the head smasser. Ten steps behind him I walked, leading my group with the yellow and white armbands. Behind us walked three smassers and, behind them, six pairs of horses drawing wagons filled with supplies for headquarters. Our officers were far in advance with their cars, motorcycles and bicycles.

"Hey, Tibor!" Joska shouted.

"What?"

"This march isn't very reassuring, is it?"

I slowed my steps until Joska caught up. "No," I said, "but we have no choice, so just let's march in good order and try to ignore all these Arrow-Cross."

"We are," he said. "Hopefully, they'll ignore us too."

* * * * *

So far they had. Since leaving Rimaszombat, our anxiety had grown with each kilometer we traveled to the west. The Russians were advancing and we were moving away. The relative stability and routine of casern life under Koranyi had changed to perpetual uncertainty. The fences and walls of the caserns had been barriers and symbols of our lack of freedom, but also had served as protectors from the outside world, not unlike mental barriers we erect to protect our egos, either with aggression or withdrawal, and keep our sanity. Since the days of Galanta, and even before, we had lived with different degrees of anxiety about the future; the next day, the next step, the next moment. We always trod a narrow line between a hostile civilian world and packs of fascist military jackals. We had to project self-assurance to hide fear and anxiety. I was constantly conscious of my behavior in order to give an appearance of compliance and strength while masking my true feelings. With this "self-assurance," I had to convince our smassers that it was normal for me to command the Jews instead of them. They, the "superior" race, should supervise and act through me. To maintain this balance, I had to be extremely vigilant concerning when to bend and when to stand firm; how to diffuse conflicts, and how to anticipate and head off trouble. A fraction of a second in making a decision could make all the difference. In such a state of mind, simple, otherwise trivial matters, take on importance, and incidents with no serious consequences stand out in memory decades later as important events.

Now that Koranyi, Dr. Miklos and some of the more sympathetic officers had abandoned us to more barbaric smassers, and we were surrounded by fascist troops, our fears and anxieties increased. Nobody would talk about them, but apprehension was written on every face and found expression only in very laconic terms; "Shit! we're in trouble."

A few kilometers in front of us, a column of trucks appeared on the dusty macadam road, led by motorcyclists who ordered everybody to make way and move to the side. We moved, but the wagons could not get off the road so easily. Everything stopped. I knew we might be in trouble even before one of the motorcyclists yelled. "Hey, Jews! Off the road or I drive through you!"

I looked at Sergeant Boros for directions. "Off the road!" he yelled.

"We already are, idiot," I thought.

"The wagons, move them now!" The motorcyclist yelled.

Barabas ran forward to me. "Tibor, we'd better help these idiots, otherwise we'll get into trouble."

"What can we do?"

"Just taper down the soft shoulder of the road enough so that the horses can gradually step down and then step back up. A few guys on each side can keep the wagons from turning over."

"You're a genius!"

"No, I just saw it done before."

The motorcyclist was talking now to our sergeant, obviously searching for a solution. I approached them.

"What do you want, Jew?" the motorcyclist demanded.

I ignored him and saluted. "Sergeant, sir! I have a way to remove the wagons from the road, with your authorization."

Barabas' plan worked perfectly, and the trucks passed, to our immense relief.

We continued our march toward Celldomolk, where we arrived with nothing worse than bruised egos from anti-Semitic insults hurled by passing fascists. It was dark when we arrived, almost as if it was planned to sneak us into towns and cities with the least possible visibility. Man and beast, we waited, tired and hungry, in a school courtyard. The peasants, who had never expected such a journey (which normally would have taken them only a half day) were particularly annoyed. They became allies in adversity and cursed our smassers to hell simply and squarely, whenever the latter tried to push us or them around more aggressively.

"Who the hell do you think you are?" yelled one of the older ones menacingly at Boros. "You barefoot peasant commandeering all these decent people!"

We were slightly embarrassed and very fearful of how Boros would react, when in the dim light Koranyi's silhouette appeared behind the loaded wagons. "That's all right, Pa. We'll take care of that." He approached and shook the old man's hand. "Thank you for helping us." He turned to us: "Let's get settled in for the night."

The two-story school building was the nicest place in which we had been quartered. Morning light poured in through large windows, and the winter sun warmed body and soul. We were ordered to assemble in the courtyard, and the entire camp lined up to listen to Koranyi give the orders of the day. "This will be our headquarters for the foreseeable future. We will share it with different military units. I expect perfect discipline. Every leave from the camp will be granted only with individual authorization; there will be no exceptions. The classrooms already marked XI KMSZ are our quarters. People with yellow or white armbands (he would not say Jews) are not permitted in any other part of the building."

We unloaded the wagons and said goodbye to the cart drivers with a surprising degree of real emotion on both sides. What a great feeling to shake those rough hands and feel a heavy pat on the back. "Keep it up fellas. This won't last long," one of them said. He pulled his hair forward and covered the two ends of his big mustache, leaving just toothbrush bristles, like Hitler. "The painter is kaput," he declared.

But no, he was not. In spite of incessant bombings and the Russians' advances, he promised to fight to his last man, to gain for himself Valhalla in his own demented Wagnerian saga.

It was bitter cold early in the winter of 1944 to 1945. Our first assignment was to dig trenches around the school's perimeter. Narrow, deep trenches against bombs, we supposed. "It's surely not to deter the Russians," Robi remarked.

"Don't be so sure." Joska retorted, "Just remember Sergeant Kovacs, who attacked the Russian tanks with his sword."

* * * * *

In his New Year speech, Hitler again blasted the Jewish-Bolshevist alliance of his imagination. But while he was barking his madness, the allied forces were pushing back his armies on all fronts. The Russians occupied Olevsk, only ten miles from the Polish border. They broke through Van Manstein's position and occupied Kirovgrad, near the Dnieper River, in the beginning of January. By the end of January, they had conquered Novgorod and Tosno, which at last permitted normal communications between Moscow and Leningrad.

Early in February, we heard news of great celebrations in Moscow for Russian successes in the Ukraine. Their forces came together in the Korsun-Shevchenkovsky area. They also reached Brestlitovsk, from where the Germans launched their original attack against the U.S.S.R. Great battles were fought for Kirograd and, in mid-February, the Russians penetrated Estonia despite strong German resistance. In Italy, the Germans put up tremendous resistance; nevertheless, the U.S. 10th Army and 34th Division occupied Cervara. Much fighting continued in the Anzio region.

The French also participated actively, with the 3rd French Expeditionary Corps relieving the U.S. 45th Division. And General Juin's forces were stabilizing the north flank of the U.S. 5th Army. On January 10th, the trial of nineteen Italian fascist leaders ended with eighteen death sentences, including one for Ciano, the Foreign Minister in Verona.

At the end of January, U.S. and British forces finally occupied Anzio and Nettuno bays. Allied aircraft dropped millions of leaflets announcing the imminent liberation of Rome and exhorting the Italians to help the Allies as well as they could.

Miki and Bela reported this news to us as their assigned duty. They gathered their information from all sources and wrote it down on scraps of paper. Getting the news was becoming more and more difficult. Although even Hungarian fascist newspapers were forbidden to enter our area of the school, they paid off smassers in order to read important news or catch remarks and segments of conversations, and would invent statements about likely occurrences to provoke a yes or no reaction. These were risky enterprises, as they were accused more than once of spreading false rumors, a major crime. Somehow, the BBC news still reached us, but we never knew how. "The BBC said ...," is all Miki would say.

Bela was telling us with great sadness in his voice of the Allied bombing of the monastery at Monte Cassino. "Big deal," many of us retorted. "You sound as if they murdered your mother. It was probably full of Germans."

"Whatever the case, it was the shrine of a culture and Christian civilization."

"Yes, a culture, a civilization which brought upon humanity, at least in this part of the world, more suffering with their intolerance than any other cause," Shmuel argued with unusual vehemence. "If the Germans used it to shoot at the Allies, then it became just another military base and a target. I won't waste any sleep over it for sure."

"Joska, you don't have anything to add?" I asked.

"You wouldn't bomb the Louvre because some Germans are hiding there or even shooting from it, would you?" Joska responded.

"Monte Cassino is more than a museum of Christianity. It's a powerful symbol of a faith which has persecuted Jews for centuries. I won't cry about it," Shmuel responded.

"I think you should, just as I do, seeing Jews at the Wailing Wall of their demolished temple, or as I would at the destruction of the Akhabar Mosque," Joska confirmed.

"Maybe in another time, but now I have to cry for my family, and fear for my life as a result of all they do in the name of Christianity." Everyone fell silent. Shmuel concluded. "That's all we need now, some break in our ranks." Robi yelled angrily, "Don't fear, destiny has held us together pretty tightly!"

Bela again began to give us the news. There was more talk that Eisenhower had met his commanders to discuss future strategies. Everybody assumed the meeting concerned the invasion of France. (This meeting was the planning of "Operation Overlord", the invasion of France). A conference of French colonies took place with de Gaulle. Perhaps the French would finally get organized, and help the Allies as well as themselves.

At the other end of the world, we gathered, the battles continued in the Pacific. The Marshall Islands, Roi and Namour Atolls were mentioned by some radio news. In China, Roosevelt was putting pressure on Chiang Kai-shek to attack Burma, but Chiang was demanding more and more financial and material aid before he would budge.

Argentina broke off relations with Hungary, as well as with Rumania, Bulgaria and the Vichy government. A good sign. The German ship was sinking; the rats were fleeing.

Churchill announced in the House of Commons Russia's intention to establish the Curzon Line as future border with Poland, and to compensate the Poles to the detriment of Germany. The Polish government in exile vehemently protested the idea.

The world was afire, and we just dug useless trenches in the bitter cold and watched the heavy American bombers and fighters fly day after day in "peaceful" formations to a murderous mission somewhere. They came right on schedule every day. The military units stationed in Celldomolk had anti-aircraft guns in different places in the city. They held drills and trained dozens of idle units to man the guns, but never tried to use them ... fortunately. The planes flew with their heavy murmur as they approached, and roared like an earthquake as they passed overhead. In spite of the danger, we felt confident. They were our eventual liberators.

We saw fear creep into the eyes of our guards and the fascist soldiers around us. They, too, sensed the beginning of the end. Some acted nicer to us, others much worse. Some imagined we could guide the planes by sending signals, so they redoubled their vigilance. Occasionally, we played their game by not denying the possibility, or by hardly noting the planes' approach. And the B-6's kept coming by the hundreds. We kept count as they passed slowly with their heavy loads, while their fighter escorts were crisscrossing their path at tremendous speed. And we counted them on the way back. Having dropped their bombs, they moved faster now. Usually, they were fewer in number. We knew they might take different routes after they unloaded their bombs, but we knew many never returned.

* * * * *

Cleaning our quarters, the officers' quarters and the rest of the school, holding useless drills spiced with punishments, and digging trenches was our daily occupation. Gradually, we became the servants of the entire school population. Small units of men were constantly requisitioned from Koranyi, who felt it better to comply than to refuse. Our egos had long since gone, and life became a matter of making the best of a bad situation. We did it to survive, I guess, but I like to reserve this word for matters of more importance than shining the boots of a lowly fascist who then kicked you with them. I would not do it myself, however, I sent one of our men. I continued to be responsible for implementing orders, and so retained leverage over who to send to what mission. I was able to deny one request to satisfy another of a higher priority. Thus, I was able to send Moricka and the weaker men to latrine cleaning, an undignified but safe place for the day, and send the stronger ones to unload supplies. To be fair, I alternated them with kitchen duties or assignments as officers' orderlies.

Koranyi's and Miklos' orderly was always a soldier, for good reasons. First, that was normal practice; second, Koranyi did not want to appear that he was favoring Jews, for to be an orderly in normal circumstances was a favor, with many advantages if you had a decent boss. Through his orderly, Janko, Koranyi received a pretty accurate reading of the mood of the troops. Still, the incidents with the fascists in the building multiplied, and their almost routine requests for personal services became arrogantly aggressive. I tried to limit the number of orderlies available in the pool, so Koranyi and Miklos took on "second orderlies" to chop wood and take care of other duties.

It was a cold morning in late February. Coal as heating fuel, although rationed, had almost disappeared and was replaced by wood. I dispersed the men in my unit to their different duties, mostly to chop wood, to be delivered by peasants. Suddenly, an Arrow-Cross, about twenty-two years old, yelled at me. "Hey you, octato, or whatever the hell you are, give me a man to carry up that wood!"

"I'm sorry, but all the men are gone for the moment."

"Okay, then you come."

"I'm sorry, but I was ordered not to leave my post."

"What post? Where is your post? The middle of this court? Move, damn it!"

I didn't. He ran toward me and stopped chest to chest, nose to nose. "Who ordered you here? Who is your officer?" he yelled in my face.

One of our smassers, the day officer, observed the scene from twenty-five meters away. He did not intervene, and the smile on his malevolent face displayed his satisfaction with my situation.

After a tense few seconds of hesitation mixed with fear, I pointed at him. "Sergeant Otto is my superior." The day officer was surprised and obviously perplexed at the new turn of the situation. Suddenly, he was my superior, so he needed to make a decision.

I will never know what went through his head. Maybe some concern about Koranyi's reaction. Maybe he understood that the Germans were losing. Maybe he had a simple reflex of routine. "He is under my command! He stays here!" he said with authority.

"Get out of my way," the Arrow-Cross yelled, pushing me aside vehemently as he stormed off.

When I related the incident in the evening, most of my friends were happy at the outcome, but Shmuel was concerned about retribution.

"We must maintain the established structure even with the risks, if we want to maintain any control of our lives," Joska stated, and Miki agreed. "Obviously, we have no control over our destiny, but we live one day at a time, and to have some autonomy in our daily lives could have great significance. The alternative is to be at the mercy of vicious smassers who will exploit any opportunity to impose torturous discipline."

The Russians advanced in leaps and bounds all through March, 1944. Dreams of escape and eagerness to do something with our lives intensified. It was important to maintain the illusion of some freedom of action. But illusion it was.

As the Russians conquered more territories, more people, mostly Arrow-Cross units, crowded into the Dunantul. The Russian Ukrainian front crossed the Dnieper River. Some ten thousand Germans were killed and thousands more captured at Nikolayev. Overall, the Germans were driven back to where they were in 1941, just after the invasion of Russia. They occupied Rovno in Poland and offered a separate peace treaty to Finland, which was rejected.

The politics of Hungary by this time were extremely confusing. Homan Balint, a historian and philosopher, prevailed over other politicians. It was agreed that the Allies were too far away to come to help if Hungary decided to cross to the other side, as the Italians had done. Nobody wanted to align Hungary with Stalin and the Russians, so the necessary alliance with Germany was maintained. However, many moderates kept in constant contact with Britain and elsewhere in order to explore other possibilities. Even right-wing politicians (but not the fascists) feared outright occupation, and tried to satisfy Hitler's demands by providing soldiers, assuring safe passage for German troops, and imposing restrictions on Jewish life. Homan Balint, for example, although personally not an anti-Semite, pursued anti-Semitic politics because the "nation's interest" required it.

Hitler knew all about the contacts with the enemy powers. He did not trust the parliamentary multi-party system of Hungary, and decided not to risk a change of sides by Hungary. But we knew very little about these events. All we knew was that there was a heavy concentration of German troops around Vienna and in southern Hungary. Various excuses were offered, but everybody felt the invasion of Hungary, an ally of Germany, was just a matter of time.

The morning of March 20th, as we were lining up for work assignments, Miki and Bela raced to join us. Out of breath, and with great excitement, they told in whispers that Germany had occupied Hungary as of the previous day. The news was quickly passed throughout the ranks. The smassers already knew, and it seemed as if their chest swelled a little, and their attitude became more arrogant.

Only some of them appeared confused. After all, Hungary had lost its independence.

But independence is a rather abstract concept. The symbols of state like the flag, Horthy as head of state, and most other politicians remained. Their dilemma was this: "Now we've got you Jews, Koranyi or not, but somehow the Germans have got us too." That turn of events could mean the Russian front for them, with or without the Jews.

Edmond Viesenmeyer was named the new German Ambassador, with the full power of action invested in him by Hitler. Within days of the occupation headed by General Von Weichs, arrests began of prominent Jewish leaders, left-of-center politicians and labor leaders, a total of some 4,000 people. The speed of the occupation, against which there was considerable official protest but no armed resistance, enabled the occupiers to lay hands on lists of "subversive" organizations (with the help of collaborators) almost instantly. On the tail of the occupation, Adolph Eichmann arrived to implement the "final solution" of the Hungarian Jews.

* * * * *

As we were sitting on our cots wrapped in any cloth or rag we could find against the cold March evening, we discussed the events we still could not believe. Could the Germans continue to hold out? Many, like Lajos and Weissberg, questioned the validity of the news we were hearing. "Yes, the Russians are advancing," Weissberg argued, "but what of the new secret weapon the Germans are talking about?"

"Bullshit!" Miki retorted. "It's just talk. Look at this Konyev is at the Dnister River surrounding the German forces entrenched in the Pipel marshes. The Red Army is in Galicia, Vatutin is in Tarnopal, and Churchill on the BBC speaks of panic in Germany's vassal states."

But the Germans still occupied Rome, where they executed hundreds of civilians because a partisan attack killed a few Germans. The Russian front was important, but with regard to our fate it was not everything. Whether by virtue of incredible luck or exceptional circumstances, the integrity and humanity of one man, Koranyi, had sheltered us from the worst atrocities, while the world was preparing for the greatest battles in history about which we knew almost nothing.

After the invasion of Hungary, we were more often confined to our headquarters, and we gained news with much greater difficulty. We knew vaguely that an increase in French resistance to the Nazis was attributable to de Gaulle having become Commander-in-Chief of the Free French Forces. We heard of the bombing of Rumanian oil fields, the Russian success in the Crimea and their capture of Yalta and later Sebastopol; and that in Italy, Victor Emanuel had resigned in favor of Umberto. The Russians reached Rumania and Czechoslovakia. Again so close, yet so far.

Signs of the Third Reich's imminent collapse were everywhere, yet we learned the hard way that this did not mean the war would soon end. Large territories still in Germany's hands included all of Western Europe and part of Eastern Europe. And there was the secret weapon the Germans kept bragging about. Was it propaganda or reality? Was it an atomic bomb? In spite of the Allied successes, we were full of fear and uncertainty.

After winning major battles in Italy, in Cassino, Allied Forces in Morocco and Algeria broke through German lines in May, opening the road to Rome. Rome itself was captured just two days before the Allied landing on June 6, 1944, in Normandy. "Operation Overlord" began bringing the relief to the Russians for which they had pressed the Allies so hard.

June 6th, my brother's birthday, and I wondered where he was. Was he as lucky as we were here, or was he suffering in another camp somewhere? Was he tortured or hungry? Was he still so good natured, so loving, always befriending everyone, or was he dying somewhere on the Russian front? He was the one who demonstrated his love so easily to our parents and friends and was loved in return. He kissed them or hugged them at any time, while I did so only on special occasions. I was the intellectual and was more respected than loved.

And how were my parents? Where were they? The last time I saw them was in April, thanks to a special permit from Koranyi. I remember approaching our house on Servita Street with apprehension. They did not know I was coming. How were they, and how would they react to me?

They broke into tears when they saw me. The house was a mess. They were packing to move into the designated Jewish ghetto in the neighborhood of the swimming pool. The outside wall of the pool was one of its perimeters. It was an evil corruption of “my pool,” where I had spent my early youth, and which had been the source of so much satisfaction and pride, and the place where I learned early the meaning of fair play and sportsmanship. But what was the meaning of those concepts today? Nothing!

My parents were sorting necessities for survival from souvenirs. Mother kept repeating with tears in her eyes, “Why is this happening to us? Why is God punishing us? We didn’t do anything wrong! And where is your brother? Who knows if we ever will see him again?”

Father was just nodding in resignation, his lips set in a strange, disturbing smile, as if he knew everything that was and everything that would be. “The passage is difficult,” he said. “But God will help us,” and he put his arm around my mother consolingly.

“God!” I yelled, “What God? Whose God? We are his chosen people? For what? For slaugter? For pogroms? To expiate the sins of humanity? There is no God! Not for us. Save yourself. Everybody is on his own. Father, please come back with me to the camp. You know about our commander. You’ll be safer there for a while. We’ll bring Mother to the family in Budapest. My permit is only good until 10:00 tonight. We have to get ready.”

My father just pulled my mother closer and continued to smile, a little stunned by my proposition. “No, son, I will not take one step away from your mother.” We did not know it, but at that moment they chose death.

Mother started to prepare the table for the afternoon meal.

The city’s Jewry was in turmoil; the mood of Gentiles was disconcerted expectation. The day went fast. I visited Grandmother and some relatives; same fears, same tears. I returned home. I tried to encourage my parents with the belief that not all camps are the same, that there was still some hope. We cried. I kissed them and hugged them for the last time.

SURROUNDED AT CELLDOMOLK

Deportation began at the end of April; mass deportations started on May 15th, and by July 10th the only Hungarian Jews to be found were in Budapest. Some 450,000 people were banished from their homes, relocated to a place from which they would never return. Most unbelievable is the fact that we still were not aware of their destiny.

The distance to Hangony from Eger is not great, but with the slow trains and having to change in Fuzesabony and Miscolc, it was midnight before I arrived back at the casern. The guard was more than happy to put me in the cooler for reporting late.

We settled again into our meaningless routines. It was difficult to determine and accommodate the shifting moods of our guards: would they go easy on us, or be harsher in view of the new events? And our own shifting moods? Sometimes we would be elated about the successes of the Allies; at other times, desperation would set in, as we were squeezed between two major fronts and unable to join either one.

Events moved very quickly on the fronts during those months. After the initial landing in Normandy, every inch of territory had to be conquered over stiff German resistance. Nevertheless, by August the Allies had occupied Cherbourg, Caen, and Nantes. They reached the Loire by Mid-August and opened a third major offensive in Provence called "Operation Anvil," with the U.S. 7th Army and France's 2nd Army Corps headed by General de Lattre de Tassigny. The Russians continued their great summer offensive in Finland, occupying Viipure and insuring Leningrad's safety. In Italy, the Allies reached the Arno River and occupied Florence.

The Germans launched their first secret weapons in June. The V-l rockets rained on England, raising the morale of our guards. In July, the attempt on Hitler's life skyrocketed our morale, which was then crushed by the announcement of its failure. Our spirits rose again in August with the Warsaw uprising, and were again dashed by the lack of help from the Allies.

The brutal termination of the uprising also ended all hope of extricating ourselves from our situation. We could only wait for destiny to catch up with us. Our moods were swinging wildly. Many grew depressed about the seeming futility of our life. Mihaly, the most unlikely one among us, advocated action even if it would end in disaster. Surprisingly, he found many followers, but their action created only dissension among us, and unnecessary challenges to the guards. Mihaly and his group ignored reality: our precarious well being depended on the good will of one person, Koranyi.

* * * * *

"You Goddamned Jews! You did not win the war yet!" yelled Sergeant Kovacs, red in the face. He hit Mihaly with the flat of his sabre, while ordering him to run, frog jump and push-up. I did not know how long this had been going on, but when I noticed them in the courtyard, which was now our drill field, Mihaly, who was close to exhaustion, was staggering to his feet. From a short distance, we observed the scene with fear. So did the smassers, but with satisfaction.

Joska stepped next to me and, in a low voice, worriedly asked what we could do.

"Nothing," I said. "I don't know what happened, but my gut reaction is that to interfere now will bring disaster."

But Joska went forward. "Sergeant sir, my brother has a weak heart, please ..."

"Good! Do you have one too?"

"No, sir."

"Then join him! Up! Down! Up! Down! Where the hell is your octato? Fetch him right now," he said. Mihaly took two steps and collapsed. I moved forward from the corner of the building, forcing myself to be quiet. "Octato," he yelled, "Line up all the Jews in five minutes! Move!"

"Yes, sir!"

By this time, the entire casern population was gathered around the drill field or was observing from the windows of the administration building. I noticed Koranyi watching too.

Even a few gendarmes were mixed with the jubilating smassers. "Because of a few setbacks for the heroic German Army, you think you have won the war? That will not happen! But if it does, you will never see it. Down! Up! Down!" I stood as usual on the side, some ten yards away. "You, too!" he yelled at me. After a few seconds of hesitation, I joined in. The torture went on for almost an hour. Many fell, exhausted. The worst part was that, for the first time since we left Galanta, the magic of our system was broken by my participation in the punishment, rather than leading it. It showed the difference.

Finally, dismissed, we waited for Mihaly to recuperate so we could find out what had precipitated the whole thing. He wouldn't tell us, but later his brother explained that Mihaly, angered by being commanded by a smasser to shine Kovacs's boots, responded that the war had been lost, and that it would be better for him if he befriended us. We were stunned. How could Mihaly, introspective, intellectual, a lawyer by profession, be so utterly stupid? Or had he simply cracked up?

In the barracks, our council got together to discuss how we should react. Obviously, everyone needed to be more careful when talking with the guards. Also, if we were to give up the octato system, incidents like this one would surely multiply.

"Let's act as if nothing happened. Tibor should take command as usual. If ordered again to undergo discipline, as he was by Kovacs, he should refuse to participate and hope for Koranyi's intervention."

"Thanks," I said, "you know what you're saying? I should disobey a direct order. How can Koranyi protect me? I'll be dead before he finds out."

"Let's not exaggerate," Joska said. "It's risky, but that's what we want you to do."

"That's crazy," I protested.

"Let's show hands," Joska said. It was unanimous, all against me. I was to refuse a direct order if the situation required it.

"You got your answer?" Robi whacked my back so hard with his ususal "delicate" affection that I almost fell forward.

"Thanks."

I was unable to sleep most of the night from fear of the consequences if I should disobey. I created hundreds of scenarios. If Kovacs says this, then I will say that. What if other smassers ask me to execute their orders too? I imagined myself court martialed and shot.

I woke up in a sweat, hoping I had dreamed all of this. The morning trumpet was almost a blessing, as it would end this mental torture one way or another. We lined up as usual for the daily drills, which I conducted under the supervision of the smassers. Suddenly, Kovacs showed up.

"Move them faster! You call that running? They're walking like sleepwalkers. I'll show you how to wake them up!" And he took over. My moment has come, I thought. "One, two, three, one, two, three, faster, faster," he yelled. Usually, I did the exercises with my group, but this time I stayed next to Kovacs running in place. He looked at me harshly. "I want you to keep up the pace. I'll observe you. Guard, make sure they're not sleeping here."

The crisis had passed, I thought, but within three minutes he was back. "You don't see those laggards?" he yelled.

"Yes, sir, but they can't keep up!"

"I'll show you how well they can keep up! Guard, take those four for special training."

They picked the weakest ones, like hungry wolves that isolate the sick or young from a herd of gazelles. Rich, flabby Moricka, Weissberg, Shmuel and Mihaly were taken to a corner of the drill field and exercised to complete exhaustion.

We took Moricka to our barracks on a stretcher and assisted the others by pouring cold water on them. They were shaking.

As we were heading toward the barracks, Kovacs stopped me.

"Yes, sir?"

"You have to be tough. When we go to the front, it won't be fun. You people had better be in good shape." It sounded to me like an excuse, an apology.

"Yes, sir."

As everybody tried to shake their fatigue and nurse their blisters and sores, Joska, who was always looking at the big picture, said, "Listen, everyone, if we can retake the command tomorrow, as it looks like we might, then today was worth it."

"Shut up!" most answered him angrily. "All this is your brother's fault."

"You realize that to re-establish credibility, I now have to be tougher than Kovacs and punish people just as hard. How do I explain that to everybody?" I said.

"We'll all explain it," Joska said, "and I volunteer to be punished."

"Anybody else?" I asked.

"I knew it! Fuck you all!" Joska spit out.

"I'll be next," Robi said.

"You're on," I told him. "Does anyone else volunteer to be punished?" A dozen hands went up.

Events were moving at a furious pace on both military and diplomatic fronts. By mid-August, the Russians had reached East Prussia, and in September they concluded an armistice with Finland. The Germans arrested Petain because he refused to resign from the government. On the 25th, the Germans surrendered Paris to General Leclerc. The U.S. Army, which made it possible, entered the city a few hours later. By September, Brussels was liberated, as well as Liege.

When the Russians marched into Transylvania, threatening Hungary, General Lakatos created a new provisional government and declared it ready to negotiate Hungary's surrender. Nobody in our camp, Jew or Gentile, had ever heard of General Lakatos. The Russians kept pushing forward. Bulgaria and Rumania, in quick succession, signed treaties with the Allies and actively took part on the Russian side in attacks on Hungary and Czechoslovakia.

But the Germans were still far from surrendering. In early September, they launched the first V-2's at Britain, Antwerp, Brussels, and Liege with devastating effects. Maybe they were really close to producing an ultimate weapon which would change the outcome of the war. They concentrated great forces in Hungary for a counter-attack. By the end of September, the Hungarian and German Armies were fighting on a second Ukranian front; but now the Russians were at the Rumanian-Hungarian border, and the first Hungarian town, Mako, fell to them.

* * * * *

Since June, Hungarian Jewry had been pratically eliminated from the countryside, having been deported to the infamous death camps in Poland. We heard rumors about them which we found unbelievable, but which later proved to be horribly accurate. Now, the pressure on the Jews of Budapest mounted. On June 17th, the government announced where the ghettos would be located and declared that all Jews had to move to them. Within the ghetto, a curfew kept everyone inside at night and permitted the inhabitants to go outside the boundary only between two and five o'clock in the afternoon.

In July, the Swedish diplomat, Wallenberg, arrived in Budapest and tried heroically to save as many Jews as he could by granting them Swedish citizenship.

On October 16th, Szallasi, the head of the Nyilas party, through an agreement with Wiesenmeyer, came to-power and formed the first Arrow-Cross government. Adolf Eichmann returned immediately to Budapest from Berlin with one assignment: to liquidate all Hungarian Jews. As Szallasi took power, Hungarian moderates were negotiating with Russia to cease resistance to their advance. Meanwhile, the Russian army kept advancing. On October 20th, it occupied Debrecen, Hungary's third largest city. Szallasi, at Hitler's orders, called for evacuation of the Hungarian fascist troops as well as the civilians. The fascists frightened the population with tales of horrible killings and rapes by the Mongol hordes in the Russian army. People believed it, packed their belongings hastily, and left their homes without really knowing where to go. They also ordered the transfer of all machinery, supplies, agricultural stocks, grain, meat and able-bodied persons to the Dunantul (west of the Danube) and Germany. Negotiations with the Russians broke down, Molotov declared that Russian forces would fight the Hungarians as they fought the Germans. At the same time, those Hungarian emigres, including an uncle of mine, who were communists and who had fled to Russia decades ago during the Horthy regime, now returned to take over and lead the liberated territories. At the end of October, the Russians had crossed the Tisza River and the fight for Budapest had begun.

* * * * *

The city of Celldomolk was cracking at the seams. Every square foot of space with a roof was full of people; extra rooms of houses, and apartments of local citizens had been requisitioned either by the army or by local fascists. The refugees were frightened. Years of constant propaganda had them believing that every civilian caught by the Russians would be killed, maimed, raped or, at best, shipped to Siberia. They poured into the small remaining unoccupied territories west of the Danube. Chaos and fear were everywhere.

It had been weeks since we learned of the deportations and forced marches to Austria and Germany that had passed through the border town of Hegyeshalom, leaving dead and injured all over the road. As the Jewish high holidays approached, we feared our own deportation. Tension, restlessness and irritability caused severe arguments among our people. It seemed as if everybody wanted to be left alone in order to concentrate on his inner feelings, to remember his family, to rekindle past emotions, to revive and relive five thousand years of tradition, and to supplicate God for answers, seeking the meaning of thousands of years of suffering and persecution.

The daily routine over, we filed into our quarters in absolute silence. Shmuel, for the third time since Galanta, called for a "minyan" (the minimum ten Jewish adults) to start the Rosh Hashana service of the 5705th Jewish New Year. We all gathered around him, except the three white-armband Christians who stood awkwardly in a corner. Shmuel had no prayer shawl, but he always wore "tsitsis" under his clothes, and he now put these cloth fringes on his shoulders. He took up his prayer book and started the service. "Baruch ato adonoy ..." Within a few minutes there was not a dry eye, except for those of Shmuel, who, stronger and more confident than ever, raised his voice to heaven affirming his unshakable belief in his God and another new year. For the ten days between Rosh Hashana and Yom Kippur, the Day of Atonement, a sad melancholy which no amount of fascist aggression could penetrate dominated our mood. As we assembled a second time for the Yom Kippur service, Joska went to Shmuel. "I want to join," he said.

Shmuel just nodded. "Of course. Everyone is welcome." When he chanted the ancient, hauntingly beautiful Kol Nidre, nearly everyone broke down. We sat on our cots overwhelmed by emotion. Whether orthodox, agnostic, converted Christian or atheist, we were all overcome by those chants. When Shmuel went on to say the Kaddish for the dead, the pain for most became unbearable. The Kaddish was said for all those who had succumbed to inquisitions and pogroms. For me, it was perhaps also said for my father and mother; I didn't know whether they were dead or alive. Finally, Shmuel lifted his now tearful eyes to heaven, clasped his hands on his chest and, swaying left and right, concluded with "Sh'ma Yisrael ..."

Every day at the same time, American bomber squadrons passed overhead to unload devastation somewhere in Hungary or Austria. They often took off from Italy to land in Russia.

On November 4th, Szallasi's government was sworn in. The next day, all of us, including guards and officers, were ordered to line up at the courtyard of the school. Commander Koranyi, accompanied by two fascists, one in a regular army uniform, the other in a green shirt and Arrow-Cross armband, goosestepped to an elevated podium. Actually, the other two were marching, proud as peacocks, while Koranyi moved between them with small fast steps to keep up, his head bobbing, and with a sly smile on his face.

"Soldiers and auxiliary units (that was us), our great leader, brother Szallasi, has taken the helm of the Hungarian government. He will lead this nation to great victories at the side of the great German people. All defeatist attitudes, spreading of false rumors, black marketing and other crimes against the state will be severely punished. We expect your full cooperation. Let us now swear allegiance to our great leader. Raise your hand and repeat. I ... solemnly swear ..."

Finally, we were dismissed. Robi, in a low voice, laughingly said to me, "Now you can put the green and white Arrow-Cross armband next to the yellow one. It's a nice color combination."

"That's right," Joska said, "we swear allegiance to the guy and regime who wants to destroy us. It makes sense according to their logic."

Unavoidably, our little group of yellow armbands became too visible in the sea of green shirts. The only way we had been able to stay on our side of the Hungarian border was by becoming the personal servants and legmen of fascist officers, doing cleaning and maintenance chores in their headquarters, offices and barracks. But more and more often, and at higher and higher levels, our presence was questioned. Why were we not on the Russian front, now near Budapest, or in the German labor camps?

Koranyi and Miklos called Joska and me to their office. The commandant was unusually formal, and drawing on his cigarette more and more nervously.

"I believe we did our best to protect your group from these jackals. We're questioned daily by the Nyilas officers about your presence. We believe the end of our association is near. It's best if you prepare your people for this eventuality."

"May I ask Commander Koranyi if that means we will be deported to Germany?"

"I believe so," he answered.

Trying to overcome my shock, my mind raced through idea after idea. How could this be avoided? After a long silence, I nervously asked, "May I make a proposal, Commandant Koranyi?"

"Talk," Miklos prompted.

"It's only late November, but it's already very cold. And the winter is yet to come. We have no fuel. Everybody is cold and we're burning everything we can find. If my unit could go up into the hills in the nearby forest to cut trees for you and the fascist officers, we would be out of sight and it could be presented as labor necessary to help the war effort."

"It's quite distasful to me to give in to them," Koranyi said. "Where is our pride?"

"It's here and here," I replied, pointing to my head and heart. "My pride is in trying to save fifty-five people and myself. You don't understand, sir ...," and the tears started to wet my eyes as I thought of Coach Frederik's warning from so long ago in the swimming pool of Budapest: "First survive; after comes everything else."

"Okay," Koranyi cut in. "I'm willing to help. How would you like it done?"

"If you could give us the work assignment and authorization on paper, perhaps also signed by a self-interested fascist, we would take our chances. We will need a uniformed guard too."

He was scratching his head. "Think over your plan and see me tomorrow. We'll talk about it then."

"That was a good idea, Tibor. It may work for a while," Dr. Miklos said.

"A while might be enough. Maybe that's all we need now. The Russians have passed the Danube on the south end, and Szallasi has moved the government to Sopron. If we can hang on long enough, the Russians may finally catch up with us."

That evening, we got together with our group to discuss what to do. We agreed that the best thing would be to disappear from view as fast as possible. But how would we get food and shelter without coming back to the quarters in the school every day? If we could find a sympathetic, reliable guard it would be much easier. But who? We went back to see Koranyi the next morning with our request to be supplied weekly, at the time we would deliver the cut wood. We also asked for field tents to sleep in. He smiled. "Everything is agreed to and will be ready for your departure. Your guard will be Corporal Rac."

We were shocked. We stared at Koranyi in disbelief. He continued to smile. Rac was the guard who, when Barabas and I tried to contact the partisans in Hangony, had threatened us with severe punishments at the perimeter of the camp.

Suddenly a light flashed through my mind. Why was he in the same area? Could it be that he had the same intention we had? "We trust your judgement, sir."

"Here's a pass for you and Barabas. Corporal Rac will go with you. You can go to reconnoiter. Find some accommodations, and I will provide two wagons and horses to haul the wood. I'll also use them to send weekly supplies to you."

The next day, we went out of the city into the surrounding forest we knew little about. The snow, rain and slush gradually became deep snow as we struggled up the mountain side. These were not high mountains, perhaps five or six hundred meters at the most, but they were very steep and rugged, with deep caves. some containing stalagmites. Covering them was a forest, primarily oak, with some pines here and there accenting the white with their evergreen.

We talked to villagers on the way up in order to find out as much as possible about the area. They recommended that we try an area where some commercial logging had been done many years ago. Puffing uphill, we were forced to stop more and more often to catch our breath, when finally, some two kilometers from the main road, we found a clearing of low bushes in the heavily wooded forest. We tried to find a dirt road leading to the long-deserted logging area, but in the knee-deep snow it wasn't easy.

It was noon, and the sun broke through the haze, bathing the area with light and bringing haloes to the trees and mountain peaks. We gulped down the fresh air. We were breathing freedom.

"Corporal, sir, I guess you're not too happy to be assigned this grueling task," I suggested cautiously. Barabas gave me a look clearly indicating his desire that I shut up.

"I wasn't assigned; I volunteered. Koranyi talked to me about the need for wood and I volunteered," he answered cautiously. And after a few seconds of silence, he added, "We're in the same boat, fellas!"

We were surprised and puzzled. "I don't understand," I pressed. "You're not Jewish."

"No, but we have the same goal. We all want to defeat the fascists. Now listen to me, damn Jews. I'm telling you this, but I want your word that it will stay between us: I'm a communist at heart. I don't belong to the party or underground, but I want to help." With a hearty laugh, he stretched out his hand to us. We grabbed it as drowning men grasp at a straw. It was a break in the icy hostility which had surrounded us, especially in the last few months.

"Listen guys, I know your game of octato and I must do the same. I have to yell louder than the others, and punish more excessively too."

"We understand. Thank you. Just one more thing," I said. "I would like to explain the situation to Joska."

"That's okay."

We ate a delicious lunch. From our rucksacks came good bread with lard and paprika, and we heated our ersartz coffee over an open fire. "Okay, now let's look around and see if we can live here. We need to find a good place to set up our tents because any time now it could become very cold," Barabas suggested.

We started scouting the area for a place to pitch our army tents, when we came upon a large structure, something like a shed, with a collapsed roof, partially thatched, partially corrugated metal, which stood up, more or less, on half rotten logs. Inside and around it we found odds and ends: half-collapsed saw-stands and rusted axes left behind by loggers.

We started to dig in the snow like archeologists looking for a lost civilization. We found a few pots and pans, broken wagon wheels and rotten ropes, and gathered them with delight. "This is it," Barabas announced confidently. "It's a palace; there's enough timber here to fix it. It can house all of us, but we must return with some stoves so we can heat it."

"This is good news. Let's start back and report to Koranyi," urged Rac.

* * * * *

"You are indeed lucky," Koranyi told us, "so let's strike while the iron is hot. It's becoming more and more crowded here. Corporal, we will all assemble tomorrow morning at 8:30."

"Yes, sir!" and he saluted.

The evening was a mix of excitement, fear and expectation. We worried about what the change would bring, yet we all felt it would be better to be out of sight and to put some distance between us and our protector. More and more, the fascists were asking openly how we could still be there, while thousands of other Jews had long ago been deported across the border. In the morning, we lined up in the courtyard, guards and all. Fascist onlookers surrounded us, staring down from the windows. With the now familiar ceremony, the brass faced us.

Koranyi started to speak in an unusually loud voice, and without the usually present cigarette butt between his lips. "The trench digging around the perimeter has now been completed, and we can put all available manpower to better use. Our fighting soldiers are battling the Russian advance on Budapest and along the Danube, alongside the German army. Many of their headquarters have now moved to the Dunantul and need logistical help. So I command, effective immediately, that the XI KMSZ headquarters personnel be assigned to the duty of alleviating the shortage of heating and cooking fuel. They will be placed in logging camps in the neighboring forest under the command of Corporal Rac. Every week, the wood will be collected at the end of the logging trail, which they will restore. Food supplies for the group will be given at the same time. I expect maximum effort from all. Corporal Rac, you will report to my office immediately. Other officers are dismissed until further notice."

We spent the rest of the day preparing ourselves as best we could for this tough assignment. We hoped the Russians would catch up with us soon. We mended clothes and shoes while we contemplated our chances for survival.

The snow on the mountains was already ankle-deep, and it was only the end of November. Luckily, we were well fed and our civilian clothes were still in relatively good shape. The headquarters tailors and shoemakers, the Jews who took care of our officers and guards legitimate or illegitimate needs, also were able to spare (that is, to steal) leather soles and other material for our needs. They would stay at headquarters, but no one knew who would be luckier. We loaded the wagon with picks, shovels and axes, plus a week's food supply of bread, lard, dried vegetables, pork sausages and meat, and we received a camp stove attached to the wagon. We were ready to pull out the next morning.

At 7:00 A.M., we were assembled in the courtyard. A nasty mixture of rain and snow was falling, making our departure miserable. The pair of old horses at the front of the wagon looked like soaked rags, hanging their heads almost to the ground. Koranyi again came with his officers and sub-officers to exhort us to do a good and useful job. He handed the necessary papers over to Rac, and we were off. Koranyi and his entourage had done an excellent public relations job, justifying the need for this activity and its benefits for all military in Celldomolk, especially for those in the school.

We marched out in proper military order, three to a row. I led, and Corporal Rac walked at the unit's side. Fascists in the school, and some of the guards who surrounded us couldn't help themselves, adding a few last vitrioloc insanities: "Okay, the bastards at least will do something useful for a change."

"Now you'll see what working really means."

"Keep moving. It's getting cold here; send us wood."

"Stay away from us in those woods."

"I don't care why, I'm happy you're going," One yelled after us sarcastically, "I just can't stomach all these Jews around here!"

"The sentiment is mutual," Joska murmured to me.

As soon as we passed through the heavy arched doors of the courtyard, Corporal Rac came up to me and pushed three pieces of paper into my hand. "Put these in your pocket. We'll talk later."

We marched through the small city with no more trouble than a few nasty remarks thrown at us. Some people seemed puzzled to see there were still Jews around. One big, fat fellow addressed Rac and asked, "You bring them to Germany? Good! They'll learn there." We reacted to nothing, just kept marching in proper military cadence.... Finally, we were out of the crowded city and on the outskirts. The main road became a narrow two-lane strip filled with potholes so deep that we had to help the horses by pushing the wagons through.

The dirt road was soggy from the bad weather. As it started to go slightly uphill, we took turns straining next to our companions-in-arms, the good old horses.

We were marching now in less orderly fashion, but we still maintained a military rhythm. It was easier to march that way. After some two hours, we came to the beginning of the lumbering trail. The drizzle solidified into fine snow crystals. Ten minutes later, the temperature dropped to below zero centigrade; everything was snow. We stopped to rest at a small clearing. We each took a deep breath, taking in the fresh air, and exhaled with a long sigh, cleansing our bodies and souls of ugliness, hate and pettiness.

"Corporal, sir, what are these papers you gave me when we left?"

"First of all, you can drop the "sir" and "corporal" bullshit, except when others are around. Koranyi gave me one command document and work authorization, with date and everything legal. I have it. The others are blank copies, in case we accidentally separate and you meet fascist units, MP's or gendarmes. You can use them at your discretion and at your own risk. Neither Koranyi nor I know anything about them. Understood?"

"Yes, I understand and thank you for your help. We won't forget it; that is, if we survive. May I ask you a question? In Hangony, when we came back from outside the camp perimeter, you yelled at us viciously and threatened us with a court martial. Now, you're helping us at great risk to yourself. Why?"

Chopping wood in the forest

"I yelled because I was surprised to be caught there by you. I, too, was looking to escape to the partisans. You get it? I'm no fascist. As I told you, I'm communist. So just let's be done with it." We shook hands, then he turned around and yelled, "Let's get going, you motherfucking bastards! Our officers need the wood! Ready? Go!"

We started up the path trying to follow old tracks to make it easier on the horses. I had the feeling that we pushed more than they pulled. After two hours of marching, pushing and resting, we arrived at the collapsed shack at about 1:00 P.M.

Most of us were in pretty good shape physically. We had been able to leave behind at headquarters the weakest and sickest, together with the artisans and cleaning personnel, who remained under the leadership of Fred, the old-timer we originally met in Hangony. He had become a very important source of news and intelligence, not only about the troops around us, and those who were still at headquarters, but also about the friends we left behind. To establish regular contacts with him was high priority, but for the moment the highest priority was to establish camp and to figure out how to keep ourselves warm that night.

"Okay, Tibor, it's all yours," Rac said to me laughingly. "Don't forget that we have to deliver the wood."

"All right then, let's get organized. Hey, Barabas, Miki, come over here. You're engineers, and although I don't think we'll have a much need here for electrical engineering, you have to create quick and livable quarters for tonight." Within less than an hour, everybody was in position, cutting timber to prop up the shack, cleaning the snow, setting up the kitchen, cutting holes and digging a latrine far from the shack. Fortunately, the ground was only slightly frozen at the surface.

But the bedding was a big problem. We had brought with us straw bag "beds", but no straw, and we could find nothing to fill them with. Rac agreed that tomorrow the wagon must go back to fetch some straw. I was concerned about sending back an empty supply wagon, so I assigned six men to produce half a cord of wood to take back to the school.

By the end of the day, we had everything organized. We set up the pup tents inside the shack, which now had an open fireplace in the middle. We laid down that first night like sardines, wrapped in our blankets, close to each other in order to keep warm on the frozen dirt floor. After a few sinister jokes, we drifted off to sleep.

The morning came slowly, as if the sun was showing its face only because it was being pushed by the tired arms of an unseen colossus. It was cold, and the latrine was far. The sun started to paint the snowy trees a crimson red.

The sketch book! Where was my sketch book? It had settled somewhere in the bottom of my rucksack. I had not touched it for some time. I was inspired to sketch a few mosaics of recent events. Since yesterday, I had developed an illusion of freedom and dreamt exhilarating, refrshing dreams. Illusions sometimes are as important as reality. They can make the world seem better than it is or block out ugliness for an hour or a day, as they generate hope for tomorrow. Tomorrow may bring reality crashing down even harder. So be it. I still wanted to dream.

I returned to my bed with some difficulty, since the one-sardine space had closed in quickly. I nudged Joska and Miki apart. Before I was too settled, Rac, for whom we had prepared a tent in a comfortable corner alone, stuck out his head in the midst of a big yawn. "Hey, fellas, it's time to move and get organized. Weiss! Is the kitchen stove crackling yet? Tibor, where are you? Get the men ready in an hour or so."

We were ready. Barabas and Miki designated the first trees to fall. Three men surrounded a beautiful oak and, as their axes made the first blows, I felt we were commiting a crime. A new routine was established and we became more and more expert at logging, more and more productive in destroying nature. There was perfect silence all around, except for the echoes of axes hitting their targets, the crash of falling trees, the sounds of frightened deer escaping into the bushes, and occasional gun shots from distant hunters. Daily, almost on the hour, around 11:00 A.M., the heavy, rumbling, flying fortresses passed overhead on their way to destinations somewhere in Hungary, somewhere in Budapest, where the Germans were now encircled by the Russian army.

We felt good seeing our saviors pass unchallenged, but there was also a little pinch in the heart, knowing that they might have to destroy my street today, or Joska's tomorrow, eliminating a tangible tie to our youth. But that was the price we had to pay. We got used to the planes, and even waved, wishing good luck to those unseen warriors. But one day things were different. "Look over there," Robi yelled. White puffs, like little clouds, burst around the slow moving heavy bombers. We gathered together excitedly. The puffs must have been from the anti-aircraft guns near Celldomolk. Suddenly, the fast flying "chasseurs" which always surrounded the bombers and were criss-crossing the sky at tremendous speeds, came very low, and we heard their machine guns not too far away.

"Give it to them, Yanks!" Robi yelled. "Give it to them!" But in an instant, one of the little white puffs hit the monster flying fortress and, like a drunken soldier, the plane zigzagged faster and faster to the ground. We clearly saw a parachute open. With a tremendous bang, the plane hit the ground somewhere in the fields; but as far as we could see from behind the tree line, the crew had escaped the blast. The rest of the squadron continued as if nothing had happened, except for one plane, which peeled off from the group and, after making a big circle, came back, surrounded by two or three "chasseurs." Within a minute, we heard a long whistle and a tremendous explosion, then a second and a third. The noises of destruction echoed in the valley. Then, quietly, the flying fortress made another lazy circle and flew away to rejoin the squadron far off on the horizon. "Give it to them, Yanks!" Robi exclaimed. "Give it to them," I murmured to myself.

* * * * *

They gave it to them, but in the process, they gave it to five young kids between eight and twelve, who were playing on a sidewalk in Celldomolk, rolling marbles. Their heads had been blown off by one of the concussion bombs. Their death became a fascists' propaganda tool. "What about those innocent kids?" Robi asked, seeing my ambiguity about it.

"It doesn't help to dwell on it," I said. "They just happened to be in the wrong place at the wrong time. Chance encounters. For one with the love of his life, for another with a bomb."

The days passed. We got straw for our bedding. We figured out that sliding the timber down to a lower point in the forest and cutting it to size there saved a lot of labor and transportation time. A week passed quickly, and our first official work orders ran out. But we had a greater concern: too many fascists had learned about our existence, and either came to steal our product or, if they passed accidentally, were amazed that there were still Jews left in this small area of western Hungary.

Once or twice, the head of a fascist unit asked for our papers, and Corporal Rac explained to him that we had overstayed our permit by a few days in order to finish the job. Rac was told to get on with it and to get rid of those Jews. Almost two weeks into our stay, what had been an unoccupied area was crowded with people roaming around. Small and large units, evacuated civilians, and locals all searched for food. There was no more to be requisitioned from the farmers or local people. People were hoarding everything they could lay their hands on, and cutting wood for themselves in the surrounding forest.

Our situation was becoming perilous. We had a meeting with Rac to try and figure out what to do. We agreed that he would return to headquarters and we would start to use the blank permits. We set up a location where we could meet with him at night, but during the daytime we would move from one place to another, so we would be less likely to meet marauders. For the next three weeks, we moved to increasingly inaccessible places in the mountains, but it became more and more difficult to avoid contact with troops, which now included German soldiers. One day, we suddenly found ourselves face to face with an Arrow-Cross unit of some fifty men, armed to the teeth.

"Where is your guard?" the lieutenant yelled, addressing nobody in particular. I presented myself as the octato (they were familiar with the KMSZ system), and explained that our guard had temporarily returned to headquarters, and that until he came back I was in charge. "And where is your permit?" he asked cynically. I flashed the first phony permit. "I don't want to see any Jews without guards, damn it! You bastard spies, you're probably the ones who directed the American bombing of Celldomolk. Did you?"

"No, sir! We have been cutting wood here for the army under guard for the last two weeks. We don't know what's going on outside."

"I don't want to meet you again without a guard or I will take care of you," he yelled.

"Yes, sir, but it's not our decision ..."

"Shut up! You heard what I said!"

We were scared to death. They left, but our fears remained. We brainstormed within the inner council. "There's not too much choice," I said. "Tomorrow we'll go a few kilometers further, perhaps over the crest to the other side of this mountain. Maybe we'll be able to see better and avoid any troops moving around us."

The next day, we went over the mountain, and what we saw was frightening. Troops of all sizes were marching into the valley, pushing frightened refugees off the road, pillaging everything from the small farm houses around the road.

I gathered our group. "Listen, fellas, I think it's better not to make any noise here by cutting timber. I suggest we remain as inconspicuous as possible; let's just duck. Let's disperse in groups of six around the area. Be on the look-out for danger. If any group sees some unavoidable trouble, chop at the trees; three ax hits, three counts of pause, three ax hits, three pauses. If your group gets caught, acknowledge that there are other groups cutting trees according to our orders, but you don't know exactly where. You were assigned to that spot. Everybody agrees?"

"Ya, ya, ya."

"Good. Then, then at 4:00 P.M. every day after it has started to get dark, we'll return to this camp by groups."

Corporal Rac came to our camp that night on the cart which shuttled to headquarters with the wood. He brought very bad news. We gathered around the open fireplace in the shack. "I don't know how to say this," he stated, "but you have to come back to headquarters tomorrow. The lumbering assignment is finished. Koranyi, Miklos and other officers were ordered to Szombathely by the fascist military authorities. They were threatened with court-martial unless you were immediately deported to a German camp."

The silence of the surrounding forest on that late December night was unbelievably noisy compared to our silence. The sound of the slight wind cracked the weakest tree branches, and whistled through the shack's crevices and openings sounding like thunder. An occasional boar rushed through the bushes, some rodents worked the snow to find some sustenance underneath, and the forest's other inhabitants went about their business.

We sat without saying a word for what seemed like hours. "So that's it!" Robi broke the silence. Some remained silent; some had tears in their eyes.

"Where are the Russians?" I asked in almost a whisper.

"Not too far," Rac said. "They may save you. They may save us. Koranyi surely will gain a few days for organizing, preparing, and the like, before giving the order."

"What's the true situation on the fronts now?" I asked Miki and Bela. "Has your miraculous source of information dried up?"

"Not quite, but it's more difficult to be sure. My source stayed in Celldomolk," Miki said. "Corporal, can you help?"

"Both the Russians and the Western Allies have been proceeding spectacularly since October. The Russians under Malinovsky were headed toward Szeged and Budapest, seeking to conquer southwest Hungary. As you know, Horthy was arrested in mid-October because he had tried to get Hungary out of the war, even though he rescinded his orders the next day on the radio."

By the end of October, the 2nd Ukrainian Army and a few Rumanian battalions had crossed the Tissa River and occupied Kecskemet after heavy street fighting. In early November, they occupied Cegled and Szolnok too, but the Germans and Hungarians put up great resistance everywhere. After three weeks of bitter fighting, the Russians occupied Csap, the very important rail center near Budapest. At the end of November, Pecs and Mohacs had also been overrun in the south with the aid of Yugoslav partisans. But the Germans stubbornly defended the rest of southern Hungary and held up the Russian advance for months.

In northern Hungary, the 2nd Ukraine Army conquered my home town, Eger, on November 30th. Then Miskolc, an important industrial city a few miles from Eger, also fell. The 3rd Ukraine Army, which had crossed the Danube on the south, was now heading north. It reached Lake Balaton, leaving little of the country still controlled by the Axis. Soon after, a major concentration of Russian troops formed east and west of Budapest, and the Germans' intent to defend the city to the end became evident.

The Germans brought up reinforcements from Italy and the western front. To lose Budapest, the pillar of the German south front, would force Hitler's generals to retrench throughout their western and southern fronts. By mid-December, Budapest was almost completely surrounded. The government, which had withdrawn to Sopron, ordered Budapest's Jewish ghetto closed. Some 70,000 people inside were forced to abide by even more severe restrictions and curfews than they had previously known. Some western countries, including Sweden, Switzerland, Spain, Portugal and El Salvador—even the International Red Cross—tried to come to the aid of individual Jews, with "protective" letters. A nice gesture, but too little, too late.

Guderian, the German commander on the Hungarian front, ordered the destruction of all industry, transportation, communication equipment, and the means for supplying water throughout the city. Deserters and university students who did not respond to the draft were hanged. They executed the writer, Bajcsi Zsilinszky Endre, one of the politicians from the old nobility who had tried to organize a resistance. The Commnunist Party organized in Szeged and other reoccupied areas. They also made room for other parties, and the Kisgazda Party (small landowners party), with Balog Istvan as its president, became influential. On December 22nd, a temporary government headed by Dalnoki Miklos Bela was created. On December 29th, Budapest was completely encircled, and the Russians broadcast an ultimatum to surrender. This was followed by the sending of delegates under a white flag, who delivered the written ultimatum. On their way back to the Russian lines, the delegates were murdered.

Retribution was swift. The Russians advanced mercilessly. Tens of thousands of Germans and Hungarian fascists who defended the hills of Buda were murdered. Heavy fighting erupted in the city, in the streets and in the houses. Escaped witnesses told of seeing Russians in the basements of homes, setting up their telephone wires, while Germans were on the upper floors, still shooting across the street. On the 31st, Dalnoki's provisory government of Hungary finally declared war on Germany.

All this was encouraging, but we still could not make contact with the advancing Russians. Although for the last two to three months all the fronts had been moving forward, we were only a couple of days away from the dreadful prospect of being handed over to the Germans.

We heard about Rommel's suicide, the successes of Yugoslav partisans and Roosevelt's re-election, and that for the first time the U.S. super-fortress B-29s were bombing Tokyo. Generally, we knew less about the battles of the Pacific, just some names and places. We heard about the fighting for Formosa, where hundreds of airplanes and warships were lost by both the Japanese and the Allies. We also heard reports of MacArthur in the Philippines.

A treaty of alliance was signed between France and Russia in December, although its meaning was rather difficult for us to understand, since they were Allies. That was the good news. The bad news was that Germany organized a heavy counter-attack in the Ardennes. General McAuliffe was asked by the Germans to surrender around Bastogne, and his famous message to them was "Nuts!" Eventually, the German advance was overcome at the Battle of the Bulge. Our last news from Hungary was that Malinovsky was five miles from Budapest and that the Russians had occupied Miskolc. The Russians were advancing to the Czechoslovakian border on a wide front. Many refugees were talking of extraordinary violence occurring between the Danube and Lake Balaton.

* * * * *

"It's late fellas. We have to break camp tomorrow and get back to school. Maybe we'll hear some better news."

It was one o'clock in the morning when we lay down on our straw cots to try to sleep. Only Lajos stayed awake, to feed the fire and try to keep the bitter cold at bay. By the erie light of the open fire, in a half dream, I thought I saw Lajos go up in flames, and conjured up frightful images of the Inquisition, of gas chambers, and the mass executions of our loved ones.

It was nine in the morning when we started down the hill. We marched more or less in formation, two or three across on the narrow paths, with hardly a word spoken all morning. With heads hanging, our sad caravan of fifty men, four horses, two wagons, camp equipment and the last firewood, inched slowly toward Celldomolk. Behind us we left our "cherished home" and "freedom", a snowy, cold but splendid isolation.

We stopped to rest before entering the town. To go through town in this terrible mood and appearance would give too much satisfaction to the surrounding fascists and anti-Semites. That they would see beaten, frightened Jews revolted and frightened me. I knew in my gut and from experience that such scum of humanity did not respect weakness, and certainly did not root for the underdog. Their strength would lie in our weakness, if we let them see it.

I stood up on a large rock. "Attention!" I yelled. Everyone, including Rac, looked around to see if anybody was approaching. "There's nobody around, but listen to me.. We can't go back in this state of despair for all of them to see. We can't give up hope either. I know everyone thinks we lost another opportunity to escape, but where can we escape to among this hostile population? Let's organize into military order, three across, heads up and we'll sing as we march. Yes, sing! Okay, everybody?"

"Yeah, yeah, I guess you're right," was the unenthusiastic answer.

"Okay, then. Corporal, we can go!"

We entered the town marching and singing "Ritka arpa ..., Ritka rozs Ritka ..." The town was much more crowded than when we left, a chaos of milling humanity. We appeared to be the only organized, orderly group. Koranyi and a few officers sympathetic to us stood at the big arched door of the school. We stopped and lined up in front of him in the courtyard. Koranyi thanked us for providing the wood, then he continued, "Return to your quarters immediately and be ready for a long march in the next few days. Do not leave your quarters unless you are ordered to. Dismissed!"

He called Joska, Bela, Janos, Miki and me into his office, where Dr. Miklos and Lieutenant Toth were sitting on either side of his table. Koranyi was drawing on his cigarette, but deeper than usual, the smoke burning his squinting eyes.

"Corporal Rac has probably told you, there's nothing more I can do for you. All the fascists in Szombathely, as well as those here, know about you. You're probably the last KMSZ unit left on this piece of Hungarian territory. I have irrevocable orders to deport you for further work assignment to a German labor camp across the Austrian border. I'll provide you with all the food you can carry. Repair all your clothing and boots. I'm sorry; I failed. We all failed. Lieutenant Toth will command you with Corporal Rac. Dismissed!"

After a long silence, with choking voice, I squeezed out "No, sir, you didn't fail. We thank you from our hearts."

After the shack in the snowy hills, our accommodations in the school rooms seemed luxurious. "Let's enjoy it while it lasts," Robi said, throwing himself on top of his cot. The rest of us lay down slowly, deep in our thoughts and worries.

A little later, a few of us gathered around Robi's cot. "Is there anything else we can do?" Lajos asked.

"Just stick together as long as possible and be of support to each other."

"I understand we'll have a long march to our destination," said Barabas. "Who knows to where? What will happen to the weak guys like Moricka, or Shmuel and the others?" Silence. I stole a glance at Moricka in his corner. He was staring at the ceiling with frozen eyes, expressionless.

"Look," I said, "our preparation won't take too much time. With our few possessions we can be ready to march in a half-hour. Everybody should make sure to have some empty bags to stock with food. Koranyi will surely provide us with as much as we can carry. For my part, if I carry any extra weight, it will be food. We can do no more. Let's try to sleep."

I tried, but in my mind I kept rearranging the contents of my rucksack over and over. Finally, I decided: one change of underwear, a blanket, eating ustensils and canteen, the small cardboard box which I had put in my rucksack in Budapest before leaving for Galanta, a few pencils and my sketchbook. The sketchbook! I got up slowly from my cot. It was almost midnight, and carefully, without disturbing the others, I visited the toilet. There, in the light of a fifteen watt bulb, I started to sketch furiously in small mosaics the events of the last few weeks and months. It was like writing a testatment: cutting timber in the snowy landscape, comrades sleeping like sardines in the shack, fearful confrontations with fascist thugs, Koranyi with his cigarette butt and oversized nose, the old peasant confronting our guard in the front of his wagon.

Eventually, I fell asleep on the toilet (a luxurious place compared with the frozen latrine in the hills), only to be awakened by the urgent banging of the next customer.

Writing, sketching my testament. To whom? I did not know the whereabouts of anybody, family or friends, other than these companions of destiny around me. Maybe one would survive; maybe I would survive. That's right, why not? I would survive anything except a direct bullet in the head. I wanted to survive. I wanted to see the end. I wanted to show those sketches to my children. Perhaps an unreasonable dream, but why not dream?

* * * * *

It was a freezing late December morning. We finished our breakfast of bread, marmalade and ersatz coffee. We lined up in the courtyard at the order of Lieutenant Toth and Corporal Rac. With our belongings packed, two wagons loaded with food for our journey, horses bridled, we awaited our camp commandant.

Our guards, including many with whom we had spent almost two- and-a-half years, seemed not to know what to do. Some came up to shake hands; others just looked on, leaning against the walls. Few were talking. One of the Arrow-Cross on the second floor, obviously unaware of what was going on, yelled out the window, "Hey, Jews, send me three up here!"

Sergeant Bereckei, one of the worst fascists among our guards, yelled back at him, "Shut up, damn it, and get lost!" Then he turned to me, "The bastards." It was not a bad performance from Sergeant Bereckei. Could it be possible that this mindless brute felt something important was happening here? Was it possible that he might have been saying to himself, "I tortured you and don't like the Jews, but I didn't mean to kill you?"

About 9:0O A.M., Koranyi appeared with Doctor Miklos and the rest of his staff, halting their march some fifteen yards in front of our column. "Sir Commandant, Lieutenant Toth reports the XI KMSZ brigade, fifty-five men, two wagons, none in sick bay, ready for your order!"

"There are many kinds of heroes in a war," Koranyi said. "You did an excellent job and you are a credit to Hungary. Good luck to all of you. Lieutenant! Proceed."

Toth yelled toward me, "Octato Tibor, march!"

"Attention! Eyes left! Parade march! Go! Sing! One-two-three-four; One-two-three-four. Ritka arpa, Ritka rozsa." The brass saluted, except for Koranyi, who gave a small wave. His eyes were lowered. He looked defeated with his head hanging on his chest, ready to turn back and disappear within his office.

One hundred meters outside the courtyard, we passed the arched portal of the Celldomolk school. We stopped singing, but continued to march to a military cadence. We headed west. Even our Corporal did not know our final destination, except that the first stop was Repcelek, a small village near the Austrian border, approximately forty kilometers away.

We slowed our pace to enable everyone to keep up. There was no rush but still Moricka and two others could not. They were permitted to get on the wagons, which were driven by two civilians from nearby Svab villages, not sympathetic to us at all. Speaking Hungarian with their typical German dialect, they made constant unpleasant remarks until Rac put them in their place.

What irony! I and most of the rest of the unit came from families who had been Hungarian for generations. We spoke with a juicy Paloc accent (of Central Hungary, in my case), and mostly in the Budapest vernacular, having been raised and educated like other Hungarians. We did not speak any other language, except for the two or three who spoke Yiddish. We who were filled with the literature and irredentism of our country, now had to hear abuse from this Svab minority with their distorted Hungarian and centuries of German sympathy and identification.

We reached the small village in twilight. After a steep climb, we arrived at Repcelek. Its narrow street, with little houses perched on two facing hills no more than thirty meters apart, had the appearance of a small gorge.

Light snow covered the street, and the roofs reflected a reddish sky disappearing beyond the hills. The village people were busily preparing for Christmas, carrying small pine trees or attaching garlands to the fronts of their houses. They were not disturbed by our arrival; obviously, they had seen other groups pass through. We stopped at what looked like the village square, and a short, heavy man with a big belly and big curling mustache came out of one of the houses. He proudly wore a swastika on his left arm. He talked with Lieutenant Toth a few minutes, giving him directions, if not orders. We continued another half kilometer to a large grange which had been prepared to receive us. There was straw on the floor as well as on a second level platform. We walked in like automatons, without much noise, ready to occupy our designated space. When we were all inside, Toth and Rac announced that they did not know how long we would be here, maybe three days. We ate an excellent supper, thanks to Koranyi: lentil soup, salami, lard with paprika, potato, good bread and the ersatz coffee.

Surprisingly, we were permitted to go about in the village more or less freely. The numerous German or local officials, all with swastika armbands, paid little attention to our yellow ones. We went about in groups of four or five and engaged in conversation with the local folk. Not all were Svabs, nor actively fascist, and many were afraid of the approaching front and the consequences of the now obvious defeat of the Germans. A kind of Christmas spirit prevailed. The villagers, mostly women whose husbands and sons had long ago been drafted, were trying to prepare holiday meals with the meager, rationed food and fuel. Some of us were even invited inside for a glass of wine.

As I was heading down the village's main street with Joska, Barabas, Janos and Bela, we suddenly heard tremendous sharp shrieking. It came from protesting young pigs being castrated by a middle-aged woman in her back yard. As we looked over the fence, we saw four little animals hanging by their hind legs, roped to butcher's hooks. One woman held them steady while the other, with a sharp, large kitchen knife, most casually cut away the pighood of each poor little animal. For us city boys it was horrible to see. We almost instinctively reached to protect our own testicles. "Hey, fellas, do you want to give us a hand?"

"No, thank you," we yelled back as we sped away.

* * * * *

Bandi, a good-looking, good-natured man, a team player who would regularly volunteer for my show punishments, was basically a loner. He was friendly with everybody, but he had no particular friend, although he had had his share of success with village girls in Rimaszombat and Hangony. As we were walking through the village two days after our arrival, he came out of one of the houses and joined us on the street.

"I was invited to this house for the third time now, and tomorrow the woman of the house will need help," he said.

"Is she pretty?" we asked.

"Not bad."

"What does she want help with?"

"She has an old cow and she'd like to slaughter it. There's no butcher in town and she wouldn't like the slaughter to become public knowledge. She'll give meat to whoever helps."

"So help her," we laughed.

"No, seriously, you know what I mean. Dezso, our cook, is a butcher. He can do it, but I need three more guys to hold it steady."

"It's all right with me. Talk to Dezso," I said.

Not knowing what butchering a cow requires, we volunteered. We were curious and dared each other into it.

The next day, the day before Christmas, we were ready. We went into the house and the pretty young woman gave us wine to boost our courage. Dezso walked the beast from the stable to the middle of the court, attached a strong rope to each of the animal's horns, and then called for us.

It was a much more violent scene than we had expected. Slaughtering the cow was so gruesome it almost made me a lifetime vegetarian. I would have run off and vomited, if not for the fear of embarrassment in front of the woman and my friends, although they didn't look too happy either.

"You want to eat? You have to do it," Dezso kept us in line. "Grab the ropes, two of you on one side, two on the other. Keep it steady." Then he took the ax which the woman had placed at the corner of the house, put on a big apron, and faced the cow. "All right," he yelled, "hold it steady!" With a big swing, he hit the cow between its horns with the flat end of the ax. The beast fell on its knees, then turned on its side.

"Good job, Dezso," the woman complimented. "Be fast now."

Dezso took a big butcher knife, cut the throat of the animal and bled it to death. That was the end of our endurance. We dropped the ropes and left the rest of the job to Dezso, Bandi and the woman. But the meat was delicious, and Rac couldn't believe the source of the terrific goulash which Dezso prepared for dinner.

Two days after Christmas, curfew was declared for our group. Nobody could leave the grange, including Toth and Rac. The day passed in torturous agony. We talked openly about escaping, even with our guard, but there was nowhere to go. In this part of the country, there was no organization or support for anti-government activity. We continued to dream that the Russians would make a sudden breakthrough in our direction, but that was all it was, dreaming.

Our orders finally came. We were to leave the morning of December 29th. After consulting with our council and our officers, I told the entire group that the best thing to do would be to maintain a strict military attitude; march in order, head up, chin down, salute properly, and create the impression of a well-trained, military unit, not a beaten, desperate mob. There was no dissent.

We were desperate for accurate news about the western front and the progress of the Russians. We hung our hopes on their irresistible progress and listened to every rumor. These, so far, had been pretty accurate, due to the efforts of Bela, a few sympathetic officers and the mysterious sources of Miki.

"Any last minute news?" I asked.

"Nope, and not for a while," he said seriously.

"How did you get all those accurate reports all this time?"

"I never told this to anybody, but now I need your help and need you to share responsibility. So here it is. These are parts of the radio set I've been carrying and hiding since Hangony. You remember when I had a leave to organize the electric company and the movie for the town? I got these parts in Budapest at the same time. Now you know why I selectect special corners for my beddings, near an outlet or at least an electric wire."

"You're amazing!" I exclaimed.

"Help me carry these parts and don't let anyone else know. They may be useless where we go, but who knows? Anyway, we will have no news for a while other than rumors."

"It's too bad," I said. "It's important."

Just four kilometers separated heaven from hell. Heaven was a very relative term signifying the place where our little group had had the extraordinary luck to meet Koranyi, the one man in a million who proved beyond any doubt that an individual can make a difference. A few more of those men could have saved thousands of lives. Only four kilometers. Three on the Hungarian side of the border, one on the Austrian side. As we passed the snowy hills and a few hamlets, we were promenading more than marching. We kept talking with Toth and Rac: about the war situation, about the centuries-old suffering of the Jews at the hands of Christians, about the age-old question of how a Jew can be as good a Hungarian as a non-Jew.

The two men were understanding and sympathetic to our cause for very different reasons. Rac, a communist, had the idealistic and simplistic view of the equality of all human beings. He saw conflict only in terms of class struggle. Toth was a patriot. He hated the Germans, the Austrians, and all who had tried to enslave the Hungarian nation throughout history, including Slavs, Turks and, most recently, the Austro-Hungarian monarchy. Unlike many of his peers, Toth recognized Jewish contributions to the artistic, literary, scientific, political and economic life of Hungary, and found us preferable to the invaders.

Knowing their sympathies, Koranyi had chosen Rac and Toth as our guards for our last journey. Of course, at that moment, our primary concern was to learn where we were going and what they knew about our destination.

We were heading to Csajta, its Hungarian name; the Germans and Swabs call it Schattendorf. Nobody, including Toth and Rac, had heard it before. "I understand," Toth said, "it's a very small village, but our true destination is just outside it; a large farm with a number of buildings, granges, stables, milk houses and the like. The official request to our headquarters was for laborers to dig anti-tank trenches on the Hungarian-Austrian border.

"Do you know anything about the conditions there?"

"Not too much. It's the first time for us too. I understand they don't let any of the accompanying guards past their checkpoint."

It was not good news.

We passed the border, marked only by a broken wooden pole, in perfect military march formation. We passed a Hungarian Arrow-Cross guard, who motioned Toth forward without stopping our group. He pointed toward a three-story yellow building about a half-kilometer away on the straight macadam road. We kept marching in perfect order, our hearts beating faster than our march cadence.

We kept talking to each other to try to relieve our anxiety. I led the unit, but I would drop back to speak to Joska, Bela, or Robi in the first row, then return to the front. Toth marched at the column's side; Rac marched at the rear. When we were no more than 100 yards from the yellow building, Toth picked up the rhythm of our marching steps, pulled ahead of me and, as he passed by, said, "Tibor, I will order you to stop, and you will execute the order by ordering the troops."

"Yes, sir." I was so afraid, I could hardly breathe, but I blocked everything else out of my mind and acted automatically, like a well-oiled machine, just as if we were on a drill field of one of the caserns somewhere in Hungary.

Fifty yards from the building, Toth yelled his order: "Sing!" I thought I'd faint. Was he crazy, or mad, or a fake who was just playing with us?

"Sir?" I yelled toward him in a muted voice. "Sing? Now?"

"Sing!" he answered with a gesture to calm me.

"Ritka, arpa, ritka, rozsa ..." we complied. All the windows of the buildings filled with German soldiers staring in disbelief. Many came outside, obviously wondering what was going on. Arriving at the main entrance, Toth yelled "Octato! Cut the song and stop!"

I knew what he had done, and I yelled as loudly as I could, "Brigade! Cut the song! One-two-three-four. Stop! Left turn! Lieutenant Toth, sir, XI KMSZ Brigade ready for your orders!"

"At ease," He commanded.

The lieutenant went inside the building and Rac took his place at the head of the line. The milling Germans and those in the windows were decidedly disconcerted. Their puzzlement was written on their faces: What kind of Jews are these? They're Jews all right; they have the yellow armband, but they're well-dressed, well-fed, many have Burgerli boots (a very fashionable military footwear), and they move with strict military manner.

Since we first arrived at Celldomolk, I had constantly practiced high school German in my mind. I had been required to study the language for eight years, although I never liked it and far preferred French, which was also required for eight years. But Doctor Czunya, professor of German, beat into us with military discipline every word and every damn grammatical rule of the perfect, the pluperfect and all the irregular verbs. We translated German literature and memorized poems of Goethe, Heine and Schiller. We did everything but speak. (The same was true for French, but I loved everything French). There were two snobbish ways to differentiate oneself in Hungary: in the business world, you peppered the language with German, and in the literary and art world with French. Now I wished I had studied German as diligently as I had French, for I feared these Germans. I kept repeating in my mind the way to report to superiors in German. In this I was helped by Toth, Shmuel, another comrade, Deutsch, and a few others who spoke some German. We also heard plenty of German around us during the last few weeks at Celldomolk.

Toth reappeared with the German officer. They approached us with long cadenced paces, in step with each other. Rac commanded, "Attention!" Toth saluted. Surprisingly, the German officer did too. Conditioned reflex I thought.

Toth spoke, "The XI KMSZ has done an excellent job to help the Hungarian army, and I commend you to the attention of the camp commandant." I tried to look at Joska out of the corner of my eye. Was he thinking what I was? The last thing we needed was to be singled out, notwithstanding Toth's good faith. "Thank you for your loyalty and, in my own and our commandant's names, good luck."

He shook my hand. Rac did too. I stepped forward and yelled, "Attention, heads left!" They passed us as if reviewing a parade. Slowly, they disappeared on the road back to Hungary, and with them the XIth KMSZ disappeared from our lives forever. We stood abandoned and terribly alone.

IN THE GERMAN CAMP

The German officer disappeared into the building. We stood at attention, waiting. Soon, two lesser grade officers, "gauleiters," took command. "You!" one pointed to me. "Naar links," to the left. "You!" pointing to Joska, "Naar rechts," to the right. Another was to go to a third group. We had come so far together, and now they were going to separate us. Joska and the others gestured to me to talk. Bela joined my group and immediately poked me in the ribs, "Talk!"

Suddenly, I don't know why, I stepped forward. I don't know how I had the courage. Maybe it was fear of losing the support we had given each other over the years. Maybe my emotion was stronger than my judgement. I saluted and, in my broken German, but in a strong voice, I said, "Herr Gauleiter! We have been together since 1942. We would like to stay together, and this unit volunteers for the most difficult job." Everyone was astounded. Even the Germans milling around the building and watching from the windows stopped in surprise. Obviously, never in their experience had a Jew or a group of Jews dared to ask them any favor or to address them this way. After a few seconds of hesitation, the gauleiter spread his legs apart, nested his two fisted hands on his hips, pushing his open overcoat behind, and broke out in a tremendous belly laugh. The others echoed him. After they had amused themselves a minute or two, making remarks to each other which I could not understand, he suddenly turned around, planted himself two feet in front of me, and thundered in my face a series of "Arsch loch, schweine hund," and other insanities for at least a minute. I thought he would kill me on the spot.

Suddenly, the German commandant reappeared in the building's entrance with three other officers. They were on their way to another part of the camp. As they passed us, he asked the gauleiter what was going on and what all the laughter was about. Still amused, but at attention, the gauleiter reported what I had asked.

"Was is das?" the Commandant thundered. Since he looked as if he was waiting for an answer, I repeated our request. To our surprise, he casually ordered the gauleiter, "Put them in Building B together, and have them report to the salting operation in the morning." Then he continued on his way with the other officers.

"Jawhohl!" our somewhat surprised officer responded. He turned toward us with a malevolent smile, "Follow me," he said. Although it was not issued as a military command, I ordered the unit to attention. "Right turn! March!" He looked back with disbelief and shook his head.

The sky was steel grey. Snow flurries fell from low clouds off and on throughout this moderately cold January day. We followed him, continuing down the same road we had arrived on. We had hardly marched two hundred meters when we spotted people in trenches on both sides of the road, as far as we could see. Probably inspired by our singing when we arrived an hour earlier, the gauleiter yelled to me with obvious mockery, "Sie mussen singen." We had to sing.

As we approached the first trenches, each man stopped working. Even the guards stopped yelling at them. Emaciated faces perched atop skeletal bodies. They shivered in the cold and, looking half-dead, they raised their tired heads to the edges of the trenches and stared at us with a curious indifference. Farther down the road, a group of some thirty others were dragging themselves toward another row of trenches. They were dressed in rags, held together with ropes. Old newspapers and straw poked out of the edges and holes in their shoes. Fingerless gloves displayed frozen knuckles and bleeding fingers. Many had blankets covering their heads, the corners tied behind their backs. They struggled with shovels, picks or axes carried on their shoulders, or dragged the tools behind them, making dreadful noises as the metal screeched and bumped against the rocks and frozen ground. With every step, their German guards hit them with long whips with fringed tips, used by Hungarian shepherds to round up sheep and prompt them forward. They made a harsh, cracking sound. Swearing angrily, the guards completed the scene of this funeral march.

As we passed, they disappeared one by one into the second line of trenches. Men appeared and disappeared in the trenches like apparitions. Some of them waved toward us with infinitely sad expressions. Others just nodded their heads, as if saying, "poor, miserable newcomers; their song won't last long."

And so it didn't. Not then, anyway. As we finished the "Az egri menes mind szurke," a marching folk song from Eger, the German did not prompt for more. The silence made our marching steps and the noises of picks and axes coming from the trenches sound louder in the otherwise quiet landscape. Like grave diggers, they labored in the anti-tank trenches which were supposed to stop or at least slow down the Russians, who were obviously not far away. My heart beat in my throat when I saw the worried faces of my comrades, as the reality of our situation, the same destiny of hundreds of thousands of fellow forced laborers all over Europe, sank into our consciousness.

We turned left off the macadam onto a dirt road, still marching in military cadence. Half a kilometer farther, we arrived at a large, open space surrounded by barracks, agricultural sheds, some of them two stories high. I noticed no numbers or letters as I looked for our assigned Building B. There were neither fences nor barbed wire. The square was empty, except for a few German guards at the entrances to the buildings.

In spite of the crisp, January air, and light snow covering the ground and hills, a puff of wind carried an awful smell to our nostrils. The gauleiter told me to halt. Almost by reflex, I ordered, "Attention! One, two, three, stop! At ease!" The gauleiter shook his head again, but this time I wasn't sure if it was done in mockery or with some sort of approval. He told us to wait there for further orders and disappeared into one of the buildings on our left. We waited about a half hour, with the cold penetrating our skin. The shy sun had disappeared behind the clouds and hills, darkening the sky of the short January day. Joska and Robi pointed back to the trenches we had just passed. Groups of people, from a few dozen to a few hundred, began to converge on the square. Tired, miserable men, frozen in body and soul, they did not even react to the brutal beatings of their guards, who hit them with sticks or gun butts, even kicked them for no apparent reason. As they came closer, we saw a number of them stumble and collapse. Sometimes their comrades supported or carried them; others were abandoned in the snow. Their crying, complaining, protesting voices were carried by the wind over the valleys and the camp's square for nobody to hear. We found ourselves standing in a kind of theatre of the absurd. It felt as if we were in the orchestra pit of a Wagnerian opera, observing a drama of gigantic proportions of men's bestiality to men.

Were we observers or participants? Neither, yet. We were just about to enter the scene. Men kept coming from all over the camp, thousands now converging on the square. Many had already lined up, having been beaten into orderly columns of three. They stamped on the ground to keep their tired blood circulating against the cold. Some stopped beating the ground with their feet and fell, hitting the ground with the entire length of their bodies, grasping the packed dirt with frozen fingers, never to release it again.

Within minutes, a group of people with Red Cross armbands over their yellow ones would appear from one of the smaller buildings and take away three or four bodies on a makeshift stretcher. Human beings were carried away, and hardly anybody turned around, shed a tear, or said a Kaddish for their departed souls. But as I turned around, I saw Shmuel swinging himself back and forth in short rhythmic movements. He prayed, perhaps saying the Kaddish. But how many more would he have to say?

From the doors of another small building, groups of four appeared, carrying heavy kettles. One kettle was set at the front of each column. The kettles had hardly touched the ground when the groups broke ranks and, like wild animals, ferociously attacked them, ripping off the covers, the way jaguars rip open their prey. The weaker ones were pushed away. It was every man for himself, in a chaotic melee to reach a kettle and dip a tin eating-can, up to the elbow, into the warm liquid. Those at the kettle completely disregarded the blows to their skeletal bodies from their guards' whips and gun butts; even warning shots didn't matter to them. Within minutes, the kettles were emptied. Many had never even reached them, and just walked away in infinite sadness, on staggering, rubbery legs, toward their barracks.

Joska pointed out to me a man who had a ripped blanket on his back. He never made it to his barrack door. He had just taken another weak step when his legs collapsed under him. He just lay down. We saw the vapor of his fast breath in the cold; then nothing more. He didn't move. His comrades passed. Some stopped to look at him, one took his blanket, and another gave a half-hearted wave toward the "medical" building.

We stood there in bewilderment, repeating to each other: Is this possible? Will this be our destiny? Will we end up like this, like wild beasts devouring each other, never letting Moricka reach the kettle, making a horrible spectable of ourselves for the amusement of the vicious guards? Can't we do any better?

Who could answer or would dare to? Perhaps these wretched people whom we almost despised for their unbelievable behavior were not different from us just a short while ago. "Don't judge," I told myself. "Remember Budapest, the days without food, the mental torture of the charity received in the Cafe Victoria, and the warning of Coach Frederik: You must survive first. Everything else comes after." But at what price? Here that question would be answered.

It was almost dark, and we, too, felt hungry. Many had started to nibble surrepticiously on food from our pockets or knapsacks. The crowd in the square dispersed and our gauleiter reappeared with three other guards. "Open your bags and empty your pockets," ordered one of them in German, but with an unmistakable foreign accent (I guessed him to be Horvath or Slovak). I repeated the order in Hungarian. When the guard saw and smelled the terrific Hungarian kielbasi, lard and paprika that began to appear, he broke out in a sinister laugh. "A kurva zsidok," he swore at us in a broken Hungarian. "Look what they stole from the Hungarian people. No wonder they're so fat. But we will take care of you. Don't you worry about it. Take all this," he ordered the other guard in German, "and give it to the fighting men."

After having been relieved of our most precious cargo, we were ordered to follow him to the two-storey grange. He motioned us to a space of about sixteen square meters between wooden pillars made of four-by-fours. On the floor and in the loft above were two other groups of prisoners. These would be our quarters.

A long, narrow, broken table stood in the corridor in front of our quarters. At the guard's order, a prisoner came forward.

"Fetch their ration for tonight," he ordered.

Within a few minutes, the prisoner returned with a small canvas bag. The gauleiter grabbed it and banged it on the table. "Here are your rations. You line up tomorrow morning at seven in front of the entrance. Is that clear?" He turned and left us.

After a long day, we were alone. Alone, that is, save for the company of hundreds of prisoners who, immediately after the gauleiter's departure, surrounded us. They assailed every man in the unit with questions, begged for clothes, or offered cigarettes in exchange for our rations, to the point where we felt under siege.

We beat back their attack, and regrouped to sort out our thoughts. I opened the canvas bag and, to the dismay of all, found four loaves of pitch dark bread made of who knew what, and two rolls of "salami," about which we knew less. There was bitter chicory awaiting us in the kitchen. After looking in consternation at our ration for a few minutes, Robi said with a laugh: "So divide it, Tibor. Better you than me."

I was able to provide a three-quarter-inch thick slice of bread for each man, but even by cutting the thinnest possible slices, there wasn't a whole slice of salami per person. "Don't worry," said Robi, "I saved a few sausages." So had I. Surprisingly, most of us had risked punishment by keeping some of our send-off feast. Thus, we were able to supplement our ration that first night.

* * * * *

For a while, the population of the barracks buzzed with activity; the miserable prisoners offering, negotiating, bargaining; trading cigarettes for food or clothing, gold or silver rings for cigarettes, coins for rags. Unbelievably, in spite of all searches, gold jewelry and gold, and French or Austrian coins were available. One could trade three coins for a double ration of bread or ersatz sausage.

One man approached us with real food: a good-looking ham, potatoes, sugar in small cubes, plain fat in little jars. He offered us an echange for gold, good boots or other clothing, but we refused. We were not hungry enough yet.

"Where did you get that stuff?"

He smiled mysteriously, "That's my business."

"He pays off the guards," another interjected, somewhat angrily. "He gives them too much. He ruins the market."

"Did the guards give this to you?"

"No, no, you'll see. It's complicated. When you're hungry, come see me first," he said, and disappeared into the darkness of his cubbyhole, some fifty feet away on the second floor.

As the tired buzzing gradually quieted down, the moaning, sobbing and crying of the sick and dying rose. Some called for help, some for food, others called for their mothers or wives with desperation, but to no avail.

In spite of the cold, the terrible stench assailed our noses and throats. Our guts heaved, almost to the point of vomiting. Still, we tried our best to settle down in our new home. We gathered around my bed, to put our heads together and see whether there was any way we could improve our situation. None had any idea. Few of us had real hope. "We may not be able to do anything," I said, "but at least we can resist becoming wild animals, and killing each other for another little crumb. I know I won't, and hope that you won't, either. Maintaining our group's discipline can help us to maintain every individual. I suggest we immediately establish a rotating order as to who gets to eat first. Let's promise; no, swear, that nobody will break the order." Everyone agreed, and I volunteered to be the last the following morning. There was a sense that just by making this small decision, somehow, we had taken into our hands at least a little bit of our destiny.

We finally settled down to sleep. Before I drifted off, I thought about Coach Frederik's "survive first." Did I speak a minute ago against that basic premise of his, which had served me well so far? I did, but would he have given that advice if he could have foreseen all this?

Since Budapest, I had carried in my bag the terrycloth swimming robe of III KET TVE, partially as a souvenir, but also because it was comfortable to sleep in. I had slept in it every night since my recruitment. This night, I held on to it as a child holds on to his teddy bear. I wrapped it tighter around me and fell asleep.

The morning came so fast, it seemed I had not slept at all. As soon as I regained consciousness, I felt my legs, groin and back itching. I began scratching myself in a frenzy. As I looked around, I saw everybody doing the same thing. Everybody, that is, except the ones who did not move at all. The "Red Cross" had been busy since early morning carrying away the dead. Four, five, six ... but I stopped counting and turned away almost in self-defense. Most of them had died around 4:00 A.M., I was told, the coldest part of the night, and the lowest point of the body's resistance.

I climbed out of my space and headed to the latrine. More dead. The hand of one man hung in a ditch full of excrement. The stench was unbearable. The latrine consisted of two long ditches, each about seventy-five feet long. On either side, long pieces of wood were held up by cross bars at seat height. One had to be careful, and strong, not to fall into the ditch.

In the main yard, two fork-pitched wells provided water to the animals' drinking trough, which we used for washing and drinking too. At 7:00 A.M., after having learned a new routine of personal hygiene, we lined up in perfect rows behind our kettle. There we collected our ersatz coffee, a piece of bread and a portion of some sort of lard with a tiny piece of meat attached to it, if one was lucky. At 7:30, our gauleiter appeared. "Let's go," he said in German.

"Attention! Left turn! March! Left, right, one, two," I commanded.

He looked at us incredulously. "Are you people crazy?" he seemed to be saying; but at the same time he took up the rhythm of our marching steps. For a while, we went back on the same road we had come in on, and we saw hundreds of prisoners disappear into large ditches, five to ten meters wide and deep, that stretched as far as we could see.

"A system of anti-tank barriers against the Russians," Barabas said mockingly. "I saw thousands working on similar fortifications at the Russian front near the Don. The Russians pushed a few broken down tanks or other vehicles, plus assorted debris, into the ditches, and their tanks rolled over them."

We followed our gauleiter off the main road and onto a small path leading to a pine forest. The pines looked like thousands of Christmas trees decorated with millions of small diamonds, as light snow crystals reflected the rays of the early sun. Ten minutes off the main road, we arrived at a perfectly camouflaged low building about thirty meters long. We followed the guard into this warehouse. The interior was divided under three signs: Ammunition on the left, Food and Supply in the middle, and Salt on the right, piled up to the ceiling in fifty-kilogram jute bags.

"Here's your job. You volunteered for it," he said sarcastically as he pointed to the salt pile. A few minutes later, two trucks arrived, and we were ordered to begin loading. "You!" He pointed to me, "get me six men on each truck. Everyone else get a salt bag, and keep it moving!"

It looked as if he had accepted my octatoship, but I felt a little guilty acting as supervisor and not pitching in with the heavy work. So I went to the back of one truck and helped the weakest ones swing the heavy loads onto the vehicle. Joska, Robi, and Mihaly passed by, struggling with a heavy load. "Keep away," they said, "It's more important that he doesn't take direct and complete command of us."

I continued to help at the truck but, at the same time, I commanded the rhythm and speed of loading.

Carrying salt bags on your shoulders is the worst, nastiest job you can imagine. First, there is the weight itself. Second, salt doesn't conform to the shape of your body the way a grain sack does, so it is difficult to balance. Third, little by little, the salt eats through the jute bag, through the protective empty bag you've thrown over your shoulder and, finally, through your clothes and undershirt, if you have one. It starts to itch, then burn. You feel the salt in your nostrils and throat. You can't keep from coughing. You could drink a gallon of water, but there is only the canteen you filled in the morning. Moricka, Deutsch and two others were unable to carry the bags at all. Before I realized this, the gauleiter was yelling to move faster. He began kicking and hitting the ones who couldn't lift the bags. "Herr Gauleiter, maybe two can carry one bag," I said, without realizing that two would only partially ease the task. But at least I had diverted his attention and gotten them some rest.

By the morning break, all of us were exhausted and hungry. The half hour rest, the small piece of bread with some kind of kasha accentuated our hunger. Some felt light-headed, others complained of stomach pains. Having perspired under the heavy loads, everybody was shivering in the January cold. By the end of the workday, around 3:30, we had loaded four trucks. It may not seem too much for fifty people to have done, but the guards seemed satisfied. I imagine most of the people we had seen could not lift a bag on their own.

How long could we do it? I wondered. Day after day, for almost two weeks, this was our routine. But after a week, we could load only three trucks a day, and soon after only two. The gauleiter yelled a lot, and would hit one or another of us, but he accepted my leadership and our discipline. On three occasions, he even ordered double rations for all of us, a godsend, since by this time every last little piece we had saved from Koranyi's kindness was gone.

The hunger became more and more painful, but the first week was the hardest to endure. At every mealtime, the hunger pangs became increasingly unbearable. We couldn't think or talk about anything else. Some managed better than others. Robi, Shmuel, Miki and I held out best. Others experienced extreme weakness and dizzy spells. But somehow our bodies got used to it and settled down. By the third and fourth week, we knew we were starving, but it was somehow more tolerable. Everybody felt very weak, our movements were slowed, and we lived in a permanent daze, listless and tired. Only some especially shocking event or the vicious barking of the guards somehow made the adrenaline flow for a few minutes.

As we finished the last load one night, our gauleiter announced that we had finished the salt job. The next day we would begin digging in the trenches like the others. So far, we had been unable to figure out from where all this salt was coming, or where it was going, but we surely welcomed the end of our dealings with it. Maybe fresh arrivals would continue the loading until their strength was also depleted.

The next morning, after assisting in the removal of the now more and more numerous dead, and collecting our rations, we followed the hundreds of others toward the rolling hills to dig. We still marched in military order and to a cadence, but we were much slower than before, and even staying in line took great effort.

Our natural tendency was to slow down, sit down, or drag ourselves along like all the others, but we had decided that to give in to fatigue would be the beginning of the end. So we kept going like automatons. It helped because it was our choice.

We were directed to a section of a half-dug trench that curved around a hill, in which our unit disappeared to about shoulder height. I stayed outside, working at the rim, supposedly surveying my men to make sure they kept digging. The relatively few guards for long stretches of the trenches walked quickly or ran back and forth, with machine guns swinging on their shoulders and pistols hanging at their sides, while submachine guns were placed alongside the trenches three to four hundred meters apart.

It took some fifteen minutes to patrol the three to four hundred meters of a section, so my duty became to warn my comrades, who could not see out of the trenches, that guards were approaching and they needed to look busy. However, as the days and weeks wore on, all of us became more and more listless, and even speaking became a chore. It became harder even to look busy. The earth was frozen and so rocky in places that often we could hardly make a dent in it all day.

Between each round of guards, the men in our unit leaned against the trench wall, losing themselves in an obsessive daydream about fabulous meals and describing in great detail, memories from gourmet restaurants. At lunch we feasted on imaginary delicacies.

Besides this main topic of conversation, we often turned to philosophy and religion, or the purpose of existence. We covered everything from tribal rites to Aristotle, Maimonides, Kant, Spinoza (a favorite of Jews who could not decide between God and Nature), Spencer, Marx, Sartre and Einstein, for good measure.

Shmuel's constant lamentation and argument ran this way: "It's all God's will; we're sinners; we haven't observed his laws ...." It infuriated many of us. His blind belief, in spite of the uneven justice, baffled us as much as the injustices committed against us.

"There's no such thing in nature as just or unjust," I insisted angrily. "It's not just or unjust that the predator kills its prey, that the powerful impose their will over the weak, whether nicely or brutally, by subterfuge or openly. That's the way things are; that's the world's way." Chance encounters, circumstances, momentary association at a point in time and space, self-preservation or survival, all of these created, destroyed or recreated new situations, I argued. Sometimes there was the appearance of determinism: that existence has reason. But nothing was determined. Even minute variations in chaos could create trends, highly probable occurences, but they were not preordained. Directly observable cause and effect existed only on a small scale, not on a global one.

"But the universe, nature, is too beautiful, too orderly to be the result of random happenings," Joska said in defense of Shmuel.

"There's no such thing as beautiful or ugliness, either. The walrus is beautiful to another walrus, but not to you. Is it beautiful that our comrades die like flies for no natural reason? I don't think so, but maybe it's beautiful for Hitler."

"I'm sorry for you," Shmuel retorted. "What will sustain you in this time of our trials?"

Joska and Mihaly were looking at me to answer, as if they approved of Shmuel's questions. "I don't have the answer, but that doesn't change the question. Maybe the search itself is the answer. I agree it's hard to live my way, and I envy you who can believe."

"Hey there! Move it faster!" I yelled as loudly as my weakened voice would let me. The returning guard was getting too close and had noticed that there was little digging in our section.

"What's going on here? Almost nothing has been done," he yelled at me.

"There are big rocks underneath, sir," I pointed to one. "It's slow going."

"So dig around!" and he moved away.

We took a deep breath. "Let's dig a little," I said. "Maybe it is so determined from above."

* * * * *

Days followed days into weeks. The routine was similar, except for more beatings, more hunger, more disease, and more death. By mid-February, the deaths had mounted into the hundreds and my unit suffered its first casualties, four in one week. Dysentery and typhoid fever reached epidemic proportions and took heavy tolls on the weakened populaton. We suffered from hunger, the bitter cold and the millions of ticks, which, beside spreading disease, drove us out of our minds with itching over the entire body. Sleep was not sleep anymore, but resigned exhaustion.

Dezso was a quiet and good comrade, who always went along with the majority. Just before the ghetto population was removed from the Gyongyos area, he had obtained permission from Koranyi for a leave. He had persuaded his father, "Uncle Jeno," to escape from the ghetto and come back with him to our camp, sure that Koranyi would accept him in our unit. So he came, which saved him from sharing the tragic fate of the Jews headed to Auschwitz. Now, two weeks after his fiftieth birthday, this second week in February, 1945, he lay dead next to his son. Dezso woke up around five o'clock that morning with tears in his eyes. He was quiet, stunned, as he made the announcement of his father's passing. Shmuel barely had time to say the Kaddish before they took him away.

Moricka got dysentery, dreaded by everybody. Death was almost certain within three days of the first symptom. The acceptance, the resignation of the sufferers to their fate was unbelievable. People painfully joked about it: "Okay, pal, you're a goner. But don't worry, we'll follow you soon." Two others died of dysentery the same week. I believe people were too weak, too tired to be hysterical about it. Death was a fact of life. The survivors cried, prayed, and hoped that the liberators would arrive in time, but who knew when they would come.

The march to and from the trenches became slower and slower, yet still we marched in order, as if chanting the cadence would move our legs, or as if the shovelling of one moved the shovel of another. The hunger periodically made us delirious. Deep in the trenches, I asked Bela and Miki jokingly what they had heard lately, reminding them of their duties of old times. To my surprise, Miki, with a mischievous glint in his eyes, said he would have some news in a day or two. "How?" I asked stunned. "That's my business," was all he answered when I asked him where it would come from.

As we talked, I had failed to notice the German officer with a sergeant behind him, who had sneaked up within twenty meters of us, obviously supervising the overall operations. He saw that many of my men were leaning against the trench wall, a few even sitting in the bottom of the pit. I froze. I didn't know what to do. Just as a reflex, I yelled "Auf! Genucht!" All right! Enough!

The officer charged forward furiously, fuming like an enraged bull and shouting at the top of his lungs, "Judische shweinen!" Jewish pigs! Leaning forward at the edge of the trench, against the small, but muddy hill, the wings of his long overcoat folded back, he reached for his pistol. At the same time, the sergeant took his gun from his shoulder and cocked the trigger, ready to shoot. The officer pointed his pistol directly at Deutsch, who had not gotten to his feet quickly enough. "Du shwein!"

"Herr Oberfuhrer! I permitted five minutes of rest to those three because of the heavy digging around that rock."

"You? You permitted it? There is no rest for anybody besides lunch, do you understand?"

"Jawohl! Herr Oberfuhrer!" And I saluted.

Waving his pistol dangerously in his hand, he charged further ahead, running on the edge of the trench to surprise people. Deep sighs escaped from our chests.

After the officer was out of sight, Deutsch approached me, tears running down his face. "Thank you for saving my life," he said. The others were nodding approvingly. Did I really save his life? I don't know. I hardly knew what I did at all. Some reflex made me talk. Later, I shook inside when I realized that I had taken the blame. What if the officer had turned against me?

This was not heroism. It was fear. Fear of seeing a comrade bloodied, of seeing his head blown to pieces. Out of that fear, you do something. Anything. Without thinking of the consequences.

So, how to answer his thanks? With something stupid like: "Jah. That's all right. You're welcome. I'm glad I could do it."

Another day had ended; for another day we had survived. We dragged ourselves back, marching in cadence—in a very slow cadence—and lined up for the evening meal of hot soup (that is, hot, greasy water with a few potatoes swimming in it, if you were lucky enough to get any in the cook's spoon). Still, we kept strictly to the order of our rotation, a miracle in the chaos surrounding us.

Lajos, Peter, and Zoltan fainted standing in their row, without attempting to push ahead or ask for help. Robi, Bela, and Joska collected their rations, brought the food to them, and poured it into their mouths. Afterward, all six returned to their places in line.

Suddenly, Peter, a nice, intelligent guy, a pharmacist in civilian life, jumped out of our line-up and, swinging his plate, ran into the middle of the chaos, swearing in Hungarian and German, staggering from left to right. He began to menace guards and an officer. I yelled with all my strength, "Peter! Get back!" He wouldn't listen. Something had snapped in his brain which could not be mended. "Peter ... !" I yelled. Bang! Bang! The officer shot him in the face at point blank range.

"Poor Peter," we all thought. Shaken, we again lined up for our rations.

Digging anti-tank trenches

* * * * *

Dysentery and typhoid ravaged the camp. By the third week in February we had lost twenty-two of our original unit. I kept repeating to myself obsessively, I will not die unless they shoot me like Peter.

Ironically, in the midst of the dysentery epidemic, I was constipated, and I was thankful for it. But my strength waned, I had dizzy spells, my legs were rubbery, and my body sometimes shook uncontrollably. Small sores appeared on my legs; they had started as a discoloration of the skin and would not heal. Despite it all, I kept marching and leading the cadence, staring toward the horizon for the Russian liberators to appear, or marvelling at the Allied bombers as they passed overhead. They were on their way to smash the German war machine. Could we hope for anything to give us relief?

"Give me the radio parts I gave you," Miki demanded, "and don't ask any questions." I pulled them out of a hole in a rotting beam which was holding the roof over our heads. "Okay," he said. "Maybe we can get some news. Wish us luck."

Miki would not admit to anyone except me that he had a radio, so he always began his reports with something like, "I overheard a guard ...." There was a report of a major Luftwaffe attack on Belgium, Holland, and France: some 800 German planes destroyed 156 Allied aircraft. Most of them never got off the ground. The danger of an attack on Bastogne had passed.

In Budapest and throughout Hungary, the Germans had put up tremendous resistance to the Russians' advance, even as the latter clawed their way through the southern part of the Danube around Szekesfehervar. Bitter street fighting continued in the capital.

On January 20th, the provisional Hungarian government signed an armistice with the Allies, but in the southwest the fighting continued tenaciously. The Germans held desperately to the small but strategic airfields around Szekesfehervar. Even at the end of January, a German and Fascist garrison still held out in Budapest, commanded by General Luger, launching an attack north of lake Balaton in an attempt to reclaim Budapest.

The news of the tenacious German resistance in western Hungary was very bad for us, Miki commented. Frightening would have been more to the point. If they held out much longer, it would have lessened our chances of surviving. Either we would die right there, or they would move those who still had some strength further inside Germany.

* * * * *

Hundreds of people would disappear from our midst almost daily. Every morning, those who felt unable to march to the trenches for work would line up in a separate column in the middle of the yard. We were told they were going to be transported to a nearby hospital. We never saw anybody come back, but still people believed. In their extreme weakness and exhaustion, they had no alternative, and we never had proof to the contrary.

The camp was controlled by the German Todt organization, whose duty was to provide manpower for German industry, agriculture and armed forces. The laborers were from the enslaved nations, mostly Jews and Gypsies, although we never encountered working Gypsies.

There was a prisoner-of-war camp next to ours, separated only by barbed wire strands. They were mostly Russians, but there were also a few English or American pilots who had been shot down on missions nearby. They were in much better shape than we were and, occasionally, at an unguarded moment, would throw a piece of bread over the fence. This was a risky gesture of goodwill, which could result in the beating of the donor and death to the receiver. Any contact we had with the P.O.W.'s was punishable by death.

There was also a small group of about thirty-five Russian women soldiers whom we watched line up every morning in front of a kind of bathhouse. They wore long overcoats, with blankets around their shoulders and towels on their arms. Their ages ranged between eighteen and forty-five. They, too, were better fed and, considering the circumstances, were in a surprisingly good mood, often making sexual gestures to us. Some opened their coats to display their nakedness. Once one of them pointed her tremendous breasts toward us, fondling them as we looked on. Another turned around, lifted her coat, and bent forward to expose her gorgeous behind. They teased the half-dead, and I think they would have made love with the dead, they were so horny.

Once, just the image of a naked leg, or the sight of the upper curve of a woman's breast as she bent a little forward would have been enough to provoke a huge erection. Now, I just gazed in my trance, dizzy from hunger and pain, at a scene that appeared like a mirage shimmering in the distance. It did provoke a little erection for a few seconds, enough to remind me to be grateful that I was not completely dead. Over the next few days, we and the women became sort of spiritual comrades, waving to each other over the barbed wire as we dragged ourselves toward the trenches.

* * * * *

News of the world now came regularly, and not just through Miki. Numerous refugees passed through the town of Schattendorf. Since many of the camp people worked outside, helping the Austrian peasants, they regularly supplied rumors, based on German papers and radio reports. They also brought us black market goods, with the help of corrupt guards who charged exorbitant rates. It was obvious that Germany had lost the war, but that it would not give up for a long while. We saw ourselves trapped until we were dead, perhaps the last victims of an egomaniac who mersmerized his people into going down to defeat in the melodramatic tradition of the Gotterdammerung.

Some time during the third week in February, while perching at the trench edge, an extreme weakness overcame me. I couldn't stand, my legs folded under me. I called for Joska and Robi. "I believe I'm finished, fellas."

"You have diarrhea?" They asked immediately.

"No," I said, "but I feel feverish."

"Then it's not over. Just hang on. It's almost time to go back. A night's sleep and you'll be back in shape."

I staggered back, creeping to the cadence, "One, two, left, right," shuffling my legs like an automaton controlled by an invisible power. The next morning, I had no strength left.

With the help of my friends, I lined up in the middle of the plaza with some twenty other sick men to go to the hospital. The reviewing Todt officer, who approved the departing men every morning, usually by pointing his thumb toward the trenches or toward the opposite side of the road behind him, stopped, faced me and hesitated a few seconds. "You good for nothing, back to your barracks, three days rest, then back to work."

This same officer had on at least three separate occasions complimented my unit for our disciplined orderliness, and for volunteering for the salt mines. For some perverse reason, we were his favorites. For my friends and me, there was a message: if he doesn't let a favorite go, there may be a dreadful reason that no one returns from the hospital.

For over a week, I lay on the barrack's floor in a state of semi-consciousness. I had a high fever and passed out periodically. I was told by my friends that when everyone was out at work, the Todt officer, during his inspection tour, bent over me and, from his pocket, gave me a large, boiled potato. Another time, he gave me two aspirins. It is inconceivable that this minute gesture of sympathy, perhaps inspired by our rigorous discipline (which makes a German tick), saved my life. After eight days of my floating between life and death, my fever abated. Robi dragged me from the dark, dungeon-like barracks out in front of the door. I blinked my eyes at the pale, shy sun of the first day of March. My blue, swimming terrycloth robe had become a haven for bugs, lice and ticks. With my little remaining strength, I tried to delouse myself by cracking those carriers of death between my thumbnails.

Robi, in relatively good shape, told me about our losses. Bela, Janos, Lajos and others had died. Only twenty-one of us still could hope for the Russians' liberation.

"What's happening on the fronts? In the world? Is there any news?" Miki and Robi gave me news that was good, but not yet for us. Nothing would be good for us until we could see the Russians in our camp.

Tremendous battles continued to rage in Hungary. In Budapest, the street fighting continued block by block until Malinovsky conquered the Capital on February 13th. Hundreds of thousands were taken prisoner, yet the Germans did not give up. They mounted heavy counter-attacks from between Lake Balaton and Lake Velencei. They were trying to cut a road and evacuate a portion of their forces, but they were rebuffed. For a second counter-attack, they transferred troops from the western front. Their efforts continued throughout March, especially in the southwest, but the Russians prevailed and occupied Galanta, the place where we had been recruited. On March 23rd, the Soviet army occupied Szekesferhervar. During the last days of March, the 3rd Ukrainian Army entered Austria from the last important Hungarian city near the Austrian border, Sopron, and on March 31st we first sighted the Russians.

About the Americans and Australians in the Pacific, we heard mostly of battles in the Philippines.

The Americans carpet-bombed Tokyo, causing tremendous damage to life, and there was intense fighting for an island called Iwo Jima. By mid-March, the U.S. was virtually in full control of the island, at an enormous cost to both sides.

Robi and Miki saved the best news for last. "The Russians are somewhere in the hills." Our black marketeers, who got their supplies by working in the village for the German guards (meanwhile making fortunes for themselves by exchanging food for gold rings and coins, which the Jews had been able to hide in shoe soles, garment linings, toothpaste tubes or other places), now told of neighboring villagers fleeing from the Russians.

One of them, in a gesture of generosity, offered me half of a sugar beet which he had dug up, after it had been left behind accidentally by the last year's harvesters. Hungrily, I bit into it. A sharp, acid taste gripped my throat. I coughed and spat to clear the taste. He laughed, "Slow, buddy, just little bites, and chew it a little, then spit out the pulp." I did a little better with it. "Just do it," he encouraged me. "It's some sort of food, anyway."

* * * * *

Three days after my fever broke, I was still so weak that I could not even walk outside the door without help. Robi, Joska and I saw with bewilderment that the Germans had hauled their big, heavy guns to the middle of our plaza and built emplacements for other guns a few hundred feet away in a hole surrounded with sandbags, which the prisoners had to fill.

A few hundred Germans arrived, regular Wermacht troops, and we were ordered not to go to the trenches. "Tibor!" Robi and Joska yelled at almost the same moment. "Stand up! Stand up! Damn it! Look behind you!" Some two miles away, on the crest of the hills, above the trench system and as far as we could see to the left and right, were Russians. There was no doubt. They advanced slowly, quietly, no more than two deep. Once in a while, we heard a burst of machine gun fire, but we could not tell from where. "We may be saved," Joska said with tears in his eyes.

"I'm afraid there are too many Germans pouring into the camp. Don't forget this is the Austrian border. They'll defend it bitterly," Robi said.

"It's the same either way," I murmured. "I have no strength to move. I'll starve to death before this is over."

"Shut up!" Robi yelled at me. "You fucking idiot, you have no more fever! You move when we move. Understood?"

I had no strength to react. For the first time, I truly believed there was no more hope for me. Suddenly, a tremendous explosion shook the barracks. The Germans fired the first big gun, then the second, then the third. No more than five minutes later, an enormous explosion rocked us from some twenty meters behind the first gun emplacement. A second shell landed twenty meters in front of it, and a third one right on it. A perfect ten for target shooting.

Bodies were scattered all over. All the Germans who had been manning that gun, six or eight of them, and a lot of prisoners died. Many more were wounded, yet we cheered the Russians, even though our own lives were on the line. Let them come! Let them come, whatever may be!

The exchange lasted about an hour. Mortars exploded throughout the large courtyard, but there was no direct hit on the buildings. Shrapnel flew everywhere and machine gun fire crackled from the tile roofs of buildings. The dead and dying were inside and outside, everywhere one looked.

The Germans did not retreat from the camp, nor did the Russians seem to move. The night passed in relative calm, but with a lot of anticipation on our part. The shocks of gunfire and explosives had somehow triggered the last possible flow of adrenaline in my system. Although I could hardly walk, at least I reacted emotionally.

"We must escape, no matter the consequences," Robi insisted. Joska, Weinberg, Miki, Bandi and Barabas seconded the suggestion. But how? We still were surrounded by Germans, Horvath and Slovak guards. These guards were the most vicious, the most uneducated, savage, wild animals of the Balkans. They always tried to demonstrate that they belonged to the master race by outdoing the Germans on all possible occasions. Fearing the end of the war, they were likely to want to liquidate every witness to their obscene viciousness.

We awoke the next morning to renewed gunfire, mostly small arms, mixed with an occasional machine gun burst. There were also Russian mortars arriving from high arcs and exploding between buildings. Unbelievably, there were more German casualties than Jewish. The guards, accompanied by some Wermacht troops, stormed into our barracks and called for attention. "It's seven o'oclock. By ten o'clock you will be lined up on the square with all your belongings, ready to march at least forty kilometers. Anyone who feels he cannot make it can stay in the barracks."

This tolerance seemed abnormal to everybody. The camp would move on, and whoever wanted to stay in the combat zone could stay? The sick, the weak and the dying? Most of my unit, although starved and staggering, felt they would have a better chance to live if they moved with the camp than if they were caught in the battle. Seven of us decided to stay and take our chances. Actually, six decided, because I had no choice. They were only hungry; I was hungry and recovering from typhoid. I could not undertake the journey.

At 10:00 A.M., the hundreds of prisoners who thought they could make it started to move out. Some couldn't even march to the camp perimeters without falling. We had hugged our remaining comrades, the fourteen who decided to leave. There had been few words, but great emotion as we wished each other well. They disappeared on the road by which we had arrived, driven forward by the brutal guards to an unknown destination. We watched them from our barracks doors as they disappeared. Suddenly, coming from the opposite direction, we noticed an S.S. detachment of about a hundred men coming toward the camp. They followed a motorcycle with side car, and were packed into a half-truck with anti-aircraft guns loaded with ammunition.

"We made the wrong choice," Joska said, with unusual fear in his voice. We all nodded. With only the sick and dying left, the S.S. had no reason to be here other than to liquidate the camp. That was us.

"No!" I said. "This is your last chance. I have no strength left, but you get out. Now! There's no surveillance. The guard is gone and the S.S. isn't here yet. The Wermacht doesn't care. They're too busy organizing themselves. You have probably no more than ten minutes. Get out! Leave from behind the barracks. Just start to walk toward the Russians. You know the terrain. We've been working here three months now. Go!" I said. "You selected me to be the octato. I tell you go!"

"Okay," Barabas said, "we'll go, but you come with us."

"I can't."

"You can, damn it," and he kicked me in my rear. "Move!" he said. "Let's get what we can and get out of here. We may not have more than five minutes."

"The Russians are still on the hill. They don't seem to be moving," Weinberg interjected. "How can we make it there?"

"It doesn't matter any more. Let's just get out of here," Barabas said forcefully.

I was wrapped in my blanket, shivering in the humid cold of March, and I took my rucksack containing one item: the little box from Budapest with photos, swimming medals, a few engraving tools and my sketchpad inside it.

Behind our barracks, we started to walk, stagger and crawl toward the Russians, who seemed to be miles away. We had advanced about two hundred yards, when suddenly we heard a loud, heavy voice from nowhere, "Stoy! Stop!"

ESCAPING HATE AND DEATH

Those two hundred meters to freedom were the longest journey of my life. After some thirty yards, I couldn't go on. I sat down. The fierce March winds blew through my weakened body. My friends would not give up on me, even though they themselves were hardly stronger than I was.

"Look back there!" Robi was nudging us. "Look there, next to our barracks." We saw German soldiers trying to change into civilian clothes, caught in their underwear by a Russian advance patrol and shot on the spot. We saw half-dead Jews attacking the S.S. blindly, bare handed, even managing to kill a few, although they took the heavier losses.

Then we noticed among the Germans children as young as twelve or thirteen, no doubt recruited hastily in the village. They had put them in uniforms too large for them and had given them guns which hung from their shoulders to the ground. Although they could hardly lift their weapons, they were aiming at our comrades, who were old enough to be their fathers or grandfathers. When they pulled the triggers, extinguishing more life, it was for them like playing games of cops and robbers.

"Let's move," Joska urged. They dragged me along. Every ten or twenty meters I had to sit down, and in between stops I often crawled on all fours, like a wounded animal. Some one hundred meters away a miracle happened. We fell upon a fairly large wooden crate abandoned in the field, stamped with Gothic lettering, "ZUCKER."

We were afraid to open it. It would not have been an easy task without tools anyway, but we also feared it might be a trap of explosives. But we took our chances and, with great difficulty and much trepidation, we opened it. It was sugar. Small cubes of household sugar. Manna from heaven. We threw ourselves on the treasure like hungry jackals on their prey, but our eyes were bigger than our stomachs.

We ate very little because our stomachs, shrunken from months of starvation, just wouldn't take it. Joska and Barabas started to vomit, so we stuffed all our pockets and packs and moved farther away from the camp, fearing a sudden German advance. We chewed slowly on the sweet miracle. The sugar did help, at least momentarily.

"Stop!" the voice yelled, this time menacingly. We stopped, but could not see anybody. Finally, cautiously, the first Russian soldier we ever met emerged from his well-camouflaged fox hole. He was pointing the famous short-barrel, drum-magazined submachine gun known as the "Davay Guitar." With words and gestures, we were ordered to lower our pants. None of us spoke Russian, but Weinberg, one of my six companions in misery, had been born in Kassa, one of those cities lost by Hungary to Czechoslovakia in the Versailles Treaty. Thus, he spoke fluent Czech/Slovak as well as Hungarian and with some difficulties was able to communicate with the Russian. We were frightened and had to explain to him about Joska, who was not circumcised. After a few seconds of careful examination, he smiled and lowered his Davay Guitar.

A few minutes of discussion ensued between him and Weinberg. He told us that fascists, even S.S., were trying to sneak through Russian lines by camouflaging themselves as Jews. We told him that we wanted to get to the Russian side through the trench, the shortest way. He responded with frantic gestures. "Nyet! Nyet!" Weinberg translated his message:

"Don't be crazy. All those fields are mined either by the Germans or by us. Go around to the other side of the main road in the water run-off ditches. It's safer." Overwhelmed by emotions, we hugged and kissed our "tovarich," our friend, whose name we never knew.

As we advanced, we met more and more Russians, two or three to a fox hole. Soon there were larger units of a dozen or so. We waved to all of them to show our thanks and friendship. They did not pay too much attention to us.

Suddenly, machine gun fire erupted in the neighboring forest somewhere near our salt mine. The Russians hit the ground and waved frantically for us to do the same. As we were inexperienced in recognizing the different battlefield noises, we did not know what to do. From all around us came sporadic gunfire, machine gun fire, hand grenade and mortar explosions, shells from long-range cannons whistling overhead, and the heavy noise of bombers dropping their loads. There were also the smells of gunpowder and other explosives of the battlefield. Our reflexes were so slow that, well after the Russian soldiers were on the ground, we were still standing, trying to figure out what was going on. It may have been just a few seconds, but that's all it takes to live or die.

We struggled closer and closer to the main Russian force on the hill, hugging closely to the ditch at the side of the road our Tovarich had indicated. We passed numerous units. Finally, someone seemingly in charge—we did not know their ranks, as their uniforms all looked the same—directed us behind a disabled tank. We were ordered to strip naked and were dusted with disinfectants. All our rags were burned and we were provided with an assortment of clothing from a horse-drawn wagon. The underwear was obviously Hungarian army issue taken from some nearby army depot. Civilian clothes were mixed with Hungarian and German uniforms, and we were concerned lest we be mistaken for fascists, so we continued to wear our yellow armbands.

When we were fully clothed in this funny, but clean assortment, we were offered the chance to eat, as we hadn't eaten in a long time. One of the Russian trucks had brought three big kettles of food for the soldiers, and we were invited to join them. They welcomed us warmly with their comradeship and understanding. They prompted us to eat, but we could hardly swallow the greasy goulash-like meal loaded with big chunks of lamb.

They enjoyed it greatly and ate heartily, but we ate very little. "It's good for you," they insisted. "You need strength to fight the fascists." We ate, so as not to offend them. Fortunately, we did not take too much; many recently freed prisoners died from sudden overeating. We sat down to rest in the shadow of the disabled tank, and our welcoming Russians dispersed, going about their business of war.

And they went about it as casually as if war were indeed a business. From the top of the hill, as far as we could see, every hundred or so meters there were mortar units. Each had a crew of three or four. Upon hearing a whistle, the crew, who had been comfortably relaxing on the ground with their heads propped up on ammunition boxes, would stand up, load their mortars and, on the hand signal of an officer, would fire their rounds before lying down once more and enjoying the April sun. Then another whistle would sound further away, another three mortars would be fired, and another, and another, until the turn of the units closest to us came again.

The mortar shells, often describing a typical high ballistic curve, landed on and around our camp, just beyond the advancing Russian troops. After half an hour of continuous pounding of the area, suddenly, just a few dozen meters away, hundreds of Russian soldiers rose from the ground like young trees suddenly grown, straight out of their foxholes. They had been so well camouflaged that we had no idea there were so many. They started to march straight ahead, across the field, across the anti-tank trenches, in a slow, but seemingly unstoppable march. They held their Davay-Guitars about waist high, spewing deadly ammunition almost non-stop. This was possible only because the minefields had been cleared before the beginning of this onslaught.

The shooting of a comrade

We watched the operation from a hilltop command post, feeling a little like Napoleon overlooking his troops from the hills of Waterloo. The Russians marched on a front of some two kilometers, almost in disregard of enemy fire. We did not observe any one person giving orders. The troops gave the impression that they followed a general directive, but acted on their own.

Small units would go right or left for a while, then might back up a little, but no commands were heard, as if each conducted the action of war on his own responsibility. We were awed. These people knew what they were fighting for.

For us, there appeared to be a chaotic order, without the discipline such as the constant saluting found in other armies. Each soldier knew his duty and his responsibility. As they advanced to within half a kilometer from our former camp, enemy fire erupted. It seemed to come from all directions, and was mostly from small arms or submachine guns. Some of the Russian boys tumbled over, lay down, or jerked in bizarre contortions of agony.

Frantically, we tried to explain to a small group standing near the tank that many German S.S. were coming into the camp when we left, and that they had to be careful. They smiled, "We know. There are many more of them than of us, but not for long. Were there many of our people killed in the camp?"

"Your people?" Weinberg asked, "We didn't see any."

"Yiddishe menschen, Jewish people," he said. "The ones who left are heading to Mauthausen. Many are dying on the road."

"What is at Mauthausen?" We asked.

"Are you fools? Don't you know what's going on just a few kilometers away?"

"No, we don't." He started to explain, but his unit called him away. "I have to go. Mazel tov," good luck he said.

"Mazel tov to you too."

* * * * *

The Russians had established temporary headquarters and a hospital at the building where we had been handed over to the Germans three months before. The road was extremely busy, and Russian women soldiers directed the traffic with great authority. Convoys of trucks were unloading supplies. Tank units moved up to just behind the front line and spread out in all directions. Medics brought back the wounded from the field, most of whom were immediately evacuated by truck to the east, back toward Hungary. We learned that the injured were cared for in hospitals in Szombathely, one of western Hungary's largest cities.

Many of the supply trucks were going back to Hungary empty. We asked permission to ride along. "Nyet!" we were told. They had strict orders not to take any civilian or anybody other than their own.

The night of our liberation day fell. We were hanging around not knowing what to do. The soldiers didn't bother us. They even shared their provisions. For sleep, we lay in foxholes abandoned by the soldiers. To our surprise, they were lined comfortably with down covers, obviously taken from the neighboring villages, and had blankets and straw against the cold. We had a surprisingly good night's sleep.

The next morning, after asking advice from the Russians about the safest direction, we started walking back on the road on which we had arrived. More exactly, we walked at the side of the road, in the field, because the road itself was full of Russians advancing to the front. We struggled back not more than a kilometer. We might have been in Hungary already. We were not sure.

We fell far enough back from the front line to relax, to try to put the last two days in perspective and decide what to do next. The Russians were okay, we thought, but they did not have much time for us. They just went on with their business, so we decided to keep walking toward the east, difficult as it might be. Suddenly, furious machine gun fire swept across the road from neighboring hills or from under the cover of the forest. A Russian we had talked with two minutes before was hit in the stomach. There were at least a dozen casualties.

We ducked into the ditches, when Shmuel cried out in pain. He was lying on his back, his leg bent at the knee, which was visible just above road level. "I was hit." We turned toward him. He had been shot in the knee. We yelled to the Russian truck driver who was taking the wounded. Shmuel was now entitled to a ride. We met him weeks later in Szombathely. He may have had better luck than we had.

Small pockets of Germans remained behind the advanced Russians, and it was difficult to tell exactly where or how many they were. The Russians did not fire back immediately. Staying close to the ground, using every rock or bush for cover, the patrols headed into the forest.

"You fellows better get out of this area," a Russian yelled.

"Yes," I said to Weinberg, "but how?" Now just six in number, we continued to crawl along the side of the road back to Hungary. Weak and exhausted, we took hours to travel short distances. The heavy Russian food was difficult to digest and, even though it helped to rebuild our strength, we had to keep on the lookout for more sniper fire.

It was late afternoon when Barabas raised the question of where we would sleep. There was nothing to be seen, not even a shed in the open field. We didn't know where the next meal would come from, although the passing Russians generously gave us bread or whatever else they had. One of them even dropped a good chunk of ham off the truck for us.

As we came around a bend in the road, we were surprised to see a large crowd gathered in the field about one kilometer away. As we got closer, we saw a number of Russian soldiers ordering everybody off the road onto the crowded roadside. We assumed they were moving either some heavy equipment or their troops. As we got still closer, we noticed that the crowd was surrounded by two lines of barbed wire and guarded by Russian soldiers.

The scene unnerved us. Weinberg was elected to go and talk to the soldier in charge. When we explained who we were and where we came from, surely they would let us pass. But the soldiers didn't listen. They pointed their guns at us and waved us into the crowd.

"Davaj! Davaj! Get there with the others." They weren't interested in our explanation. Within ten minutes of joining the crowd, we realized that they had lumped together everybody who passed: German S.S., Hungarian Arrow-Cross, Jews, Horvath, smassers, soldiers, or civilians heading to their hometowns. Within this chaos, we found a small group of Jews who had been caught in the web earlier. They were organizing a petition to the top Russian to ask him to release us. After hours of negotiations, a Jewish Russian soldier arrived and lined up the people who claimed to be Jewish. His comrade, obviously not Jewish, held a big bag of bread. Safe at last, we thought. Then the screening process began.

As each man approached, the Jew started to ask questions in Yiddish. This was fine for the Poles or Rumanians: most spoke Yiddish. But most Hungarian Jews did not. If you answered correctly, you were offered a piece of bread, but when you reached for it, he would yell, "Broche, say the broche," the prayer for eating bread. Most of us knew this from childhood, but many of the white armband Jews did not. Finally, it was the test of your penis: circumcised or not. But even passing all the tests only meant that you got to join a separate group. It did not mean release.

Some S.S. and other fascists wore yellow armbands to try to pass as Jews. The Russian caught a few and shot them on the spot.

That evening, as we were milling around in our enclosure, we heard rumors that the Russians planned to ship this manpower back to Russian labor camps.

Irrespective of their origin, Jew, Gentile, fascist, or even local communists, they would be sent to a labor camp in Mother Russia. Odessa was the destination most often mentioned.

We saw the Russians let a few Jews go. We didn't know why, but we noticed that they had shown a paper to the guard at the exit. Like lightning, an idea struck me: "Barabas, Joska, Weinberg, get your hands on one of those papers. Robi! You see those apple and cherry trees? Get me a clean, neat, small branch off one. There must be no knots and it should be about six to eight centimeters in diameter."

"How do you want me to get out of here?"

"It's dark, isn't it? There's almost no guard. If there is one, just tell him you're limping and need a sturdy stick to help you walk. Move, and make a clean cut. Also, find some ink or anything else I can write with in their guardhouse. If there's no ink, look for some gluey substance. You can squeeze resin from the trees at this time of year. Look also for some blue, purple or black powdery material."

"You're crazy, and too complicated," Barabas announced quietly. "What's wrong with shoe polish? The Russians must have some." Within an hour, I had a sample pass and the branch of a cherry tree. Three men spent hours honing the end of the branch with coarse and then finer and finer gravel and dust, until the hard wood was smooth as a mirror. I copied on thin cigarette paper the handwritten lines of the pass, and a variation of the Russian hammer and sickle stamp. I was then ready to transfer it to paper. I traced over the handwritten cyrillic characters with diluted shoe polish, then pulled from my bag the little box, the last item I had added to my pack in Budapest before departing for Galanta. Stored carefully inside it were four burins of different shapes, still as sharp as they were in Budapest. With the tenderness of a lover, I started to engrave the Russian escutcheon in reverse. My five comrades surrounded me to admire my craft, and to shield me from the curious. "I'm an artist in my job, but you're a better one in yours," Robi acknowledged. We all laughed and joked for a while.

Early the next morning, our six passes and a spare one were ready. I had traced the characters, but what they spelled out we had not the vaguest idea. At 8:00 A.M., the Jewish Russian was on duty again. "Let's go for it." Joska suggested. With full confidence, we presented our passes. Weinberg mumbled something, and the non-Jewish guard of the bread bag signed on the dotted line. Those passes would prove a great asset during the days and weeks to come.

We were out of the camp again. We hurried to put distance between it and ourselves, but our weakened condition did not permit us to go too far or too fast, and we were afraid to continue on the main road. Who knew where the next check point would be?

If the sugar in the field was our first miracle, a half-dead horse was our second one. Passing a tiny hamlet which had been completely destroyed, we saw a few farm tools and a broken cart with only two wheels lying around as witness of some human labor, probably from just a few months ago. From behind a collapsed barn we heard a plaintive, weak neighing. A horse? Was it Don Quixote's Rocinante? The pathetic creature, nothing but skin and bones, stood facing us with supplicating eyes. A terrified Weinberg pointed to the hind quarters of the poor beast. There was a big, ugly wound probably caused by shrapnel. Flies surrounded it in a feeding frenzy. "Like us," sighed Joska, "another innocent victim of human bestiality, which neither he nor we will ever understand." Whoever left it behind also left a half bale of hay, but the horse was unable to reach it because of the short tether around its neck.

"Can he help us to travel a little faster back toward Hungary?" Robi wondered.

"Maybe. Let's try," Barabas suggested.

We fed him the hay, carefully cleaned the wound with water to give him relief from the flies, and named him "Misery." Misery now seemed to show a little more vigor. As best we could, we repaired the two wheels and the cart, and bridled the horse with pieces of harness we found. We held the contraption together with spit and pieces of rope, and tied a big piece of paper over the animal's wound to shield it from the flies, as well as to hide the upsetting view.

Now we were ready to travel, taking turns sitting on the cart one at a time. But where should we go? We could only head back to the same villages we had stopped at on the way to the camp, in the hope that the few sympathetic peasants would help us again. First, however, we needed food for ourselves and the horse. This forced us back to the road to seek the help of the Russians. Every attempt to get a ride on an empty truck returning to Hungary failed, but they gave us enough food to get by. They always answered our pleas with "Nyet!" and referred to their strict orders. Nevertheless, we saw people taken on in exchange for gold coins which some had managed to save or acquire.

We continued to struggle with our horse of the apocalypse, avoiding Russian road blocks, yet sometimes helped by individual soldiers. We used our passes on a number of occasions to move from one unit to another. After six days, we reached Becske, which had been our last stop in Hungary some three months ago. The town was now firmly in the hands of the Russians. Within minutes of our arrival, the townspeople went to fetch the mayor. We could hardly recognize Bandi in his Russian uniform. We jumped in each others' arms and shed tears of joy. He had survived, and in excellent shape. "Now I'm the Mayor, Mister Octato," he said mockingly. "Now I will take care of all of you."

He led us to the town hall, an old stone building where he introduced us to his colleagues in the Russian administration. Everybody treated him with reverence, like a hero. "So you talk first! How did you get this illustrious position?"

"When the Russians were on the outskirts of the town, the German rear guard was still resisting. Most of the population left; the few who remained wanted to join the Russians, but they didn't know how. Do you remember the nice little lady who took a liking to me? She had hidden me in her basement for all this time. I came up for fresh air only at night. I dressed like the local peasants, and one night we went to the edge of town. When we saw the first Russian tanks, we waved with all our might, me with my yellow armband, she with a white kerchief. They stopped and talked to us. There were already some Hungarian troops with them. We told them that we knew every stone in the area and offered to help. 'Jump on the tank,' they ordered, and we started to move. We entered Becske as liberators, and the townspeople firmly believed that we saved their town from destruction. So what do you want to eat?"

"Anything, but slowly." An old lady from town brought a big wooden plate containing bread, ham, potatoes and vegetables, and a jug of wine. We feasted and told our stories about lost comrades and those who had undertaken the march and of whom we didn't know anything more. (They never reappeared after the war, and have disappeared from my life forever; I do not even know if they are alive or dead.)

"So what's next?" Bandi asked.

"I guess we'll try to reclaim our homes in Eger and Budapest, or wherever, and see what is left, if anything or anybody."

"Don't rush, and don't hope for too much," he said. "The news is very bad. Rest a few days, then go whichever way you can. But there is no transportation to speak of, and don't forget the war is still going on."

"Can you get any news here?"

"Yes, more or less. During the last two or three weeks a lot has happened. There are Russian news bulletins, someone bought a 'Fuggetlenseg,' a revived newspaper from before the war, from the reoccupied territories, and we hear the BBC." Bandi reported that the Ruhr was encircled, and the French in Karlsruhbe were heading to the Tubingens. The U.S. First Army was heading for the Elbe. In Konigsberg, General Lash surrendered, Hanover fell, and the U.S. attacked Weimar. The second U.S. Army reached the Elbe at Magdeburg. On April 12th, Roosevelt died and Truman became the new President. We did not know too much about him.

The Russians occupied Vienna, proclaiming that their goal was the destruction of fascism, not the nation. Hungary had by now been liberated by the Ukrainian Second and

Third armies, but in Yugoslavia heavy fighting continued. Yugoslavia signed a friendship treaty with the Russians. In Italy, the battle continued in the Senio area and on the Lombard plain. We were learning geography better than we ever did in school.

And we heard the first authentic horror stories of Buchenwald. Although Bandi learned about them only through the BBC and short, sketchy descriptions in the local communist newsletter, we had no reason to doubt any more. Tears flowed from my eyes as I envisioned the details of the horrible end of my parents and others in my family. Yet, I didn't want to believe, and hoped without hope.

We remained in Becske only three days so as not to overstay our welcome. The towns-people who remained went about their business calmly. The stories they had been told by the retreating fasicsts, which depicted the Russians as looters and rapists, had failed to scare them away. They invited us into their homes. Miska Bacsi found our horse in better shape than we thought, and told me that Misery was just what he needed for the spring plowing. He would feed him well and tend the wound. "I'll give you good money and food for the road, and the Russian trucks will take you further for a few pengo."

After I had consulted my friends, we made the deal. Bandi helped to get us on a Russian truck.

"How about you, Bandi?"

"I'll stay with my girlfriend, then we'll see. I'm not in a rush to face the new realities." We hugged and departed.

We had spent three days with different families. I lived with Uncle Miska, one of the few men who remained in town. He was in his seventies and had a young granddaughter. We spent much time reliving our life experiences; his much longer than mine, going back to the First World War. For the first time in a long while, I could reflect in some security on the past months and think about my neglected sketchbook buried in the bottom of my bag.

As images sorted themselves out in my mind, I started to sketch, and continued almost non-stop for three days. Miska Bacsi looked over my shoulder, and I explained the many events, the many mosaics of my experience: the salt mine; cutting the paper-thin salami ration; the gauleiter who was just about to shoot Deutsch, but didn't; the officer who did shoot our pharmacist in the face; the chaos in distribution of food; delousing myself in front of the barracks.

"Don't keep memories," Uncle Miska warned. "They'll drive you crazy. And most of all, don't save images they'll haunt your dreams."

"You're probably right, Uncle Miska, but my mind lives in images, in drawings and paintings, hundreds of them, dramatizing what I see and can't forget. I want to share them with others, so they don't forget."

He put his heavy peasant hand on my shoulder. "Forget the past, and quickly, or you'll ruin your future." I put my hand over his on my shoulder, and we stood silently in friendship.

* * * * *

The Russian truck driver would not take us very far. His furlough took him only to Szombathely, some fifteen kilometers away. It was one of the largest cities on the Dunantul, and we thought we might have a better chance to catch a train or find other transportation there.

First, however, we decided to try to find Shmuel in one of the hospitals. Amazingly, we found him in the first one we entered. He was in the courtyard, wearing a heavy bandage on his leg, as he hobbled along on a crutch. I tapped him on the shoulder from behind. "Hey! Can't you move a little faster?" He almost fell over from surprise.

"You made it! You made it!" he exclaimed.

"Ya, so far. How is the wound?"

"Not bad at all. They operated on it and, fortunately, I was hit just above the knee, not right on it as I feared. I'm fine," he said, "but now tell me about all of you. What happened after I left?" We told our story.

After the effusion of joy, I asked Shmuel if it would be possible for me to talk to a doctor also. I still felt very weak, and was constantly feeling either dizzy or dazed. Also, the sore on my leg did not heal. Shmuel arranged for us all to be examined. Generally, the prognosis was good for us all: we needed rest and good food. The sympathetic old Doctor Schwartz told me to put salve on my wound. "It will heal, don't worry," he said.

He arranged with the mixed Russian and Hungarian administration a three-day stay of rest for us in the hospital. It was great. We felt much better, and although we could have stayed longer, we wanted to go home. We were told that freight trains left the railroad station on an irregular schedule, but they were our best bet for covering some distance. So we said good-bye to Shmuel again.

The station was under Russian military command. It was full of people hoping to catch a ride. The few long freight trains which arrived were loaded with military supplies. Some of the cars needed to be unloaded, and the Russians caught any able bodied men and women they could lay their hands on to do the job. Sometimes they offered a ride back in exchange for the work, although it was obvious they had no idea where the empty train would go or when.

After two days of hanging around, sleeping in the station, eating at a kitchen set up for refugees, and standing on long queues for everything, we finally got onto a train which was supposed to go in the direction of Budapest. But we would never know where it really ended up. After experiencing a few dozen kilometers of stopping and starting and waiting on side-tracks, we gave up and went back to walking.

The April nights were still very cold, with occasional late snow flurries. Even in daytime, when the open car was moving just ten kilometers per hour, we were frozen. We struggled from village to village on foot or riding on a peasant's cart. We were careful to avoid large concentrations of people at major crossroads out of fear of repeating our last experience on the road.

On the outskirts of a small town, we ran into a traditional outdoor market. Peasants were selling their food,—the Hungarian peasant always had food, even in the worst times of the war—live pigs, chickens, geese, as well as cheap clothing, utensils, kitchen bric-a-brac, and old furniture. Gypsies were selling horses, as they had done for centuries. "Hey, Tibor, why don't we buy a horse? Joska asked. It will help us move faster."

"That's right, with the money Bandi gave us, we'll have enough!"

With only the experience of the half-dead horse, Misery, we approached the gypsies as expert horse traders. From the moment we amicably patted the flank of one of their horses, we couldn't get rid of them. Four or five of them assailed us at once. One after the other, they showed the teeth of their beasts, which we examined carefully (without knowing, of course, what we were looking for. All we knew was that teeth had something to do with age.)

They trotted the animals up and down, pointing out the features of their legs, the curve of their backs and other esoterica. Just behind stood their women, in colorful but ragged dresses, offering mushrooms, soap powder, or palm reading, while a bunch of kids buzzed around, begging for coins. The bigger ones sawed away on beat-up violins, some with only two or three strings, and meowed in our ears for an extra coin.

We retreated for a conference and decided on one fairly good looking and especially alert looking horse. "Hey, Jansci! I called to the owner. "How much?"

"Ten pengo," he said.

"Are you crazy?" I retorted. "Five!"

"Eight!" he yelled.

"Six!" I said.

He swore by his mother, by his children, that we were buying the best horse on the market, "It's a steal for that money." That it was a steal, I had no doubt, for it had surely been stolen.

"Seven," I said. "That's it," and I offered my hand for him to shake.

"My handsome sir, it's not enough. Look at my wife with all the children. They're hungry..."

"No more," I said. "Will you shake on it?" He shook my hand and those of my comrades, who could hardly hold back their laughter. While I was bargaining for the horse, Barabas had bought another two-wheeled cart and some hay. We were ready to go.

But we didn't go too far. After some two hours of slow going, with usually two and sometimes three of us on the cart, the horse looked very tired. We spent less time on the cart, we stopped more and more, and then the horse stopped altogether. He seemed to be shaking. He hung his head, drank but wouldn't eat, and the next morning expired. The gypsy had the last laugh!.

What could we have known about the drugs and all the other tricks that are used to make an animal look good for a few hours? We were more sorry for the horse than for ourselves. But now we had almost no money, and Budapest was still more than 200 kilometers away, and Eger 120 further.

* * * * *

It took us more than three weeks to arrive at Csepel on the outskirts of Budapest. As we made our way back east, and as the Russian occupation of Hungary solidified, we saw the difference between the fighting Russian soldiers on the front line and their political organizations that were settling in the villages. The soldiers were warm, helpful, understanding of human miseries, and knew that in the shadow of death we were all alike. They appeared to us as real heroes and liberators. On the other hand, the bureaucrats, mostly Hungarian communist, hastily installed under Russian supervision, were harsh and unbending. Although we recognized that they had to be careful not to be infiltrated by returning fascists, a cruel new regime was developing.

The war was now virtually over for us, but not for millions of other soldiers and civilians.

Madman Hitler continued to resist, callously sacrificing women, children, the too young and the too old. He was now drafting twelve-year- olds into the regular army to defend his egomania. Verona had fallen to the Allies, after Mussolini was captured by partisans at Lake Como and executed with his mistress and twelve other fascist leaders. Finally, in April, the Germans surrendered Italy unconditionally

The U.S. attacked Munich and liberated Dachau, revealing the horrors committed in that concentration camp. While some Russian army units were fighting inside Berlin, practically annihilating the city and the infamous Reichstag, the great news spread around the world. On the 23rd of April, the Russians and Americans met for the first time in Targan, on the Elbe. But the news did not evoke great enthusiasm. We accepted it with quiet satisfaction, as good news that came too late for our loved ones, and in many ways too late for us too. This news found us in Csepel, as civilians without homes or jobs. We lived one day at a time, preoccupied with finding the next meal and a place to sleep. We became part of the mass of refugees floating aimlessly, aided only by the meal distribution canteens in railroad stations or in small municipal buildings of towns.

We were no longer in a rush to go home. By now, we knew what to expect. By now, we no longer disbelieved what had happened in Auschwitz, that the Jews from my home town, like most Hungarian Jews, had perished there.

"Your brother might have survived in another camp, as we did," Joska said.

"Maybe some friends in Budapest were able to hide. By intermarrying with Gentiles, perhaps they could have managed to survive," I said.

"In Gyongyos, where I came from," Barabas said, "there could be no hope, and in a small city, like Eger, there's no hope of hiding."

"How about you, Robi?" I asked.

"I had my mother and a sister; I never knew my father. Who knows, maybe the gangsters and petty thieves at Angyalfold had the heart and guts to save them." Miki and Weinberg were in the same boat.

At the railroad station's distribution center, we got a fairly good goulash, mostly potatoes, but with some meat in it, a half kilogram of bread with pork fat, and even a piece of cake. Trains were coming and going, mostly open freight cars. Passenger trains were all reserved for Russian soldiers or high ranking civil servants.

We walked back to the city's high school, which was set up for refugees. Here there were fairly decent military cots, and no questions were asked other than name, address, and destination. There were at least two hundred people in the building, but nobody communicated with anyone but their families or their closest friends. Who knew what kind of monster or torturer might be sleeping in the next bed? We did not talk much, even between ourselves. Somehow, we knew the time of separation was near, and each of us had to find his home and restart his life; none of us wanted to say it, and none of us wanted to face it.

In one corner of a classroom, on the beat-up desk of the last professor, stood a small radio giving news of the war by the Russian controlled Hungarian broadcasting service. The news consisted mostly of the Russian advance and much less about the efforts of the Western Allies, but what was announced usually was factual and correct. Miki still had his makeshift radio, less and less serviceable, which provided additional information from the BBC. So, these last days of April, we heard that Hitler had taken command of Berlin and had dismissed and arrested Goering. We listened with hope to the opening of the San Francisco Conference to write the charter of the U.N. We heard about Hitler naming Doenitz as his successor, and about Hitler's marriage to Eva Braun. "It's a good omen." Miki remarked. "He has finally realized that the end is here." On the 30th, we heard in a broadcast that he had committed suicide in the bunker of the Chancellerie. We heard, too, that the Russians had captured the Reichstag. They were also engaged in heavy fighting in Breslau, on the Baltic coast and at Austerlitz. In the Pacific, in Okinawa, Burma and China, heavy fighting also continued.

When the broadcast ended, it was late and we were tired. We headed to our beds to seek consolation in our dreams, that is, if they did not turn to nightmares. "Where do we go from here?" The ever rational Barabas asked.

"Shut up!" Robi cut him off. "We'll talk tomorrow."

In the morning, we sat on the steps of the school entrance, very close to each other in body and soul. We looked like ugly little birds with bruised feathers, warming in the early sun, each immersed in his own thoughts.

"We have come so far together," I said, "but now each of us has to go further." Silence.

A few minutes later, Barabas added, "We have to find trains or trucks to our destinations." More silence.

It was hard to imagine doing anything separately or acting solely on one's own behalf, without thinking about the others or having their support to rely on.

"We have to part," Joska said, "but we all will meet in Budapest sooner or later. Let's at least exchange our old addresses."

"But who knows what we'll find? Let's go to the station," Joska urged. "It may take days to find transportation."

We went with all our belongings, consisting of ragged rucksacks and blankets. That afternoon, a long wagon was leaving for Budapest. We heard of it only a half-hour before its departure. "That's it," I said to Joska, Miki and Robi. "You'd better take it." They nodded.

Robi, the toughest one, was crying like a baby. We all embraced and sobbed, they climbed into the freight car, and Robi squeezed out a smile between his tears. “Szervusztok, Comrades!”

The three of us who remained spent two more nights with the other refugees. We talked more about our recent past than we talked about the future, which we were unable to anticipate.

I added two more drawings to my sketchbook: the dead horse, and the departure of our three friends in the open wagon. Although all the sketches were very rough, mostly a kind of reminder for future possible paintings, Barabas greatly appreciated them: “You, at least, got something out of our misery.”

“Yes, each one is a wound engraved in the deepest tissues of my brain, never to be forgotten.”

On the third day, we found a truck going to Eger, Gyongyos and Miskolc. After two more days of stopping and starting, we dispersed to look for our families and our homes.

A RETURN TO WHAT WAS HOME

We stayed together as far as Hatvan, a major railroad junction. From there I took a train to Fuzesabony, where I got a ride to Eger on a horse-drawn wagon loaded with bags of grain, chickens in wooden boxes, and food stuffs. I sat on top of the pile in the back. After a while, the driver asked me where I had come from.

"From far," I answered. "Are you from Eger?"

"Yes, my name is Berci."

"I'm Tibor."

"Are you from Eger?" he asked again.

"Yes, from Servita Utca," Servita Street.

"Ah ... and I'm from the Maklari hostya," he said, naming a suburban area.

"What's new in Eger?"

"You know the Russkies are everywhere, and their communist lackeys fill all the government positions."

"Is it bad?"

"It was in the beginning. They raped some women; everybody was hiding; they broke into wine cellars, shooting into the larger barrels. One person actually drowned in Bikaver, he added, referring to 'oxblood,' the famous red wine of Eger. But it's better now, and if you have an officer living in your house, it means safety and protection."

It was late afternoon, a balmy, beautiful spring day. The delicate white petals of snowbells shimmered in the sun as the earth awakened from a long winter. From a bend on a hill, before descending toward the city, we saw the silhouettes of the cathedral, the Turkish minaret, the astronomic observatory tower of the Lyceum, and the fortress towering over the small one and two-story houses.

It was a beautiful picture-postcard view, holding the memories of my childhood, quiet and peaceful, the people looking like small dots. Would there be any familiar faces left, or just the furtive, guilty looks of past acquaintances, fascists, or bystanders who let my family be driven from their homes?

Berci spat on the ground without removing the straight pipe he had held between his teeth during the entire trip. "Where do you want to get off?" has asked.

"At the market place, if you don't mind," I answered.

"No, not at all. I stop there anyway. I can take you to Servita Street. It's not much further."

"No, no, thank you. I would rather walk." It was getting dark when Berci let me off. I went first to the City Hall's refugee center. I asked the policeman there if any Jews had returned to town.

"Just a few," he said. "You should go to the 'Kulturhazba,'" he added, indicating the old Jewish House of Culture in Ujvilag Street. "I hear they're trying to organize a congregation."

The first thing next morning, I directed my steps toward my parents' house at six Servita Street. I crossed the market place and passed the statue of Dobo. My steps got heavier and heavier as I approached the house. Nobody was waiting this time. With tears in my eyes, I pushed down on the door handle. Through the narrow corridor, I saw a cement reinforcement of the fortress wall, which was leaning dangerously. The little garden in the back of the house had fallen victim to the concrete. The door of the front apartment, occupied by the building's owner, opened. Mrs. Erzsi came out tentatively. Opening her arms, she gave me a hug and asked me in.

"Can I give you a glass of wine? So good to see you back." I listened to her embarrassed talk without really paying attention.

"Do you know anything about my family, Lady Erzsi?"

We sat down and she told me the details of my parents' last days in her house before they moved to the ghetto with only what they could carry.

"Stop!" I said. "I don't want to hear it. Not now! Who lives in the back? In our apartments?"

"The Kovacs," she answered. "Nice people. When they moved into the apartment it was completely empty. The fascists took everything."

"I know, everybody is nice now, but who were the fascists then," I asked, "the neighbors to our left and right, or across the street?"

"No, no," she protested, "we didn't know them."

"Where is your husband?"

"He was killed on the Russian front."

"I'm sorry," I said. A short silence. "I'd like to see the apartment."

"Please do."

I knocked at the door. "I'm Tibor Gerstl. May I look inside? I lived here before. Please." Mr. Kovacs opened the front door. I looked inside, but I did not go in. I also looked into the kitchen. "Thank you."

"My pleasure," he said.

I went back to Mrs. Erzsi. "By any chance, was anything saved?" She pointed to the table, where she had laid out all that was left of my family, the remnants of dreams and struggles, the memories of two children: a few photos and three small rings belonging to my mother.

"I took the photos from the wall," she said, "and your mother, at the doorstep before parting, gave me her rings for you boys, if you should return."

"Thank you."

"Please sit down. Do you want coffee?"

"No, thank you. I've seen enough. I have to go." We said cordial, but somehow distant good-byes.

There is a limit, I assume, to what a person can take in emotional stress without cracking up. You become desensitized as a self-defense and you go on with the business of survival. The disaster somehow doesn't want to sink in. I went to my grandparents house. Again, I saw a few things, but no people; at least not the ones I loved. The old velvet sofa which I had loved to caress with my hands and feet when I slept on it as a small child was still there. Even though I could touch it, the sofa was now only a memory.

Then I went to the Culture House. "You're only the sixth to return," said Mr. Hirsch, who was the "shames," the rabbi's helper. "We're receiving help from the city's Communist Party. There are now a few Jews in top positions. Your schoolmate Feher is the head of the Police Department. If you want to repossess your house and belongings, if you can find any, you can. There are some objects remaining. Go to the old ghetto. Perhaps you'll see something there that's yours."

The ghetto was next to the swimming pool. A disquieting, confusing feeling assailed me as I approached the small, tired old houses, now collapsed. On this side of the pool was misery, brutality and inhumanity; on the other side, sportsmanship, health and friendship. It was as if the pool was the "the holy water," which had connected both these worlds. One of the six who had returned was sitting at the entrance as a guard. "Shalom," he said.

I was a little surprised at the salutation, unusual before the war. "Shalom," I replied.

"Go in," he said, without rising from his low chair, as if he was sitting "shiva," in mourning for the dead. "Go in," he gestured, pointing his thumb behind him.

In one of the largest rooms of the ghetto, in chaotic disorder, were piled the tattered vestiges of Eger's Jewish community. There were mostly photos, with some clothing, religious objects, "teffilin," prayer shawls, and a few books. That was all. I started to dig through the pile. Almost every picture had a familiar face, sadly reminding me of lost friends and acquaintances. I began to remember the families of my schoolmates, and to relive events, celebrations, weddings, births, deaths, vacations and picnics. The pile also contained old photos with yellowed, oval matting, of long gone great-great grandfathers with big Hungarian mustaches, and great-great grandmothers with high-necked laced blouses, the glass broken across their faces.

Suddenly, my mother was facing me with the beautiful smile of her wedding day. "Here I am, son," she seemed to say. Then I saw my brother at the age of eight or nine. Then my father's strong, but anxious eyes pierced my heart. He looked at me again, dressed this time in his military uniform from World War I, war hero medals decorating his chest.

Now I searched feverishly; a few more family pictures surfaced. I grabbed them all and rushed out to escape suffocation, gasping for fresh air. I roamed the streets aimlessly, with the photos under my arm in a paper bag. Where could I hang them? I didn't even have a wall, a brick, to call my own.

* * * * *

A few more Jews returned. One, a close friend, had the infamous Auschwitz number on her arm. Either she had not seen my family, or else she would not talk about them and that place. I could not insist.

For days and weeks, I hung around in confusion, unable to do anything. Maybe subconsciously I was waiting for somebody else to return. The warm late spring brought people back to the solariums. Swimmers swam all year long outdoors in the naturally warm artesian waters. I went too.

The second week after my arrival, as I was sitting in the Culture House reception office, there appeared outside the dirty window the silhouette of a skinny young man. He was almost buried under what looked like an army tent, with a big rucksack and a large leather hide flapping on both sides. We raced to open the door and help him with his burden. My heart was pounding. Surprise and disbelief were warring inside me.

He dropped his burden and we ran into each other's arms. "Ocsi! Ocsikem!"

"Tibi!" and we cried.

My brother had returned. We stared, speechless, examining each other to make sure everything was alright, that no arms or legs were missing or no injury needed immediate care. The administrators pushed us inside with great solicitude, sighing as they registered him. "One more returned, praise God," they said. One of them dropped Ocsi's belongings inside with an incredulous look on his face.

"What are you carrying with you? What is all this, Ocsikem? Where did you get it and why were you carrying such burden?"

But he cried and could not answer me. I cried too. After a while, he quieted down. "I came from Mauthausen," he wispered. "Do you know anything about Mother and Father, or anybody?"

"No."

"Auschwitz?" he said.

"Yes."

He put his arm around my shoulder and we cried.

"Let us say the Kaddish, Mr. Hirsch said, and read for us the ancient words for the dead because we did not know this holiest of Jewish prayers by heart. We looked at each other with so much emotion that we could hardly speak.

Finally, I asked, "What's all this stuff, this heavy "bazaar" you're carrying?"

"You see, when the Americans liberated us, I became guard in a jail were they put all the Germans caught in the camp. We took care of them, I assure you. We got money and gold from them; the roles were reversed. The Americans were too good to them. They did everything by the rules; I don't believe they knew with whom they were dealing. But what could I do with money? There was almost nothing to buy. So I bought this army tent because I was sure everything was bombed out, and for this shoe leather you can have almost anything."

All of us listened with amazement. How fast our entire value system had changed. Our perceptions had become distorted. The border between legal and illegal acts had disappeared. Beating, killing, raping, falsifying papers, black marketing were normal or justified in the name of survival. Although the war was over, at least for this part of the world, those things we had learned in order to survive could not be set aside from one day to the next. We were prepared to do anything; only the fear of getting caught and hurt kept us in check.

After we settled temporarily in the empty house of my grandparents, who had died in Auschwitz, like all other Jews from Eger, our feelings could no longer be repressed, and stories of our lost family poured out like rapids rushing over a waterfall. Ocsi's road had been not unlike my own: labor camps in Hungary, ending in Mauthausen. But Ocsi had had no Koranyi to shelter him from the naked brutality of the fascist guards.

"Where can we go? What should we do next?" he asked with resignation.

"Let's just rest for a while and enjoy having found each other again. Then maybe we'll go to Budapest to find out if Bojti is there. Look at this; I still can engrave." I showed him the falsified Russian stamps. He smiled for the first time.

Ocsi had been a warmhearted, generous person, who laughed easily and had loved good times. Now, although bitter and broken in spirit, he was still beloved in town, and many wanted to help him. We spent the days in a kind of torpor, waiting for people to return, trying to find out about our fellow townspeople. How had they behaved? Could we still be friends? Did they know any details about the last days of our families? We wanted to know about the town, the swimmers, the possibility of our living there.

* * * * *

At the solarium I met Losonci, an old friend from the pool who, we learned, had behaved in exemplary fashion and helped the Russians to occupy the city by providing intelligence at the risk of his life. "I did everything I could for Miklos Steiner, but it was too late, just one day too late. I'm sorry," Losonci said.

"What are you talking about?" We sat up with anxiety.

"You don't know what happened to your classmate Miklos Steiner? He came back a few days before the Russians arrived. He hid in the attic of his family's old house. He was seen, or trusted the wrong person, and was denounced to the fascists. They arrested him and hanged him one day before the Russians arrived. I only learned of it in the marketplace, the day it happened."

My stomach turned and I felt woozy. "Let's go," I told my brother. "Thanks for what you did. We know you did your best."

* * * * *

As time went by, a few more survivors staggered back from the labor and death camps; still not enough to make a "minyan". I knew I couldn't bear to pass the empty houses of my parents and grandparents every day, and it would be better if I left soon. My brother and I talked, and we agreed that I would go to Budapest and he would stay for a while to see. "To see what?" He was not sure, but he preferred it that way.

In Budapest, there was a shortage of everything. Perhaps in the chaos there would be something for me to do. The black market between the countryside and the city was operating at its most frenzied pace, in spite of enormous risks. The Communist government punished these activities mercilessly, even ordering the death penalty in serious cases.

The Communist government that took over with the help of Russians was headed by Ferenc Rakosi. He had lived in exile in Russia for nearly fifteen years with many other Hungarian communists. Like them, he had to flee the Horthy regime, under which the Communist Party was illegal and Communists were pursued mercilessly. Now, with Russian help, the Communists occupied most major government positions. Among them was one of my uncles, a political commissar in a textile manufacturing company in Russia (a trade of which he knew nothing). In Hungary he had been a printer, with a trade that had a strong, mostly socialist union. Now he preferred the black market to the government.

Despite the dominance of the Russians, other parties were tolerated at this time, like the "Kisgasda," the small landowners party, which enjoyed the majority of votes in Parliament, and the Socialist Party. The government purposely let inflation rage to the highest it had ever been in history. Prices changed within hours. A loaf of bread cost in the million "pengo" range.

Although black marketing was one of the most serious crimes, government agents disguised themselves as black marketeers to buy gold and silver jewelry from desperate former members of the middle class, who sold it to buy food for their families. Precious metals would constitute the basis for the new money, the "forint." Since I had neither gold, silver, pengo nor forint, this was of no great concern to me. I would not sell my mother's little gold ring, even if my life depended on it; I would rather rob or kill.

While we tried to pick up our lives in Eger or Budapest, the war continued to rage. Although the news from the fronts was good, the fighting didn't seem to end. Neither did we wish it to end until the collapse of the Third Reich and final surrender of the barbarians. Finally, Goebbels killed himself and his six children; Krebs, who had asked to surrender, committed suicide; Borman escaped; and Weidling surrendered Berlin. In Reims, at Eisenhower's headquarters, Germany signed an unconditional surrender. Truman declared May 9th V.E. day. In spite of the cease-fire on May 9th, fighting was still going on on the Russian fronts. Finally, the Germans surrendered to the Russians at Karlshorst, near Berlin, and Tito liberated Zagreb and Trieste. Now, with the help of old schoolbooks and newspaper maps, we were better able to locate far away places in Asia, and news of Nepalese troops parachuting into Rangoon became more meaningful to us. By the end of May, heavy bombing continuously struck Tokyo and rumors flew of the U.S. invasion of mainland Japan.

* * * * *

After some two and a half weeks together in Eger, my brother and I said good-bye again. I left for Budapest with the understanding that within a few weeks he would join me. It took two days for the train to cover 150 kilometers; I spent a night at Fuzesabony waiting for a connection. The train was loaded with men carrying rucksacks, women with large baskets, and animals: chickens, geese, even pigs. There was no glass in the windows, and it was so crowded that people lay flat on the top of the train.

We pulled into the Keleti, the eastern station, or what was left of it. The "fin de siecle" glass vaults had all been broken, and the steel structure holding it together was badly damaged. I headed to Rozsa Utca, where an elderly relative had once lived. It seemed like my best starting point. Entire neighborhoods had been carpet-bombed. The Royal Palace on the hill of Buda and all seven bridges over the Danube were wrecked. Only one bridge had been temporarily repaired, to enable the Russians to establish communications between the two halves of the city.

To my great surprise, I found my relative at the address on Rozsa Street. Like so many buildings all over the city, half of his house had been bombed out, and the other half was dangerously crooked. This distant relative, named Pista, was in poor health and was the only survivor of his family. He invited me to share his apartment while I reorganized my life. I began by registering with the Jewish organizations in the city in order to get some help in my search for surviving relatives. At the Place Bethlen, the synagogue was still standing. It had become a center for returnees and repatriates. There I learned that Koranyi had survived, but was under arrest in Rimaszombat, charged with being a labor camp commandant.

I tried in vain to contact other labor camp survivors who might testify in his behalf, but the Bethlen Plaza organization knew about his heroic behavior, probably unique among Hungarian officers. When I told them I had served under him, to my surprise they already knew. They also knew I had once had a fiancee in Rimaszombat who might have survived.

"You should head a group of witnesses, a rescue team, as soon as possible," said a tall, good-looking man in his 50s, whom they called the "Fejes," referring to his stubbornness, ability and leadership.

Travelling to Rimaszombat was no simple matter. It meant crossing borders again, dealing with Russians and Czech border guards. "I'll go," I said, "but I need one or two weeks to organize myself here. Meanwhile you must try to find some of my comrades, like Joska, Robi or the others."

I tried to return to my old flat on Damjanics street. The once familiar streets had been made unrecognizable by the constant American bombings. A street sign on a pole atop rubble pointed the way. My flat was on the street level of a six-story house, whose top was completely gone. But the flat itself still stood. The concierge, who had been installed by the communists, was in reality a block watcher, whose duty it was to report any anti-communist activities or disturbances. After a short exchange of arguments, I was able to repossess my old flat which, despite its bare walls, comforted me with its memories. It felt almost like finally being at home.

The search for my labor camp comrades was fruitless. I visited their old addresses in Budapest, and tried institutions and newspaper ads, but I could not locate anybody. It was almost unbelievable that after so many years of close friendship, I would never see them again. We had simply disappeared from each other's lives. Yet I needed help on Koranyi's behalf.

My childhood girlfriend, Cica, and her mother had survived in Budapest. I found them in their old apartment. They were making every effort to join a son who had lived in America since 1935. We renewed our friendship, but just as friends. I told them about my fiancee in Rimaszombat, and Cica started to date men with American connections, which pleased her mother. Nevertheless, their dinner invitation provided a welcome contrast to the meals in community kitchens.

Mostly at the mother's prompting, I tried to re-establish a normal life. However, I was still very weak, and the wounds on my legs had not healed. I made a number of visits to the famous Jewish hospital, where even the fascist leaders had gone for treatment, up until the last minute before they were evacuated. They told me my legs would heal slowly. I also struggled with occasional dizziness and constant anxiety about the future, which the doctors promised would heal even more slowly. To overcome the physical injury, they recommended returning to swimming; for the psychic wounds they recommended beginning to design again. With anticipation as well as trepidation, I headed to the Isle of St. Margarite, to the national swimming complex. The Margarite Bridge was half-submerged in the Danube, its broken steel girders sticking out of the water like hands imploring for help. I carefully walked across the temporary bridge, built by the Russian military. It was called "Mancika," a cynically affectionate diminutive for the name of the bombed-out old bridge.

The pool facade and the surrounding greenery, which had always been shiny and spotless, now looked dirty and unkempt. The main racing Olympic pool was cracked, I was told, by the nearby bombardment and the constant shelling from Buda to Pest. Nevertheless, people were lined up at the ticket window. In the past, the personnel had known almost every swimmer and it was seldom necessary even to show your team's or club's identity card.

Now, from behind the glass enclosure an employee asked for my identification. "I'm Tibor Gerstl," I said, "from the III Kerulet. I'm back for the first time since the war."

"Sorry, you have to have your card or buy a ticket," the young man said.

"I was the goalie of ..."

"I'm sorry, you have to buy a ticket."

"Let me just look around in the locker room, to find some friends," I insisted.

"Okay, but fast."

I found nobody. Unfamiliar young faces stared at me, wondering what this old guy was doing there. I turned back, said thanks to the young man and, with a terrible sickening feeling, lined up for a ticket. I still hoped to find somebody I knew well inside, but I met only a few old acquaintances from other clubs. They introduced me to the new coach of my team, Mr. Kalmar, who welcomed me and invited me into the newly forming club. Once again I had an identification card. I began a workout for both the backstroke and water polo. But it wasn't the same.

I left the pool depressed, but I kept repeating to myself that I must go on. Mr. Frederik's message was again ringing in my ear; "You must survive first." It had a different meaning now, yet it still seemed to be valid. Where was he and where were my other teammates? Somebody must have survived.

Yes, I must survive. Or must I? So many didn't. What was there to live for anyway? For love, which I had tasted just enough to want to have? To have a family of my own? Oh, no! I did not need to bring children into this miserable world, to expose an innocent life to the horrors and misfortunes that I and my family had gone through. I faced poverty, discrimination, uncertainty. I couldn't forsee the future, so how could I know what a son or daughter might become? Another Einstein or Leonardo? Did I have the right to deprive the world of such a treasure?

I arrived at Damjanics Street, having passed dangerous looking characters amid the rubble teeming with scavenging dogs and cats. Day by day, my mood sank lower and lower. I became listless and could hardly eat. Exhausted, I did not react to anything, but I knew I had to help Koranyi, and this finally shook me out of my lethargy. I decided that I did want to live, and would try to return to my old job.

One morning, automatically and without much conviction, I headed toward the Rakoczi Plaza, looking for the small side street where my tutor in graphic art, Zoltan, lived. I knew his labor camp unit had been wiped out, so I didn't expect to find him. I knocked at the door. A young woman invited me into the small, neat apartment. Gone was the beautiful disorder of my bohemian artist friend. Gone were the pots and jars full of color, and the messy walls which were used as sketch pads. "No," she said, "he didn't come back."

"I heard he died in Russia somewhere. How about his wife and baby?" I asked. "They weren't Jews,"

"We don't know."

"Thank you for letting me in," I said.

As I was reaching for the door handle, she said, "Mr. Gerstl, I found a few drawings in the closets. Do you want them?"

"I would like to have them." She handed them to me. As I browsed through them, Zoltan's presence filled the room. This was what was left of him, of his humor and talent, his vibrant bohemian character. All was there, in my hands. Then I discovered a drawing of my own. "Thank you," I said.

Ever since I had arrived in Budapest, I had an urge to go to my old engraving job at Mr. Bojti's, but I was also reluctant to return to the old routine, if I could avoid it. It is a curious paradox that you can have peace of mind when you don't have options, and are ordered around, but when you have freedom to explore any option, that freedom can create stress and anxiety. Nevertheless, I preferred freedom, since ultimately one had to provide for oneself, and make ones own choices. Actually, I had fewer options than I imagined. The pressure to eat tomorrow was a persuasive decision-maker. I could continue to live on supporting organizations like the JOINT, but that did not suit me. So I decided to seek out Mr. Bojti.

"Tibor! My boy!" he exclaimed, as I opened the door to his office. He hugged me and squeezed my arms, right and left, to make sure that I was real and that no parts were missing. Peter rushed out of the workshop, his green visor still on his head. Geza came more slowly, leaning heavily on a crutch.

"What happened? Is it serious?" I asked. Without a word, he pulled up the left side of his slacks, revealing an artificial limb from the knee down. Why should this happen to the nicer and more understanding ones? I saw a tear in the corner of his eye.

"Any news of our mini-Hitler?" I referred, of course, to Janos.

"Not so far," they told me.

"I would rather see him humiliated, beaten, than dead. I was wondering, did he get the message? Did he learn?"

"People never learn ," Bojti said. "You can learn engraving, not character or humanity."

"Is your family all right?" I asked. "Your wife was Jewish."

"She still is. Everything is fine. What's to tell? We survived: the bombings, the house-to-house fights between the Nyilas and Germans against the Russians, the lack of food, the building collapsing over our heads. And we've survived the Russians too ... so far," he said with disdainful humor. "Talk!" he demanded.

"I will, I will, but slowly. For the moment, I need a job."

"The bench is there. Get on with it."

"I'll show you I can still work." I showed him the false Russian shield engraved in the branch of the hard apple tree.

"Good job," he said. "You're hired!" and he slapped me on the back and laughed.

"We may need another one like this to get us out of here," he whispered, giving me a significant nod.

* * * * *

It had been no more than two weeks since I had settled down to a routine of some normalcy. Work, swim, time with Cica and her mother. Mr. Bojti poked his head around the door, "Tibor, come out. There's a visitor for you." I came to the office. I couldn't believe my eyes. My visitor was none other than Edit, from Rimaszombat.

"Edit! You're back!" We rushed into each other's arms. As she wrapped her arm around my neck, my eye was drawn to the row of blue tattooed numbers. The poor girl, I said to myself.

Edit had survived Auschwitz. She caught my eye. "Yes," she said, turning her numbers toward me, "but please don't ask any questions. Not now, anyway. I'm here, that's all." She had the fleshy appearance which was a temporary condition of many who had survived the death camps: bloated, rather than fat; puffy-faced, a reaction to sudden eating after starvation.

We celebrated finding each other, but it was a bitter celebration, tinged with the memory of our families and friends. Bojti took us out for lunch and gave me the day off. That evening, I returned for the first time to my favorite restaurant on Kiraly street, which had been my salvation many times before the war. It was a little mom-and-pop operation with excellent home cooking and, most important, generous credit when I needed it so badly in the past.

When we entered, Aunt Sophie almost dropped the bowl of hot soup she was carrying between the tightly packed tables. She put it down at the nearest table and embraced me, her eyes wet, burying my head in her voluminous chest. "You're back, thank God. Sit down, both of you, here, and tell me what has happened to you. But tell me first what you'll eat. It's on me."

"You know, Aunt Sophie, my old favorite, pasta with poppyseeds."

"Coming up, my boy." Dinner was wonderful.

Edit and I went to the flat at Damjanics street and spent the night in bittersweet remembrance of our recent past, especially the times at Rimaszombat. Edit would not talk about Auschwitz.

We took it for granted that our love affair would continue. She still considered herself my fiancee, although I accepted this situation with some hesitation. We were happy for each other, although perhaps, too careful about the other's sensibilities. We made love with frantic desperation, as if there would be no tomorrow, or as if to affirm that we were alive, that we were real.

* * * * *

After a few days, Edit brought up the one subject I had painstakingly avoided so far. "What's your plan, Tibor?" she asked at night, when we were holding each other, relaxed after some wonderful lovemaking.

"I have none," I said. "I just live."

"I want to go back to Rimaszombat," she said. "I heard news about Pista and Zsuzsa, my second cousins who survived. They're living in our house. They found the building intact, although completely emptied. Would you come with me?"

"It's not simple," I said. "Rimaszmombat is now Czech again, and I have no papers."

"Unless you make some," she laughed.

"And my job. What will we live on in a small town like that? On the other hand, Koranyi needs my help, so I'll probably come."

"Are you coming because of Koranyi or for me?" she asked, offended.

"Of course for you, but I can't live there permanently. We'll come back to Budapest."

"That's all right, maybe after a few months. We'll see."

When I told Bojti about our plan, he shook his head in disbelief. "You've hardly warmed up here and you're going again. Haven't you had enough of this unsettled life? Let her go to take care of her affairs, and she can come back. It's too risky to cross the border now. The Russians control everything and, of course, the Czechs have never been sympathetic to those of us from the mother country."

"I know," I said, "but it's my duty to her and to Commandant Koranyi."

"How about your duty to yourself?"

"After this is done, I'll settle down. Will I have my job when I come back?"

"Yeah," he said, "you will."

"Thanks."

"So when do you go?"

"Within a day or two." It wasn't difficult to get false papers at a time when thousands of refugees from all over Europe were moving in all directions. I packed my few belongings, not much more than a change of underwear, some clothing and blankets, and the box which had accompanied me everywhere since my departure for Galanta: it was my bridge to the time before the war, with the photos of my family, the swimming medals and the engraving tools. Edit hadn't much more.

* * * * *

In July 1945, I was again at the railroad station. My fiancee and I waited for an open freight train heading toward the border. A train came, and within minutes was invaded by a mass of humanity fighting to board. I pushed Edit up first, another guy pulled her in, then I jumped up. It was standing room only. We were so crowded that we breathed into each other's faces. There had been an early heat wave, and the wagon smelled horrible. We were most anxious that the train move and clear the air around us. Finally, we heard the whistle and the traditional "All on board!" The train's rhythm and jerking movement shook everybody into place. I felt Edit's warm body pleasantly close, closer than was really necessary, and we embraced with satisfaction.

A half-hour or so into the journey, people started to loosen up, and conversation began between little groups squeezed together. It was as if people had decided that they must either like their neighbors, or else throw them overboard. The war and the Japanese resistance dominated the conversation, which was carried on by shouting over the noise of the rattling wheels and creaking cars.

Strange, far-away places were on the lips of concerned people. The U.S. Army was progressing everywhere, while kamikaze bombers caused great damage to lives and ships. Finally, on July 5th, MacArthur announced that the liberation of the Philippines was complete.

Yet on everybody's mind was concern about a secret weapon. It was obvious that an atomic bomb was a possibility. Although Germany was down, they could have passed the secret to their Japanese allies. The Americans must be working on it feverishly too. The wildest rumors provoked irrational fears of annihilation of the world by either combatant, but many dismissed this doomsday prediction as ridiculous and impossible.

* * * * *

After some five hours of stop-and-go at every hamlet, only eight of us remained in our car. We came to the final stop about one kilometer from the Czech border. "Everybody off!" the conductor yelled. A total of some twenty people assembled from all the cars.

Three freight cars and a passenger car with broken windows stood behind the dirt-encrusted, aged locomotive. The engineer and driver, dripping oil and coal soot, also got off, then all of us were lined up for inspection by Hungarian and Russian soldiers. Edit grabbed my arm, "Here it goes again," she said with a deep sigh.

I proudly showed my forged papers of Czechoslovakian citizenship. There was no problem with the papers, but one of the Russians pointed to my "burgerly boots" and ordered me to take them off. I took off one, thinking that he wanted to inspect it. Then he pointed to the other. He quietly sat down on a broken wooden case, took off his own shoes and shoved them to me. "Take them," he said. "It's okay for you." When I pretended not to understand that he wanted to steal my boots, the Hungarian soldier explained that I had better quietly accept the trade if I wanted to cross the border instead of being arrested. So, urged by Edit, I took the shoes, which were twice as big as my own, and badly worn.

When we were ordered to walk the distance to the border along a small footpath beside a cow pasture, I took the shoes off and walked barefoot through the high grass, and we laughed.

The Czech border guards and even the Russians there were much nicer. They let us pass easily. We got on another train soon after crossing the border. This time we rode in a passenger car. It was a short ride to Rimaszombat. As we approached the station, my heart started to beat a little faster. Would I see any trace of the action we had taken on the railroad tracks before we left? Would anything remain of the derailed German train headed to the Russian front? Edit confirmed the effectiveness of that action, and now both of us tried to spot the scene of our success. There it was, two burned-out cars that had rolled into the ditch from the slightly elevated track, lonely witnesses to our most meaningful act during the whole war. Maybe it was not as important to the world as what others may have done, but nevertheless, I felt proud.

We passed the casern and rolled into the familiar station. It was only slightly damaged. The only change I could see was the sign which now read Rimavska Sobota. After rather unemotional greetings were exchanged between Edit and her distant relatives Pista and Zsuzsa, she introduced me to them.

From the first moment, it was obvious that there was no great love lost among the cousins. With Edit's reappearance, they lost their claim to the ownership of the house for which they had been hoping. Nevertheless, relations remained civil, if chilly; the house was big enough to accommodate both families comfortably. Pista and Zsuzsa were civil servants, quiet but fairly intelligent, and I developed a rather friendly relationship with them. Occasionally, they would ask if we were getting married. To my hesitant answers, they responded with thinly veiled negative remarks about Edit, which I chose not to hear.

My first order of business the day after our arrival was to discover Koranyi's situation. I soon learned he was in the county jail. With the help of the recently returned Jewish leader in town, I had little difficulty getting information about his case, although the local Communist authorities refused to speak Hungarian. Following a delay, I was finally given the authorization to visit him. After having been frisked, I entered the visitor's room. There was no separation between the prisoners and visitors in this political section of the jail.

Suddenly, Koranyi appeared in the door. A burly guard walking behind him made his already slight frame seem even smaller. He had lost a lot of weight, and his nose looked twice as big as before. But to my great surprise, he still had a cigarette butt hanging from his lips. "Dear Commandant!"

"Tibor! My octato!"

We exchanged laughter and tears, as we hugged each other. "What a terrible thing to see you here after all you did for us." I made sure that I spoke loudly enough so that the guard and plainclothesman could hear, just in case. "How are you treated? Is there enough food? Who is your lawyer?"

"Everything is fine, except my having to be here unjustly. As for a lawyer, I have none. My actions alone should be enough to speak on my behalf. Truly, even so, I hoped that one of you would show up."

"I never thought you could be so naive, if you'll excuse me. I'll get you a lawyer immediately."

"I have no money, Tibor. I lost everything."

"Don't worry about that, I'll get money from the Jews of Budapest, or I'll get you a Jewish lawyer."

"How about the others? Joska, Bela, weren't they lawyers in Hungary?"

"I found no trace of them."

"I'm terribly sorry," he said.

After a half-hour of reminiscing, we heard the guard announce that the visit was over and that I had five minutes to vacate the premises. "I'll be back tomorrow, and I guarantee you will be out within a week. We won't let you down."

Edit's cousin, Zsuzsa, was a great help in establishing contact with the judiciary. With the aid of a local lawyer who was not Jewish, some local witnesses, and my testimony in a courtroom where Koranyi was not even present, we were able to obtain his release. Three days later, he was unceremonioulsy let go. It had been just over a month since his arrest. He started to express his gratitude, but I interrupted him, "No, Mr. Koranyi, we thank you for the lives you saved by delaying our departure to Germany. We'll be in touch again when I resettle in Hungary."

I walked with him to his house, a small, unpretentious dwelling, four walls and a roof on a side street in the center of town. Only his vizsla dog, which his neighbors had cared for in Koranyi's absence, welcomed this hero home.

Slowly, Edit and I walked to my new home with sad and confused emotions. I, who had been condemned by the Germans to die, was walking the streets of the former labor camp, trying to restart my life. Just a few streets away, a paragon of human decency must also piece together a shattered existence with the help of just a few of us. Shouldn't somebody have shouted out to the world the glory of this man, and hung some kind of flag of righteousness over his house? But that was not the way of the world, which took the good for granted while continuing to accept the ugliness.

* * * * *

Heading back to Edit's house, our house, I encountered a few familiar faces. One, a policeman, had formerly worn a Hungarian uniform which was now replaced by a Czech one. Recognizing me, the plump, jovial man smiled. "It's bizarre," he said, "but it's the same job for me, no matter which uniform I wear. How are you? Will you settle here with your fiancee?" He gave me a conspiratorial nudge.

"I don't know yet," I said. "For the moment I'm just visiting." I wished him well, and we said our good-byes.

Days and weeks passed and I could not even consider looking for work or undertaking any job. I was in the country illegally and too many people knew my status. Zsuzsa reported that the administration was considering new registration of all residents to stop the flow of refugees. She advised me not to show myself outside too often until I was ready to decide where to live.

My situation became more and more difficult. Police began to stop people on the streets to verify identification cards and travel visas. Soon I couldn't leave the house. Edit did all the shopping, petitioned the Jewish resettlement organizations for help, and tried to restart her family's soda factory. But most of the time we were at home, daydreaming about our future, or making love every time the boredom threatened to become too obvious.

I felt suffocated by our gilded cage. "Listen," I said one evening, "I love you, but I must do something with my life. In this small town there's nothing for me. Let's go back to Budapest, where I can continue to work at Bojti's."

She refused to go with me. "I have to take care of the house and settle things with Pista and Zsuzsa. You go, make a little money and come back, then we'll get married and decide where to settle. In a month or so, I may have my soda business running well enough for us to make a living from it."

I left again, this time using my legal Hungarian papers as a repatriate. I promised I would be back no later than September, and one way or the other we would soon be married. Bojti had plenty of work and there would be no problem returning to my old routine of work, swimming, and seeing a few friends at night.

Just five weeks after I left, Edit sent an urgent letter. Koranyi had been rearrested and they needed my testimony as well as that of anybody else I could find. I still could not locate anyone from my unit, so I would have to travel alone. When I explained the situation to Bojti, he agreed once more to keep my job waiting for me.

This time, I could not risk crossing the border at the regular checkpoint. Instead, I got off the train at a small hamlet and crossed the border at night on foot, in view of the railroad track in the fields. My false Czech papers were in my pocket, just in case.

I arrived at Edit's house early in the morning. She had known I was coming, but neither of us knew how or when, so there was a big surprise celebration. On that very day, Koranyi's second trial had begun. It followed the same procedure as the early one, but with different judges, and I realized that Koranyi's biggest problem was not what he had been doing in the labor camp, but simply his status as a Hungarian officer rather than a Czech one. The trial was more like a hearing. The Czech judge found it hard to believe that a Hungarian officer could behave so decently. There was nothing spectacular about his trial; a few questions, that was all. I gave my deposition, as well as the few Jews who had returned, and was satisfied to hear that he would be released shortly. We were relieved because, guilty or not, under the communists someone could languish in prison for years without a hearing at all.

Edit had organized the soda factory with some old hands, and it had begun to produce a fair amount of seltzer. We could now talk seriously about marriage. I still argued that it was not the right time, but mostly I did not want to settle down for good in Rimaszombat. We enjoyed the four days following my deposition, and felt secure enough to venture out together. We went to a restaurant where we ate, danced, and had a very good time. As we were leaving, a policeman stopped us on the street and asked to see my papers. There was no point in showing him my false papers; it seemed he was waiting there for me and I did not want to aggravate the situation. I told him I didn't have the residency papers yet. "I'm sorry," he said, "you have to follow me to the police station."

At the station, I had no choice but to tell the truth. I was arrested. Edit cried, and we kissed good-bye for what we hoped was only the night. "Don't worry," she said, "you'll be out in no time. I'll see Mr. Weisman, the lawyer." Less than an hour later, I was taken to a room next to the police station office. It had two army cots, a table, two chairs and iron bars on the window, which were mainly for show, because one could easily push over the whole wall of crumbling masonry. At this late hour, there were only two police officers in the headquarters: the one who arrested me and the heavy ex-Hungarian officer whom I had spoken to on the street. I learned now that his name had been changed from Janos to Janovitch.

"Hi, Tibor! What the hell happened to you, ending up here?"

"I have no papers."

"Listen," and he leaned over his desk, motioning me closer and shielding his mouth as he whispered. "We knew you were here illegally, and we've known about your romance for a very long time. We're sorry, but take my word, we had to arrest you."

"You had to? Why?"

"Look," he said, "we can close our eyes to your being here as long as we have no problem with you, but you were denounced by an official letter, signed and all. So we had to do it."

"Who denounced me? And why?"

"I can't tell you. It could cost me my job, but I can tell you that Edit has had other suitors since you returned to Hungary."

"Shit, that's all I need to know now, with all my other problems."

"Look," he said, "just relax. You're free to move around here, but please don't escape. Do you give your word?"

"Yes," I said.

"Probably Edit can easily arrange a temporary stay of your deportation."

"Don't be so sure. You know Czech authorities have no love for Hungarians."

Edit visited me every day. Some days she visited twice, and one time they let her stay overnight. "Have fun," the ex-Hungarian officer said as he closed the door to the my cell. We spent a wild, wonderful night, ignoring the police next door, but finally I could not hold back, and questioned her about the suitors.

"I don't deny it," she said. "Occasionally, I go out to a movie or Saturday evening dance. I hoped you would understand that after what we've been through, I can't close myself in. But I have nobody but you. We must hope you'll be out soon. Then we'll do everything together."

I was not fully satisfied by her answer, or the casual way she claimed her right to be free in my absence, but there was no choice other than to accept it. I put the best face to it I could, and we separated at six o'clock in the morning in a stressful mood.

Two days passed, then three and four. Edit came daily, once with a lawyer and twice with Zsuzsa. Zsuzsa argued that I would be better off returning to Budapest and having Edit follow me there. She promised to take care of the house with Pista until everything got settled. It may have been a truly generous offer, but I felt she had ulterior motives, so I was on my guard. The Friday afternoon after my arrest, my policeman friend called me out of my cell. With a grave face, he unfolded an official paper. Without a word, he pushed it into my hand. It was in Czech, but I knew from his face what it said.

"You're expelled, effective immediately. We have to take you to the border tonight." I was speechless from surprise but, strangely enough, I was not really upset. "Do you want me to call Edit?" he asked.

"Yes," I said, "I would appreciate it." I felt relieved, even liberated. For weeks I had been constantly on my guard. My life had almost always been indoors, except when I was working in the courtyard or taking a rare late evening walk in the neighborhood. The long period of inactivity had affected my nerves, creating an anxiety which was not relieved by the occasional compensation of sex.

But at least I drew one benefit from the long hours and days spent alone. Since my liberation by the Russians, I had never permitted myself to dwell on or truly face what had happened to me or my family. It was not a conscious decision, but a reflex of avoidance which made me constantly escape to activity. Now that I was forced into inactivity, mental images in minute details made me relive stages of my life, especially since 1942. The war was still not over for me, and I returned to my sketchbook to put my memories on paper, so as never to forget the hurt and suffering. Never would I forget the kindness of simple country people, the savagery of the human beasts I encountered, the passage through the Russian camp, the devastation of the small villages, the separation from my comrades of three years, or the clandestine travel back and forth over the Czech border, for which I was now detained again.

* * * * *

The Americans were still locked in war with Japan, and I was on my way to Rimaszombat, when the explosion occurred whose echo travelled all around the world: the first atomic bomb dropped on Hiroshima on August 6th, by order of President Truman. It had been obvious for some time that the race to produce this ultimate weapon was on. We had believed that the Germans were the ones closest to achieving it. Even when the Germans were beaten, we were not sure whether Japan was in the race to develop and implement this weapon of unknown destructive power.

We had put our trust in American technology, but were less assured of America's willingness to implement it. Now, I was not sure whether to celebrate or be frightened. I guess I did both. I knew, everybody knew, that a terrible new weapon system was unleashed on the world. It was fearful. But I applauded the heroes of science and technology, Einstein, Oppenheimer and Teller, for their brilliance, and for being first. I was especially proud of Teller, who was a Hungarian Jew. The end of the war was now in sight. On the 8th, the Russians declared war on Japan, on the 9th, the second bomb annihilated Nagasaki, and on the 10th, Japan agreed to surrender.

The Russians fought their last battles with the Kwantung army, which suffered a loss of more than 700,000 men. The Russians ended their role in the war by concluding a treaty of alliance with China. On September 2nd, the Japanese signed surrender papers on the U.S.S. Missouri in the bay of Tokyo. The war ended and the problem of peace began.

* * * * *

My own problems were continuing, if not getting worse. "So what do you want to do?" my police friend asked.

I was to be dropped at the Hungarian border by my police friend and another guard. Then I would be on my own. Edit arrived about an hour before my official expulsion with all my belongings in an old cardboard valise and a corrugated box tied with ropes. The policeman showed her in and closed the door. We embraced, tears in our eyes, no words able to form on our lips. Long minutes passed. "Do you have any idea who could have denounced me in so cowardly a way?" I finally asked.

"No, maybe Pista or Zsuzsa. They may think that I'll go with you and leave them the house."

"Will you rejoin me in Budapest?"

"Yes, as soon as I settle the question of the house, either by renting or selling it, and if you promise me we'll be married." I promised, and said that I hoped a month or two would be sufficient to settle the business and the house.

"Do you have all my belongings packed here?"

"Yes, everything," she said.

"All right then, I am counting on you. Let's relax now until they come to fetch me, then we'll say 'au revoir' here, and I'll write you tomorrow as soon as I arrive. We were sitting on the edge of the bed, holding hands and exchanging kisses, when my police buddy knocked on the door to announce that it was time. I was escorted by the two policemen to a pick-up truck and I waved good-bye to Edit. I did not know then that it was forever.

* * * * *

When we arrived at the border it was dark. We stopped on the Czech side. My police buddy asked if they should hand me over to the Hungarian guards, or if I would prefer to cross on my own and avoid them. I felt tired, jittery, and disgusted from the constant running and hiding. "Hand me over to the guard. I have the papers to repatriate, again. I see no problem."

"Okay," he said, "let's go, then."

We entered the shabby guard house, signed some papers in Czech and Hungarian, shook hands warmly, and the next evening I was back home on Damjanics street in Budapest. "I'll leave the unpacking for tomorrow," I said to myself. "I'm too tired now even to stand. A good night's sleep will put everything in better perspective."

I woke up refreshed and started to unpack. As I did, I became more and more nervous. "Have I missed it?"

For the third time, I searched through my few belongings item by item to no avail. My heart was racing as if disaster was about to strike. My small, special box, which I had carried with me everywhere since 1942 like some magic talisman, never once letting it out of my sight, was not there. I got panicky. The photos of my family, my swimming medals, the engraving tools were all missing.

"But why am I so upset?" I asked myself over and over. "Edit will be here in a month or so, or she can mail it, although I wouldn't trust the postal services across the border. She just forgot. It's not so terrible," I rationalized. "The war is over. I don't need the tools now, and I can buy others if I need them." But the photos and medals were the bridge to my past; they had enormous sentimental value to me, and those particular engraver's tools may have saved my life and had certainly spared me a lot of possible suffering.

I sat down immediately and wrote a letter, then a second and a third in succeeding days. My letters were answered, but what was most frustrating, I never received an answer about the box. Finally, weeks later, Edit wrote that she couldn't find it. I thought I would go berserk, and I was ready to confront the border guard again. But I didn't. To travel, I needed money, so I went back to Bojti and my brother to ask for help. They persuaded me to be patient; I would get the box back. I tried to be patient and I tried to believe them.

* * * * *

Neither my brother in Eger nor I in Budapest was able to achieve more than a subsistence level of existence, in spite of our hard work and talent. No salary kept up with the galloping inflation, and often only the black market provided the edge to a better life. The capital was hungry for everything: food, cigarettes, coffee, shoes, nylon stockings. The countryside had almost all of these, and did not need nylon stockings. While black marketing was a major crime under Communist government, with penalties including death in more serious cases, it flourished, often with the help of occupying Russian soldiers, who were paid off handsomely to look the other way.

Ocsi had many connections and friends with links to the breadbaskets of Hungary. He knew well the peasants in and around Eger who sold grain, fruits and livestock. Pigs were often killed illegally to be converted into black market sausage, kielbasi or ham. My brother bought a bunch of these products, which he loaded into a cardboard valise and covered with a few stray rags of clothing. He brought them triumphantly back to my Budapest flat.

"How many kilos is that?" I asked.

"Fifteen," he said. "I paid only twelve forints per kilo."

"Not bad," I said. "It's worth at least thirty-five here. I have enough friends at the pool, and Bojti is also reliable. Let's get a scale to weigh the cuts, and by tomorrow even the scale will be sold."

The friends came, and others too, like hunting dogs following the exquisite aroma of excellent Hungarian salami. In a very short time, we had sold half of it, measuring it out in quarter, half, or one kilo portions. Then we realized that something was wrong. It didn't add up. We had sold only eight kilos, yet almost nothing was left. We had learned a lesson the hard way. "You were fooled," I said to my brother.

"When did you buy this salami?" one of our friends asked, "a week ago? That's it. It dried out. They load it with water when you buy it, then the water evaporates and here's what you're left with."

My brother began to swear profusely. "I'll kill the bastard!"

"No, you won't. Just pay them less next time and accept this as a lesson in business." Although painful, it was a good lesson: different trades required different skills. And we had earned after expenses almost fifty forints. After we had made a few more profitable trips between Eger and Budapest, the meat supply dried up altogether.

But there were other opportunities. Our small city had other assets, like the flourishing cigarette factory, which restarted almost immediately after the Russian liberation. The Russian soldiers and the Hungarian male population smoked like Turks. The lack of production elsewhere in the country turned these cigarettes into hard currency for sale or barter. While I never smoked, my brother, who did, reported that the quality was awful. Even so, and although they had no brand name, he sold them like hot cakes. His connection at the factory was able to sell him cigarettes in bulk, packed a hundred to a carton in gray cardboard boxes.

He sold these mostly to Russian soldiers, particularly to Boris. Neither Ocsi nor I was very shrewd in business. We were too naive and honest in our dealings, so we were often taken in by unscrupulous people. One incident almost ended in disaster. "The first time I took the cigarette boxes from the factory," Ocsi explained, "I automatically passed them to Boris without counting them or checking their content. The next time Boris came to my apartment to pick up the cigarettes, he opened a box, emptied it on the table, and started to count. It held eighty-five. I was embarrassed. Then without saying a word, he took another, and another: seventy-six, ninety, eighty-two. I got red, I was furious, and I feverishly started to count them myself, when suddenly he pulled out his service revolver and, with an avalanche of Russian curses, pointed it at my head. He wanted all his money back from every precious deal. I tried to explain that I had no money and that it was not my fault, but he was adamant, and a little drunk too. Finally, through all the difficulties of the language barrier, I begged him to let me go to the factory and fetch the missing cigarettes and then some. He agreed to that, but planned to stay in my room until I returned. I did not go home for a day, until I could reach my contact and talk him into making up for the shortage. When I got home, Boris was lying dead drunk on my bed."

Soon after this incident, someone else discovered that cigarettes sold better with brand names, and soon all kinds of false brand names appeared. My brother asked, "Tibor, can you make me a stamp with a nice engraved shield or something to put on my cigarettes?"

"You're crazy," I said, "It's illegal and dangerous. You know how the government reacts to black marketing."

But my brother had no other income. There was no time for custom, haute couture tailoring, so, with some trepidation, I did as he asked. I engraved nice little escutcheons and fancy cursive types, imitating or just inventing trade marks. The cigarettes sold for a high premium, especially in Budapest.

* * * * *

My life settled gradually into a more normal, but somewhat boring routine. Work, swimming; work, swimming. The water polo team of III KER was recreated, but of those who had been there in the old days only Fred came back. It was nevertheless my only refuge from the harshness of life, and from my recurring thoughts of the recent past.

The war was over, but in all of Europe there was a constant movement of homeless, displaced people, migrating and wandering from country to country. Jews who tried to leave behind the fascists in their birthplace, to escape those people who had participated in the destruction of their families, often shared trains with fascists fleeing communist retribution. Tens of thousands were on the road trying to find a new home, a new country, any place where they could settle their tired bodies and fulfill their dreams, dreams often no more complicated than to be left alone to live in peace.

I was in my homeland, in my old environment, but I was not home anymore. The people around me, my compatriots, were the killers of my family. Was it the man I just passed on Kallay Street, or the guy sipping his coffee on the cafe terrace who had closed the freight train door on my parents? Was I still Hungarian at all, as they taught us we were in my childhood, in school, in the Levente? Could I really be proud of my Hungarian heritage? What difference did it make that my great grandfather, and who knows how many generations of Gerstls before him, had been born in Hungary around Eger? Did that really make me Hungarian? Did it matter that I had grown up on the poetry of Petofi, Arany, Vorosmarty, Ady, or on the music of Liszt, Kodaly and Bartok, or that my heart beat faster for the Olympic victories of the Hungarian teams? Did that make me Hungarian? Not to them.

But you can't get out of your own skin. With the disaster which befell the Jews, it was obvious that the only home of their own Jews would ever have would be Israel. How ironic it was that, while a Hungarian Jew, Theodore Herzl, had founded the Zionist movement in Vienna, many of the assimilated Jews in Hungary were actually fighting it. "We are Hungarian first, of Jewish religion," they would argue. "We should not have other allegiances," we were told, and rabbis with Zionist connections were often censured by their congregations.

Now all our hopes were with the Zionist movement. We admired the heroism of the early settlers in Palestine, felt the hardship of the first kibbutzniks, and gloried in their success against the English, the Arabs, and even nature, as they irrigated the mosquito-infested swamps which filled our dreams.

It was an open secret that, since the end of the fighting, Jews from Eastern Europe were crossing borders everywhere. They would travel from Poland to Rumania, from Rumania to Hungary, then to Austria, then from the Russian occupied zone to those of the Allies. Many had the ultimate goal of reaching Palestine,but not all. For others, the goal was the U.S., Canada, Australia or South America. The common purpose was to rebuild a life. Passage across the borders was relatively easy due to widespread confusion and loosely guarded check points. However, as the newly established communist government took hold and got organized, borders became tighter, and travelling more and more difficult.

Nevertheless, there was still a certain amount of tolerance toward a people who had suffered so much and were returning to their homes from far away places, often with no identification papers.

I thought more and more about going to Palestine, but could not imagine myself living on a kibbutz. That life was fine for those who wanted it, but I have always been a loner, far too individualistic, and I was not sure I would be able to fit in. Still, I would have done whatever I could to help those who chose to make the "aliyah," the decision to immigrate. I felt homeless at home, and guilty for not joining the "alyiah" and participating in the building of the Jewish homeland.

* * * * *

1945 passed with enough trauma for individuals, nations and political groups to last a lifetime, as we all searched to establish a new life, new alliances, new philosophies. During that long winter, I survived a nasty bout with pneumonia and was relieved when the awakening spring renewed my strength. Letters from Edit were increasingly scarce, but I did not press her to write more often. If it were not for my anxiety about my box, I probably would have ceased communicating with her altogether.

Inflation raged as the Rakosi government tightened its hold on the country's money. Opportunities for economic advancement practically ceased to exist. I renewed my friendship with Cica and her mother, who was now chasing American millionaires again for her daughter. I dated many girls, which made me appear a rou•, but inside I felt only loneliness. My heart's desire was to settle down with a decent girl and build a family. But who had a family? Very, very few. So I put all my energy into work and water polo, and lived from day to day.

One beautiful spring afternoon, I finished work and was on my way to the pool on St. Margaret Island, when a stocky, medium-sized man with reddish hair, a prominent nose and thin, determined lips stopped me at the corner of Kalay and Kiraly streets. "Are you Mr. Gerstl?" he asked. "I'm Mr. Zeltzer. I would like to speak to you. Would you have some coffee with me for just ten minutes in that coffee shop there?"

"I'm sorry," I said. "I have no time. But who are you? And what do you want to speak to me about?"

"I'm a devout Zionist," he said, "and so are you. We need your help."

"How can I help? I need help myself."

"Can we sit down for ten minutes?"

"Okay, but for no longer."

The coffee shop was noisy and crowded. He had a table reserved (very unusual in a coffee shop) near the window looking out to the Nagykorut.

"I represent an important Zionist organization. Our goal is to help the 'aliyah' and you can provide an invaluable service to our Jewish brethren who want to go and rebuild Eretz Yisrael." He leaned over the table, his steel blue eyes seeming to penetrate into my brain, into my being. "You must help us."

"No, I must not," I retorted. "I don't know you, and I don't know how you want me to help."

"Are you for the 'aliyah' Mr. Gerstl?"

"Yes, I am."

"Are you for the building of a Jewish homeland in Israel?"

"Yes, I am."

"Then we have no difference of opinion. That's all I wanted to know from you. I thank you for your time."

"Where is your organization, Mr. Zeltzer?" I asked.

"I'm sorry," he said, "I can't tell you that now, but I will see you soon, if you don't mind. In the meantime, here is the telephone number of this coffee shop. You can reach me here if you wish. May I ask for your telephone number?"

"No," I said.

"I'm sorry," he said. We parted, offering cordial but formal good-byes.

Two days later, Mr. Zeltzer was waiting for me at the same corner. Again, he asked to talk with me. I could not resist the combination of supplication and the strong call to duty. I was to help realize the Zionist dream of a Jewish homeland, and he was now ready to tell me how I could help.

"May I call you Tibor?" he asked, as we sat down in the coffee shop at the same table as before.

"Sure," I said. At the same time, I noticed that the same two people as before were sitting at the next table.

"You see, Tibor," he started, "we know you from your activities as octato in the labor camp. You did an excellent job there with your group. You protected your people. We know you from Schattendorf too, and the way you escaped from the Russian camp on the roadside. Now you have to help our people, yours and mine, escape to Palestine."

"How do you know all this?" I asked, somewhat stunned at the way my private life seemed to be such public knowledge.

"You were not unobserved. Actually, although your stamp did an excellent job in fooling the Russians, it may not have passed our inspection. Just remember, they depended on advisors for Jewish and Hebrew."

"May I meet these people? It wasn't you. I don't remember you."

"No, it wasn't me. I'm not authorized to tell you anything more. As a matter of fact, all this was told to me, and I'm not sure myself who the advisors were, but only that they were ours."

"All right then," I said, "spit it out. What do you want?"

"We need stamps. Excellent, perfect replicas of the rubber stamps of some agencies."

"What sort of agencies?"

"Well, some are foreign agencies and some are Hungarian. We need visa authorization stamps and the like."

"They're too intricate in design, with their escutcheons, griffins, eagles, bears and whole menageries. You need to be an artist to do a good job of it."

"You're the artist, Tibor."

"Are you crazy," I exclaimed, "haven't I suffered enough? Why should I risk prison and who knows what, just on your word?"

"Your misery, and mine, and that of all the other Jews was in the past. What I'm talking about is the future. The future of our people. We need men in Israel who can build, and who can fight the English and the Arabs. Doesn't what we went through convince you that this is what we must do?"

"Yes, I know, but ..."

"Then help us do it."

"I would help you, but I have no equipment for fabricating rubber stamps, and I won't involve Mr. Bojti, my boss, who has helped me all these years."

"Of course not. As a matter of fact, we insist that you do not tell him, but you can use his equipment at night and on weekends. We're well organized, and with one big push we can have everything we need."

"Am I also to copy passports or official papers?" I asked.

"That's taken care of by others. It's already done, and it's not your concern. One more thing," he said, "we'll pay for your work and your expenses."

"Keep your fucking money," I almost yelled at him. "If I do it, do you think I'd do it for money? Is there any amount of money you can offer to equal such a risk?"

"Sorry, sorry," he protested. "I was told to offer it. It wasn't my idea. I'm sorry."

"But I'll tell you what I need. I want proof of who you are, and who is behind you."

He pulled a wallet from the hip pocket of his trousers, carefully peeled away the leather of an inside pocket, and took out an identification card of the Haganah. I was so impressed that I almost stood up and saluted. "Okay," I said. "Tomorrow show me what you need, then I'll see."

"Would you wait just a few minutes, please." He stood up and disappeared through a service door: the two men at the next table disappeared too. In a short five minutes, he returned and handed me an envelope. "Open it at home, alone," he said.

* * * * *

I anxiously opened the envelope and carefully laid the contents on the table. On two pieces of paper were fairly clear impressions of the seals of the immigration offices of Austria and Hungary, two temporary identity cards, one Czech, the other Rumanian, and the seals of their repatriation offices. My heart started to beat faster. These weren't small things. "If I get caught, if Bojti sees and reports me, if the police uncovers the organization, no one will know me and I will be sacrified. But here is a way I can be of use to my people. I'll do it. I'll try to do it so perfectly that nobody will ever be able to tell the difference."

I started to organize myself the next day. I figured that I could do the most difficult engraving at home: the double-headed eagle of Austria, and the Hungarian shield with its intricate crown of St. Stephan on the top, the cross bent at a specific angle and flags arranged in a complicated fold. However, setting type, especially in circles, requires the appropriate typeface, brass supporting rings, machine molds, and vulcanizing the rubber; these things had to be done in the shop. The mental preparation was the hardest part of the job. To hell with the risk involved in doing something illegal. Was what they did to us legal? Perhaps from the fascist point of view. Man makes law and pronounces it legal at his convenience. As for morality or humanity, who cares! In our future country we will write the law and decide what is legal!

To assemble the necessary typefaces and to hand engrave the ones unique to those seals and documentations took more than two weeks. I made good progress with the figurative elements. It was time to put it all together. Zeltzer, after waiting patiently for a week, was on my neck almost daily. "People in Rumania and Czechoslavakia are waiting for these documents," he urged. "We have too many people crowded into Hungary, and we have to move them to Austria and beyond. The opportunities are narrowing daily. Small groups are able to cross borders when we pay professional smugglers to move them, just as they do coffee, sugar, cigarettes or any other commodity. But that's not enough. We have to move masses, thousands at once, officially. Don't you understand?"

"Yes, I do, but you have to understand that one error on my part can jeopardize all those people, and us. This weekend, I'll be ready to go to the shop to finish the molds and vulcanize the first stamps."

Saturdays, we worked half a day, and Bojti often did not come in . As his trusted employee, I had a key to the shop. I told all my colleagues that they could go, and I would put things in order. Then I prepared everything for Sunday. I did not want to waste time in a shop that was supposed to be closed. I would probably need about two hours to accomplish my task.

Before I left, I released the latch of the small horizontal window at street level. The shop on Kallay Street was a fairly modern building, with a concierge who lived on the left side of the staircase. Six steps down on the right side of the entrance hall was the entrance to the shop. I would have to go through the window if I couldn't sneak by the concierge.

At 9:30 in the morning, I was hiding on the opposite side of the street, waiting for Mr. Kovacs and his wife to leave the house for Sunday mass. Their teenage daughter would be left in the house, but she never paid too much attention to what was going on. Finally, they left, so I did not need to use the window. I entered the shop easily, and immediately applied myself to the task ahead.

Late that night, I called Zeltzer at the coffee shop, my urgency due partially to the excitement of creating the work, and partially to fear of keeping the materials with me. Surprisingly, he was there. The next morning before work, I delivered the goods. Over a week passed before he cornered me again.

"How are things going?" I asked.

"Good, very good, for that matter," he said. "You're a real artist; the papers passed all inspections. They were put to good use. More than a hundred people crossed the border and made a good trial run. But listen, Tibor, we need more, more of the same and some new ones."

"Are you crazy?" I yelled at him angrily. "I've destroyed the molds."

"But you have the engravings?" I nodded mutely. "Then redo them. It's a must! Thousands are waiting. Do you want them on your conscience?"

"Okay, okay, give me the damn things you need." For the next three weeks, I was in the shop almost every Sunday and finished more than a dozen stamps.

It ended one beautiful Easter Sunday. I was toiling feverishly, as had become my Sunday custom. A new mold had been completed, and I was just about to start the vulcanizing press when I heard a key in the shop's entrance door. I froze. Before I could touch the hot plaster composite on the hot metal base, Bojti was facing me with obvious surprise. "What are you doing here on a Sunday, Ti?" Before I could reply, he had moved closer and he had his answer.

"What is this for?" I gave a short and honest answer. He became furious. "That you're willing to ruin your life with this stupidity is your business, but you have no right to ruin me and my business. I still have a family, even if you don't." I said nothing. He grabbed a scraper and demolished the mold in seconds. Next, he threw the typefaces apart. But when he looked at the eagles and flags, a sudden change came over him, "Terrific job, you could put your talent to better use."

"Am I fired?" I asked.

"I don't know," he said hesitantly. "I don't want to hear your story. I didn't see anything, but this has to be stopped immediately. Give me your key and get out."

That was the last engraving of any kind I ever did in my life. The next day I came to work as if nothing had happened. Bojti never said anything more about it. When I broke the news to Zeltzer, he was upset, but he thought he had enough material to keep people moving.

By this time, trainloads of Jewish refugees were moving across Hungary, mostly to Vienna's Rothchild Hospital, which was set up to receive, feed, and clothe people before reprocessing them to new destinations. The movement of such a mass of people obviously did not escape the authorities' attention, but we speculated that as long as the Russians did not put pressure on the Rakosi government, the movement would be tolerated. From the Hungarian government's point of view, the more these potential troublemakers left the country, the better it was for the government. However, as this exodus began to take on major proportions, the Russians saw the severe loss of manpower and, more important, the loss of brain power that it represented. They put pressure on all their Eastern European client states to close their borders. Which the latter did almost completely, but only almost.

* * * * *

It was a beautiful, balmy, late May evening. I was unusually relaxed, considering my generally tense nature. The flowers were blooming on St. Margaret Island. Tulips, narcissus, geraniums stood in formal flower gardens, and wildflowers and plants overflowed everywhere. The aroma was intoxicating. Lovers embraced on benches under the darkness of huge wild chestnut trees, and soft dance music filtered through the trees and forsythia bushes from St. Margaret restaurants.

I had just come from the National Swimming Pool after my daily training session, pleasantly tired after a good workout. Although I had a dinner invitation at Cica's house, I lingered on the island, jealous of lovers, eyeing the people on the dance floor, where body moved rhythmically against body to the slow tango. "When will my turn come?" I thought about Edit, Agi, Cica and others, but none of them was the person I waited for.

Yet I was not feeling bad. I felt proud of what I had done recently for others, for Israel, even though almost nobody knew about it. I knew I had done a good job, and that it had been the right thing to do. I was trying to answer the question I raised for myself hundreds of times: whether or not to join the "aliyah," to go with the many I had helped to reach Palestine. But I still could not decide. I walked leisurely across the Mancika bridge, enjoying the fresh breeze over the Danube, arriving a little late for dinner. After a pleasant meal and good conversation, I went for a short walk with Cica along the shore of the Danube, where we embraced lovingly and dreamed about our uncertain future.

We parted around nine o'clock, and I took the tramway at the Western Train Station to near the Liget, the Central Park of Budapest. From there I walked through the dark, half bombed out streets to Damjanics street. The main entrance to my building, which was controlled by a concierge, was still open. As I walked through the door, I noticed two men at the opposite corner of the rectangular inside court, near my flat, walking back and forth. When they saw me coming, they stopped and started to talk to each other. I had a sick feeling in the pit of my stomach, but I tried to ignore them as I took the key out of my pocket and headed to the door.

"Are you Mr. Gerstl?" one asked, rather politely.

"Yes, I am."

"Tibor Gerstl?" he said more emphatically.

"Yes." He shoved his secret service identification in my face, shining a flashlight over it. His partner repeated the procedure. "We have a search warrant to check your flat."

"What for?" I tried uselessly.

"We'll tell you shortly, but we assume you already know."

"No, I don't." I tried again to convince them and myself of my innocence.

"Okay, Mr. Gerstl, let's go inside and not draw attention to us from the whole house." With a heavy heart, I turned the key. The lock rattled loudly against the evening's silence. I turned the handle slowly, deliberately, nervously, as if there could be time to delay the inevitable. Eventually, the door opened. I turned the light on, and immediately as they entered, one said, "We're proceeding to search." They started to examine the flat systematically. They peered meticulously into every drawer and closet, looked at every scrap inside and out. Miraculously, they had not found the sheets of imprints on paper and two reverse engravings, which weren't hidden, but lay on an open top shelf with a few books.

"So where are the rubber stamps, Mr. Gerstl? Why don't you help us? It will be easier on you and on us." He had an undisguised menace in his voice.

Even before I could answer, his partner exclaimed with satisfaction, "Here they are, Jancsi!" (which was certainly not his real name). "Here they are! Take a look."

"You said you didn't have any, Mr. Gerstl," the first one said in a harsh voice.

"These aren't rubber stamps; that's what you asked for," I answered.

"Come on, Mr. Gerstl. We're not that stupid. Are there any rubber stamps, or more of these prints or molds in this place? But before you answer, I warn you, if you don't help and we find more, we will have to become more aggressive in our search."

It was obvious what "more aggressive" meant. "No, there are none," I answered.

"So then where are they?"

"I don't know."

"All right then, you will come with us and answer a few questions."

"Where are we going?"

"You'll see."

"Should I take anything with me? Will I be back tonight?"

"We don't know. Your return depends on your cooperation. Let's go," he said.

I looked around my ransacked room, turned off the light, closed the door, and turned the key slowly again. Groups of two and three neighbors stood watching in the outdoor corridors. I saw a few pointing in our direction, obviously discussing what may have been happening to their neighbor. However my neighbors may have felt in the past, they surely were no friends of the secret police. Since the concierge knew who had come for me, by now so did all onlookers. They were careful to stay in the shadows.

We walked down Damjanics street, past Bethlen street. We turned onto Andrasi. This was the most prestigious address in Budapest, with its upper end in the Liget, at the "Szabadsag," or Freedom Plaza. The center of the plaza was dominated by statues of Arpad and the tribal chiefs, the founders of the Hungarian nation, on horseback.

Freedom Plaza. "Whose freedom? Freedom from whom?" I wondered. From the Slavic nations? From Roman, Turkish, Hapsburg or German domination? Freedom from the Fascists or the Communists? Or now, more likely yet, freedom from the Jews deported and exiled?

We walked down Avenue Andrasi, passed the Korond, on Rozsa Street, where the only survivor of one branch of my family lived. I had no doubts about where we were heading. For nearly all of the half hour's walk, the secret police said almost nothing. I walked between the two to their cadence. To the few shy questions I asked, they made no answer. They did make a few remarks about Jews who emigrated from Hungary, rather than staying to build the new socialist country, but I did not react. When they talked, their tone was polite and conversational, but my thoughts were far away, on my destiny. I felt fear and anxiety again. Any brush with the secret police was no laughing matter. About two blocks from our destination, I asked if I could call from the telephone booth on the corner, hoping to reach the organization. "No," was the answer, "maybe from the station."

Andrasi ut 60, at the turn of the century, was the home of a well-to-do Jewish bourgeois whose family had since been dispossessed. Later it became the infamous headquarters of the Hungarian Fascist Party, the nerve center of the Arrow-Cross' secret police. The pleasant looking two-story baroque building was solidly built. From the foyer, a wide staircase led to the second floor main offices, and a narrow staircase led downward into what might have been taken for a basement or wine cellar. It had been transformed into a dreaded place, where Jews, communists, and other enemies of the party were brought for interrogation, torture and death.

The victorious Communists had taken it over as the headquarters for their own secret police, and many of the Fascists who had been upstairs before, now were downstairs, interrogated according to the same methods they had practiced just a few months previously. Here, I was surrounded not only by Fascists, but by all the new enemies of the people and the party, who could be anybody who had been denounced: heads of political opposition, black marketeers, "Kulaks" rich land owners, outspoken religious leaders.

I was led to a small room where I had to check my belongings, belt and shoelaces included. These were sealed in a brown envelope on which I put my name and address. All of this was done almost without a word. My two detectives simply disappeared without a sound, and a third detective in civilian clothes appeared. He said I was to follow him, and I did.

We headed down the narrow staircase, which went far deeper than I had expected. With every step down, I grew more anxious. Up to that point, I had been concerned but unafraid.

With great naivete, I had believed that although what I had done was illegal, people would understand my motives and I would soon be freed.

I was now facing a big, heavy, dark steel door. My jailer turned the key and the door opened with a menacing noise. "Get in," he said, and pushed me forward as I hesitated, trying not to stumble over the threshold into the murmuring darkness. It took a few seconds before my eyes adjusted to the dimness, broken only by a single dim electric bulb dangling from the twenty-foot high ceiling.

I stood frozen as the door closed behind me. The eerie light dimly revealed three rows of bunks along the facing and side walls. A long, narrow table with benches, all made of rough wood, stood in the middle. Suddenly, a painful cry rose above the hum of whispered conversation. "Ah, my back, my leg, my back...," came plaintively from the darkness.

"Hold on, buddy," someone called, "it'll pass. Try to sleep."

None of the twenty-five or so people there seemed to notice my presence. Finally, someone sitting on the edge of the second shelf of bunks asked if I was new. "Yes," I answered.

"So take a bunk. There's a space here."

"Thank you, I'll just wait a moment," I said, as I sat down on a bench at the long wooden table in the center. Minute by minute, I became more panicky. My heart was pounding and thoughts were scampering through my brain. "Where am I? Who are these people? If they are fascists, they deserve to be closed in here to pay for their crimes against humanity. But what crime against humanity have I committed?"

About an hour passed. It was late night when the door opened and a screaming, crying mass, once a man, was tossed inside the door. "Okay, okay," someone yelled, as he sleepily and reluctantly came to help.

"Give us a hand," someone said to me. We dragged the badly beaten man to his bunk.

"I don't know how he survives, getting this every night," one prisoner said to another.

I spent the night at the table, trying not to settle down into the bunk they showed me. I didn't want to accept my situation. But by so doing, to whom was I demonstrating my revolt? Some were asleep, others were crying out their pain. As for me, nobody cared.

The food distributed in the morning consisted of ersatz coffee and bread. It stirred up the other prisoners a little, but shortly they settled back in their bunks, waiting in that windowless and airless cell.

After awhile, a few came to talk to me. They asked my name, but did so in a way that made it clear they only wanted a name to address me by, not my true name. All knowledge of any kind could be used against you. Still, curiosity was strong, and they asked what I was in for. "Helping Jews to go to Israel," I announced proudly.

"Hey, Arany," they called laughingly toward someone in the dark depth of his bunk.

"Come here. Here's a Zionist colleague of yours."

When Arany and I had been left alone by the others, he said "My real name is Golden (Arany is Hungarian for gold). I was working on the transports."

I had never met Golden before, but I had heard about his activities. Golden regularly accompanied trainloads of people with false papers, sometimes numbering in the thousands, from Budapest to Vienna's Rothschild Hospital. His group organized and disciplined the people on the trains, and were troubleshooters in case of a dispute at the border. Many of the passengers hardly knew what was happening to them; others knew only that they wanted to get to Israel, and wanted nothing and no one to get in their way.

"Do you have any news about others?" he asked.

"I met only one person," I said. "I don't know anything."

"Oh boy," he sighed, "our entire organization has been discovered and arrested, some twenty-four people from top to bottom. Our headquarters were in the Bethlen-teri Temple. They infiltrated the organization. They knew everything. What did you do to end up in here?"

"It's better if you don't know," I said. "They may beat it out of you."

"They'll beat it out of me anyway," he retorted. So I told him.

"Congratulations," he said. "You did an excellent job."

"Do you know where the others are, and if my contact is here?" I asked.

"I believe everyone is here in this building. That's all I know."

Two hours after our conversation, they came to fetch him, and I did not see him again. Two days passed and no guard even asked my name. On the third night, about ten o'clock, a detective came and ordered me to follow him. We emerged from the dark, narrow staircase to the well-lit main floor, and went up the beautiful, wide marble stairs to the second floor, into a spacious, well decorated office with a big mahogany table and comfortable armchairs. Nobody else was there, and after the detective made me sit down, he left too. My fear of the unpredictable vied with the small hope that I would be given the opportunity to explain my case. Not knowing what they knew about my activities, I decided not to volunteer anything.

After about five minutes, a medium-sized, well-dressed man with a Mongolian-style mustache hanging over his thin lips entered. My heart almost stopped. I recognized him immediately as someone I had seen before in the labor camp, but I could not remember his name. He took two steps forward, stopped for a second, continued, then stopped again behind his armchair and grabbed it with both hands, observing me all the time. I stood up, partially as a reflex toward authority and partially as a way of trying to communicate with him. I did not know whether to smile, talk, or stand at attention.

"Sit down," he ordered, cutting off my hesitation. "Your name... address...," and so he went on with the routine questions. All the while, I kept telling myself that he was a Jew from one of the labor camps and he had recognized me.

"Are you a member of the Zionist organization?"

"No," I said. "I'm not a member of anything, but I am a Zionist."

"Shut up," he said quietly. "What was your role in the conspiracy?"

"What conspiracy?" I asked.

"So, you're difficult," he said. He opened a drawer and put on the table the engraving which the detectives had found in my house. "Did you do these?"

"Yes."

"What for?"

"For a customer, as a private, freelance job."

"Did your boss know about it?"

"No."

"How many of these counterfeit stamps did you make?"

"Just those."

"Really?"

"Maybe a couple more. I don't remember."

He opened his drawer, pulled out a paper bag, and emptied a dozen rubber stamps on the table. "How about these?"

"Yes, I did those," I acknowledged defiantly. The game was over.

"You committed a crime for the wrong cause," he said, repeating what I had heard from the arresting detectives, which was obviously the party line. "You should be working to build a new socialist society so that fascism cannot raise its ugly head again."

He stood up and, with determined steps, walked to the door. Before leaving, he turned. "You're lucky," he said with significance, which made me understand that, indeed, he remembered me. He closed the door and I never saw him again.

A few minutes later, another officer came. "Follow me," he said. I was returned to the cell. Before closing the door on me, he, too, repeated, "You're lucky."

I spent the next week and a half in that dark cell. Nobody called me. I did not know if my brother or Cica or anybody else was aware of my arrest. Few people in the cell talked to me, but I overheard enough whispered conversations to learn that many important Fascist leaders were in the building, some even in this very cell. They were beaten or otherwise tortured regularly, mostly at night. Although I was convinced that they were indeed criminals, it was difficult to witness the pain and to hear the agonizing cries of another human, even one who had himself behaved like an animal. Were these people really human? Did they belong to the same species as I? How were they able to inflict and enjoy the suffering, the torture and the killing of Jews? How had the Jews become, in their eyes, so threatening that, few Jews as there were, they felt the need to annihilate them?

The days passed infinitely slowly. My anxiety increased with every passing hour and day. Would they leave me for months without ever saying a word to me? One day, when I was almost at a peak of desperation, I heard the door open. "Tibor Gerstl," a guard called. He led me to the same counter where I had checked in. My belongings were returned, and I signed a statement saying that nothing was missing. I was convinced that I was finally free, when, instead of telling me to leave, the guard commanded me into another room. In that room were several other people. Among them, I recognized Mr. Zeltzer. He came to shake my hand. "Are we freed?" I asked.

"No," he said, "We're being transferred."

"No? No! No ... No ..." My heart sank as I kept repeating that one word to myself. For the first time, I met my "co-conspirators," and for the next ten minutes, while waiting for the paddy wagon, I learned a little bit about the organization I had become a part of, whose members were all small, but important gears moving the machinery of the exodus to Israel. Three of them were the transport train commanders, one was a printer and supplier who provided special papers for documents, and Zeltzer was the Haganah's envoy. All of them had been beaten and "moderately" tortured, whatever that meant. The other seventeen members, most of them at the top level of the organization, had either been liberated or set free until trial, Zeltzer explained.

Nervously we tried to explain to each other what had happened to us, and what we said during our interrogation, when our cacophony was interrupted by two guards. We were ordered to line up in single file, one arm's distance behind each other, and walk straight to the wagon. "No talk among yourselves or with anybody else," one of them ordered. "Understood?"

"Yes."

"Proceed!" he commanded.

We started to file out, with one guard at the front and one behind. Surprisingly, we were not handcuffed. I was in the middle of the group. When our first "chaver" crossed the threshold and emerged on the sidewalk, "Hatikvah," the hymn of the Zionist movement and later of the state of Israel, rang out on the street. I could not see yet what was happening outside, but my chest swelled with pride. I straightened my shoulders, lifted my head and, with romantic enthusiasm, walked out the prison doors.

Proud and defiant, some twenty Zionist youths were singing: "Koolod beliva, penima ..."

The paddy wagon closed on us. We were heading to the Marco Street Prison, which covered a city block and contained judiciary offices. It was an old, well maintained institution which had formerly been used for common criminals. As we disembarked, we saw another group of people waiting for us at the main entrance. There were family and friends and, with a big sigh of relief, I spotted my brother, Cica, and the uncle who had returned from Russia. We could only wave at one another, but they shouted encouragement, trying to reassure us that they were working on our release. It was already reassuring that they knew our whereabouts.

Within minutes, the massive door of the prison had swallowed our little group. After a routine reception, we were separated and led one by one to different cells in different parts of the prison. In a daze, I followed my guard up staircases, through long corridors, and down still other staircases. Cells lined the sides of every walkway. All closed. Here and there someone could be seen peeking through the peep-hole.

Finally, we stopped. The guard advised me to behave, and not to create trouble or agitate. Then he opened the door and I entered a strange, frightening and almost incomprehensible world: a 15 x 15 foot cell, whose furniture consisted of a toilet bowl, a small table, one chair on the door side, two bunk beds along oppossite walls, and one bed under a small window. The window was covered by iron bars, and was six feet above the floor, so that I had to stand on my toes to see outside. The stench was that of a never aerated gymnasium.

In the hot cell sat six almost naked men, their eyes riveted on me. The mouths under those eyes bid me a noncommital welcome.

For seconds I could hardly move, and just stood with my back against the closed door. One husky guy, after carefully appraising me, pointed with his thumb to the lowest cot on the left side. "Thanks," I said without really knowing why or for what I thanked him. Maybe for helping me to make a decision to take another step inside. After five minutes of absolute silence, my cellmates grew more animated. Four of them started to play a card game using scrap paper; one went to look out the window, standing on the cot under it. The sixth picked up a small piece of handwritten paper and read it over and over.

Suddenly, the husky one threw in his cards and turned to me. "Talk," he said.

"Talk about what?" I asked uncomfortably. They laughed.

"What are you here for?"

I did not know what to answer, but I felt that answer I must. "It's complicated," I said, "but basically, false papers."

"Ah, that's all," they said disappointedly. "Money?"

"No."

I learned very fast why they were there without asking a question.

The entrance of a newcomer gave them a reason to tell their stories, some with boisterous pride, others with discouragement. The only commonality among their stories was a lack of luck. "I prepared the break-in perfectly," one said, "and my stupid partner drops one of his gloves and they tracked us down." All of them were there for different degrees of stealing: robbery, aggravated assault, mugging, breaking-in and trespassing. But there were subtle legal differences between those activities, which they knew better than a lawyer would, and which they explained to me in great detail. They were proud of their expertise in the law.

"I measured the fence carefully," one explained like a science teacher. "It was less than three meters; which means I was stealing, a misdemeanor, and they want to send me up for robbery. Are they crazy? They won't get away with it," he said indignantly. Their stories distracted me momentarily from my own misery, but as the evening approached, I grew more and more tense, and I spent the first night sleepless, exhausted.

I could not help but think about Robi in the labor camp. A professional criminal, yet a wonderful, warm comrade, who would not hesitate to take great risk to help others. I wondered about the redeeming qualities of my new comrades. For them, what they did was normal, and they did it casually, as I would go to work from nine to five. We both accepted the normal business risks. What made them any different from anyone else? At least, that's the way they talked.

Environment, peer pressure, poverty, education, different value system, quick buck? I am not a criminologist, but I feel the answer is all of this, and none of this. Maybe it's biological, some chemical imbalance in the brain, which robs such people of patience, agitates them, reduces their resistance to the temptation of immediate gratification.

What I could understand the least was their willingness to lose their freedom so casually. They seldom blamed or praised the police. They assumed responsibility for their acts. "I was lucky; I was stupid; next time I'll do better; a partner goofed, that's all." So what was I so upset about after just one day?

The transfer to the Marco gave me both hope and fear. First, it was definitely better than being at the secret police headquarters. Second, I hoped that if Zionist lawyers could not have our case dismissed, at least they could bring the matter to trial, and then either the case would be dismissed or I would learn my sentence. Sometimes I felt I would be better off being sentenced than living with the uncertainty.

Then, immediately, the fear would take over. Who knew what sentence they would dish out? The criminal aspect of my action was insignificant, relative to the political aspect of it, and that was dangerous. If they decided I was an enemy of the state, they could treat me the way they treated the fascists.

The days went by with unbearable slowness. A week passed and then a month. June turned into July and still nobody had even asked my name. I was not allowed visitors. My only contact with the outside world was through food packages which were permitted to be sent into the prison. They were delivered to the cell after meticulous search for illegal objects or letters. No one knew what else was being taken by the guards.

My cellmates did their best to teach me how to survive and even to enjoy myself occasionally in prison. They showed me how to write a message with bread paste, on cigarette paper thin enough to be laminated between layers of the name tag on the food basket, or wrapped in fat and worked under a chicken skin, or hidden in the seams of undergarments. They taught me Morse Code signals, to communicate with fellow prisoners by hitting the naked water pipes; one strong and one or two quick blows, with the proper timing. We took turns looking out the window and observing the women prisoners during their half-hour walk in the courtyard below. The women knew they were being observed from each window and they loved it. They did their very best to show their legs, their buttocks, their breasts, in unguarded moments. Although it was against the rules even to be at the windows, the guards were fairly tolerant. I guess they themselves enjoyed the sight of women on display.

My cellmates were all in their twenties, except Uncle Pista, who was about forty-five. The young ones were quickly aroused by the sexy show, and shamelessly jerked off at the window, grabbing the iron bar with one hand and balancing on chairs stacked on the bed for a better view. My stomach turned until I got used to their behavior.

The Judiciary Building's inside corridor faced our cell from the opposite side of the courtyard. There was public access, so wives, girlfriends and family came to the large windows to wave, and wait for us to acknowledge their presence. That was where I saw my brother for the first time in almost six weeks. I was amazed by the warmth, the hope generated by the simple sight of a person who cared.

I was frustrated by the lack of news about my case, and I asked the husky guy to help me establish communication with my brother. "Don't worry, man," he said, "it will be done in a few days." Through his basket post office, he sent my brother's address to his girlfriend, who found my brother and taught him how to communicate.

Two days later, I got my first message. "They are working on your case. I have also hired a separate lawyer. The food is from Cica. No news from Edit." Immediately, husky taught me how to swallow the note if the guard suddenly opened the door. "Never recognize the note as yours. Ever," he punctuated.

Every weekday morning at 8:30, cell doors were opened with a big clash. The corridors became animated. Guards from the judiciary department came to pick up prisoners who were to stand trial. Every morning I sat on the cot, facing the door, hoping to be called, but the weeks passed and I never heard my name. Those hours from 7:30 to 8:45 were hours of my greatest mental torture, vascillating between hope and disappointment. I worried that I no longer existed in the prison's records.

Then, one day the door opened and an unknown guard called my name. My heart beat faster. Finally, this was it. Hurriedly, I repeated in my mind again, just as I had one thousand times before, the answers to any possible questions. "Follow me," he said. "We're going to the Judiciary Building." We went from corridor to corridor, and up and down stairs, before we finally stopped in a corridor on the main floor, where most of the cells were open. Another guard took charge of me and explained that I had been given the privilege of working in the prison's office, and would be returned to my cell every evening.

I thought I was going to collapse. I turned white, my legs felt like rubber. "What's wrong?" the guard asked, puzzled. "It's a privilege!" I was overcome by disappointment; I had been so sure I was being taken to stand trial.

Notwithstanding my conscious effort not to be absorbed and swallowed by the system, I did settle down to the daily routine, and blended into that strange environment. My job consisted of retyping legal documents. I could not type, but I soon learned on the old machine how to type with two fingers as fast as I could. My new fellow workers were all intelligent professionals, many of them lawyers, doctors, teachers. One older man, the "chef de bureau," distributed the documents in the open cells and we, too, were free to move around in that corridor. On the left side of the corridor were our offices, and on the right side five or six cells were open, each with a guard in front, guarding a single prisoner.

I was quickly warned by my colleagues not to approach them. They were war criminals, condemned to death, waiting for either their appeal or their execution. Once more I was amazed at how casual people's attitude could become about life and death. How casual they had been about exterminating the Jews just a few months ago, and how casually and naturally they accepted that the new regime would want to exterminate them.

What could that middle-aged man with the round face and potbelly be thinking now, sitting on his cot gazing into space, while-awaiting his execution tomorrow morning? Did he feel any guilt, or did he believe he had done the right thing? After all, the Jews and communists were just like vermin to him. How did he feel now, being so powerless in the face of those he had judged, who became his judges. One man was quiet until the priest came; then he broke down crying, yelling, refusing to leave his cell. Some threw themselves to the floor, kissing the boots of the guard, shamelessly seeking pardon. Still others were defiant, and walked to the gallows, head high until the last two steps, when they collapsed or grabbed the post behind them with their manacled hands. Those vermin who had dispensed death to innocent people were the greatest cowards we had ever seen. No Jewish prisoners during my war experience had ever begged for their lives by kissing the boots of their torturers. If not heroic martyrs, at least they had accepted their fate with dignity.

On the fifth day of my office employment, around eleven o'clock in the morning, the "chef de bureau" called me aside. "Accidentally, I suppose," he said, "the papers of your case came through my office to be copied. If you want to read them, here they are." Of course, I wanted to read them.

I retreated to a corner near the high window and stared avidly at the four-page document on the stationery of the Judiciary. As I read through the lengthy description of my case, spiced with legal jargon and references to laws, regulations, penal codes A and C-123, code XYZ-351 and the like, my eyes blurred and the blood drained from my brain.

By the third page, I had to stop. I asked for water to ease my throat, which had become so dry I could not swallow. The three cellmates, the "chef de bureau" and the prison guard were all looking at me; others from the neighboring cells peeked in too. "Bad news?" they asked. I nodded.

"Please leave me alone for a minute," I asked. They withdrew, and I continued to read. When I arrived at the end of the document defining my act as "a crime against the people," and saw that the prosecuter had proposed a fifteen year prison sentence, I broke out in a sweat, my body tingling with pins and needles. I almost passed out. They came back to console me, to tell me that it did not mean anything, that they had seen many documents like that, and that nothing had happened as a result of them.

After more than an hour, the "chef de bureau" came to me with a big smile and patted me on the back. "Forget the whole thing," he said. "It's just a joke." They all broke out in a big laugh, including the guard. They explained that the document was of their own making, as a way to have a little fun. I could not believe it; I thought they just wanted to calm me down. So finally they tore up the document, and explained to me how the scheme was to be played on the next newcomer.

It took a long time to recover from the shock and accept that it really was a joke. It had looked so real, written by my cellmate lawyers to whom I had told my story, and my doubt lingered for days. What sort of sadistic pleasure could intelligent, educated people draw from the fright, the mental torture of another human being? What kind of pleasure could they derive by using their knowledge of law against a fellow prisoner? Were they any different from the people in the criminal cell section, who scared newcomers with mock attacks, or by hiding pins in their cots and laughing at their pain? Certainly not; indeed they were much worse. It was scary to see how easily people could be mobilized against a defenseless person or group. Wasn't this the human baseness in which the possibility of another holocaust was rooted?

Now that I had paper and pencil available, I decided to continue to add to the memoirs of my life. Meanwhile, I longed for tranquility, for the basic routine of a steady job, for marriage to someone I loved, and for the resumption of my swimming and polo. I desperately desired an end to the misery and deprivation which demanded to be expressed through my sketches. But obviously this was not yet to be.

With great reluctance and hesitation, I started to sketch my cellmates lying on their cots, playing cards, or sitting on the toilet. Then I went back to my arrest at Damjanics street, the dark dungeon of the secret police, the incredible cruelty of my lawyer cellmates and, finally, back to the days of my escape to the Russians, when I was crawling on all fours from weakness. No, the war was not over for me; the struggle for a more decent, quieter life continued.

* * * * *

The hot days of July and August made everyone more edgy. Small-scale skirmishes between prisoners were part of their daily routine. Everybody was an irritant to everybody else. We were not even allowed out for a walk, so we turned our energy against each other. My only exercise was to go to my office cell and back to the criminal quarters.

In the midst of our boredom, Pista's liberation in mid-August was a great event. A nice fellow, he had burglarized only a few houses. He knew the rules: that is, to do his work during the daytime to avoid violating the early curfew. It was decreed that anybody caught committing armed aggression of any kind after 8:00 P.M. would be sentenced to an automatic death penalty.

His replacement arrived soon after he left. A young gypsy, about nineteen, good looking, strongly built and smiling. "Talk!" Husky ordered with authority. The youngster knew the rules of the prison and talked without hesitation.

"I tried to rob an army depot at night."

"Are you crazy?" Husky yelled at him with reproach. "Don't you know the decree? They'll hang you, idiot!"

At that, the gypsy broke down, crying, lamenting his misfortune, swearing and damning all authorities. He went on for hours until he fell asleep exhausted. The very next morning his trial took place. The verdict in such cases was either guilty and death or not guilty and free. When he was brought back to the cell late in the afternoon, he was smiling, almost joyous. "Are you free?" we all asked as soon as he entered.

"No," he said.

"Then what, are you dead?"

"No," he said, "I got the death penalty, but it was reduced to life imprisonment."

We were speechless. "That's what you're so happy about?"

For days I turned that thought over in my mind. What was happiness? How could optimism help you through crisis? How would I behave? What was really better, a life without quality or death? But the quality of life was relative too. You could create or dream great things in prison, too. The next day he was transferred to another prison. "At least his case is moving," I thought.

A heat wave during August's last days turned the cells into a furnace. I couldn't sleep at night, but lay and waited for the morning so I could go to the office cell, which was more shaded. At 8:30, as part of my routine, but without real hope, I fixed my eyes on the door. When it opened, I wasn't excited. It could be opened for many reasons.

But this day the guard not only called my name, but ordered me to take all my belongings. "You're going to the judge," he said laconically. "You'll have a hearing."

It was the first time in three months that something had happened in my case. My brother had indicated in his latest notes that I could expect a hearing soon, but I had dismissed this as wishful thinking.

The hearing didn't last more than ten minutes. Name? Address? Occupation? The judge read the accusation, and then concluded that I had not acted for personal gain. Consequently, I would be free until the trial, which would be held at the end of September or the beginning of October. I would be advised of the date, and could not leave Budapest without authorization. "Sign here," I was told.

That was it. In less than an hour I walked through the prison gates onto Marco street. Nobody waited, nobody knew that I was free. I stood bewildered in front of the prison door. What should I do? Where should I go? I did not know where my brother was, so I headed for my uncle's flat.

* * * * *

My uncle lived near the Western Railroad Station with his third wife. He had returned just days after the liberation of Budapest with a dozen or so Hungarian refugees from Russia, on the heels of the Red Army. He had lived in Russia for fifteen years, having had to escape the Horty regime because of his communist beliefs. These repatriated Hungarians were supposed to help establish the new Communist regime under the direction of Rakosi. But the new ambition of my uncle was to get rich fast. He and others used their influence to traffic in coffee, sugar, nylon stockings, gold coins and jewelry. My hope that he would use his influence on my behalf vanished fast, but at least he had paid for the private lawyer and the telegram to my brother, which brought him to Budapest the next day.

I got in touch with Cica and her mother, and thanked them for the food they had sent to the prison. Then I spoke with Bojti, who told me about having also been interrogated. After some hesitation, he again took me back into his shop.

While in appearance I returned to my normal activities, all I could think about was the coming trial. I got in touch with the Zionist organization, whose people I hardly knew, since my only contact, Zeltzer, was still in prison. They assured me of their help and indicated that although the formerly large scale transfer of people had been reduced to a trickle, the organization still had a secondary route for the emergency use of their own members. If I chose to leave the country, it would be available to me.

They also recommended that I would be better off being defended by a private lawyer rather than by the organization's lawyer because of prejudiced judges. Our meeting was very businesslike, without heroics or praise. But just as I was ready to leave, "Max" and "Dolf," the heads of the organization, shook my hand with great warmth and, looking deep into my eyes, said, "Shalom."

* * * * *

Mr. Friedman, the private lawyer hired by my brother with the help of the organization, had been working on my case many weeks, and it was partially due to his activities that I was set free. We were only three weeks from the trial date of September 28th when he advised me that the government was not well-disposed towards my case, and he foresaw the possibility of a serious sentence. "If you're not willing to face this, you had better prepare to leave the country, if you can. I'll advise you if anything changes. Trust me, I have good contacts," he said.

As I walked home with my brother through the streets I knew so well, past familiar landmarks, somehow everything looked different. Was this the last time I would walk these streets, work at Bojti's shop, play polo in the National Swimming Pool, meet girls at the Banana Island, or pass the Victoria Coffee Restaurant? "Isn't it strange," I said to my brother, "I've never seriously thought of leaving Hungary." I wondered why, since the fever of emigration was all around us. Everybody was learning English or French, running for papers, for contacts all over the world: Jews who could no longer live next to neighbors who might have been instrumental in destroying their families; Fascists who were afraid of being caught; and moderate middle-of-the-roaders too, who could not accept the new Communist regime.

I had neither family nor friends outside Hungary. I could not imagine myself in kibbutz life, which was what Israel meant to us. Nor did I like the United States, with its grossly unequal society, racism and exploitive capitalism. My feelings and sympathies, if not my dreams—I had no more dreams—were with western Europe, in Paris, where a better balance between capitalism and socialism offered more hope for a more humane society.

My brother broke into my silent dialogue. "So what will you do?"

"There's almost no choice. We must prepare to leave the country."

"We?"

"Yes, you should come with me. After what we've been through, we shouldn't be separated again."

"Where?" he pressed.

"I don't know. It doesn't matter. Just out of the Russian controlled territories, to the west. You heard the lawyer. I will not go back to prison; I swore to that. I would rather take any risk. If my case is dismissed, we'll stay; if not, we must go."

"And how will we get out?"

"With the organization's help; I'll take care of that. For the moment, just let's act as if we assume I'll be acquitted."

The only other people with whom I shared my intentions were Cica and her mother. Cica's brother was in the U.S. They had wanted to join him for a long time and had made some attempts through legal channels, but to no avail. Hearing my plan, they told me they would like to join us, and would even pay our expenses if necessary.

* * * * *

The days and weeks passed dangerously fast. Many meetings with Mr. Friedman led to nothing positive. The answer to my every question was "maybe." I was now also in daily contact with the Zionist organization. After lengthy arguments, they agreed that my brother, Cica and her mother could come with me if they paid their own expenses.

"How will we go?" I asked Mr. Max.

He smiled. "I can't tell, my friend. When the time comes, you just follow orders without questions, understand?"

The trial, set for the 28th of September at 9:30, was now only days away, and I was still unsure whether to leave or stay. If I decided to go, it could be at a moment's notice. My brother and I had no problem getting ready; all our belongings were not much greater than they had been when we came back from the labor camp. Cica and her mother had slowly liquidated most of their belongings, and would be ready whether or not I decided to leave.

Only one matter remained to be settled. My "talisman" was still with Edit. I told my brother that I would go to Rimaszmombat overnight, and he handed me a letter that he had received in August. The letter was from Edit's cousin, Pista. In it he let me know that Edit, convinced that I would receive a long prison sentence, had emigrated to Australia with a local boy. They had never found my package, but he suspected she took it with her. I had had a premonition that something like this would happen, and concluded that it was her boyfriend who had denounced me in Rimaszombat.

I was only moderately shocked. "So be it," I told myself with disgust. "It's just another disappointment in a long series. Maybe it's just as well to put everything behind me and start a completely new life somewhere else." Yet, even so, I was really not sure I would leave unless the outcome of the trial looked bad. I have never been able to explain why I hesitated. Fear of being caught, desire not to run anymore, exhaustion, worry about starting a new life, sympathy toward the possibility of a socialist society? After all, the Russians had saved my life. Possibly, subconsciously I still felt Hungarian, attached to the familiar landscape, cityscape and culture. Any one or a hundred other reasons are possible.

The day before the trial, I met once more with Mr. Friedman, and to my great surprise, Mr. Max was there too. They told me their latest information was that the trial's outcome would be favorable, and that I did not have too much to fear. However, in case of a sudden change, I should read the instructions they handed me, memorize and destroy them. The escape route would be available for only one night, two days later. It would be my only opportunity for escape. Not Ocsi, Cica or her mother were to be told any more than necessary. Mr. Friedman and Mr. Max left me, wishing all of us good luck, and adding, "We don't want to insult you with the obvious, but if you're caught, all the arrangements were your own making. We won't know anything about it. Rest assured, we'll provide witnesses to our innocence, whatever you say."

"I understand, Mr. Max. You can count on me. Mr. Friedman advised me that if I don't want to leave the country immediately, it's better for me to attend the trial, but to stand in the gallery with the spectators. If the last information is still good, he will nod to me, and I'll show up ten minutes later with some excuse for my tardiness. If it appears that the verdict will go against me, then he'll blow his nose and shake his head. At that, I should disappear and leave the country, without even stopping at my flat."

The day of the trial finally arrived. Everything was ready for our departure. Cica was waiting for my signal at home, but my brother came with me. I don't know what induced me to take such a risk, but at 9:30 I was there among the spectators, trembling with fear, and with an inexplicable exhilaration Mr. Friedman blew his nose and shook his head.

* * * * *

"No trouble so far?" asked Mr. Korosi. We had made his acquaintance on the outskirts of the city of Sopron, where at about 8:30 in the evening we had arrived separately, although traveling on the same train. There were two other people waiting at his house. "Introduce yourselves," he said, "we'll travel together with two more people we'll pick up on the road. There's soup in the kitchen and some sandwiches; help yourselves. Rest and relax. We leave at ten tonight. Make sure you can carry your belongings."

Aranyka, Cica's mother, had come with two heavy valises and was wearing high heels. To the amusement of the others, we ended up carrying her bags. At ten o'clock exactly, a truck arrived. "Get up, everybody," Korosi commanded. We climbed onto the truck. "There must be complete silence, no talk, no noise." The truck's flat bed was covered with canvas. Before he latched the last strap he looked inside, "Relax," he said, "I'm not coming with you, but I'll meet you at 1:00 A.M. Good luck."

We felt very uncomfortable, and we were very afraid. From this moment on, we no longer knew whose hands we were in or where we were heading. After more than an hour's ride it felt as if we had left the road. We were shaking, jumping and sliding in the truck. We peeked under the canvas and saw that we were indeed rolling through an open field.

At the edge of a small forest, in the middle of high bushes and grassland, we came to a halt. The driver ordered us off in a subdued voice. Within minutes Mr. Korosi appeared, followed by a small black and white dog, which was a mixture of at least three different breeds. "This is Marci. You'll follow him on this foot path in absolute silence for about twenty minutes. I'm not coming with you, but I'll meet you again at the end of the road." It was a beautiful night with millions of stars overhead and, fortunately, no moon. An intoxicating aroma of wildflowers lay over the sleeping earth.

My heart was heavy. So was Aranyka's valise, which I carried. She was hopping and panting, her high heels catching in the soft earth. After fifteen minutes, the dog we had been following stopped suddenly, sniffing left and right. We immediately jumped into the bushes, lying flat, as we had been instructed to do. After a few minutes, branches and leaves cracked under approaching steps. We were trying to stay as silent as death, when a man called out quietly, "Marci, Marci." He patted the dog. "It's okay, fellas, you can continue. I'm a friend." He was carrying a heavy bag, and it was obvious that we were following the path of smugglers. "Just be careful now. You see those little lights pointing in three different directions, but very close to each other? That one is the Hungarian border guard, the one to its right is the Czech, and the one to the left is the Austrian."

Now we were really scared. Why hadn't Korosi told us about all these guards? Perhaps just for this very reason. We might have been too scared even to start. At this point, there was no way back.

We followed Marci under the bushes for another fifteen minutes until the path led onto a wider road. There again we heard the call for Marci. He started to run, but we knew where and why. His master was there. "Okay, fellas, no problems? Be calm, you're in Austria. Follow me."

In spite of the great risks ahead, our arrival was a small but imporant victory, one we could feel good about. Still, the west was very, very far away. In addition to crossing the Hungarian border, we had to cross many more: from the Russian occupational zone to one of the Allies' zones; then from Austria to Germany, and from Gemany into one of the hospitable countries, Holland, Belgium, France or Italy. We had no idea how we would do this, so we were happy to follow Mr. Korosi to an oxcart half loaded with bags and boxes, waiting for us under the trees. We loaded our belongings and Aranyka on the cart, and followed it without even asking where it was heading. The important thing was to move away from the border area as fast as possible.

After walking for almost two hours behind the oxcart, we were dead tired, when we finally stopped at a crossroad and had our first chance to relax. On one corner in front of a dimly lit inn, a truck was waiting for us with soup and sandwiches. After a half hour's rest, we continued our journey. Around ten in the morning, we arrived at our first destination, the Rothschild Hospital in Vienna.

Finally out of Hungary, but still in the Russian zone of occupation, I felt only half relieved, mostly because of the circumstances of my escape from trial. I felt like a hunted animal. I was always on my guard, and alarmed at the slightest innocent questioning of a stranger. The place itself was a hospital before, but now looked more like a casern. The corridors were full of people speaking languages of every Eastern European country, plus Yiddish and some Hebrew, all arguing, gesticulating and milling around in constant commotion.

On our arrival, we were deloused and provided with food and shelter. For four days we could only hang around, while gathering information about opportunities to go further, talking or negotiating with officials. Then, by chance, I met an aliyah organizer who knew about my activities and my trial in Budapest. "Thank you for what you did," he said. "How can we help you? Where do you want to go?"

"I have no idea, except out of the Russian occupational zone," I answered.

"Are you ready to go tomorrow?"

"Sure, we are."

"Then be ready at eight in the morning. Shalom."

We were given food, train tickets and new identity cards. At nine, we were on a long train heading west. We passed gorgeous mountain views of Steyer in the Austrian Alps. The ticket inspection gave us some jitters. In every uniform we saw danger, but then that reaction passed. We had hardly taken a deep breath when, inexplicably, the train slowed, and then came to a halt in the middle of nowhere.

We looked out and saw Russian soldiers boarding the train. We were not too far from Linz. One more inspection, we sighed, and we are out. By no stretch of the imagination did we look like casual Austrian travelers. Refugee status was stamped all over us. But at least when the Russian officer asked my name, address, and where I was going, I could answer in German with details corresponding to my false papers. Fortunately, that was enough.

The Russians got off and the train picked up speed, when a man whom we thought we had seen in the hospital came in from another car. "We're in the American Zone," he said. "I'm Herb, from the organization. Wait for me at the station." I felt as if a huge weight had been lifted from my chest. All in the group hugged each other, and I could not contain my emotions any longer. I broke down and cried. The fear and insecurity that had been accumulating for months burst through the gates of passivity or overactivity which held them back, but what if ... what if?"

At the station, Herb gathered some fifteen people from the train and led us to an American truck. We drove directly out of the city a few kilometers to an American displaced persons' camp. Over the entrance gate a sign read, "Greenshelter Lager".

* * * * *

We settled into our new home, army barracks again, but quite different from the others I had known. Here we were given new blankets, clothing, excellent food and clean beds. Clearly, we were in a new world; but we still could not leave the camp without permission.

We had made our journey so far without a penny, and without legal papers. To be able to move around now we needed money. Aranyka helped a little, but it was not enough. The black market flourished in the camp. In Linz and the neighboring towns, there were shortages of everything, while the Americans seemed to have goods in the military warehouses in endless supply. They had money, chocolate, cigarettes, preserved fruit of all sorts and concentrated milk, which I loved. My brother had made good money by transforming blankets into winter coats; now I earned a good supply of canned food, predominantly Spam, for painting the Officer's Club. Aunt Aranyka and Cica concentrated their efforts on obtaining preferred visas through Cica's brother in America. I applied myself to learning French, to refresh my eight years of French studies at the Dobo High School in Eger.

My situation with Cica became tense and bittersweet. We were lovers of a sort, yet we worked for opposite goals. Her mother still dreamed of an American millionaire, ostensibly for her daughter, but mostly as insurance for her own future comfort. We seldom talked about our inevitable separation, but it was understood.

The weeks passed. I made friends with a few officers, one of them a Hungarian born American who told me that in Linz there was a Hungarian water polo team composed of refugees. My eyes lit up. "Please help me to get there," I begged. He arranged for trips on the service truck back and forth to Linz.

When I entered the pool, I could not believe my eyes. Two of the seven players, Cele and Fules, were from my home town, and I knew all the rest from Budapest. None of them were Jewish, but as far as I knew, none were active fascists either, but were simply people fleeing the communist regime. All of them jumped out of the pool, greeted me warmly and, after chatting a few minutes, Cele yelled, "So what are you waiting for? Get in the goal!" I felt almost at home. I obtained a permit from the camp to go to practice twice a week.

Six weeks passed. Cica and Aranyka expected their visas any day. I became restless as I realized that my brother and I could not stay there forever. New people were coming in, while others left our camp to go to facilities closer to the west. We learned through the grapevine how to move around. We made friends who knew more.

Every day someone would decide he had been there long enough. It was time to travel to Frankfurt or Munich or elsewhere. But travel wasn't that easy. To use the train one needed a travel permit from local authorities. After minor difficulties, I obtained one for both my brother and me. It was issued for Salzburg.

We set our departure for three days later when, unexpectedly, a response arrived to my brother's letter, from a friend in Belgium. My brother opened it and jumped for joy. The letter read, "Advise you come here. My address is Rue Jourdan. My phone is...," signed, "Bule." Bule had been a close childhood friend of my brother. How he got to Brussels we didn't know. But we knew one thing immediately: for the first time since the end of the war, we had a direction and an address to go to.

The adieu wasn't easy. I walked with Cica for hours in the cold November evening, reliving our past. I was chagrined at not being able to offer her any future for a long time to come, especially one good enough to satisfy her mother. With sobs and tears we wished each other good fortune and kissed for the last time.

Early the next morning, Cica and her mother left for Munich, legally, to fly to America. Two days later, we took the train to Salzburg with some new friends. I felt strangely free. Except for my brother, I had nobody in the world. I felt as if I were floating like thin air up on the snowy mountains. We possessed no money or papers, and travelled from shelter to shelter, Jewish municipal and American. "But the road is open," said one of our new friends. "There are only two more borders for you to pass."

"Yes," I said, "but it's six hundred kilometers to Brussels."

"So what," he answered, "you have no time?"

By hitchhiking, jumping on trains without tickets, climbing-on oxcards or horsecarts, and by helping smugglers, we made it to Germany. We passed through Garmish-Partenkirschen at night in a camouflaged truck, and ended up in Munich at the Deutsche Museum. The once famous Pinacotec now displayed a human palette of refugees in every possible mixture of nations and languages. There were no pictures except the picture of the terrible results of war. Displaced persons from all over Europe searched for somebody, for their families or friends. They ate at the military kitchen and slept in filth, not knowing who might be asleep next to them.

Three days were more than enough of that exhibition, so we went to Ulm. I did not neglect to visit the beautiful cathedral with its single spire, which looked as if it had grown straight out of the ground. Again, we grew tired of not being "home." Very tired indeed. The weather turned bitter cold. The first snow began to fall on the cities and towns. We needed to rest, to settle down somewhere.

During our travels, we had heard about a good American displaced persons camp in Traunstein, a city in the mountains of Bavaria. It would be difficult to get there in the snow, but we had little choice. "Let's try," we encouraged each other.

Traunstein is one of those gorgeous picture post card towns in the high mountains. The snow was knee high as we struggled over the last few kilometers to the camp's entrance. Although it was evening, the sky was clear, and the moon lit our path. We asked permission from the American guard to enter the camp. "Sorry," he said, "we can't accept any more refugees without papers. We have no more room."

We insisted, implored and explained, to no avail. We were trying to figure out what to do, when a group of three refugees passed through the gate. We explained our problem and they advised us not to worry, but to go around to the back and climb the fence. Once someone entered, the Amerians would not expel him, and in two or three days they would issue a pass for a temporary stay. That's what we did.

We settled quickly into the new routine, which was the same as the one at Greenshelter-

Lager, with one exception: we found no black market. We spent our time gathering information about how to travel to Holland, Belgium or France. Invariably, we were told how easy travel was, but nobody could provide us with specifics.

More and more we wanted to reply to Bule's letter, but were unable to give a return address, as we were constantly on the move and telephones were unavailable to civilians. We shortly learned that there were many Hungrian Jews in the camp. One of them was named Laszlo. We told him our story just as we told it to almost anybody, in the hope of finding help. "I think I can help you," Laszlo offered.

"How?" we asked.

"I may be able to connect you to your friend."

We were astounded by his self-assurance. Or was he pulling our leg? "Would you explain, please? There's no civilian phone service as far as we know."

"But there is military communication. Just come to the office complex around eleven at night and knock three times at the door to the telephone room. Try not to be seen, if possible. Come alone."

The American military switchboard was manned at night by Hungarian-Jewish refugees who spoke fluent French, English and German. However, on the military lines one could speak only English or French, and getting connections was very difficult. To reach Brussels, one had to connect first with Antwerp, then Paris, and only from there to Brussels. Since I spoke no English and only broken French, and our friend in Brussels spoke neither, we had to speak Hungarian. "Listen," Laszlo explained, "speak fast because they'll cut the line."

That night and the following two nights we made at least ten calls. Each time it was arduous, and each time, after a minute or so, we heard a voice say, "Please speak English or French or I will disconnect." Then we would be disconnected. So we would redial over and over.

After three nights, we had constructed a complete road map with the help of Bule. We were jubilant. We might finally be nearing the end of our journey. At least we would be safely in the west. There was no legal way for us to travel, so on December 20, 1946, we packed our rucksacks, blankets and as much food as we could carry, and hit the road again.

* * * * *

We traveled by train to Koln without tickets, avoiding inspections by jumping from car to car, and at small stations sneaking past the train guards. The city was preparing for Christmas, but we saw only a few candles in the windows. We weren't sure whether this was due to lack of electricity or lack of festive spirit as well.

We were amazed by the way precision bombing had destroyed everything in the city except the famous Gothic cathedral, which now became our hotel for three days. The priests welcomed all refugees, touched maybe by the Christmas spirit, serving hot soup and providing shelter in the caves of the medieval cathedral. Hammock-like canvases hung from the walls to accommodate as many people as possible. The walls were damp, the air warm, and the atmosphere suffocatingly humid in spite of the winter. The air reeked of urine, and rats ran on the floor, while overhead loamed the stark serenity of the Gothic cathedral.

On Christmas Day, just a few of the city's people came, mostly the elderly, and the priest in his gold-embroidered stole said mass. "For whose souls?" I wondered. But it was a shelter, and the soup was hot.

"What should we do?" my brother asked with sarcasm as we lined up for the morning soup, "Say a 'broche' here or cross ourselves?"

"Very funny! Eat the soup and let's get out."

Our friend Bule's last message on the phone in Traunstein was to avoid passing into Belgium through Aachen or Monshau. Too many people were using those routes, surveillance was heavy, and many people were arrested. He told us instead to find the village of

Crossing the Belgian border

Kalterherberisch, just south of Monshau, and to call him when we crossed the border. It was easier said than done, as we found out.

On December 29th, the sky was grey, and snow began to fall as we left the cathedral. Our best hope for reaching the border was to hitchhike. Truck drivers, and peasants with horse-drawn carriages or oxcarts, were often helpful. They would offer a ride and give directions and information about where refugees or repatriates could find food and shelter. We were not lucky in our travels, and it took us two days to reach the border town. Our arrival in knee-deep snow had to be timed for the late afternoon, after darkness had fallen, so as not to raise suspicion in the small village where everybody knew everybody else.

It was six o'oclock, December 31st, New Year's Eve, when we walked down the main street, past the few people who were outside shoveling snow in front of their small houses. The ones we asked were very helpful in pointing out the road to the border. Our intention was obvious and they wished us good luck. I guessed they were more than happy to get rid of strangers. "This road into Belgium has no German border guard," they told us.

* * * * *

A two lane macadam road crossed the border east to west from Germany into Belgium in normal times. Now, heavy "Spanish horses" (barbed wire rolled over cross legged stands about four feet high) blocked the road at both ends of the no-man's-land. The road itself was elevated some three meters above the surrounding field, which was criss-crossed with barbed wire. The only way we could pass was by hugging the side of the road. For half an hour we observed the movements of the Belgian border guard. He passed each section of this territory regularly, at ten-minute intervals. He would begin at his guard house and walk around the bend, where he would disappear for four or five minutes. Then he would return.

"Okay, Ocsikem, this is it. We've come so far, and can't retreat. We'll start crawling for three minutes as soon as he disappears, then we'll freeze flat against the roadside and try to use the few evergreen bushes to hide behind. Be ready. We move at his next turn. If he spots us, we'll give up immediately, rather than risk his shooting at us."

It took almost a half hour to cover the one kilometer of no-man's-land. We crawled through the snow to the border. As the guard made his turn, we scrambled past the Spanish horses on the Belgian side and jumped into a deep ditch on the opposite side of the road. We had crawled a few hundred meters through the roadside ditch when we heard a car approaching. We camouflaged ourselves with snow as best we could and remained rigid. A jeep passed, its searchlight scanning the field just over our heads. New border guards moved to their posts. We were frozen and hungry, eating snow to quench our thirst. Finally, the car went away.

Not too far away, we saw a small building with a neon sign reading Cafe-Brasserie. My brother pleaded, "We must take the risk of going there to warm up, and try to get some hot food. If not, we'll never make it."

"You're right. Let's try."

We approached the small establishment carefully. We peeked inside and saw, through a small opening of the drape, a room decorated with balloons and crepe paper. Uniformed men stood drinking beer, laughing and talking. "We can't go in here," I said. "They look like the border guards, and the others dressed in short black capes look like Hungarian postmen." They were gendarmes, as we learned later.

We saw another faint light in the window of a farm house. Out of desperation, we decided to try there, and had to knock for a few minutes before the farmer opened the squeaking door just a crack. We asked him for shelter for the night, anywhere in the stable or in the barn. My German was good enough for him to understand and he let us in. "You crossed the border?" he asked.

"Yes."

"We've seen others, too. Don't worry, it's all right."

His wife and daughter came into the room. "Bonne Annee," they said. "Come eat with us and then you can sleep in the stable." We thanked them a hundred times.

They were so nice we could not believe our good fortune. "Isn't this a trap?" my brother kept asking me.

"They may denounce us, but there's nothing we can do now. We must rest, whatever happens," I said. "How far are we from the border, Monsieur?"

"It's just there, maybe two hundred meters."

I began to panic. "How can it be so close? We were running almost an hour."

"Yes," he said, "probably parallel to the border. If you had continued on this little road, you would have arrived back in Germany."

The next morning, I told the farmer about our friend in Brussels, and about our need to call him. "The only phone is at the post office in town. You can call from there."

"How could I dare go into town?" I said.

"My daughter will go with you. It will be no problem."

The teenage daughter was happy to help. We went into the town, and passing people saluted us left and right, "Bonjour, Bon Nouvel An ... Gelukkig Niewjaar."

The telephone rang for the third time before a sleepy voice answered. "Bonne Annee," I said.

"Hey, you idiots, did you have to come on New Year's Day? And you had better change your accent. Where are you?" The next day Bule arrived to pick us up.

When he offered to pay our hosts for their trouble, they refused. "What wonderful people," I said. "And I was afraid they might denounce us."

"There are human beings here," my friend said in Hungarian, "not animals, like there." Bule pointed to the other side of the border.

By nightfall we were dining at his flat on Rue Jourdan, relating our adventures. With the help of our friend and Jewish organizations like JOINT, we got settled. Only one more step was needed to start a new life. I went to the Maison Communale de St. Giles to ask for a permit to stay in Belgium. From behind an office window, a middle-aged, jovial man called, "Next!" I approached and, in broken French, I asked him for the permit.

"Your passport?"

"I'm sorry, but I don't have one."

"Travel papers or identity card?"

"Non, Monsieur."

"How did you come into the country?"

"I walked across the border with my brother."

"But, Monsieur, you can't do that," he said with mild indignation. "I may have to arrest you."

"But I came from so far," I stuttered. Perhaps he saw the fear on my face.

He shook his head. "Just wait a minute," he said, as he disappeared into the office behind him. Through the partially open door I saw him consulting with another gentleman. He came back. "You were lost," he said, "and accidentally walked across the border?"

"Oui, Monsieur."

"That's different," he said, as he filled out a paper: "Le soi-disant Tibor Gerstl...," permit to stay three months. "It can be renewed," he said. "Have a good stay. Next!"

I had tears in my eyes. "You see," I told my brother, "there really are human beings here. Can you imagine this happening back in Hungary? That man understood our problem in a minute and wanted to help, casually, naturally, without even realizing what a great thing he was doing. At least in my eyes, he represented everything I have ever dreamed of." He was, for me, Western Europe.

* * * * *

One man can make a difference: Koranyi, Dr. Miklos, the Communist corporal, the farmer at the border, and this man behind his office window each proved that. How beautiful, but also how terrible that truth is, because Hitler and the likes of him can make a difference too.

I went home with warmth in my heart. Bule and Ocsi had left the house together. It was good to be alone. I couldn't know what the future would bring, but for the moment I felt peace and security. I picked up my rucksack and the small cardboard valise from the corner of the room. I took out my few belongings, straightened out a shirt and a pair of briefs, and hung a pair of slacks on the back of a chair, trying to restore the invisible crease.

I pulled out my sketches, the mementos of my recent past, and laid them on the table and the floor. I gazed at them as at some strange happenings. Little by little, my tired eyes closed and the sketches took life again. Each one was a piece of the mosaic of my life, to be fitted into a greater picture. Turning, melting into each other, they appeared suddenly inundated by an eerie cosmic light. Streams of life-giving blood oozed from the hurt of each sketch, collected into a river, a flood, trying to annihilate the past. I woke from the dream, but the images remain ... forever.